ASHES OF THE REVOLUTION

Nathan G. Alexander

Cover design and maps by Wouter F. Goedkoop

ISBN 978-1-0673977-0-8 (paperback)

ACKNOWLEDGMENTS

I started writing *Ashes of the Revolution* during the beginning of the Covid pandemic in 2020 and was finalizing it for publication when I was diagnosed with cancer in 2025. It's been a strange few years! There has been much personal, professional, and global upheaval in that time – but also a lot of good, too. The book, I think, reflects it all.

Many people have contributed over this time to getting the novel where it is today. I am grateful to the following people who offered valuable feedback on the manuscript or tips on the publication process: Millie Abecassis, Kim Corvi, Ben Hiemstra, Tim Hoare, Dawn Hollis, Krishna Patel, Nathan Pellerin, Todd Tavares, and Andrew Whyte. Thanks as well to the community at the Ottawa Writers' Group for their support and encouragement.

Particular thanks is due to João F. Silva who gave feedback on an early draft but also gave me important info about the self-publishing process. (Check out his fantasy series, the Smokesmiths!)

Jolanta Komornicka proofread the novel and saved me from a number of errors, including an excessive amount of exclamation points! (Oops!) Wouter F. Goedkoop of the Voyager's Workshop created the cover art as well as the maps, and went above and beyond in both cases.

I am indebted to colleagues and friends at the University of Ottawa who have supported me in various ways during this strange time, including Lori Beaman, Hinna Hussain, Karel Leyva, Edmundo Maza, Brenda Montero, Heather Murray, and Patience Otitoju.

Special thanks to Ashley Laverty, who selflessly helped me so much in the wake of my cancer diagnosis. I will always appreciate it.

I also want to thank the entire team at the Ottawa Hospital

Cancer Centre, particularly Michael Vickers, my oncologist; Liz O'Brien and Kathy Cowan, my chemotherapy nurses; and Oguzhan Serce, the research coordinator for the clinical trial I am part of. I am grateful for their kindness, compassion, and professionalism. I feel so fortunate to be under their care.

Finally, I would like to thank my brother, Matt Bourassa, and my parents and step-parents – Joan Alexander and Barr Huether, and Chris Alexander and Brenda Alexander – for their love and support… and, well, everything.

DRAMATIS PERSONAE

Main characters and their families and associates

- **Charlotte of Evesbury**: Noblewoman and secret supporter of democracy; alias, Silver
  - **Brondin, Earl of Evesbury**: Charlotte's younger brother
  - **Allegrette**: Brondin's wife
  - **Willien of Marchal**: Charlotte's husband and scientist
  - **Jacqueline of Evesbury**: Charlotte's mother

- **Yanis Haller**: A former pamphleteer, exiled and made to serve as a soldier for his criticisms of King Aramal
  - **Jackson Mylner**: Yanis's mentor and publisher of *The Voice of the Working Man* newspaper
  - **Calina Gray**: Scientist accompanying Yanis's unit's mission
  - **Ronar**: Soldier in Yanis's unit
  - **Vinzent of Highfalls**: Noble commander of Yanis's unit
  - **Nadeni Lichenxu**: Activist from Iron Town
  - **Clem Lake**: Fellow soldier and Revolutionary Defense Force officer
  - **Devon Black**: Revolutionary Defense Force officer

- **Dellirea Zendar**: Princess and heir to the throne of Estenland
  - **King Aramal Zendar**: King of Estenland, father of Dellirea
  - **Queen Bravala Zendar**: Queen of Estenland, mother of Dellirea

- **Dario, Duke of Prencroft**: Aramal's lead advisor
  - **Andamar the Great**: Aramal's father and previous king, deceased
  - **Meritoria**: Sister of Bravala
  - **Yuvela**: Closest friend of Bravala
  - **Lochmar**: Brother of Aramal
  - **Rodnel, Count of Summerstone**: Royal engineer
  - **Kephalos**: High Priest
  - **Omephas**: High Priest
  - **Phantos**: Author of *The Book of Oqci Critically Examined*, deceased
  - **King Sera**: Estenland's king, several centuries ago, deceased

- **Samuel Nox**: Scientist and professor at Iron Town College; alias, Eston Miller
  - **Greta Esant**: Samuel's student
  - **Robert Grim**: Samuel's student
  - **Professor Kelson**: Senior Professor at Iron Town College
  - **Michael of Highstaff and Adar of Winslough**: Noblemen who sell Nox sacred creatures
  - **Will and Olive Hunt**: Peasants in Farnestead

Estenland Politicians and Family

- **Quinneas Raeil**: Lawyer and radical politician
- **Koralo, Count of Ulsted**: Nobleman and moderate politician
- **Selver Bronn**: Railway industrialist and supporter of democracy
- **Richard, Duke of Saundley**: Wealthy nobleman and conservative politician
- **Solorina of Saundley**: Wife of Richard, Duke of Saundley
- **Aldred**: Son of Richard, Duke of Saundley

- **Tressa Smith**: Radical politician from Iron Town
- **Aran Potter**: Radical politician from the countryside
- **Penn Harper**: Lawyer

Friezzians

- **Hyazaral VII**: King of Friezzia
- **Anderyl**: Hyazaral's son
- **Yunolarol**: Anderyl's son
- **Lady Fondyrel**: Noblewoman at Friezzian court
- **Mikazal**: Famous Friezzian artist, deceased

Religion

- **Oqci**: Mythical figure reputed to have brought the sacred creatures to Ogard; pronounced "oak-chee"
- **Mazir**: Wife of Oqci

Soldiers of Oqci

- **Sun**: Alias of the leader
- **Sky**: Alias of a Soldiers of Oqci member

Groups and Committees

- **Great Chamber**: Estenland parliament that can be called to counter the monarch's power
- **Emergency Committee**: Smaller body composed of five members and formed to temporarily act for the Great Chamber
- **Revolutionary Defense Force (RDF)**: Military force established to protect the Great Chamber and its members
- **People's Army**: Renamed Revolutionary Defense Force

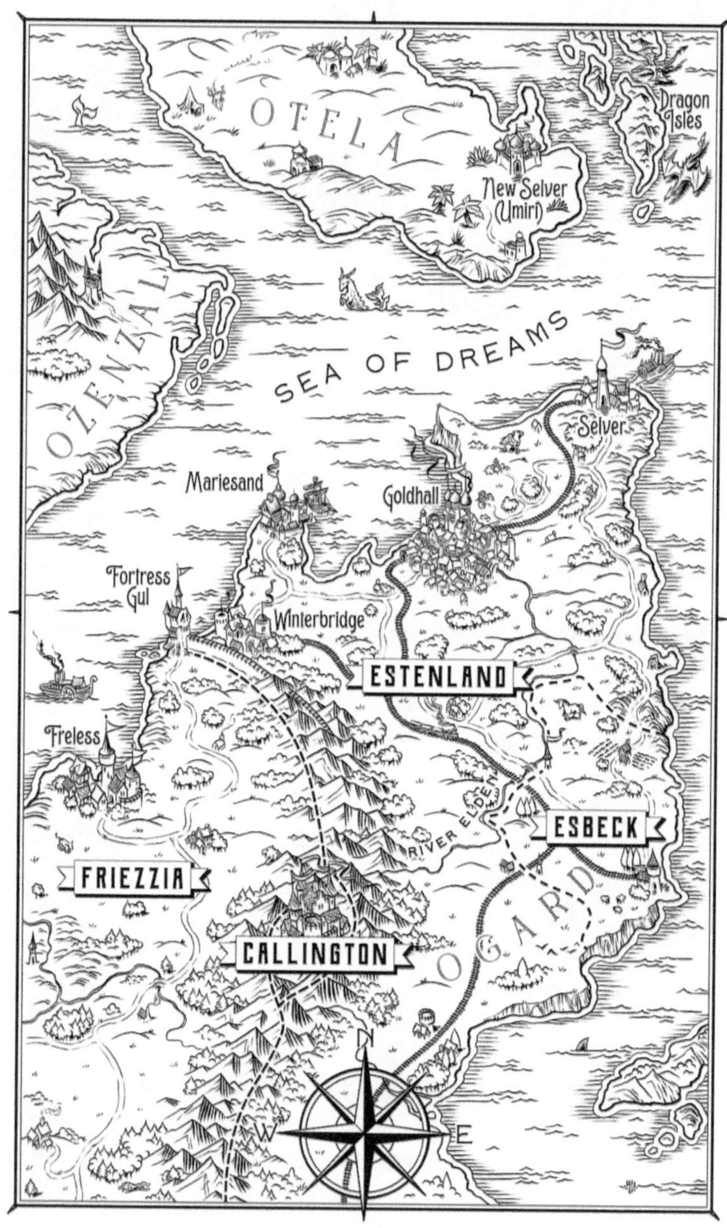

OTELA
New Selver (Umiri)
Dragon Isles
SEA OF DREAMS
OZENZAL
Selver
Mariesand
Goldhall
Fortress Gul
Winterbridge
ESTENLAND
Freless
RIVER ELDEN
ESBECK
FRIEZZIA
OGARD
CALLINGTON
N
W
E

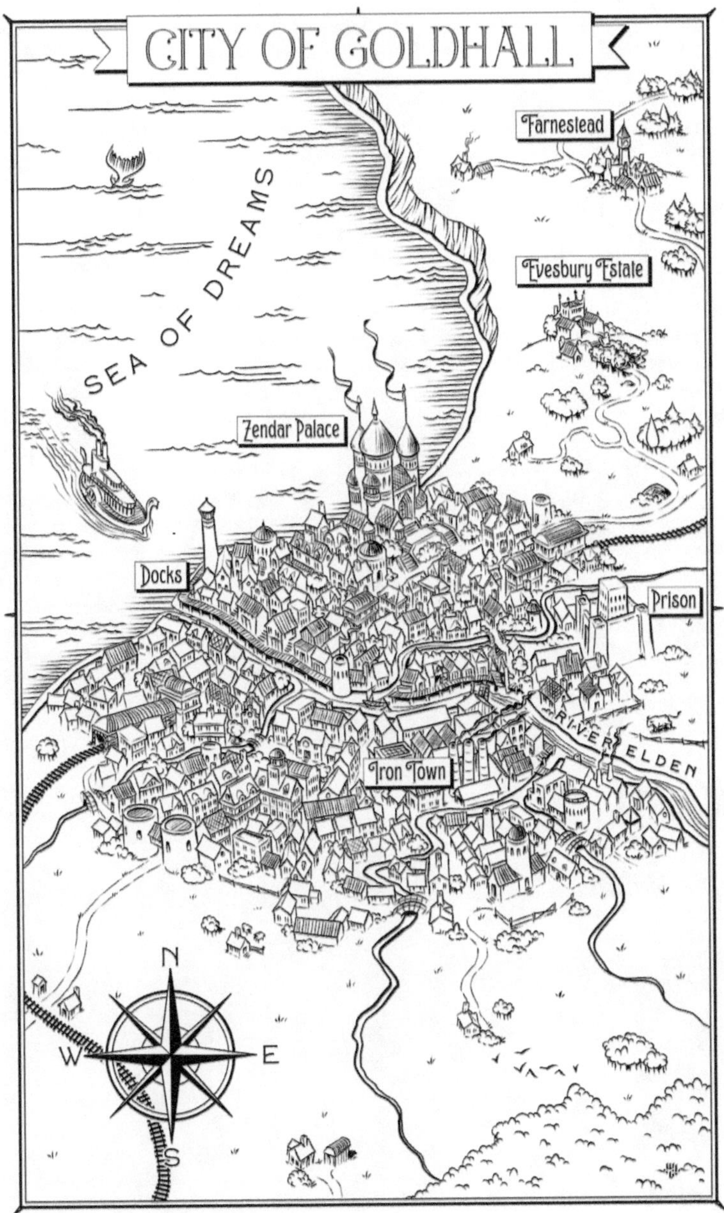

CITY OF GOLDHALL
SEA OF DREAMS
Farnestead
Evesbury Estate
Zendar Palace
Docks
Prison
Iron Town
RIVER ELDEN
N
W
E
S

CHARLOTTE

"I believe you may be lost, my lady," said the hulking doorman.

Charlotte *was* a curious sight, she supposed.

"I believe not," Charlotte replied. She extended her hand and grasped his, placing her thumb upon his middle knuckle, tapping twice, then sliding her middle finger across his palm as she relinquished her grip. This softened his menacing look. "My map-reading abilities have never once failed me," she said with a wink.

"Apologies, my lady," he said, amused. "In these times we must be careful, you understand. Please, do come in."

Charlotte entered the building – the meeting hall of the Working Men's Benevolent Association – located amidst the tenements of Iron Town. She walked toward the chattering coming from the main hall and dropped a generous donation into the collection box upon entering the crowded room. The clinking of the coins brought a surprised smile to the face of the woman guarding the box. Most of the attendees evidently did not give so much as Charlotte.

A steady hum of boisterous conversation filled the room as attendees waited for the meeting to begin. The men – for it was mostly men – were as well dressed as could be expected given their relative poverty. The suits they wore, if somewhat threadbare, were carefully pressed for the evening's meeting. Even though Charlotte had foregone her golden bracelet and aletolium necklace, she looked out of place in what was, to her, a relatively modest green dress.

On the program for this evening was a lecture by Jackson Mylner on the anonymously written book *The Downfall of the Monarchy*. Much of the conversation of the waiting audience surely concerned this text.

Charlotte approached two men in discussion, one of whom was holding a copy. "May I take a look?"

The older man looked her up and down before deciding she must be safe. "Of course, my lady."

"I have heard a great deal about it," she said, "but have not yet had the opportunity to hold it in my hands." She ran her fingers over the embossed words on the spine and flipped through the pages. Inside were arguments not only for democracy, but for the end of monarchy altogether. The faults of King Aramal were carefully detailed, and even the story of Oqci and the sacred creatures was revealed as but a fantasy.

Charlotte lifted her eyes from its pages. "Have you any idea of the author?"

"Well," the man said, lowering his voice, "I have it on good authority that it is by Mylner." His gaze turned to the old guard of the movement himself, who stood in the centre of a small crowd, with someone whispering in his ear. "That said," the man continued, "he has officially denied it. But, then, how could he do otherwise?"

"Very prudent," Charlotte said.

The other man, probably in his thirties, nearer to Charlotte's age, interjected, perhaps wishing to show off his knowledge. "My friend, I have heard it is by Quinneas Raeil. A close associate of mine knows him well, and he told me that it came from Raeil's pen. But," the man added seriously, "you did not hear this from me."

"Whoever the author is," Charlotte said, careful to hide her amusement, "they are surely someone very brilliant. To that, we can all agree."

"Indeed," they said.

The frantic chiming of a glass drew their attention to the podium. There stood Mylner, flustered. "My friends, we must exit," he implored. "Hurry! I have received an urgent notice that a convoy of police will be here shortly."

Police? Dear Oqci. If Charlotte were discovered here…

Panicked cries sounded as the crowd thumped down the corridors to the backdoor exit. Charlotte joined the group as if she were a dinghy swept along in the current. Pressed against the others in the tight hallway, her heart pounding, she struggled merely to keep pace and not be trampled.

The group burst out the door and into an alleyway. Charlotte's comrades raced to their dwellings, yet the heavy galloping from the carriages signalled the imminent arrival of the police.

Her fellows might not all make it to safety in time, she realized. A plan instantly formed in her mind. Charlotte ran back through the building – even as others urged her not to – and out the front entrance. Her shoes clacked on the cobblestones in the quiet night air as she dashed to intercept the police before they drew closer. Down the empty streets she ran with all her might until she spotted the convoy.

"Help! Help!" she shouted as she ran in front of the lead carriage, nearly out of breath.

It halted at once, and the carriages behind barely managed to avoid colliding with those in front. Two constables descended in a rush and appeared stunned when they saw Charlotte was not at all like a usual Iron Town dweller.

"Praise Oqci!" she said, running to one of the constables and grasping his collar. "Praise Oqci! Why, I was just taking a walk and became lost in my thoughts and before I realized, I had found myself terribly mixed up. And now I have not the slightest idea where I am!"

The two policemen could only stare at her, dumbfounded, as other police poured from their carriages, dressed in their sharp blue uniforms.

"Who is this lady?" shouted one of them.

The constable looked at Charlotte then back at his superior. He sighed. "She is only a lost noblewoman."

"A lost...?" said the police captain, exasperated. "Help her find her way home. Everyone else, let us continue on our way."

The captain and the others began to climb back inside their carriages.

"Oh, goodness," she said. "Why, I hope I did not prevent you from any important work."

The captain stopped his movement and turned back to her.

He stifled his frustration – he was, after all, addressing someone above his station – and said, "We had heard there was a meeting of radicals. But worry not, my lady. You are in no danger."

"Radicals? Oh, praise Oqci that you found me in time. How frightening!"

Charlotte could delay them no further without raising suspicion, and she hoped she had given her comrades sufficient time to escape.

The others returned to their carriages, while the two remaining constables looked dejected to miss the adventure. "Step aboard, my lady," one said. "We shall take you to safety."

Charlotte ascended into the rear of their carriage.

"You must learn to be more careful," the constable said, turning back to her.

"I shall be in the future," she said. "Praise Oqci! If you hadn't found me, well, I know not what I would have done." As the policemen fixed their attention forward, Charlotte grinned at her ruse. "Constables, would you take me to the centre of Gold-hall? I have a cab waiting there."

YANIS

Yanis's boots crunched upon the white sand as he stepped from the boat, alongside the other soldiers and explorers. An idyllic tropical island with sandy beaches and lush trees appeared before them.

He glanced back at Calina as he joined the other soldiers ascending the sloping beach and entering the bright green forest, filled with leafy palms, tangled vines, and the scent of fruit trees. Exotically coloured birds, the likes of which did not exist back home in Estenland, fluttered back and forth between the trees, chirping pleasant songs.

Yanis and the other soldiers cut their way through the dense forest, blazing a path for Calina and the other explorers on the mission. Surveys of the coast of New Selver had been the primary task of Yanis's unit, but this was the first time they ventured to explore the chain of islands off the coast.

As they embarked deeper into the forest, an unusual stone block buried amidst the greenery caught Yanis's eye. He reached down and hoisted it up. "Calina, look!"

She came from behind him and took it from his hands. She held it up and squinted to examine it. The block was a solid cube, a bit larger than one of the coconuts from New Selver. It was in perfect condition except that one of the corners was chipped. "Amazing," she said. "Why, it appears manmade. Yet how could that be? The natives in New Selver insisted these islands were uninhabited."

Calina called over one of the porters to gather the block to be taken back to New Selver for further study. Yanis stood back and watched as she gave instructions, her reddish-brown hair standing out against the green backdrop.

As the other soldiers pressed on ahead, Yanis lingered with Calina. He rested his hand upon her waist as they continued walking. Back in Estenland, this kind of intimacy between an unmarried man and woman would be frowned upon, but here, at the other end of the world, greater liberty was afforded in these matters.

"Hmmm, it seems as though there are more," Calina said, stepping assuredly through the vegetation to collect another of the blocks, similar in size to the first one. "This is wonderful. Look!" This one, too, was handed to the porter for further study.

As they advanced, they encountered more and more of the greyish blocks streaked with turquoise. Some even formed incomplete structures. A geological survey of the islands was all that was expected from this mission. Yet already Yanis realized this was a major discovery.

"Highly unusual," Calina muttered as she and Yanis stopped near one of structures, about two stories high, mostly intact save for a collapsed wall.

Yanis ran his hands through the weeds and brush that had grown up around the stones. "There used to be a society here," he said, mostly to himself.

From Calina's thoughtful expression, Yanis could tell her mind was turning quickly as well, considering the implications of these ruins.

"To think," Calina said, winking, "a vile and treasonous criminal like yourself, here, discovering a civilization lost to history."

A smile came to Yanis's lips. "You should be careful to be seen with me."

Their noble commander, Vinzent of Highfalls, approached from behind. "Let us advance further inland," he said, and added with a grin, "there will be time for cavorting later." He marched on.

Calina and Yanis looked at each other and suppressed their laughter as if they were school children who had been scolded. But there was hardly any malice in Vinzent's voice. Indeed, he had taken a liking to the two of them. Being self-educated, Yanis stood above the other criminals and fiends Vinzent was given to mold into soldiers. And Calina differed from some of the older, more self-important scientists who accompanied them on their missions.

Yanis hurried ahead to join the others, who continued cutting through the brush. Birds and insects chirped and buzzed all around them. His brown uniform was already becoming damp from the sweat and clung to his body like a second skin. Yanis wiped his brow. Even as he had been in New Selver for several years now, he believed the climate would always be much too hot for an Estenlander.

"Over here, Yanis," Calina called from another of the structures. This one, mostly undamaged, was the tallest they had encountered so far. She climbed her way through a thicket of trees that had grown around and inside the structure.

Yanis tilted his head up. His heart beat more quickly watching her climb. "Be careful, Calina."

"Worry not," she called down.

Years of colonial adventures had a tendency to make one less averse to risk, Yanis knew. Yet a flutter of anxiety passed through him as she climbed ever higher.

Perched atop one of the structure's ledges, Calina ran her hands over its stone wall. "The turquoise streaks in the blocks must be aletolium," she shouted down to him.

Before he could respond, the sun overhead grew dark, and they were plunged into shadow. The steady whirr of chirps and buzzes ceased. The whole party stopped and stared skyward.

High overhead, a huge silhouette glided in the air. Massive wings spanned the length of a small ship. Protruding from the body were a long snout and an even longer tail.

This was no bird. Some sort of… gigantic flying lizard?

Could it be? A… dragon?

Yanis and the others were frozen, transfixed at once by the magnificence and horror. Awakening them from this temporary stupor, the creature screeched loudly and contorted its body toward the earth.

Yanis scrambled to find cover in the dense jungle as the dragon flew toward them. Their party scattered. At the last instant, just before it would have crashed into the ground, the creature rose again as it flapped its wings, producing a powerful gust of wind that knocked Yanis off his feet.

He stood uneasily, aching from the fall. His eyes darted to find Calina. A moment ago she had been standing atop the stone structure. But no more.

Dear Oqci! Where was she?

"Calina!" he cried, to no response.

Before he could investigate, the massive green dragon, high in the air again, circled back for another go at them. Yanis retrieved the rifle from behind his back. As he fumbled with the powder flask, another soldier shouted, "Get down!"

Yanis ceased his attempts to load the weapon and dove away as the dragon rained a breath of fire upon them. In an instant, the lush jungle was an orange and black inferno. The smell of charred trees filled Yanis's nostrils, and he coughed as he again struggled to his feet.

The creature emitted a deafening roar, shaking the ground.

Yanis scanned the jungle and was horrified to see some of the members of his party reduced to nothing more than blackened corpses amidst the burning greenery. Yanis stumbled toward the structure where Calina had been standing just moments before. It was now no more than a pile of smoking rubble.

"Yanis," Vinzent shouted above the boom of the creature's cries. "We must go!"

Fighting for breath amidst the smoke and ignoring the commands, Yanis climbed atop the ruined structure and frantically cleared away the stones. Block after block, boiling hot to the touch, careened down the small mountain of debris as he threw them aside. "Calina!"

But no response came from beneath the rubble.

Vinzent grabbed his arm. "Yanis, now! We're going to be killed if we stay any longer."

Yanis pulled his arm free, never turning from the rubble. "I cannot leave her!"

Vinzent tugged Yanis with all his might. "Yanis, we must leave now. That is an order."

Yanis continued to ignore him. He heaved a large rock away,

but it was no use. With another pull, Vinzent awakened him to reality – as did an ear-splitting screech from the creature above.

All around was panic. Soldiers rushed past, hurrying for their lives. Yanis joined the charge, with Vinzent's hand clasped tightly around his arm the whole way. They bounded over fallen branches and across the uneven terrain in a haze of flames and smoke. Several more of the dragons, large and small, circled overhead.

One soldier fired a shot. An anguished cry came from above.

Yanis's heart pounded as they exited the thick jungle and the shore came into view. With Vinzent still at his side, their sprint slowed on the soft sand of the beach.

They climbed aboard one of the waiting boats and took stock of their situation. Less than half of their party had made it to safety. Vinzent took one final glance. "Go, go!" he shouted at the crew after seeing no one else.

Back in the boat, Yanis realized what had just happened. "We cannot leave them behind. We must go back!"

"It is impossible," said Vinzent. "We need to return to New Selver. Once we regroup, we can return for the others."

As the scattered boats pushed out to their waiting transport ship, Yanis counted ten of the dragons circling above the island. Fortunately they did not pursue beyond the shore.

Slouching forward, Yanis muttered, "We should have stayed."

Vinzent settled his hand upon Yanis's shoulder. "You know we couldn't have," he said softly. "We'd have all been killed."

3

DELLIREA

Because the afternoon weather was pleasant, Dellirea and her father Aramal walked the palace gardens amidst the unicorns and griffins who roamed freely around the grounds. A short walk would help improve Aramal's mood following the tensions at the council meeting from earlier, Dellirea thought.

As they walked a stony path lined with carefully sculpted hedges, Dellirea talked to her father about happier subjects, of her volunteer work the day before at the urban charity centre.

"One man committed himself to our faith," she bubbled. "He has become a true follower of Oqci!"

Aramal made a small grunting noise acknowledging Dellirea's words, but said little more.

She turned to look at him, though his eyes were focused on the path. Dellirea reasoned that his mind was preoccupied with the news of the dragons and the ruined civilization. In truth, she was too. How could it be otherwise? She knew not what to think about it, but she was deeply unsettled. Had Oqci not told them in the holy scriptures of only five varieties of sacred creatures? He had said nothing of dragons.

Children, like Dellirea's younger cousins, had wild imaginations and drew pictures of flying, fire-breathing lizards, but Dellirea and all other mature people understood these were fantastical.

"The Creator has blessed you with a heart of kindness," Aramal said at last, interrupting Dellirea's wandering mind. "But you must be careful, Delli. Some of those men have decidedly poor morals and may have sinister thoughts about a young lady such as yourself."

"Worry not, father," she said. "The men are harmless. You are right that some lack morals, but it is only because they are ignorant of our doctrines, and their poverty makes them unable to resist vice."

"Mhmmm," mumbled her father, plainly unconvinced.

"It's true! The convert we won was a man who had previously earned his living at a woollen mill... until an accident in the machinery cost him his right arm. After that, he could no longer usefully work. In his poverty and despair, he allowed himself to be conquered by evil. He turned toward alcoholic drink and abandoned his wife and children. But deep down, under this evil, the good man remained. It is our duty to offer him a path back to the light by teaching him the doctrines of Oqci – and so indeed he has now returned."

"Just be careful, Delli. That is all I ask. After your brother... Please, just be careful."

They continued walking. The scent of the blue and purple hyacinths in the garden, just coming into bloom, wafted up to them. The scent of springtime. The sun warmed the exposed skin of Dellirea's forearms and the gentle breeze blew her hair about her face.

She looked up at Aramal, who appeared much older than his age. His hair had begun greying already and pronounced wrinkles were forming around his eyes, surely the result of the stresses of ruling these past years.

"I apologize for raising my voice at the meeting earlier," he said abruptly. He stopped and faced her. "You remained quiet when he discussed plans to send another expedition to the island. You are growing older now, Delli, and I value your opinion."

"I can only offer my guidance," she said. "The final decision remains yours and everyone is bound to respect it." She considered her words carefully. "But I fear we must not be hasty in exploring this island. As the Duke of Prencroft counselled, if handled improperly, this mission could only increase unrest among the poorer classes. I have seen them up close and, though their hearts are good, I know that they can be easily swayed by agitators, like the author of that horrid book whose name I dare not speak. Let us instead use our resources to uplift the masses, to show them the way to Oqci."

Her father turned to face the path and continued walking with his eyes trained to the ground in thought. "Your opinion is very dear to me, Delli. And I admire your concern for the coarser segments of our nation. Yet I worry this concern will cloud your judgment when it comes time for *you* to take over the throne and lead the nation."

"Oh father, please –"

"You must understand that part of the job of the ruler is to lead our nation to greatness," he interrupted, his voice growing more forceful. "This island of dragons, I'm sure, is precisely such an opportunity. And one from which we cannot run. Are we to let Friezzia discover it? To stand back and let them claim the glory that rightfully belongs to Estenland?"

"Well –"

"No. No! I could not allow that," he bellowed. "It *must* be ours."

Dellirea knew it was fruitless to put forth a rebuttal. And perhaps he was correct, that a ruler must be concerned with national greatness. He, most of all, was constantly reminded of that. Dellirea contemplated a nearby clearing where a half dozen winged horses grazed, a fraction of the sacred creatures who made the palace grounds their home. Some of them had come from Friezzia, captured following her grandfather's victory during the Great War. What was more, all around them – in the garden, throughout the capital, throughout the country even – were statues of Andamar the Great that commemorated the triumphant victory.

They stopped in front of one with Andamar posed atop a winged horse, looking out with a determined expression.

Slowly gazing up at the white marble statue, Dellirea's father said, "I wish to be remembered for something as well. To do pride to the Zendar dynasty. To have my own statues. To be known as one of the greatest kings in our history."

In that moment, Dellirea's heart softened for her father as she recognized the immense burden that weighed upon him.

"You will be," Dellirea reassured him, tenderly grasping his hand. "You are a wise leader who cares for his people. They will always love and respect you for that."

Aramal smiled warmly before putting his arm around her shoulders and pulling her close.

4

SAMUEL

"Ladies and gentlemen," Samuel said, stepping to the centre of the lecture theatre. "I have here on my desk two skulls. On the right is the skull of a deceased nobleman who donated his body to science. On the left is the skull of a pauper, recently dead by suicide, donated by the city coroner. Might I have a volunteer to come and tell me what differences they perceive between these two skulls?"

Samuel looked out at the rows of spectators. Tonight, as he did once a week, he opened his anatomy lectures to the public. Samuel's regular students were there, of course, but some of the newly moneyed classes were also in attendance, curious to see this eccentric professor whom they had heard so much about, even if it meant descending into the slums of Iron Town.

Samuel spotted an eager newcomer in the second row raising his hand. A well-dressed young man with a confident expression.

"Come and take a look, my friend. Have I seen you before?"

"No, this is my first time attending," he said, as he rose to his feet. "But I have done much reading on the subject of anatomy and consider myself a student of the discipline."

"Excellent, excellent. Now, tell me what you see here."

The man bounded to the front of the room, flashed a smile to the audience, then bent down to examine one skull and then the other. Samuel resented the smugness of those of this man's class, but he could hardly be mad at them for long, since they flocked to his lectures – much more popular than those of his colleagues or the stodgy old professors at Etterburg – and provided him with an income he had never thought possible in his youth.

Stroking his chin in such a way as to give the impression of thoughtfulness, the man began, "The one on the right, that of the nobleman, is a superior size. A larger cranial capacity indicates a more well-developed brain, whereas the smaller size of the one on the left, the pauper, shows limited mental development. Perhaps the result of inferior stock or poor education. Or a combination of both."

"Excellent," Samuel said, nodding. "Continue." Samuel winked at Greta, his prize student. She smiled knowingly back at him from her seat in the crowd.

"Hmm," the man went on, "I believe this bump here at the crest of the skull on the right might indicate a particular aptitude for charity." Gaining more confidence, the man continued, "And these ridges on the forehead of the left skull might indicate an undeveloped control of the impulses. This pauper was perhaps a drunkard, unable to master his urges."

"Very astute observation."

The encouragement only made the man bolder. "The proportions of the facial bones and the jaw of the skull on the right are very much in harmony. This might well indicate a talent in the arts. Whereas that of the left seems decidedly out of balance. The poor man probably struggled to compose fluid sentences, let alone to express complex or beautiful thoughts."

"Very good," Samuel said, clapping his hands. "Very good indeed. I hope everyone was taking notes. And you said you were self-taught?"

"That's right."

"Even more impressive in that case."

The man stood tall with an earnest smile, looking out at the crowd like he thought himself some kind of great genius. In the audience, Samuel's students glanced back and forth at each other, suppressing their grins.

"But," Samuel said, pausing for effect and raising his index finger, "there is just one thing."

The students could barely contain their laughter. The man's grin gave way to a look of fear.

"Yes, there is just one thing I should have mentioned… The skull on the right is, in fact, that of the pauper. The left is the nobleman."

The audience erupted with laughter and applause. Samuel

looked out to the crowd to sweet Greta, who too bubbled with laughter.

The man's face grew red. He looked as though he wanted to curl into a tiny ball.

"That's all right, my friend," Samuel said, slapping the man's shoulder in a good-natured way – even though inside Samuel was delighted at the man's humiliation. "It happens to the best of us. But it is with this knowledge that we learn an important lesson. We learn the value of humility and the power of suggestion. Scientists must learn to stifle any preconceived ideas and approach everything with a fresh mind. I thank you for giving us the opportunity to learn from your mistake. Now, let us give our friend a round of applause."

Samuel bowed to the man and joined in the applause. The man, with his dignity slightly recovered, although still bruised, returned to his seat.

As THE LECTURE concluded and the audience filed out, Samuel gathered his materials and carried them back to his lab, pleased with his trick from earlier. He returned the skulls to the glass cabinets, which contained specimens from across the animal kingdom. Through the study of these specimens, he would one day add his name to the history books. His theories would one day reveal all.

The so-called sacred creatures! Brought down from the sky by Oqci? Ha!

But it was still too dangerous, too scandalous, to think of publishing. One day, however!

A knock at Samuel's door interrupted his musings. Two men, dressed in crisp three-piece suits with top hats, appeared at the door. They introduced themselves as Michael of Highstaff and his brother-in-law, Adar of Winslough. Highly unusual. Noblemen did not typically take an interest in the subject of anatomy, least of all Samuel's lectures.

"Dr. Nox," Michael said, in an accent Samuel couldn't quite

place, "it may surprise you, coming from noblemen such as ourselves, but we have followed your lectures closely."

"We are with you in science," Adar added, "and politics."

Samuel could hardly believe such words coming from nobles. But perhaps his ideas were having a greater impact than even he had imagined.

"The purpose of our visit," Michael continued, "is that we believe we can contribute to your scientific research. Recently, one of our unicorns fell ill and, despite our best efforts, sadly did not survive."

"I'm sorry to hear that."

"Indeed," said Michael. "It was a terrible tragedy. What we propose..." He stopped to clear his throat. "What we propose is for you to examine the creature's body."

"I... But... Such a thing is forbidden by law!"

"Worry not, Dr. Nox," Adar said, moving closer and lowering his voice. "We come to you in secret. The only people who know will be the three of us in this very room."

"The question is whether you will agree," said Michael. "But the longer you wait, the greater danger we shall all be in."

Samuel knew not what to say. He had never before contemplated dissecting a sacred creature. Procuring a specimen had always been an impossibility...

All his theories about the animal kingdom made sense. They were perfect, elegant. Yet there was just the matter of the sacred creatures. They were the final piece of the puzzle. If only he could solve it... He would be known as one of the greatest scientists of all time. No, the greatest ever! And he would win the love of Greta.

The men edged closer. "Well, Dr. Nox? What is your answer? Will you examine the creature?"

Thoughts flew wildly across Samuel's mind. Of the triumphs, yes, but the dangers also. To be found desecrating the body of a sacred creature? The harshest penalty would await anyone caught.

But great men of science always took risks, did they not? And no one would ever know but the three of them in that very room. He could perform the dissections at night, Samuel reasoned, when the lab was empty. Discovery would be impossible.

But would it? Even the smallest mistake could unravel the entire enterprise. One of his students, bumbling in his cabinets... Another professor working late... The list of potential dangers was great.

"Dr. Nox? Please, we must have your answer," said Michael, who nervously checked his timepiece.

Samuel took a long inhale. Curse the dangers!

"I shall do it," Samuel said and extended his hand to the two men.

With the handshake, they settled on the deal. Tomorrow evening, just after sunset, they would bring him the body of their unicorn.

5

CHARLOTTE

The horse-drawn carriage jostled Charlotte this way and that as it traversed the bumpy streets of Iron Town. Her heart slowed to its normal pace and the ride became smoother as she neared the centre of Goldhall. The perfect escape! And hopefully her subterfuge had distracted the police long enough to give her comrades a chance to avoid capture.

Charlotte requested the police carriage drop her two blocks from the King's Society of Philosophy.

"Thank you ever so much, constables," she said, as she alighted. "Praise Oqci!"

The men could only smile at her, speechless – too smitten for words, Charlotte reckoned.

Before they had a chance to inquire into her name, or anything else for that matter, Charlotte hurried through the backstreets toward the old philosophy building and slipped in the side door. She checked her timepiece. Perfect.

She made her way through the building corridors, walking purposefully so as to not invite conversation from anyone still lingering inside, and immediately out the front doors. There she found her own carriage, patiently waiting, just where she had left it several hours ago.

"An agreeable meeting tonight, my lady?" said her driver.

"As ever," Charlotte said, satisfied that he suspected not a thing.

As they made their way through downtown Goldhall and back to her estate, as they passed through ever wealthier neighbourhoods, her mind could not turn away from the earlier events. Charlotte had narrowly avoided capture through her quick thinking, but now that the thrill had dissipated, she wondered if she had not been foolhardy to put herself in danger in such a way.

~

THE FOLLOWING MORNING, Charlotte found her brother Brondin sitting in the dining room, waiting for breakfast to be served. His wife, Allegrette, and the baby were still in the nursery, Charlotte surmised.

"How was the philosophy meeting last evening, dear sister?" Brondin said casually but eyeing Charlotte with suspicion.

"Excellent," she said flatly. "Much great discussion."

Brondin was three years younger than her, yet Charlotte still had trouble imagining him as anything more than a child.

"Very good," Brondin said. "And which paper was discussed?"

"Its contents would be beyond your grasp," she said, "but Milton presented a paper on his preliminary theories of logic."

"I see," he said, as Charlotte's mild insult sailed clear over his head. "And did you see Lord Marjorie there? I believe he was attending as well."

"Hmm," she said, "our paths must not have crossed."

"Indeed, they must not have. He regularly attends the meetings, yet when I mentioned you in conversation last week, he told me he rarely sees you there."

"Perhaps we sit in different parts of the seminar room."

"Is that so?"

Charlotte ignored her brother's question as one of their servants brought her a cup of tea. Outwardly, she appeared calm, yet inwardly, she was growing irritated at this inquisition. Her breathing quickened. What was he driving at?

Looking across at him, she even became bothered at how similar they looked. His brown hair was a shade darker than her own, but his features were becoming more refined, even attractive, as he became an adult, much as hers had.

"Charlotte," he said, his expression serious and his tone quieter so that none of the servants could overhear, "I asked our carriage driver to watch you closely last night. He reported that only a moment after you entered the building of the society, you exited from a side door and caught another cab. Wherever were you going?"

"Spying on me?" she whispered angrily. The thought of him catching her in a lie was bad enough, but she quickly realized that she could be in grave danger if her true destination were discovered. "How dare you!"

"I knew I was right to be suspicious," Brondin said. "Now where were you? Were you off gallivanting with some man? You *are* married, don't forget!"

"It is none of your concern." Charlotte looked around the room, ensuring that none of the servants were eavesdropping.

"It is my concern," Brondin said, "since, with father gone and mother unwell, someone needs to look after you. Your husband evidently won't. But I suppose it falls to me, even though I have my own family to look after now. Charlotte, you cannot go around risking scandal upon our family name by going Oqci-knows-where every night."

"It's none of your concern," she repeated and rose from her chair. "I shall hear no more of this. Do not tell mother and do not speak of Willien. We ought not even be married."

She called out to one of the servants who waited in the nearby kitchen that she wished to have breakfast upstairs alone and left Brondin behind before he could say anything more.

6

YANIS

Yanis lay upon his cot, staring at the ceiling of the barracks. Little breeze entered through the window, so the room was hot and smelled of sweat.

It had been a week since their ill-fated voyage to the island. Yanis could think of nothing other than the tragedy of that day. He could not extricate the horrible images from his brain. Nor the feelings of guilt from which he could find no relief.

He and Calina had been together only six months. But those months were the happiest of Yanis's life. She was a rare person, someone who saw the best in everything. No darkness tinted her view of life. To her, life was too full of joy for her to be bothered by anything else for long. So different from how Yanis viewed things. Being with her was like the coming of a bright and sunny day after months of rain.

They had first encountered one another when his unit was posted to accompany the scientific explorations around New Selver. Yanis was intrigued: someone like her, also from Iron Town, becoming a scientist. To his surprise, she was intrigued by him too, when she found he was more learned than the other soldiers. And when she found what he had done to deserve the punishment of exile.

It was unexpected that they should ever be together. And Yanis could hardly believe his good fortune when they were.

His mind kept replaying the moments before the dragons attacked. There she stood, atop the stone structure, running her hands over the mysterious blocks. Just then, they were plunged into shadow, as high overhead the terrible creature flew through the air.

And that was the last he saw her.

～

IN THE PALM-THATCHED tavern that evening, Yanis sat amidst the other soldiers in his group and imbibed the potent native liquor, made from a local fermented root. He liked how it warmed his insides, and so he paid little notice to the burning it caused in his nostrils or how it made his eyes water. Listening to the gentle waves crash onto the beach just outside, he happily glugged down several cups, which the tavern keeper eagerly refilled.

The group had already received the news that King Aramal intended them to return to the island once reinforcements had arrived from Estenland. The dragons and the ruined city were too great a prize to be left alone. A dozen warships and a force of a thousand men were to join them for the mission. Even a contingent of priests was making the voyage.

But it all seemed senseless to Yanis. And if he died on the mission, he would hardly mind. In fact, it might even be preferable.

Whenever Yanis began to feel any kind of emotion welling up inside, he brought the wooden cup to his lips. He was content to drink in silence as the others laughed and carried on conversation. He had nothing to say to those other men. Most of them had either been so poor as to need to join the army in order to survive, or they had been convicted of some crime like theft – or in Yanis's case, offending Aramal's sensibilities with his pamphlets.

But the soldiers from his group hooted and hollered at some of the native women who also frequented the place, interrupting his solitude.

The world was already spinning as the alcohol took effect. Yanis lost count of how many drinks he had taken. And he was growing ever more agitated with the brutish behaviour. "Must you act like such fools all the time?" Yanis exclaimed to the soldiers at his table as they persisted in whistling at the women. "Have you no decency?"

"Cheer up, Yanis," said Ronar, a drunken buffoon from his unit. Ronar shakily rose from his chair and placed his arm around Yanis. The stench of liquor on his breath was overpowering. "Missing Calina, eh pal?"

Yanis resisted this provocation as some of the other soldiers chuckled.

"Look around, my friend," he continued, gesturing at the rest of the tavern. "There are plenty of whores here to help take your mind off her for the evening."

"You… You simple-minded dolt!"

Before Yanis could think, he rose to his feet and shoved Ronar onto the table, nearly tipping it over and sending the wooden cups and bottles of liquor clattering down.

"Whoa, whoa!" cried Ronar, as the others in the group shouted for them to stop.

Ronar sprang back up at Yanis, and they both collapsed to the wet dirt floor.

The next moments happened in a blur. Yanis climbed on top of Ronar and threw a wild punch as hard as he could. His fist grazed Ronar's face before connecting with the solid ground. His knuckles stung from the miss. As Yanis recoiled from the pain, Ronar flipped him over. Just as Ronar cocked back his fist, Yanis grabbed his shirt and dragged him to the ground.

Before Yanis knew what was happening, two soldiers had pulled him up and restrained him. Ronar, too, was held back by another pair.

Yanis shouted incoherently to be released. But the room was suddenly spinning. He could barely stand upright without the soldiers' help. All the liquor in his stomach was suddenly forcing its way up.

YANIS'S HEAD POUNDED, his mouth like cotton. He opened his eyes a crack, before shutting them once more. What happened last night? His last memory was the furious tavern owner, in his broken attempt at the Estenlanders' tongue, demanding that they pay for the damages to his shop as the other soldiers helped Yanis away.

Dear Oqci.

Yanis willed himself out of his cot and to breakfast. There

were few soldiers there yet. He sat alone, drinking some cool tea to quench his thirst.

Ronar entered and approached Yanis. His eyes were blood-shot, his hair wild and unkempt. Yanis imagined that he hardly looked any better.

"Sorry, mate," he said. "Listen, I had a bit too much of the natives' grog last night. Shouldn't have said what I said."

"Think nothing of it," Yanis grumbled.

"Thanks, mate." He slapped Yanis on the shoulder and returned to his table.

Some apology!

Yanis observed Ronar across the room. Like Yanis, he had come from Iron Town and had been sentenced to serve time as a soldier, in his case for convictions of theft and public drunkenness. Yanis hated that he would forever be associated with the likes of Ronar. But he knew he had no choice but to serve alongside him in the coming mission.

YANIS and the others in his unit waited upon deck. The largest of the chain of islands once again appeared over the horizon as their ship approached at dawn. The goal was to capture at least one juvenile dragon alive and bring it to Estenland.

As they drew ever closer, Yanis could only think of Calina. It had been two weeks since the first expedition. She and any others were surely dead by now. Still, in the back of his mind was the possibility, however slim, that they might find survivors. Whenever he felt the slightest tinge of hope, however, he did his best to blot it from his mind.

With all of the ships in place, and the sky a purplish-red, they approached ever closer.

A group of priests assembled on the deck of the warship, all dressed in their blue robes and wearing aletolium pendants. It was said that priests possessed the strongest connection with the sacred creatures, so it was reasoned that they might also be able to connect with the dragons. At least, that was the theory. They bowed their heads and chanted, asking the Creator or Oqci or whoever for assistance. Yanis shook his head at the absurdity of their mumbled chanting.

Yanis waited anxiously while breathing in the sea air. He wondered if this was not a certain suicide mission, let alone whether they could actually hope to capture one of the dragons.

7

SAMUEL

Samuel had slept awfully the previous night. His rash was flaring up again and he could not cease the scratching.

His thoughts continued to turn to the possibility that lay before him. If… if he uncovered the secret of the sacred creatures, when he walked down the street no longer would he be known as the eccentric, balding professor, with his well-known side whiskers, or as a mild amusement for members of high society. No, he would be hailed as a genius: Articles would be written about his ideas, those old fossils from Etterburg would attend banquets in his honour, and the entire pretense of Estenland's unequal system would come crashing down. And best of all, he would win Greta's love.

No! He mustn't get ahead of himself!

Samuel awaited the arrival of the two noblemen that evening, constantly checking his timepiece throughout the day. But they arrived promptly, just after sundown. Just as they had agreed.

The noblemen wore the same suits as yesterday, now slightly wrinkled. Slightly odd, but no matter.

Samuel's eyes focused instead on the large trunk they rolled along behind them. After exchanging pleasantries, the noblemen opened it to reveal the well-preserved body of a unicorn. They transferred the body atop one of Samuel's dissecting tables. The unicorn was majestic, even in death. In the gaslit laboratory, its white coat still shone and its horn sparkled.

On the side of the unicorn, however, a section of its coat was stained a dark brown. Lifting up the creature revealed a hole in its neck surrounded by dried blood.

"Unfortunately, we had to shoot the creature when it became clear it would not recover from its illness," Michael explained gravely, noticing Samuel's concern.

It was a shame, but otherwise the cadaver was in excellent condition.

Samuel ran his hands over its soft coat. This was the closest he had ever come to a sacred creature. The nobles and priests would sometimes walk them through the streets, but the chance to actually examine one up close was something Samuel could never have imagined when he was young. This could be his passage to fame. To respect.

He almost forgot the two noblemen were still there, so engrossed was he with the creature. "Gentlemen," Samuel said, "I cannot thank you enough. I realize the tremendous sacrifice you have made to bring me your unicorn. I shall not disappoint you. From this specimen, I shall be able to unlock great mysteries."

"We do hope so," Michael said.

Samuel bowed to them and awaited their departure. However, they continued to stand silently in his laboratory.

"There is one final thing, however, which we need to discuss," said Adar. "We shall need a payment of 1,000 crowns, to ensure we are justly compensated."

"What?" Samuel said. "Why… we did not agree to that when we spoke yesterday! You said this was in the interest of science. I shall agree to no such payment!" He stopped. This lacked all sense. "What kind of noblemen are so in need of money that they need to extort it from a poor scientist like myself?"

"Dr. Nox, please, you are hardly a poor man," said Michael, his tone suddenly menacing. "We are well aware of your finances. As to why noblemen such as ourselves need the money… It's better if you know as little as possible. We are sympathetic to you, so we ask that you be sympathetic to us as well."

Both of the men stepped toward Samuel and backed him into the corner of his lab. They came so close that they and Samuel almost touched. They smelled of having gone days without washing, their skin coarse and dirty up close. They stood silently glaring at Samuel, awaiting his response.

"I shan't pay it," Samuel said, trying to his best to sound firm.

"Is that so?" said Michael. "In that case, the police would be very interested to learn that you have a dead unicorn in your lab. And what was the penalty for desecrating the body of a sacred creature…?"

"Death," Adar said. "Death by hanging."

"Yes, that's right. Death by hanging."

Samuel could say nothing. He was finished. Everything he had worked toward, all the hardships he had endured. To climb from nothing, to reach heights never before imagined by someone from his background, and for it all to come crashing down, at the hands of these so-called… nobles.

Nobles? How could he have been so foolish to believe that?

"Don't despair, Dr. Nox," said Michael, seeing the defeated look on Samuel's face. With his finger, he lifted up Samuel's chin. "We can still have a fruitful partnership. We supply creatures for you, and you do what you wish with them. These creatures will make you famous, will they not? And we shall have been appropriately rewarded."

Samuel looked again at the unicorn cadaver upon his dissection table. There was a certain logic to what he said. Perhaps it could be fruitful. Perhaps Samuel could perform the dissections, publish his findings anonymously at first, and when they became accepted, announce he was the author and be hailed a hero. On the other hand, the risk was great. Receiving dead creatures from these scoundrels…

If he reported the men right away, Samuel thought, perhaps he would be spared. But would the government show him mercy? Would they even believe him? They might just as soon lock all of them up. Or worse.

And what a great chance he would be wasting! This was the kind of opportunity upon which to build a career. The kind of opportunity that could change the face of science.

Risk be damned! Samuel was a man of science at heart. And progress in science came from taking risks, he knew. He told the men he would accept their deal. Samuel would pay them the fee, even though it represented a substantial portion of his monthly income, in exchange for the unicorn, and more creatures to come.

8

DELLIREA

That afternoon, Dellirea's lessons in the Friezzian language were cancelled, by reason of her teacher falling ill. But privately Dellirea was delighted by the turn of events, since this afforded her the opportunity to join her mother, her aunt, and some of the other noblewomen at court for card playing and tea drinking. Dellirea was unsure if playing cards was appropriate, especially since the five types of cards each contained a picture of one of the sacred creatures. She wondered if this was not blasphemous. Still, she stifled her reservations since it meant a chance to spend time with these sophisticated women.

Dellirea walked through the gardens to her mother Bravala's new residence, off the east wing of the palace. Her mother had built it recently to serve as a private residence to escape the hectic life of court, especially the rumours – entirely false, Dellirea knew – of her decadent spending.

As Dellirea entered her mother's chamber, before the others arrived, she found her mother gazing at some landscape paintings of the Esbeckian coast that adorned her room and provided her with memories of home.

"Isn't it just beautiful, Delli?" she asked, looking at one with brilliant blue water splashing onto the beach below the rocky cliffs.

"It is indeed, mother."

"You know, you can swim in the sea all year round in Esbeck," she said wistfully as she turned to her daughter. "And you can eat the finest seafood whenever you wish."

"It sounds lovely." Dellirea had only ever visited Esbeck a few times, and she had to admit she preferred the more moderate climate of Estenland, although she did not express this opinion aloud.

"I said to your father that we must try to visit more often," Bravala said, turning back to face the painting. "I miss my home very much sometimes."

"I understand." Dellirea moved closer to her mother and clasped her hand. It saddened Dellirea to think of leaving home the way her mother did. Bravala had been only a few years older than Dellirea was now when she came to Estenland to marry Aramal as part of an alliance to affirm diplomatic ties between the two nations. Dellirea could only imagine how painful it was for her mother to leave so much behind.

Their discussion was interrupted by boisterous chatter coming from the hall, indicating the arrival of the other women. Fortunately, Dellirea's mother had not left all of her family behind in Esbeck.

As THEY GATHERED in the drawing room, the women stood out from the typical Estenlanders that could be seen at court, with their blonde hair and dainty features, common among Esbeckian nobles. Dellirea had inherited the blonde hair, but not their delicate features, which created, in her opinion, an unharmonious mixture with the larger nose and eyes of the Estenlanders. But she did not care for such frivolous things as appearance. What mattered was what was in one's heart, just as Oqci said.

Dellirea had been eager to join the card-playing, yet after less than an hour, she began to wonder why she had even wanted to. In between rounds of the game, the other women only gossiped about others at court, about how this noble or that was seen making eyes at another while their spouse was none the wiser. Dellirea cared not at all for such talk.

"Is there religious significance to the dragons?" Dellirea asked, hoping to turn the conversation to substantive issues, worthy of ladies such as themselves. "Why is there no mention of them in the Book of Oqci, and what is to be our nation's approach to them?"

"Delli, please," said Yuvela, Bravala's closest friend, who had joined her from Esbeck, "your mother built this residence to get away from such talk."

"Yes," another interjected. "Let us change the subject. Delli, have you a boyfriend yet?"

"I have not," she answered. Her face grew hot. She disliked gossip in general, but especially so when it concerned her.

"Ohh, come, Delli," said her aunt Meritoria. "You are almost sixteen now! There must be someone you fancy?"

"I haven't anyone yet," Dellirea said. "I haven't thought much about it."

"Really?" someone else said. "Don't be so prudish!"

Bravala, perhaps sensing her daughter's discomfort, tried to redirect the conversation. "Come, ladies. Let us not pester Delli with such questions."

"Of course," said Yuvela. "Just one piece of advice, Delli: Make sure you marry a man with a big cock!"

All the women laughed at this, even Dellirea's mother.

"That's right," Meritoria interjected. "Don't make the same mistake as Yuvela!"

They burst out in even stronger laughter now. Some even wiped tears from their eyes.

At this, Dellirea rose and exited the room, disgusted with her mother's friends, and even with her, for allowing such crude talk.

Her mother chased after her down the hall. "Delli, I'm sorry for the ladies' behaviour. Sometimes we get carried away with our joking. None of them meant to offend you."

"That kind of talk is highly inappropriate," she said. "Perhaps it might be appropriate for coarser women, but it's hardly becoming for women of *our* status." With that, Dellirea continued to the exit.

9

YANIS

As Yanis's group neared the island, packed into their transport boat which bobbed through the waves, ear-splitting cracks from the artillery of the warships rang out behind them, followed by the distant thud of the shells hitting land. It was hoped that the dragons would be drawn out to do battle at sea with the finest ships of Estenland's navy, while Yanis and the other soldiers would move into position unobstructed on the island. Yet the dragons had not appeared by the time his boat made landfall.

The noise from the artillery barrage jarred with the peaceful crashing of the waves on the beach. Yanis filed out alongside the rest of his unit. The loss of Calina had dulled any nerves he might have had. Instead he felt only a lingering sense of duty. Duty to what, or to whom, he knew not.

Yanis and his unit marched solemnly on the same path they had blazed last time. The blackened trees they found along the way were grim reminders of the dragon's fire.

A roar in the distance stopped them in their tracks. One soldier stood next to Yanis, wide-eyed and visibly shaking: a fresh recruit, like some of the others in the unit, with no experience from the previous mission.

"Keep moving," ordered Vinzent.

"Dear Oqci," the man said, almost ready to begin blubbering. "We're… we're all going to die."

Ronar chuckled at the man's cowardice, but another roar, much closer, shook the entire ground. And it ceased Ronar's laughter.

"Let us persist," Yanis said, encouraging the rest of the unit forward.

They pushed on, even as a shadow covered them as a dragon flew past. Yanis gripped his musket tightly in case of attack.

Behind them, the capture team readied their device. Another dragon approached in the distance.

"Ready…" Vinzent called out. Yanis raised his musket. "Fire!" In unison, half their unit launched a volley as it flew overhead. A shriek from above meant a direct hit.

The dragon's pathetic cry filled Yanis with pity. The dragons were their foe, but were they not simply defending their homes? How bloody awful Estenland was, Yanis thought. He hoped they could just capture one and extricate themselves as quickly as possible.

The cracking and crashing of a warship in the distance told him that this would not be easy.

"Dear Oqci," said the nervous recruit again. "What was that?"

"Didn't sound good," said Ronar.

More dragons flew above. There had to be at least a dozen now. Maybe more.

With half the unit, Yanis fired a shot skyward. As they reloaded, the other half launched their volley. Fire again. Repeat. Yet the dragons passed too quickly to provide any hope of shooting accurately.

The gunpowder smoke hung around them like fog in the jungle, yet through it, Yanis caught a glimpse of one of the younger, smaller dragons: their main target.

The capture team scrambled into position. A modified cannon launched a weighted net into the air. Yanis's entire unit froze to watch.

The net flew upward, nearing the dragon, closer, closer…

Their eyes followed its arcing path through the air.

Closer, closer… before it finally dropped back down to the earth, missing the dragon by some margin.

"Fuck," grunted Vinzent.

The dragons focused their attacks on the warships and ignored Yanis and his group as they pressed deeper into the jungle. At last they came upon the first of the ruined structures Yanis had seen during the previous expedition. All the scattered memories of that day returned. That was where Calina had proudly hoisted up one of the stone blocks. Where they had joked and flirted. Where she had stated that the blocks could not possibly be manmade.

Moving farther into the jungle, Yanis realized that all his memories were mixed up. The piles of stone rubble all looked the same, and the charred ruins of the forest made tracing their precise path impossible.

As they passed the blackened skeleton of one of their comrades from the last mission, the recruit averted his eyes, turning his head carefully to the other side of the path.

Yanis told himself it could not be Calina. That pathetic heap of ashes in human shape? No! But he could not be certain. And even if she did not meet that grisly fate, then surely she would have been crushed under the rubble.

They would find no survivors. Yanis was suddenly sure of it. However hard he had tried not to, Yanis had allowed himself the possibility of hope. But it was gone now.

Yanis stopped on the path, feeling little need of continuing. Even a roar from above could not draw him from his utter hopelessness.

"Yanis," Vinzent shouted from some distance away, "come here."

The dragon was coming close. The others ran for cover. But Yanis remained completely still, unable to move.

"Yanis!"

A spray of fire cut through the jungle, sending shards from the stone ruins in all directions. Yanis's body stung as the shards tore through his uniform and knocked him to the ground with a thud. He opened his eyes. He was bloodied but not seriously wounded.

Bracing against a nearby tree trunk, Yanis lifted himself back up. Half their party had become freshly scorched corpses laying amidst the burning jungle, while the others anxiously gripped their weapons. The poor, nervous recruit was nowhere to be seen among the survivors.

"Back into formation!" Vinzent yelled as the dragon flew toward them again.

Yanis's instincts of self-preservation took over at last. He scrambled to join the others, moving next to Ronar, and pointed his musket skyward. He let off a volley with the rest of the group. The dragon released a wounded cry as it peeled away and flew higher above them.

Mechanically, and in perfect harmony with the others, Yanis poured the powder into the barrel, then the wadding, then the ball, then the powder into the pan, cocked it, aimed, fired. An even louder and longer shriek. Reload. Another volley.

The dragon cried out again, weakly this time. Dear Oqci. They were going to kill it.

Yet they persisted. With precise, unthinking discipline, they continued loading, firing, reloading, and firing again.

More direct hits had seriously wounded the dragon, and it flapped its wings even harder, struggling to remain airborne. Enraged, it let out another blast of fire, sending Yanis and the rest of the unit scattering away once again.

But that was its last gasp. Yanis glanced skyward. The dragon flapped its wings desperately before letting out a long moan and beginning a freefall toward the earth. Instinctively, Yanis sprinted through the trees as fast as possible. Within seconds, the whole earth shook as the beast crashed down.

Yanis collapsed into the dense vegetation. His body throbbed with pain from yet another fall. Turning back, he saw a wall of green scales. Several dozen paces away lay the dragon's huge, lifeless body. Yanis climbed to his feet but doubled over. His ankle! He had twisted it from the fall.

An anguished cry near the dragon made him hobble quickly to help. There was Ronar: alive, but his legs were trapped under the fallen creature. He was in a delirious state, barely conscious, whimpering in pain. Thinking of Ronar's crude remarks at the tavern, part of Yanis wished to leave him to die.

Yet he knew he couldn't.

"Ronar," he said. "I shall free you!"

Yanis pushed up against the side of the dragon's scaly green torso – slick and hot – attempting to create enough space to free Ronar. But its body would not budge.

"Yanis?" Vinzent said, rushing over to him. "Hold on."

Together they grabbed some fallen logs and hastily wedged one under the dragon and another under that log, constructing a lever. With all his weight, Yanis pushed down on the log and managed to displace the dragon's body just enough for Vinzent to pull Ronar to freedom, even as his legs were badly mangled. In the distance came the signal for retreat.

Vinzent and Yanis lifted Ronar from the ground. Ronar could place no weight on his useless legs. The retreat signal sounded once more.

Vinzent looked around him, seeing no one else. "We'll be left behind!"

"We can do this," Yanis said. "Hurry!"

Yanis carried Ronar's upper body while Vinzent carefully cradled his legs. They moved through the forest, Yanis's ankle throbbing with each step, but he couldn't stop. He couldn't leave another person to die on this island. Not again.

Ronar, moaning indecipherably, had little awareness of what was happening. The signal came again.

"Hurry!" Yanis shouted.

Yanis and Vinzent, moving even faster, reached the beach at last. They placed Ronar upon the ground and waved their arms frantically for the others to wait. A group of remaining soldiers saw them and rushed to help carry Ronar to the transport boat that would carry them to one of the last remaining battleships.

"Dear Oqci," Yanis said to Vinzent, as they both climbed aboard. Yanis wiped away the sweat from his forehead. The boat rocked in the waves as it departed.

The scene at sea was chaos. All around them, survivors hung onto floating wreckage and lifeboats scuttled away from flaming ships. Scattered artillery fire from the remaining warships continued as the dragons pursued their retreat.

Vinzent could only shake his head, undoubtedly glad to be alive. Yanis supposed he was too.

10

DELLIREA

Dellirea was awakened by frantic knocking at her door. She had been sleeping lightly, having fallen asleep knowing such a situation was likely. The expedition to the Dragon Isles had happened earlier that day, but there was still no news by the time she had gone to sleep.

She dressed hastily and joined the others in the council chamber. It was still several hours until sunrise.

The expression on Dario's face was grave, which did not bode well for the meeting.

Her father entered the room, and everyone stood as he marched to his seat at the head of the table. "Well?"

Dario, the Duke of Prencroft, cleared his throat. "Your Majesty, I'm afraid the mission… was not successful."

Aramal and several others around the table sighed, but Dellirea stayed silent.

"We received a telegraph message from our outpost in New Selver an hour ago," Dario continued. "The dragons' attacks were too great. We were forced to retreat." Dario looked down at the table, avoiding eye contact. "What is more, the dragons destroyed most of our warships. Hundreds of men were lost, including the entire contingent of priests."

Murmurs filled the chamber. Tears began to well up in Dellirea's eyes at the thought of those brave men lying in a watery grave at the bottom of the sea. It was all so terrible. No, she told herself. The fallen men joined Oqci and the Creator in the Cloud Kingdom as distinguished martyrs of the faith.

"There was one positive development," said Dario, interrupting the murmurs.

"Oh?" said Dellirea's father.

"The first expedition to the island located a number of stone blocks seemingly used to construct buildings in an ancient city.

They will soon arrive in Goldhall where our royal scientists will begin to examine them."

The idea interested Dellirea since the island was previously thought to be uninhabited, but it hardly made up for the tremendous loss of life. And the news appeared to do little to raise the spirits of her father, who sat resting his cheek against his hand.

"But," continued Dario, "tests in New Selver determined that the blocks contain large quantities of aletolium."

At the mention of aletolium, the rarest of rare metals, Dellirea noticed her father's eyes grow wide.

DELLIREA's younger cousins eagerly tore open their presents for Descent Day. Of course, Dellirea no longer believed the stories about Oqci's lion Abeqex coming to bring presents for children during the night as she once did, but her cousins still believed.

It had been several days since the tragedy at the Dragon Isles, yet Dellirea hoped that this Descent Day would brighten everyone's mood. Dellirea, her mother and father, and her aunts and uncles all watched the joyous scene from their chairs. A wistful smile came to Dellirea's face listening to the children's excited chatter as the silk paper was thrown away revealing boxes of sweets, stuffed toy animals, and games. Was it not, after all, only a few years ago when she too lay awake the previous night, wondering what Abeqex might bring her?

Aramal nodded at their servants, placed patiently at the edge of the grand sitting room. They rushed forward to collect the discarded paper while the children, seated upon the red carpet, clasped their gifts.

After presents, the family gathered for worship at the palace temple. Dellirea took her place at the front beside her father and mother as the other worshippers made their entry. The dimly lit interior and the coolness of the stone focused her attention on contemplating the descent of Oqci many centuries ago.

Kephalos, dressed in his blue robe, ascended to the pulpit. He folded his hands and closed his eyes. Dellirea and the others did the same.

"O Creator," he said, "today we celebrate the glorious descent of your messenger Oqci from the Cloud Kingdom. We thank you for sending him. For allowing him to bring the sacred creatures and the holy doctrines which guide and enlighten us."

Behind Dellirea and her family sat the other priests, and behind them the major noble families who resided at court. Further back was the area reserved for the common people.

"In this world," Kephalos said, "as Oqci explained, we recognize that we have obligations and duties. From the lowest peasant to the highest noble, we all have our duties to perform, and doing so will be rewarded with eternal life in the Cloud Kingdom."

When Dellirea was younger, during the Descent Day worship, she would think only of the feast of roasted duck and moonberry pie that was to come. But now that she was older, she appreciated more and more the meaning of the holy doctrines.

She hoped that the people at the back of the room understood their importance. She hoped as well that the nobles took Kephalos's words to heart. Too often, she thought, they did not do enough to fulfill their duties to the common people.

As Kephalos continued his homily, Dellirea looked at her mother and father. She was ashamed to worry that sometimes they, too, overlooked their duties.

11

CHARLOTTE

Copies of newspaper clippings were spread across the desk in Charlotte's study. She delighted in keeping track of the mentions of that "horrid," "shocking," "terrible" book, *The Downfall of the Monarchy*. Perhaps one day she would look upon these clippings fondly, once the monarchy was but a distant memory.

What the dragons meant for the future of the monarchy was something Charlotte could not yet discern. Like all other Estenlanders, she had been drawn to the reports of their discovery and the bungled attempt to capture one of them – even as government censors tried their best to suppress the stories. If King Aramal succeeded in taming a new kind of sacred creature, his reputation would be forever assured. If he failed, however...

And what did the dragons mean for the tales of Oqci? It seemed as though the fate of the Estenlanders' religion, their government, their society were all in a state of change. History was no longer just what one read in books; it was something to be lived through. And Charlotte realized she was playing a small part in it.

Charlotte's optimistic musings for the future were disturbed as her eyes passed over a headline in the morning's newspaper.

Fear gripped hold of her. No. It couldn't be true!

"PRINTER OF TREASONOUS BOOK FOUND DEAD IN CALLINGTON."

Charlotte's grasp tightened on the newspaper. Suddenly living through history did not feel so exciting.

As she read on, she learned that the cause of the printer's death had been ruled the result of poisoning. Dear Oqci. The government of Callington, anxious to defend their nation's cherished freedom of the press, protested to Estenland's ambassador. Aramal's government officially denied any responsibility, yet Charlotte was sure his agents were behind it.

The poor man! What a great shame. And yet, he knew the risks. He knew the risks as well as Charlotte did.

Her chest tightened as she contemplated what this meant. Was the government now closing in on her? If the king's tentacles could reach into Callington, could they not reach her, too?

Charlotte threw the paper down in frustration and brought her hand to her brow. Why did she ever write such a book? Why? Why was she so foolish?

No, no, she reassured herself. She had taken great care to remain anonymous. She had arranged a chain of carriers who delivered the manuscript to the printer in Callington, all ignorant of each other, the contents and destination of the package, and most importantly the identity of its author. Tracing her would be impossible. Wouldn't it?

～

CHARLOTTE DID NOT WISH to leave her room, such was her worry. Terrible nightmares haunted her sleep. The manner of death was different each time, but her fate always remained the same: Poison slipped into her food. Neck snapped on the gallows. Bludgeoned in the streets by agents of the king.

From her room, she anxiously watched visitors coming and going. Several days after learning of the mysterious death of her publisher, as she kept watch, a carriage arrived at her estate and two blue-uniformed policemen stepped out. Her brother Brondin walked out to meet them. The police bowed to him before they shook hands and made pleasantries.

What were they doing here? Was this the end for her?

Her mind raced through the scenarios. Despite her precautions, if the police had managed to trace the whole series of carriers it might be possible to find her. From there, she was sure to be executed. Her palms and underarms grew sweaty, and she could barely keep from shaking.

Charlotte tried to maintain her composure as she crept down

the stairs, gripping the banister tightly and making sure to stay out of view.

The policemen and her brother went through the house and into the back gardens. She tiptoed behind them at a safe distance, looking out at them talking and gesticulating, particularly toward the menagerie where the family kept their sacred creatures.

The two constables and Brondin walked into the menagerie and inspected the outer fencing. One of the constables squatted down and examined the ground. He motioned the others over and the three carried on an intense conversation with much pointing this way and that. What were they doing?

After what seemed like an eternity, the police shook hands with Charlotte's brother and departed.

It was silly, Charlotte thought, but she instinctually looked skyward. Thank you. Thank you.

Once the police were gone, she confronted Brondin in the foyer. "What were the police doing here?" she choked out, her mouth still dry.

"They're launching an investigation of you," he said with a serious look on his face.

Charlotte's heart came crashing down. "What?" she mustered in a weak voice, her legs feeling as flimsy as wet paper.

"You are white as a ghost," he said. "I'm only kidding!"

Charlotte's nervousness gave way to fury. She shoved him. "Don't do that!"

"Get a hold of yourself, Charlotte. It was only in jest," he said. "No, they came for a serious matter. It concerns our sacred creatures. Several weeks ago, one of our unicorns went missing. I reasoned it must have slipped through a hole in the fencing, yet I could find no such gaps. Then another went missing last night!"

"Dear Oqci."

"This morning, when I discovered it missing, I found some footprints nearby their pen. It seemed as though the ground had been disturbed, and that someone tried to remove the traces."

A wave of relief washed over Charlotte, knowing that the

visit had nothing to do with her after all. But her relief turned into worry for their sacred creatures. "What did the police say?"

"They said that a handful of other noble families have also reported creatures missing. Possibly democratic radicals."

This did not sound right. No radicals she knew were in the game of kidnapping sacred creatures, but she could hardly say so. "That's awful."

"Yes," he said. "I believe they will be looking more closely at these radicals now."

This gave Charlotte considerable fright, yet... their poor creatures! The entire story of Oqci bringing the creatures with him from the clouds was silly, of course. There had to be a logical explanation. But whatever their origin, Charlotte loved her creatures and shuddered at the idea of harm coming to them.

Such fond memories she had of her beloved winged horse, Silver Justice, whom she befriended when she was younger. The name embarrassed her now, but she was only a child then and she believed almost religiously in the principle of justice. Riding Silver Justice high above their estate was the rare distraction from her rigorous program of education. It was one of the few happy memories from her childhood.

IN THE FOLLOWING DAYS, Charlotte kept a watchful eye on the newspapers but saw nothing about democratic radicals or missing creatures. What if Brondin had been lying and the police *were* investigating her? Would he do that? Should she confide the truth to him?

No. It was too risky, she reasoned. She was not sure he could be trusted.

And she couldn't disturb her mother with this. Learning that her daughter was the subject of a police investigation... No, with her illness, it would simply be too much for her.

SAMUEL

Under the microscope, Samuel saw it again. That same distinctive pattern in the cells, this time in the cells of a sea goat. That same pattern that kept appearing in all his dissections of the sacred creatures.

Earlier that evening, the two "noblemen" had brought him the sea goat cadaver, his first of that variety. True to their promise, they had somehow been procuring a steady supply of sacred creatures over the past weeks. Indeed, Samuel's partnership with them had grown almost congenial, if not for the small fact that they were technically extorting money from him. But he was acquiring the creatures he needed for his research. Unicorns and winged horses were most common, but they even brought one each of a winged lion, a sea goat, and a griffin – the cadavers of which were housed, away from prying eyes, in his lab's basement storage vault.

These days, Goldhall was in a frenzy over talk of the dragons. Their existence made his research even more pressing. Yet how did they fit into his theories? Much to Samuel's dismay, knowledge of them was thus far limited to the crude observations of soldiers, all entirely untrained in biology – or even worse, priests!

Samuel contorted his arm behind him to scratch at that terrible itch upon his back. His skin ailment had been growing ever worse since he had first met those two men. The rash covered most of his back, his legs, his arms. Even small patches upon his face. It had never been quite this bad. Not even in his youth.

No matter. Samuel checked his timepiece. Two in the morning. The only time when he could be sure to be alone in the lab, when he could be sure not to be discovered.

Samuel returned to the microscope to observe the distinctive cells. This sea goat would make eleven creatures in total that he had dissected. In every one, there appeared the same unique markings in all of their cells: dozens of jagged lines that danced wildly across the nucleus, far more than could be observed in the cells of normal creatures, like the common horse.

He moved to his notebook, where he drew a careful reproduction of what he saw under the microscope.

But what did it all mean? And were the dragons connected in some way?

Stories about the divine origin of the sacred creatures were a load of rubbish, made up centuries ago by priests to control the credulous masses, Samuel knew. But how to explain these markings? Were they proof of the divine? Or was there some other explanation?

13

YANIS

The scenery, from jungles to plains to rocky hills, whipped past as the train travelled south from New Selver. During the dragons' attack, Yanis had twisted his ankle, and it had become badly swollen on the trip across the sea. While he was not so badly injured as to be rendered useless, Vinzent of Highfalls graciously had him sent back to Estenland, along with the other injured soldiers, in the first wave of retreat from New Selver. Given Yanis's heroism in helping Ronar, Vinzent said that he deserved it, even despite the orders that had exiled him.

Among the injured crowded into the railcar was Ronar, who was now conscious and in good spirits, although it seemed probable he would lose the use of his legs. Yanis sat on his cot across from Ronar's as the train chugged along.

"This man," Ronar said to no one in particular, while proudly pointing at Yanis. "This fucking man! He is the one who saved my life."

Yanis cared not for the attention, least of all from Ronar. Yanis had saved his life, but he still found him uncouth.

"I did what anyone would have done," Yanis said quickly.

Fortunately, the other soldiers mostly ignored Ronar as they stared blankly at the countryside zipping past. The railcar was hot and sticky in the warm climate of Otela, and it stank of urine and sweat. Long-legged flying insects bounced stupidly against the windows.

Yanis was already anxious for the journey to meet its end. They would soon reach the south of the continent, then there would be the ferry ride across the Sea of Dreams to Estenland.

As the nurse came through the car, Ronar excitedly said, "Nurse, my mate here killed a dragon."

"I did no such thing."

"You did. When it was flying down at us, you pulled out your musket." He dramatically pantomimed aiming a gun and firing. "Bang! With one shot, you took the bastard down."

"That's not how it happened at all," Yanis protested. "Our entire unit was shooting at it."

"Nurse, he's just being modest," Ronar insisted. She paid him no mind as she went about her work, but some of the other soldiers began to turn their heads toward Yanis.

"Is that true?" one of the soldiers asked.

"It's absolutely true," continued Ronar before Yanis could object. "I was there. Saw it with my own eyes. And when the dragon fell to the earth and crushed my legs, my mate here saved me."

Some of the other soldiers examined Yanis with interest. Most of those who were on the island had been killed in the fighting, and there were few left alive who could verify what had actually happened.

∽

THE TEDIOUS JOURNEY by rail and sea seemed as though it would never end. Yet at last, Yanis arrived in the bustling port at Goldhall.

It had been over three years since his exile, and because he no longer had any fixed dwelling in the city, Yanis had sent a telegram to Jackson Mylner arranging accommodation. Jackson generously agreed to provide a bed for his first several nights.

When the ship landed, Yanis stepped on to the stone pier and made his way to land: Home.

He hobbled as quickly as he could through the crowd of people lugging heavy suitcases, embracing long-lost friends, or rushing to catch the next ferry. Amidst the chaos, Yanis spotted Jackson. He had less hair than Yanis remembered, and it was entirely white now. He wore his familiar vest, which fit a bit tighter than before. A warm smile came to Jackson's face when he saw Yanis. He rushed over and shook Yanis's hand vigorously before taking hold of his suitcase. "Welcome home, Yanis," he said. "Come, we shall take the new tramline."

This was, Jackson explained as they made their way through the masses, recently installed by the city. A line of shabbily dressed people formed outside their car, the one with the cheapest tickets. Yanis was the only passenger in military dress.

"There have been a great many changes in our fair city since you left," Jackson continued as they boarded. "Life moves along as ever, but more on all that later when we have a chance to speak freely. Tell me, how are you?"

There was so much to tell. Yanis had sent the occasional letter, but how much made it past the censors, he knew not. Probably little. Yanis told Jackson about his time in New Selver and the travails of colonial life. When it came to his relationship with Calina, he stopped. It was too painful to speak about. Better to omit it altogether.

The tram creaked and groaned as it made its way twisting and turning through the streets of downtown Goldhall.

Yanis hesitated when describing the most recent encounter with the dragons. He explained how their group fired upon a dragon and killed it, but that one of the other soldiers told tall tales about how it had been Yanis who fired the fatal shot.

"Well, did you?"

"I believe not. But my memory of the attack is scattered. Everything happened so quickly. At first, I was quite sure that Ronar was exaggerating, but the more I think about it, I wonder if it is I who is mistaken."

"You did something heroic whatever the case," said Jackson. "Saving a man's life, particularly someone with whom you had quarrelled. That is honourable."

Jackson looked at Yanis with pride. He had taken him in as an apprentice at his printing shop many years ago when Yanis was still a teenager. Yanis became something like a son to him. Jackson had never married or had children. The government press had spread rumours that he preferred the company of men, but he had never told Yanis if it were true, and Yanis had never asked.

As they exited the tram and caught a cab into Iron Town –
Jackson's neighbourhood, Yanis's old neighbourhood – the city
began to change. The cab bounced on the uneven cobblestones.
The amount of garbage littering the streets increased. The
people were thinner and poorly dressed, and the smell of sewage
and factory smoke occasionally filled one's nose. Still, it was
home.

~

ARRIVING in Jackson's small apartment, above his ground-floor
printing shop, Yanis set down his suitcase. The apartment was
sparsely furnished, and handwritten notes and copies of his
newspaper, *The Voice of the Working Man*, were strewn about
most surfaces.

Yanis was eager to rest; it had been a long journey. But
Jackson insisted on conversing more now that they had privacy.
From under his floorboards, he retrieved a slender book and
placed it in Yanis's hands. *The Downfall of the Monarchy*, he read
on the cover.

This little book, Jackson explained, had been causing a great
commotion in the city with its arguments against the monarchy
and the doctrines of Oqci. Government agents scrambled to the
discover the author, but in vain.

"Do you know who the author is?" Yanis asked as he
skimmed the pages.

"Some people seem to think it's me," laughed Jackson. "But of
course it isn't. You know I wouldn't do something so foolish!"
Jackson's face quickly turned red and his jovial expression
disappeared. "I'm sorry, Yanis. I didn't mean to suggest that your
own pamphlet was –"

"Not to worry," Yanis said.

But as Yanis looked down at the small book, he shuddered to
think what would happen if the author were caught. His own
pamphlet was much more reserved than this one – and for that
he had been exiled halfway around the world.

Jackson took the book back from Yanis's hands and returned

it to its hiding place under the floor. "Listen, Yanis," he said, "I know you must rest, and I shall let you in due course, but tomorrow evening a meeting is taking place. I wish you to make a speech if you feel comfortable."

"Is that wise?" Yanis said. "I am hardly a great orator, for one thing. For another, Lord Highfalls, my commander, did me a great favour allowing me to return to the capital. I am still not technically a free man. If I were discovered making speeches on behalf of democracy..."

"That is all true," said Jackson, "but we have real momentum now. The monarchy is more unpopular than ever. With the publication of the anonymous book, with the disaster of the dragon mission... I..." He struggled to find words, thinking he might have offended Yanis once again.

"No, no. You are right. And I know you meant no offense."

Jackson smiled. "I just believe it would be important to have your voice there. To have someone who saw the dragons up close. To have a real military hero. Yes, you must join us!"

Yanis could see that Jackson could not be convinced otherwise. And Yanis was also growing to like the idea himself.

14

CHARLOTTE

Charlotte's worries had become too great. Brondin's comment that the police were investigating her continued to haunt her. There was one person she knew she could confide in, however: her husband, Willien of Marchal. They swore vows to each other, did they not?

Arriving at his estate, Charlotte was ushered into the gardens by one of his servants, who greeted her with surprise, as her presence there was a rare sight nowadays. The servant led Charlotte through the maze of plants back to Willien, who was crouched next to a flower bed and surrounded by garden tools and glassware for his specimens, as usual.

Willien, a large, lumbering, but gentle man, rose from the ground slowly when he saw Charlotte. He had a puzzled look on his face.

"If it isn't Lady Evesbury," he said, using the surname to which she had since reverted, even as they remained married. "How can I help you?"

"There is no need for such formality, Willien," she said. "I have come to confide something to you. I am unsure whom else I can tell."

His expression turned serious. "Of course, Charlotte." He led her to a place deeper in the gardens where they were certain to have privacy.

She took a deep breath. "Willien, have you heard of the book, *The Downfall of the Monarchy?*"

"I have heard of it," he said offhandedly, "but its existence has had little effect on my life."

Charlotte let out a snort of laughter. She knew he cared not for politics, or much else truly, so long as it did not interfere with his plant experiments. "Well," she said, "I am its author."

"What?" he said. He was animated with more concern for

Charlotte than she had ever before seen. "What do you mean you are the author? Do you know what would happen if you were discovered?"

"Keep your voice down," she said. "I am well aware of the risks, but I only wished to ask if you had heard any rumours. Brondin gave me a great fright several days ago. He said the police were investigating me but quickly told me it was but a joke."

"Dear Oqci," he said. "No, from what little I have heard, the author's identity remains a mystery."

"Very well. Brondin also said that two of our sacred creatures have gone missing. There have apparently been other cases of missing creatures as well. Have you heard anything of this?"

"Now that is true. At a meeting of the King's Society of Biology last week, in private, members discussed several cases of missing creatures. It has caused something of a stir. But no one is sure who is behind their disappearance or for what purpose they are being taken."

Charlotte nodded. At this, she was relieved. Brondin had been telling the truth about the creatures, which led her to hope talk about an investigation of her was only a cruel joke.

"Willien, thank you for your help," Charlotte said. She hesitated. "I... I regret that our marriage did not unfold as we had hoped, but I value your counsel."

"Is that everything?" Willien said, no doubt anxious to return to his plants.

"Please don't mention this to anyone."

"I'm not daft," he said. He paused and once again appeared struck by concern. "Just be careful, Charlotte."

"I shall. Thank you, Willien."

~

As HER CARRIAGE returned her home from Willien's, she crossed the boundary into her family's lands – or Brondin's lands more accurately, as he inherited them upon the death of their father. The carriage weaved its way along the stone paths, surrounded on all sides by fields of wheat, barley, and pasture for sheep and cattle. On these lands, held by Charlotte's family for generations, dozens of peasant families farmed and in turn paid the Evesbury family their share of the produce, as well as their taxes to the government, something from which Charlotte and her family were exempt. It was a deeply unjust system, but it was one from which Charlotte knew she could not yet break free. In time, however, she pledged to right those wrongs.

When she drew closer to the house, Charlotte noticed Brondin standing outside, waiting for her with a disturbed look on his face. But she also wondered if that was not merely his normal expression.

Alighting from the carriage, Charlotte walked past him and inside. "Charlotte," he said, following behind her, "we must talk. It is urgent."

She spun around. Her heart rate quickened to a furious pace. She had been relieved after having visited Willien, but no longer.

"Let us go someplace private," he said.

Charlotte's mind raced imagining what this could concern. If there were no investigation, then what? More news about their sacred creatures?

They walked into an empty sitting room and Brondin shut the door. He wore a grave expression. "When we spoke about the police some days ago," he said, "I noticed the colour completely disappear from your face. My joking evidently gave you a great fright, like you had reason to be nervous of something. And I thought more about your suspicious whereabouts for so many evenings."

"Come to your point."

"I apologize for the invasion of privacy, but I was concerned about your behaviour. I went into your study and looked through some of your things."

Charlotte's knees became weak as he held up a small pile of newspaper clippings.

"In a desk drawer in your study, I found these. They all concern that heinous book calling for the overthrow of the monarchy."

Horrible thoughts about the printer in Callington flooded Charlotte's mind. Was she next?

"What is the meaning of all this?" Brondin asked.

"How dare you!" Charlotte exclaimed. "How... how dare you!"

"Why do you have those?" he demanded, his face growing animated. "Tell me now. Are you a sympathizer of the author? Are you a sympathizer of the radicals?"

"I am under no obligation to answer your questions. Shame on you for spying on me."

"If you refuse to answer," he said, "then I shall have no choice but to contact the police and tell them that I suspect you of supporting radical activities."

"You devious slime!" she shouted. "You would turn in your own sister?"

He said nothing as he slowly walked toward the door.

"Brondin, wait!"

At the threshold of the room, he turned back and looked at her.

"Don't do it," Charlotte said, weakly. "Please."

"Why not?"

Charlotte composed herself. "Because I am the author of the book. If I am discovered, I shall surely be sentenced to death. So, please..."

Brondin stared at her with his mouth open, his eyes wide. He slowly shut the door.

"You! You are the author? No, I don't believe it. My own sister... arguing such horrible things!" He began pacing around the room. "Have... have you no thought of what this might unleash? How these ideas could infect the common people? What harm this could do to our family name? How... how could you be so stupid, Charlotte?"

She grasped for words to answer his charges. But none were forthcoming. Her prized rational abilities failed her. She was silent.

He stopped his pacing and stared at her. "Do you have nothing to say for yourself?"

Explanations, rebuttals, and arguments bustled about in Charlotte's mind, but she could not find the right phrasing. At last, she said simply, "I wrote the book. And I believe strongly in every word."

He could only stare at her in horror. As if she were some kind of demon rather than his own sister. "I shall not turn you over to the police," he said, resuming his pacing. "That is one grace I shall grant you. But I never wish to see you in this house again. Ever! I must think of Allegrette. And my son. I shall not have you infecting my family with your vile ideas!"

The thought of leaving home filled her with despair. But what choice was there?

"If you wish me to leave, so I shall."

"That is precisely what I wish," Brondin said. "And do not be tardy."

15

DELLIREA

"A great luncheon has been prepared for your birthday, Delli!" said Dellirea's mother excitedly as she greeted Dellirea in her room that morning. "We shall have the finest meats, cheeses, fruits, seafood from Esbeck, cakes –"

"Oh dear, mother," Dellirea said, "I... I'm afraid I had already planned to volunteer at the charity centre today."

"But," she said, "today is your birthday! And... and you would wish to spend it amongst such... such people?"

As her mother said the words, Dellirea's brow crinkled with disbelief. She lowered her head and said nothing.

"Oh, Delli," she said, "I have offended you. I'm sorry. You know, I only wanted your sixteenth birthday to be special."

"Worry not, mother," Dellirea said, realizing she had been too curt. "Perhaps we shall have the celebration once I return?"

"Oh yes," she said. "Yes, of course! I shall tell everyone that it will be delayed until evening. And also, I wished to give you something." With an eager smile, she held up a jewel box and passed it to her daughter.

Dellirea opened the lid, revealing a brilliant turquoise necklace of polished aletolium stones. "It is beautiful," she said, taking the necklace into her hands and running her fingers along the smooth stones.

"Come," Bravala said, "let me put it around your neck." She took it from Dellirea's hands and moved behind her. "You can wear it to the charity centre."

"Oh no!" Dellirea said, spinning around before her mother could place it upon her. "I mustn't wear it there! Those people... some of them are so terribly impoverished that I would feel guilty flaunting such wealth. It would be vain. Obscene, almost."

"Oh," her mother said, her eyes lowered, her smile erased. "I suppose I understand."

Dellirea realized she had once more gone too far in her protests. "I'm sorry, mother." She grasped her hand. "The necklace is very beautiful and I shall be sure to wear it tonight."

THAT EVENING, after Dellirea returned from a fruitful day spreading the doctrines of Oqci at the charity centre, the feast awaited. Gathered next to her mother and father on either side of her were her aunts, uncles, cousins, and other nobles from court. In the grand dining room, dozens prepared for the feast.

Just as her mother had said, it was a sumptuous banquet. As Dellirea regarded her fellow diners, talking and laughing with their mouths full of food, sucking back oysters, guzzling wine, she could not help but turn to her work just hours ago, providing food to those whose ratty clothing hung upon wiry frames. Those for whom such a feast would be more than they would consume in a week, or even a month. It seemed almost like gluttony, a fault which Oqci warned against.

"Isn't this just delicious, Delli?" said her mother, who slurped her chicken and vegetable potage.

"It is indeed," Dellirea said, bringing a spoonful to her mouth too.

The taste was sublime, yet she had not the appetite of the others, and with her bowl still nearly full, a servant came to remove it and placed a new course in front of her.

Dellirea told herself that to feast in such a way was a privilege of being royally born, a privilege that was only legitimate if the duty to provide for those born lesser was fulfilled.

"Let us propose a toast to Dellirea on her sixteenth birthday," said her father, rising from his chair, "one of the finest, most pure-hearted souls to ever grace our world. How lucky are we to have her!" He paused, struck with emotion, since Dellirea knew he thought of her departed brother in the Cloud Kingdom. Yet her father's face grew more steadfast as he persisted. "And how fortunate our nation is. One day Dellirea will be queen. And what a fine queen she will make. She will lead our country to greatness and continue the Zendar reign!"

Dellirea looked at him and smiled as the well-wishers echoed their support. But she could not help feeling that the celebration was inappropriate at a time like this.

DELLIREA KNELT in the palace temple, completely empty at this early hour. The birthday feast from last evening had been pleasurable, yet much weighed upon her mind. The discovery of the dragons and then the terrible loss of life from the failed mission. It seemed as though no one had even considered it during the joyous feast yesterday.

Eyes closed, hands clasped together, she prayed to Oqci for guidance. Was their course correct? Were they doing enough to fulfill their duties to the common people? Or were they becoming entangled in a foolish quest?

A rustling on the altar interrupted her thoughts. Who was there?

She opened her eyes and looked up. It was High Priest Kephalos, busying himself at the altar, arranging the candles.

It was, she recalled, around her birthday last year when Kephalos had replaced the previous high priest, who had suffered a heart attack. In a year's time, however, she had yet to warm to him. His views had always been somewhat unconventional. He was known for his scholarship, studying the Book of Oqci in its original language, yet also for interpreting some of Oqci's words as metaphorical, rather than literal – something of which Dellirea was unsure.

He startled when he noticed Dellirea watching him. "Your Highness," he said, "I did not realize you were there."

"Nor I, you," she said. "I was only praying quietly."

"Very well. I shall not disturb you."

"No, I would rather appreciate your company."

Kephalos nodded and descended the altar to join her.

"I should have thought you would have been resting after the feast last evening," he said. "I do hope your birthday was agreeable."

"It was indeed," she said. "Yet I awoke early this morning and could not fall back asleep."

"What troubles you, Your Highness?"

"I was only thinking of the past tumultuous weeks. How much loss we have suffered. Hundreds of souls, representing our nation, departed from this earth. Yet I fear the loss has not been sufficiently acknowledged. There has not even been an official period of mourning. Perhaps it would be valuable for you as high priest to lead our nation in the process of grieving."

Kephalos sighed as he leaned back in his seat. "I have decided against it," he said quietly.

"But why?" Dellirea asked. "Did those men not die for our country?"

"It is for reasons you are not yet old enough to understand."

"I am now sixteen years old," she said, becoming angry with him. She cared not for his strange views about their faith, nor for him treating her as though she were a child. "Surely you do not think it best to refuse to acknowledge the sacrifices of those men? The bodies of *your* fellow holy men lie at the bottom of the sea. Are we to simply ignore them?"

"Please, Your Highness," he said. "Their deaths pained me too. I lost many friends."

"Then why can we not mourn them? I don't understand."

Kephalos hung his head, seemingly unwilling to answer.

Dellirea stood to leave. She wished no longer to be in his presence if he refused to speak.

"Wait," he said, as she began to exit. "Your Highness, I suppose you are right that you are older now. You deserve to know the truth. But please do not think ill of your father for what I am about to say."

She returned to her seat, unsettled. The morning sun was now risen and light began to stream through the stained glass windows.

"Your Highness, I made a similar observation to your father

on that matter. That we should hold a mourning ceremony for those souls we have lost."

"And his response?"

"Unfortunately, he thought it would only draw attention to the failure of the mission. To have a formal mourning period, he thought, would only give the people further cause to doubt his leadership."

It couldn't be true. Her father would never do such a thing. To think only of his perceptions rather than the duty to mourn those fallen for their country!

"I am sorry to relay such news," he continued. "Please do not be harsh on him for it. And please do not let on that I told you. He is a good man. I know he is only trying to do what is best for our country."

Dellirea knew not how to respond. And she did not completely understand. How could her father be so cold that he would simply act as if those fallen souls did not exist?

"I should leave you to continue in prayer, Your Highness."

"Thank you, High Priest, for your candour."

He bowed to her and returned to his work at the altar.

SAMUEL

Atop Samuel's dissection table, lit brightly by the overhead gas lamps, sat the body of a large species of lizard from the continent of Otela. This particular species came from the tropical climes of New Selver. Around the table gathered ten of his best students, Greta among them, all of them dressed in white coats.

It was not a coincidence that he had chosen to lead the students through a dissection of this creature for the morning lesson. Many students were drawn to the prospect of how this lizard might compare with a dragon, a comparison Samuel hoped they'd make and one that he did nothing to discourage.

"How is it possible," one of his students asked while Samuel made an incision into the lizard's scaly skin, "for a dragon to have evolved naturally?"

Speculations about the evolution of species was a taboo subject, but in his classroom, no topic was forbidden. There was more tolerance for unconventional views at Iron Town College of course, but most of the professors there longed for recognition and acceptance from the professors at Etterburg University, even if they did not say so aloud.

But, Samuel wondered, did they not realize that those old fossils at Etterburg would never think to lower themselves by listening to anything those from Iron Town had to say?

"What is the alternative?" Greta asked, raising an eyebrow at his question. "That Oqci brought *them* from the sky as well?"

The students chuckled at this, as did Samuel.

Oh, sweet Greta. A young woman after Samuel's own heart. Smart *and* beautiful.

"I just cannot surmise how it could be possible," the student continued. "Why do we not see evidence of similar creatures elsewhere? Why are there fossils of early lizards but no fossils of early dragons?"

"This is a potentially serious flaw in the theories," Samuel said. The thought of it called to mind his terrible skin irritation, and he resisted the urge to scratch at the burning itch suddenly making itself known. "I believe that when further study of the sacred creatures is possible, we shall begin to understand this mystery."

How Samuel wished to spill out all of his ideas to his students, to tell them of his dissections of the sacred creatures and everything he had found. But the danger was still too great. Soon, however. Soon!

LATER THAT NIGHT, as Samuel lay awake contemplating the earlier conversation with his students, he resolved that he must prepare to publish the results of his findings thus far. It simply could not wait. With the dragons in the public eye, the research would be more relevant than ever. In the morning, he would begin drafting his article.

After Samuel slept restlessly for several more hours, the first signs of light began to poke through the curtains. He climbed out of bed, ready for work. As he arose, he noticed that the white sheets were stained in several places with dried blood. Blast! He must have been scratching again overnight and accidentally broken the skin. No matter.

He put on his robe and opened his apartment door to find the morning newspaper waiting in the hallway. He flipped through the pages as he prepared his coffee. The paper did its best to put a positive framing upon the debacle of the dragon mission, but to no avail. That should blunt the arrogance of Aramal the Incompetent!

As Samuel continued leafing through the pages, however, a headline jolted him from his stupor: "POLICE APPEAL FOR ASSISTANCE IN SACRED CREATURE THEFTS." This was curious. Deeply curious.

As he read on, his breathing accelerated. And his body began to itch all over. According to the article, various noble families had, over the past several months, reported their sacred creatures missing. What was more, two suspicious men had been spotted near several of the sights and gunfire had even been heard on the nights before the creatures were discovered missing.

The connections began to form in his mind. Could the two men in question be his so-called noble collaborators? Could it be true? There was always something sinister about them. Samuel never queried whence they acquired their creatures. He tried his best to block out of his mind any possible answers, none of them good.

As he considered the consequences, the gravity of the situation became ever clearer. How long could the men remain free, with the police gaining evidence against them? It was only a matter of time. When they were inevitably caught, Samuel reasoned, it would not be long before the police were pointed toward Samuel.

He was shaking. The itching was growing worse.

If he was found to have dissected the creatures' bodies… If the police knew, if the public knew! He would be ruined. Ruined! His career would be finished. Worse than that, he would be bound for the gallows.

"My skin," Samuel moaned to himself. "My cursed skin!"

Samuel strode to his medicine cabinet and pulled out the sulfur. His hands were shaking so much he could barely get the lid off. Once he did, the familiar stink of rotten eggs wafted up to his nose. But he needed it.

What to do? What to do?

He hastily unbuttoned his shirt and removed it. The liquid burned as he slathered it over his broken skin, but it ceased the itching.

He would deny knowing anything about the men. He would say he knew nothing of the thefts.

No. No. That would do nothing. With the testimony of the

men, with the specimens in his lab, he would only reveal himself a liar.

Destroy his findings? After everything he had gone through? The hours of toiling in the middle of the night? No, he couldn't! No. There had to be another way.

YANIS

The meeting took place the next day at the Working Men's Benevolent Association. Yanis knew the place well, although like everything else in Estenland, it had been years since he had laid eyes upon it.

His first time there was as a teenager. His parents had forced him out of the house for daring to question Oqci's teachings. Yet Jackson took him in. It was Jackson who introduced Yanis to the democratic movement, who brought him to this meeting hall. There he heard people talk about things he had never before imagined. Radical things about the equality of all people and the injustice of the monarchy.

His life was altered, forever. From then, he knew which course he must take.

Jackson and Yanis entered the building together, with Yanis hobbling along on his still-sore ankle. As soon as they entered, everyone in the room gravitated toward Jackson and he spoke easily with them, treating even strangers as long-lost friends.

Once the meeting got underway, Yanis waited anxiously in his seat, picking his nails, as he prepared for his turn. Jackson was at the podium giving his introductory remarks and holding up a copy of *The Downfall of the Monarchy*. But Yanis could not focus on what he was saying. His sweaty hands gripped the notes for his speech.

"Many of you know Yanis Haller," he said. "He was unjustly punished by the government and forced to spend years in exile for his supposed crimes."

The audience jeered.

"The government forced him into dangerous and futile missions, but he served honourably. Even heroically. He partici-pated in both voyages to the Dragon Isles and saved one of his fallen comrades from certain death." Jackson lowered his voice and raised an eyebrow, as if letting the audience in on a secret. "And some even say he *killed* a dragon."

Yanis was surprised by this last statement, but the crowd applauded as he limped to the podium. He gazed out at the crowd, which regarded him excitedly. Yanis wasn't much of a speaker, preferring instead to express his ideas on paper.

"Thank you, Mr. Mylner, for the warm introduction. But I must correct the final point. It is true that I was involved in the expeditions to the Dragon Isles, but I did not kill any dragons."

The crowd deflated upon hearing this, or it appeared so to Yanis. Perhaps they wished it were true, but he couldn't allow them to have a false impression. He found it hard to look out at the crowd after this, instead focusing upon his written notes.

"My experiences on the island are not something I would wish on anyone," he said. He did his best to recount the first expedition – naturally avoiding reference to Calina – then the second. Yanis even told how he saved Ronar from being trapped under the dragon's body.

A hesitant glance up at the crowd made him realize, to his surprise, that they had been following his words with rapt attention. "Our illegitimate government was reckless in launching the attack," Yanis said, gaining newfound confidence. "They show no regard for the lives of our countrymen, or of any other people! The monarchy must fall!"

This elicited applause and cheers of "hurrah!" as he stepped away from the podium.

"Bravo!" said Jackson, returning to the stage and shaking Yanis's hand. "Bravo!"

Having successfully delivered the speech, Yanis wished to return to his seat, but one young woman, a few years younger than himself, stood from the crowd before he could. From her complexion, Yanis could see that she was not from their country – perhaps from one of the colonies. "Could you speak about the injustice of Estenland's continued rule in Umiri?" she asked.

"I believe that the people of New Selver... or Umiri, rather...

should be free," Yanis said. "They desire freedom as much as we do. If we care about freedom here, we should also support their freedom there."

This produced some cheers in the crowd, but also some hisses.

The woman nodded at Yanis's response but gave a foul look at those who jeered. A devious smile came to her lips at the controversy she had caused. "You all recognize that it is wrong for the king to rule without giving *you* a voice," she said to the crowd, "but some of you seem unable to extend this same principle to those who have a different skin colour – especially to the so-called 'Deniers of Oqci.'"

This only caused more murmuring in the audience. Yanis admired the woman's boldness, her bravery, the way she refused to be intimidated by the crowd, even as she was one of the few of her gender and skin colour at the meeting.

Before the atmosphere grew more heated, Jackson called for order. "Friends, let us remain united!"

The woman smiled at Yanis, knowing she had made her point, and sat down. Yanis was ready to do the same. His nerves had been frayed from the speech and he wished to withdraw from the eyes of the crowd.

AFTER THE MEETING CONCLUDED, Jackson and Yanis walked back to Jackson's flat. "The people loved your speech," Jackson said, patting him on the shoulder.

"Why did you add that bit at the start about me killing the dragon?" Yanis asked. "I'm not offended, only curious."

"It was just a bit of fun," Jackson said. "These people, you know, they have so little excitement in their lives. This is why they reach for those ideas about Oqci and the sacred creatures. It gives them something to hold on to. Something to brighten their lives. But perhaps we can also supply them some excitement, some wonder, can we not?"

As they walked amidst the tenement buildings, some packing families of several generations into a single, windowless room, Yanis knew that Jackson was right. As usual. For those whose lives were a constant struggle for survival, what harm could it do to give them a bit of hope, even a bit of fantasy?

SAMUEL

Samuel needed to act quickly. Any day now, his supposed noble collaborators would be caught by the police. And they would point the finger at him!

He arranged a meeting with Quinneas Raeil, a lawyer known for his sympathies for the radicals and for his integrity. Samuel had never met the man, but he would surely know what to do.

"Dr. Nox," Quinneas said, smiling warmly as his assistant led Samuel into his office. He was considerably taller than Samuel and dressed in a sharp green coat, which matched his striking green eyes. He had a thin face with shoulder-length black hair. "I have followed your work," he said. "It is a pleasure to meet you."

"I… I confess my surprise that you've heard of me."

"You are too modest, Dr. Nox. I always keep up with the important people in our fair city."

Samuel glanced about his office, which was decidedly learned. Leather-bound books filled every shelf and exotic prints from far-flung places in Otela hung upon the walls. He had, like Samuel, come from a humble background and worked hard to raise himself from obscurity, from poverty. He had even adopted the name Quinneas, instead of simply Quin, his birth name, as a way to disguise his poorer background. But he inhabited the more refined name with ease.

He motioned for Samuel to sit. "Now, how may I help you?"

Samuel explained the entire situation. The first encounter with the men. Being forced to take the creatures. The police investigation closing in on them.

Quinneas stroked his chin in deep thought for some time before beginning: "Here is what we shall do. We tell the police you have information on the men. No more than that, only that you have information. We demand absolute immunity from any prosecutions that might arise from the information you have.

The police want nothing more than to solve this case. They will be eager to grant immunity. With that, you will tell them that you believed all along that these were benevolent noblemen, as devoted as you to the cause of science. It was slightly unusual, you thought, but you had no reason to suspect they were stealing the creatures. You trusted in the good judgment of these noblemen and did not think to question them. Now, I can well imagine that it will be difficult for someone of your stature to lower yourself in this way, but make sure you emphasize that final point."

It was indeed hard to stomach for Samuel. Passing himself off as a naïve fool, blindly doing as nobles told him! It would hurt his pride, but if it were necessary, he would do it.

"If I do all this," Samuel said, "I shan't be charged? Could such a deal even be trusted?"

"You will not be charged," Quinneas assured him. "And the deal can be trusted. The police would never get cooperation again if such deals were not respected. However, it pains me to say, Dr. Nox, that your career may be permanently damaged. You will avoid prosecution, but eventually the details will emerge and you will not be looked upon fondly for desecrating the corpses of the creatures."

The thought of losing his career, losing everything he had worked for...

"There must be some other way?" Samuel asked, almost pleaded.

"You must prepare for the worst, I'm afraid. As far as I see, you have two choices: you confess to the police now and risk your career. Or, if you delay, you risk your career... and your life. I know it is difficult, Dr. Nox. But the sooner you tell the police, the better it will be."

IT WOULD BE the ultimate humiliation. For Samuel, someone who was born into poverty, who worked his way up from nothing to become one of the most brilliant scientists in the country, to degrade himself like this! But he saw no alternative. Quinneas was correct.

Together, Quinneas and Samuel went to the district police station, an austere grey building. Uniformed constables rushed this way and that, but they were ushered into the superintendent's office immediately upon Quinneas explaining that Samuel had information about the case of the missing creatures.

The superintendent listened closely to Quinneas's request for immunity. He eyed Samuel skeptically but agreed to the conditions. As Samuel told his story, the superintendent flitted his moustache, giving the impression of disbelief.

"You truly thought these men were nobles?" he asked once Samuel had finished.

"Yes," Samuel said, as convincingly as he could manage. He gripped the arm of his chair, fighting the sudden need to scratch all over.

"And you never questioned that what they were asking was a crime?"

The itching was growing even worse. Samuel took a deep inhale to steady himself. "I never thought to question them. I assumed that nobles always acted with the best of intentions. I could not believe that nobles would ever ask me to do something illegal."

Samuel hated himself for allowing such stupidity to flow from his mouth, but he had no choice.

The police superintendent stared at him for several seconds, trying to look deep into Samuel's soul to determine whether he was telling the truth. "Very well," he said at last, evidently not completely believing his story, but having no way to disprove it. "You must be more discerning in the future, Dr. Nox."

Samuel nodded, refusing to respond to this crack at his intelligence.

"In the meantime, we shall post constables outside your lab just after sunset. This is when they bring you the creatures, yes?"

"That's right."

Soon it would be over. Soon he would be free from these travails. Even if he had to degrade himself in the process. He had done the right thing. The men were criminals and were harming innocent creatures, he told himself. They deserved to face justice.

Samuel could only hope his career would be spared in the process.

As he walked homeward from the police station, Samuel was at last free to scratch. It felt like ecstasy as he gave into the urges.

Soon it would all be over.

CHARLOTTE

Perhaps Charlotte secretly wanted to be discovered. How else could she explain her carelessness? Feelings of shame circled in her head as she hastened to throw clothes and other belongings in suitcases. She knew she needed to leave today, even as Brondin had allowed her a week. Her only option was to go to Willien's and thence determine a more permanent place to live.

After her hurried packing, she nudged open the door to her mother's perpetually darkened room. Slivers in the curtains let in only tiny beams of light. The room smelled unpleasant, Charlotte was embarrassed to notice. Her mother's illness caused her a great deal of digestive problems to which the doctors could find no solutions, and the smell of vomit and body odour was not fully masked by the lavender scents the servants placed about the room.

Her mother lay still in bed when Charlotte opened the door. Charlotte was unsure whether she was even awake.

"Mother?" she said quietly.

Her mother rustled beneath the blankets and slowly pulled them away from her face. As if the hint of light from the doorway were blinding her, she shielded her eyes. "Charlotte? What is it?"

Charlotte did not wish to disturb her in her weakened state, so she remained ambiguous. "Mother, I wish to inform you that I shall be living elsewhere for now. I have decided it is best."

"Why is it best?" she said, sitting up.

"I think it is best to have time on my own, that is all. I shall go to Willien's in the first instance."

"Well," she said, her voice growing more animated, "so long as this is your idea and not Brondin's. No matter what the law states, no matter about his wife and child, this is as much your home as it is his! Do not let him dictate to you."

"Shhh, I know," Charlotte said softly. "I know. It is my decision."

Charlotte bent down and kissed her mother's cheek, withered from years of suffering from the illness.

The thought of deceiving her regarding the reason for her departure filled Charlotte with sadness. As she slowly exited and shut the door to her room, she wondered whether she would see her mother again.

~

ARRIVING AT WILLIEN'S, Charlotte was once again led outside to meet him, this time in a different section of his garden.

"Two times in one day?" he said, rising from the flowerbed. "I shall record this in my almanac as a historic day!"

Charlotte could not bring herself to laugh at Willien's joke. If it was indeed a joke. Her situation was far too grave. When she explained it to him, he shook his head in a knowing way, and agreed that she could stay.

They were after all still married, so it was hardly inappropriate. And perhaps it would even quiet some of the nobility's gossip about them. Willien was fifteen years Charlotte's senior and by his age – at the very latest – one was supposed to have a wife and family. The fact that his marriage was unsuccessful led some to make unkind jokes at his expense.

When they had realized things between them were not harmonious, they talked of divorce. But this would only create scandal. And there was no simple process by which it could be achieved, except by permission of a senior priest. Charlotte living at Willien's estate would at least give the appearance of a normal relationship, for a time.

SAMUEL

Samuel paced around the lab, doing his best to avoid scratching, even as dozens of places on his skin burned. He gripped the edge of the table tightly to occupy his hands.

The superintendent checked his timepiece. "They are now ten minutes late. If you alerted them in some way –"

"They will be here soon, I am sure of it," Samuel replied.

There was no way for them to know a trap had been set, of course. They had notified Samuel of a fresh winged lion specimen, and he expressed his desire for it.

He checked his own timepiece and eyed the superintendent. The man glanced around the lab, looking at Samuel's glassware and instruments, and muttered something under his breath as he shook his head, probably imagining the horrors of Samuel's blasphemous experiments. Positioned in the adjoining lab were a group of constables waiting to apprehend the culprits at the crucial moment.

"Let us have faith in Oqci," the superintendent said as he checked his timepiece once more. He eyed Samuel with a sardonic look. "I suppose you have no such faith."

To that, Samuel said nothing. He knew it would be unwise to enter into a discourse on the various fallacies and logical contradictions found inside the holy text.

A rap upon the door interrupted the awkward silence. At last!

The superintendent hurried into the side lab and left the door slightly ajar.

Samuel's two "friends" dragged behind them a large trunk on wheels. Memories of that first fateful night flashed into Samuel's mind. Adar and Michael betrayed no suspicion on their faces.

They had grown so accustomed to the routine that few

words needed to be spoken. With the trunk in the centre of the room, they opened it to reveal the lion, its eyes resting peacefully in death.

Samuel went to collect the money for their payment, even as he knew they would not be keeping it. And nor would he.

Samuel began shaking as he opened the drawer that contained the money. His fingers were so sweaty he had trouble separating the bank notes. As Samuel counted the notes in his hands, some slipped from his fingers and then the rest came fluttering down to the floor.

His heart pounded as he knelt down, scrambling to gather the fallen notes.

"My… my apologies, gentlemen," Samuel croaked with a dry voice.

"What is the matter, Nox?" said Adar.

"No matter," he said as confidently as he could. "No matter at all." He scraped up the notes into a messy pile in his shaking hands and walked slowly to his two former allies.

They wore scowls upon their faces. But when he extended the notes, Adar readily accepted them.

"They're all sweaty," said Adar in a disgusted tone. He shook his head and turned to Michael. "Such a curious man."

Just then, the lab door burst open. "Halt!" shouted the superintendent. The other constables rushed out with pistols drawn.

Adar and Michael flinched, but before they realized what was happening, they were surrounded.

"You are under arrest for murdering sacred creatures and selling their bodies."

Samuel stood like a statue, watching the entire scene unfold, as if he were watching it all from above, floating outside his body.

"You scoundrel, Nox!" cried Michael. But the sound washed over Samuel without eliciting a response. Further protests from the men made no impression, like they were speaking a foreign tongue.

The constables circled the men and restrained them as they continued cursing.

Samuel was frozen. But he knew the ordeal was now behind him.

~

THE ARRIVAL of the newspaper the next morning was what Samuel awaited. All night, he had tossed and turned, wondering whether his name would be kept from the papers.

The headline of the front page announced in giant letters the capture of the sacred creature murderers. He had already discerned the newspaper would have had just enough time from the capture of the men last evening to print an article. He anxiously scanned the text, which stretched across the entire front page, for his name.

Cursory details of the men as well as a recounting of the mysterious disappearances of the creatures were to be found. But the words "Samuel Nox" were not. Perhaps he would be spared after all!

The men were, of course, not nobles at all. Their real names were Cam Fletcher and Kalum Reed, Samuel learned from the article. "Michael of Highstaff" indeed. They were nothing more than a bunch of lower-class rascals.

As soon as they were captured, Samuel read, they spilled their guts, trying to implicate the other. It seemed as though Fletcher, an impoverished and irregular worker from the Iron Town slums, had, out of spite, killed the unicorn of a noble family with whom he was acquainted. He had apparently done odd jobs on their lands during the harvest season. From there, having acquired a taste for crime, Fletcher recruited his friend Reed, and they continued to kill the creatures of other noble families just outside the city.

Samuel basked in his good fortune that the newspaper said nothing about them selling the bodies of the creatures to him. How the two men learned of Samuel, he knew not, but he surmised that perhaps one of them had come across an advertisement for a lecture of his.

The first day of coverage in the newspaper gave Samuel

hope. Was it too much to ask that his name be kept out of the papers?

~

THE NEXT DAY, Samuel entered Iron Town College's anatomy building with optimism in his steps. But outside his office door was stationed Professor Kelson.

Kelson wore a stern look on his face. He simply held up a copy of that day's newspaper as Samuel approached. The headline on the front page read: "NOX DISSECTED MURDERED SACRED CREATURES."

No! It couldn't be true.

Kelson handed him the paper, saying nothing. Samuel's eyes frantically moved over the article. He was not painted as malicious but as hopelessly naïve. The article read, "Dr. Nox claimed that he thought the men were nobles, donating the bodies of these creatures for science. He did not question the men when they suggested he dissect the bodies." An editorial comment added, "Dr. Nox is either a liar or an imbecile. Whatever the case, we would all to do well to hear no more from him."

Reading the article as the professor looked on, Samuel's mind raced for a way to rectify the situation.

"It's… it's not true," he stammered at last.

"What's not true? That you dissected the creatures?"

"I… I…"

"You knew exactly what you were doing in accepting their bodies," said Kelson. "Maybe you convinced the police you were a fool, but I know you better, Nox. You might be a knave, but you're no fool."

Samuel struggled for words. The itching was coming back again, everywhere.

"I have convened a meeting of the anatomy committee for later this afternoon," the professor continued. "There I shall propose a resolution to have you removed from the college. I have already spoken with some of my colleagues and their opinions on the matter are one with my own. I suggest that you not contest our decision, and, please, spare our poor college any further humiliation." He shuddered. "Just imagine what the scholars at Etterburg must think of us now. Please, don't make it any worse for our humble institution!"

"I…"

Before Samuel could summon a response, Kelson receded down the hall, his hands clasped behind him.

DELLIREA

Despite the failure of the dragon mission, Dellirea's father had been in a happier mood in recent days, for reasons Dellirea could not divine. The blocks from the island had arrived in Goldhall and preliminary examinations confirmed their high concentration of aletolium. Could this be why?

Aramal called for a meeting of his council. Not in the council room as usual, however, but in an open field just outside the palace grounds.

Dellirea marched alongside the other council members, in a state of confusion and amusement, onto the dry grassy field. The late summer sun warmed them, and they laughed as they speculated about the possible reasons for meeting in such a strange location.

"So Aramal, what are we doing here?" asked Uncle Lochmar.

"Just wait," Dellirea's father said, looking like a child on the morning of Descent Day. "Just wait!"

Aramal introduced to the group a lanky, enthusiastic middle-aged man with floppy brown hair. This was the royal engineer, Rodnel, Count of Summerstone, Dellirea's father explained.

Then, behind a group of trees in the field came a mechanical whirring sound, like gears grinding together. Something that resembled a grey metal house appeared from the trees. The contraption was circular, its top shaped like a cone. Cannons poked out all around the lower part of the contraption. It moved slowly toward them. But how it was moving, Dellirea knew not.

Her father clasped his hands near his chest and watched with a wide grin on his face. He then took a rifle from the head of the armed forces. Dellirea was confused. And a little frightened. Her father aimed the gun at the contraption which had come to about one hundred paces from them.

"Behold," he said.

He fired a shot. A ping was heard as the bullet bounced off the side. The gun was reloaded. Another shot, another ping. The contraption continued moving, as if nothing had happened.

"What… what is it?" Dellirea asked.

"This," her father said proudly, "this is what will allow us to defeat the dragons!"

Dellirea shared the confusion evident on the other council members' faces. As the contraption arrived, a door on the side of the moving house opened and eight soldiers alighted.

"A true genius," Aramal said, motioning toward Rodnel. "He proposed the design for what he calls the 'war machine.'"

Rodnel bowed. Dellirea thought he looked like a showman from one of the travelling carnivals that visited them each summer. "Greetings, friends," he said. "The problem of the dragons vexed me considerably. How best to confront them? At first, I designed a device which would launch a net to entrap them. But this was too inaccurate. And our soldiers were still too vulnerable to their attacks. What good fortune then to have, one day while walking the gardens, a common turtle cross my path! The appearance of the turtle inspired me. Could we not design some kind of contraption based upon a similar notion?"

Dellirea and the others nodded in unison at his explanation, enchanted by this curious man.

"The war machine works thusly," continued Rodnel. "The wheels move by four soldiers pedalling inside, in the same way as one would pedal another new contraption to grace our nation, the so-called 'bi-cycle,' while the other four soldiers operate the cannons. The sloped cone roof, made of steel, provides protection against artillery fire," he said, and with a wink, "not to mention dragon fire. What is the advantage of the slope you ask? It means the absolute width of the outside is thicker than if the same material had simply been positioned vertically."

Dellirea pictured this in her mind and realized it was so.

"This is but a prototype," Aramal added. "I have already instructed our military engineers to begin building more, but we need to do this faster. Much faster! We must devote all our nation's resources to building a fleet of these war machines and an army of soldiers that knows how to operate them. With this fleet, we shall capture a dragon!"

The other members of the council looked at each other uneasily. The nation's poor still suffered and Dellirea worried that this project would distract from the more urgent matter of tending to their welfare.

"Together, anything is possible," her father went on, smiling to himself and looking at no one in particular.

"But… will this work?" Dellirea asked.

"The war machines are impenetrable," her father said. Rodnel nodded.

"But can they operate on terrain aside from a flat, grassy field?" Dario, the Duke of Prencroft, asked.

"We have not yet tested this," Rodnel said, "but the machines should be able to traverse any terrain with which they are presented."

"Even if they do work," Dellirea said, unsure if she was being too bold, "are there not better ways to use our resources?"

Rodnel appeared undisturbed by the criticism, but it was too much for Dellirea's father. His happy mood quickly evaporated and his eyes turned to his daughter in anger. "I see no better use for our resources," he snapped. "We must regain our national greatness. We must! It is our destiny!" Turning to Dario, he continued, "You must prepare notices for the conscription of all able-bodied men and women." He grew increasingly animated, gesticulating with each sentence. "The nobles and priests will be exempt of course, but anyone else will need to prove it is essential they remain at home. Otherwise I wish them to be building war machines or training for combat. They will be preparing for an epic victory. The greatest victory our nation has ever seen!"

"With respect, Your Majesty, what you ask is unprecedented," Dario said. "This kind of undertaking is far greater than anything attempted before."

"Yes," replied Dellirea's father, "but the dragons are foes unlike anything we have faced before. That is why such a step is necessary. If you do not believe you are able to carry it out, please recommend someone who can."

"No one can do such a thing," Dario said. "It is beyond our nation's capacity. To suddenly transform the entire economy to build these machines? It is impossible. What is more, the people won't stand for it."

Dellirea turned to look at Uncle Lochmar, and she could see in his face that he doubted this course, as did others on the council. No one else dared speak. Dellirea did not wish to defy her father, yet she thought of Oqci and summoned her courage, saying softly, "I fear that Lord Prencroft is correct."

"I repeat," her father said, slowly and softly, trying to hide his frustration, "if there is anyone here who feels they cannot carry out their duty, please vacate your position and bring me someone who can."

With that, he walked away from the group and toward the war machine. He ran his hands lovingly over where his shots had slightly dented the steel roof.

Dario, with a dejected expression, turned to Dellirea and the others. "We must begin preparing the draft notices."

SAMUEL

Samuel resigned himself to his fate. Knowing it was futile, he did not appear at the anatomy committee meeting. He was duly notified later that day that they had indeed voted to remove him. The department took control of his lab and all of the specimens, including the tissues of the dissected sacred creatures, which Samuel assumed would be disposed of in a sacred fire. He retained his detailed written notes and drawings from the dissections, but for all intents and purposes, his scientific career was over.

Everything he had worked toward, gone. Gone in a single moment.

In the coming days, more articles appeared about the case. Samuel was lampooned in editorial cartoons. One of the cheap rags depicted him with an idiotic grin as he held up the severed head of a unicorn, dripping blood. Samuel crumpled it into a ball and hurled it at the floor. He was sickened and humiliated by it all.

The streets were more unfriendly than ever. Samuel was forced to relocate from his apartment in Iron Town to a boarding house, under an assumed name. When walking in his neighbourhood, he made sure to wear a hat with the brim pulled over his face and the collar on his jacket high. Such was the public hatred toward him that he took to carrying a concealed pistol in case of trouble.

~

Like everyone else, Samuel had received his draft notice in the mail. Splendid. With no hope of an exemption, he would be forced into building the so-called war machines for the king, or worse, being sent to die in a hopeless quest to capture a dragon.

But today the two perpetrators of the sacred-creature murders were set to be hanged in the public square. A wicked desire to see justice done to these men compelled Samuel to attend. He made sure to keep his face obscured as he walked through the crowd. His side whiskers were distinctive, but surely no one would expect him, the hated Samuel Nox, to be so bold as to walk amongst them.

A bloodthirsty crowd had gathered in the square to watch the drama unfold. The crowd – men, women, and even children – was barely above the level of savages, dressed in shabby clothes, faces encrusted with dirt, and a stink of uncleanliness and alcohol hung about them.

They disgusted Samuel, but he found he shared their blood-lust as his two "noble" friends, barely able to restrain their blubbering, were marched onto the gallows. His heart beat faster and his breathing grew heavier as he awaited their deaths. Those men who ruined him, who caused him to lose everything he held dear. Justice would be done! A sickening delight raced through him as the nooses were placed around their necks. The one who called himself Adar began sobbing like a baby.

The restless crowd jeered at the men and pelted them with rotten vegetables. A wet green leaf from one of the vegetables stuck to Adar's face, covering his right eye, and yet his hands were bound and he could not remove it. Samuel felt at once a pang of sympathy for the men but also a strong desire, at one with the crowd, to watch them meet their ends.

Once the men were in position, the floors underneath them opened. They dropped. Their necks snapped. Their bodies went limp.

A wild cheer went up from the crowd when the deed was done. Yet the police struggled to hold back the crowd – whose bloodlust was not yet satiated – as they surged underneath the gallows to try to grab hold of their lifeless bodies and tear them down. A handful of the mob grabbed Michael's legs even as the police frantically beat them back with clubs. They pulled down on his legs so hard that his body became separated from his head. Blood splattered upon those below as his head bounced into the crowd.

Samuel stood well back, watching as others in the crowd held poorly made puppets that were supposed to represent him. Small groups formed circles and set the puppets on fire. As they lay on the ground smouldering, some of the men and women in the drunken crowd, without shame, proceeded to drop their pants and piss on the charred remains as others cheered.

Animals. Disgusting animals! To think, those were Samuel's people. Everything he had done – all of his scientific labours, to prove some kind of equality between humans – he had done for them. To climb out from their dirt and squalor, to fight to give them a chance for equality, to sacrifice everything... and for what? To be burned in effigy by those fools who had the mental capacity of farm animals!

Samuel realized he had been wrong. He had made a terrible mistake in believing that he could change things. The idea that one could improve society... Ha! One might as well try to teach pigs to read. What a fool he had been. An idealistic fool.

CHARLOTTE

Charlotte's conscription notice arrived by post. Both men and women were to fill in the notice and wait to be assigned to a unit or to be considered as an essential person able to remain at home. Of course, she and Willien knew that neither of them would be drafted. Nobles like them were far too important to be forced into combat or manual labour. Better to let the commoners do the hard work. At least, that was the government's thinking.

An emergency meeting of the democratic movement was called in response to the conscription notices. This time, Charlotte had no need for subterfuge as she took a carriage from Willien's into Iron Town, to the same meeting hall that she had attended some weeks ago to listen to the praise of her book.

Jackson Mylner began the meeting and hushed the noisy crowd. "Friends," he said, "we have found ourselves in an unprecedented time. Our king has grown hungrier and hungrier for power in his futile quest to conquer these dragons."

Quinneas Raeil, the lawyer, spoke after Mylner. Despite his middle-class status, Charlotte admired how easily he seemed to move among the working people. He strode confidently to the podium, dressed not in the grey suits worn by most of the crowd, but a sparkling green jacket and trousers. He gave a fervent speech, using much stronger language than Mylner's measured tones. "We must resist this draft!" he said. "The time is now that we emerge from the shadows and publicly show our opposition to this draft, and to this entire monarchy!"

"Hurrah!" the crowd shouted.

"Let us hear from the Dragon Slayer," someone in the crowd said. Cheers of agreement followed.

Dragon Slayer? Images of a bold, burly hero entered Charlotte's mind, but instead a rather timid-looking man with dark brown hair, slicked neatly back, approached the podium.

"Yanis Haller, ladies and gentlemen," Mylner said, "the Dragon Slayer."

The man looked slightly embarrassed by this nickname, but he stepped to the podium to signal his agreement with the previous sentiments. "I have come face-to-face with these dragons multiple times, and I have lost people dear to me as a result of their attacks." He spoke slowly in a dry, serious tone. "I have more experience with the dragons than anyone. Now is not the time for further action against them. I believe that we should demonstrate our strength in protest."

More shouts of "hurrah!"

When Jackson asked if anyone else wished to speak, without thinking, Charlotte raised her hand. She had never before made a speech in public, but suddenly she felt compelled to do so. The crowd looked at her, puzzled. They certainly had not expected to hear from a noblewoman.

"I would like to offer my support for your movement," she said, not exactly knowing how to begin. "I am Charlotte of Evesbury. I am a noblewoman, but I have long believed that our system is unjust. Why should nobles have an easier life on account of an accident of birth?"

Cries of "hear, hear" pushed Charlotte along.

"The latest actions of the king are just more evidence of his incompetence. We must end this system of monarchy. I join you in saying that we must have democracy. We must have equality!"

As the crowd cheered wildly, Charlotte considered letting it be known just then that she was the author of the notorious book. No, no, she realized. It was still too dangerous, even among this group of friends. She bowed to the crowd and sat back down.

"I would like to thank the lady for her speech," said Jackson. "Her support of our movement shows how widespread democratic ideas are becoming!"

As the meeting concluded, it was agreed that a mass protest would happen in two days. The democratic movement had never before attempted to directly confront the government, but these were special times. It was a daring plan. And Charlotte prayed they would be successful.

~

THE DAY OF THE PROTEST, Charlotte joined the group in Iron Town. Willien was not one to become involved in politics and remained as ever in his gardens, yet he expressed his support and urged Charlotte to be safe.

Quinneas and Jackson had done their best to spread the word among the people about the march and several hundred had gathered already, clutching their draft notices uneasily. The plan was to march from Iron Town and across the city to the palace, collecting more supporters along the way. Some of the crowd held make-shift weapons like sticks and clubs, and a few even had guns. These weapons made Charlotte realize the very real dangers they faced. They could be arrested. Or worse.

Dear Oqci. Was it not too late to leave?

"Come here," said Quinneas, interrupting her worries and motioning for her to join him. He handed Charlotte a green cap to wear, which he and many of the other protesters also sported. It matched, somewhat, the aletolium gems in her necklace. "You should march beside me. We should have the most respectable members of society leading the charge."

Charlotte gave him a confused look. Did they not believe in equality?

"Oh no," he said, realizing her sentiments. "This is not to demonstrate that we are better than the others. Rather, the police might be less willing to use violence against us. We can act as a shield for the people behind."

Charlotte nodded her head at the perfectly sensible explanation. But… violence? The word sent a chill down her spine. Still, Quinneas marched tall, confidently. And walking so close to him, Charlotte felt safe.

As they marched, more people poured from their homes or factories to join. A jovial atmosphere developed among the marchers. Some waved flags of green, white, and yellow – the colours of equality, justice, and democracy. A rendition of "Justice for All" added to the sense of comradery.

"This is a historic day," Charlotte said to Quinneas.

"It is a special moment," Quinneas said. "I am so happy that we have the support of someone as distinguished as yourself."

"How do you mean?"

"I know you are a great scholar at the King's Philosophy Society," he said.

Charlotte's face grew hot at this compliment, however exaggerated it was. "I'm hardly a great scholar," she said. "And you're quite accomplished yourself."

"It is true, I suppose, that I have been fortunate to become quite successful in law," he said with a chuckle. "Tell me, how did a noblewoman such as yourself come to support democracy?"

"It was the influence of my mother. She had her own ideas about the capabilities of women and wished to demonstrate that they were not inferior to men, but that with a thorough education, they could become just as accomplished."

Quinneas listened intently as the crowd of marchers wound its way through the city streets. The cleaner pathways, well-maintained buildings, and purer air indicated that they were moving farther and farther away from Iron Town and closer to the Palace district.

"She laid out a rigorous program of study for me," Charlotte continued. "By the age of seven, I was reading poetry and philosophical treaties in several languages. By twelve, I had written a two-volume manuscript on the historical relationship between Estenland and Friezzia. But my mother did not realize the directions my education would lead me. She was sympathetic to reforms allowing women greater rights and privileges in society. It was not right, she said, for only the eldest son to be able to inherit property and titles. Why not the eldest daughter? And she even supported elections in which those with property would be able to have a say in governance. But why stop at such limited reforms? Why have *any* barriers to equality? If it were true that men and women were born equal, surely it was also true that whether one was born to a noble family or a poor family should have no bearing on one's opportunities."

"Quite right," Quinneas said, nodding. "Quite right."

Police constables began to appear, clutching batons nervously. "Cease at once," one of them said, limply.

Yet they were few, and the marchers were many.

"We wish to express our displeasure to His Majesty himself," said Quinneas. "And we shall not stop until we deliver this message."

The hapless constable looked dumbfounded, and the crowd marched past him and his fellows, ignoring their vain attempts to stop the march.

As they continued walking, Quinneas turned back to Charlotte. "Your childhood must have been difficult. To have such expectations placed upon you... and such a strict program of education."

As he said this, Charlotte realized how correct he was. Her upbringing was not something she considered much. She felt emotional for a moment thinking of it but quickly regained her composure. "It was difficult. There were few diversions. I sought pleasure in flying atop my winged horse, Silver Justice, but such amusements were rare." Quinneas examined her carefully with his kind green eyes, almost like emeralds. "But," she quickly added, "it made me the person I am now."

"All is well that ends well, I suppose."

They continued their walk, and Charlotte felt a jolt of electricity move through her body when his arm brushed gently against her shoulder. She looked up at him but he appeared not to have noticed. Maybe he had not intended to touch her, but it was merely the crowd of people pushing them close together. Or maybe it was her who brushed into him?

"And you," Charlotte asked, "how did such a famed lawyer come to support democracy?"

"Ha, 'famed lawyer'! You are trying to stroke my ego, but I shan't object."

They both laughed. "I am only repaying the compliment you paid me."

"Very true," he said. "I suppose it also stems from my childhood. You may know, for it is hardly a secret now, that I was conceived out of wedlock, though my parents married before I was born. But shame always circled me for this reason. Growing up, I was teased by my peers and the adults whispered about the disgraceful circumstances of my birth. It led me to realize how cruel and arbitrary distinctions of birth can be. From then I vowed that I would wipe away all these distinctions if it were ever in my power to do so."

As he marched, so self-assured and strident in his convictions, Charlotte tried to imagine him as a small, helpless child, bullied for his parentage. It seemed difficult to reconcile that child with the confident man who walked alongside her.

WHEN THEY REACHED KARAZIN SQUARE, the crowd must have numbered thousands. Quinneas, already a tall man, climbed atop the base of Karazin's statue in the centre of the square. Steadying himself by hanging onto the statue, he spoke into a brass speaking trumpet to amplify his voice.

Protesters continued to wave the tricolour flags. And the caps they all wore created a sea of green. The police attempted to reach Quinneas, but the people on the edge of the crowd locked arms and refused to let them come near.

"Your Majesty, we gather here," said Quinneas, looking toward the palace, his voice projecting far beyond him, "to express our displeasure with this draft. There can be no more expeditions against the dragons! We must look after our own people first!"

The crowd cheered wildly.

The king, queen, and princess appeared at the palace balcony. Charlotte again thought of Quinneas as a child, and here he was, protesting in front of King Aramal himself.

Everyone began to throw their draft notices into a pile as planned. "This is what we think of the draft, Your Majesty," Quinneas said, as the pile was lit ablaze. Charlotte crumpled her own and flung it into the fire, which quickly consumed it. The fire crackled as more people moved toward the centre of the circle to throw in their notices. The smell of smoke filled the air.

The police attempted to disperse the crowd in order to extinguish the fire, but the marchers would not budge.

"We call for democracy," Quinneas continued. "We call for equality. We call for justice!" The crowd was rapturous and broke into "Justice for All" once again.

The police officers, unable to break up the crowd peacefully, looked around uneasily, unsure of what to do.

DELLIREA

ellirea's father paced on the balcony of the palace, overlooking the horrible scene taking place below. Dellirea and her mother had joined him there. A crowd as far as the eye could see packed Karazin Square. It angered Dellirea to think that the square, so named to commemorate the general who led the nation to victory in the Great War, was being dishonoured in such a way.

Even from up there, they could smell the smoke of the burning draft notices, and they could hear the amplified words spoken by one of the lead agitators.

Dellirea was stunned to see such a demonstration among the people, who all wore green for a reason she could not fathom. She had spent considerable time among the working classes through her charity work. It was true that there were some bad apples in the bunch who spread poisonous ideas, but even she had not realized how deep their poison went.

"How dare they," her father fumed. "How dare they disobey their king!"

"Why are the police just standing there?" her mother asked. "How can they allow this... this gross disobedience?"

Other members of the council hastened to join them on the balcony. Dellirea and the others looked at Dario expectantly, wanting to understand why the police stood idly. "Your Majesty," Dario began, "we fear that an intervention by the police might make the situation worse. There could be violence –"

"There *should* be violence!" shouted her father. "I want this gathering dispersed and the leaders jailed. By any means necessary. If there is violence, it will be a valuable lesson for them."

"Your Majesty, we believe that many of the people are armed.

And our police are outnumbered. If they try to intervene, it could turn into a bloodbath. One we may not win."

Aramal gripped the balcony railing as he stared out at the crowd that had now broken into song. Singing? At a time like this? Dellirea could not believe it.

"Send the griffins," her father said to Dario. "Gather them from our menagerie and send them upon the people. *That* will teach them."

Dellirea froze in horror at his suggestion. To use the sacred creatures for such a purpose… "Father, please!" she said. "Do not do such a thing. The protesters are angry because they are confused. Give them time to see that they are wrong before inflicting violence upon them."

As she looked down at the herds of people, dancing around the massive fire, she wondered how much she believed her own advice. Were these people truly capable of understanding their errors?

A flash of vengeance appeared inside Dellirea. Part of her wished to see them suffer. But she resisted this base feeling.

"Your Majesty, I agree with the princess," said High Priest Kephalos, who had joined them upon the balcony. "Our creatures are peaceful. The Book of Oqci teaches us that they are not to be used for violent purposes. Your Majesty, I implore you not to do this."

"In normal times," Dellirea's father said, "we would never use the creatures this way. But look at how far the masses have strayed from goodness. Some of them, I hear, are even killing sacred creatures for profit! Now others are demanding to overturn the divine order. No! We need to restore balance and harmony to our society."

There was to be no convincing him, Dellirea realized. Her father ordered Dario to ready the griffins.

"Your Majesty," said Kephalos, "I shall have no part in this. I resign my duties as high priest." At once, he exited the balcony and walked back into the palace, before Dellirea's father could even respond.

Dellirea admired the strength of Kephalos's convictions. She only wished she had similar courage. Instead she stood motionless with fear at what was to come.

~

SEVERAL DOZEN of the magnificent creatures, brilliant shades of black and brown with white heads, and some entirely white, were slowly led out into the square, towering above their handlers. Some stretched out their wings as they entered. Usually, the griffins' appearance filled Dellirea with pleasure. She would contemplate their beauty, the way they reminded her of the Creator's benevolence. But knowing their intended purpose, she was now filled with dread.

At first, those in the crowd paid no notice to what was happening. But, gradually, more and more started to realize. The crowd's singing grew quiet.

At once, the noble commanders responsible for the griffins gave the signal to attack.

"Look away, Delli," her father advised coldly.

But she did not. She needed to see it with her own eyes.

At their commanders' signals, the griffins pounced on the protesters, clawing at them, snaring them in their massive beaks. Blood-curdling screams reached even to the balcony. People ran for their lives. But there was nowhere to run. A wall of their fellow protesters only trapped them. There was no escape.

Dellirea shook with horror but didn't turn away. She wanted her father to know that she would not look away.

Gun shots rang out as the protesters struggled to fight off the griffins. Some threw stones or hit them with sticks. But they were no match.

One woman became separated from the mass of the crowd near the palace gates. A griffin eyed her and approached. The woman looked frantically around, unsure of what to do. She screamed for help, but no one came to her aide.

Dellirea steadied herself against the balcony, not daring to turn away, however much she wished to. It was her way of standing up to her father: letting him know that she was seeing exactly what horrors he was allowing to happen.

In an instant, the woman was tackled by the griffin. It clasped her torso in its beak and shook its head violently. Her body was torn in two as blood and guts splattered over the griffin's head and body.

Dear Oqci.

Dellirea's mother vomited at the horrific sight. One of her ladies-in-waiting helped her away. Dellirea's father watched silently, emotionless. He looked over at Dellirea with his dead eyes.

Dellirea fought back tears. She had never been so disgusted, but she did not want him to see her cry.

Within minutes, the protesters were dispersed. The griffins were reigned in. The police dragged away protesters. Dozens of dead bodies lay strewn about the square, as well as unattached legs and arms and heads. A handful of griffins lay dead as well. The grey stones of the square had turned red.

YANIS

The fire from the draft notices burned brightly. The message had been clearly sent.

Yanis stood near the centre of the crowd, next to Jackson and just below where Quinneas was standing atop the statue's base. The democratic awakening they, especially Jackson, had long hoped for was finally coming to fruition.

Suddenly, the chatter of the masses grew quieter. Screams, screeches, and sounds of gunfire came from the edge of the crowd. People ran in every direction, knocking over others or falling down. Dear Oqci, what was happening? Reflexively, Yanis started running too.

"Yanis, wait!" called Jackson. Yanis turned around. Jackson was slower in his old age and could not keep pace.

Yanis and Quinneas ran to him. They stood on either side to help him along, running arm-in-arm.

"Hurry," Quinneas shouted. "Hurry!"

Others in the crowd streamed past as a cacophony of horrified cries emanated from all around.

"Griffins!" someone cried as they ran past. "We shall all be killed!"

A screech nearby caused the three of them to spin back. A griffin stood before them, taller than even Quinneas. Its intense yellow eyes were trained upon them. The three froze beneath its gaze. Yanis could feel Jackson trembling with fright as he held him close.

More protesters rushed past, one slamming into Yanis and sending him to the ground. His rifle clattered out of his hands. He rushed to try to recover it amid the stream of escaping protesters.

Before Yanis could reach his weapon, the griffin leapt toward Jackson and Quinneas. The griffin's huge talons clawed at Jackson, who was thrown helplessly to the ground. He cried out in agony. People all around them fled for safety.

Jackson struggled in vain to fend off the griffin's attacks. His face and chest were bleeding heavily from large gashes. Quinneas rushed toward the griffin and grasped its front talon, attempting to yank it away from Jackson. As if brushing away a fly, the griffin's arm extended out and sent Quinneas flying backward. The griffin then turned its sights upon him.

Quinneas scrambled to his feet and ran. The griffin screeched loudly. It pursued him and pounced on him in a single bound.

With the rifle now in Yanis's hands, he chased after them. He took a second to lift the gun and aimed at the griffin's head. He fired.

The shot rang out and a cloud of blood misted through the air. The griffin's body collapsed on top of Quinneas. Yanis ran to him and pushed the massive beast with all his might, enough that Quinneas managed to slip out. He was covered in bits of the griffin's brain and blood.

Yanis helped Quinneas to his feet. "I'm unhurt," he insisted. "We must attend to Jackson!"

They ran to Yanis's fallen mentor, who lay lifeless in a pool of blood, his gentle face locked in an expression of anguish.

Yanis stared solemnly at Quinneas, who returned the gaze. No words were needed. They knew they must leave now before another griffin did the same to them. They joined the last of the protesters in a mad dash down the street whence they had come.

PEOPLE FLED INDOORS. The streets were deserted. Quinneas sought a doctor to attend to his wounds, which were greater than he had let on. But where could Yanis go? Return to Jackson's flat? It would be too painful – but more importantly, police would already be circling it. After the protests, the king's forces would surely go there to put a stop to his newspaper. And Yanis had absconded from his unit. He was no longer safe.

Yanis wandered the streets as if in a daze, marching south with no clear plan. He lost track of time, but the setting sun meant he had been walking for hours. As he reached the outskirts of Iron Town, he saw a face he recognized among the few remaining pedestrians. It was the striking woman who had asked the question about New Selver during Yanis's speech.

She looked at him for a moment before she realized who he was. "Come in here," she said, ushering him through a door and down into her small basement flat. "I was a part of the protest too," she told him, as they both sat down at a wooden table in the centre of the flat. "It was horrible."

"Yes," Yanis said. He could think of nothing else to say. "Yes."

His friend and mentor slain in front of his eyes. Others killed or maimed. The democratic protest, which had seemed like it was on the cusp of success, stamped out by the brutality of the king. Dear Oqci. It was horrible.

The woman, who told Yanis her name was Nadeni Lichenxu, filled a pitcher of water for him with which to bathe. Unthinkingly, without protest, Yanis removed his clothing and carried the pitcher to a corner of her tiny flat which gave at least the pretense of privacy. He stepped into the small wash basin and poured some of the lukewarm water over himself. Saying nothing – for what was there to say? – he scrubbed away the blood from his arms and torso and face.

Nadeni's attention was turned in the opposite direction, filling the tea kettle as Yanis bathed. She busied herself in silence as he sat in the basin, struggling to comprehend the events that had happened just hours ago.

AFTER EXITING THE BATH, Yanis dried himself and put his clothes back on. The shock of the earlier griffin attack had begun to dissipate and reality set in. He joined Nadeni at the table and brought the cup of tea to his lips.

"Jackson was a mentor to me," Yanis said.

Nadeni listened with a compassionate expression. She sipped from her own cup.

"When I was a teenager," he continued, "I expressed doubts about Oqci to my parents. The entire system of religion, the entire system of monarchy, it was all a sham, I told them. But they would have none of that talk. They sent me out with nothing."

"A terrible shame," she said, shaking her head.

"I had nowhere to go. But Jackson took me in. He allowed me to serve as an apprentice at his print shop. Jackson always stood by me and encouraged me. Even when I was exiled, he never wavered in his support of me. He never abandoned me like my parents had." Nadeni sat patiently listening to his story. "I'm sorry," Yanis said, "I am rambling. I am only just beginning to imagine a world without him."

"There is no need to apologize," said Nadeni, touching his hand, looking at him with her gentle brown eyes. "It is a great loss. To you personally, and to the democratic movement."

"Thank you for your kind words," he said. He took a sip of tea.

"Of course, I knew who he was, everything he did for our nation," said Nadeni, "yet I did not know him personally like you did."

Yanis looked around and despaired. But perhaps Nadeni understood his predicament. "It is not much, but you may stay here for now, if you need."

CHARLOTTE

As Charlotte returned to Willien's estate following the protests, her dress ripped and dirtied, she was in a daze. She only remembered Quinneas urging her to run while he and the one they called the Dragon Slayer helped Jackson. Charlotte just ran and ran, not sure which way she was going. She simply ran.

It was some time before she realized she was far from the square, the protesters long gone. She wandered the city before she found a carriage to take her home, or rather to Willien's.

When she arrived, she found Willien waiting for her. And… Brondin. What was he doing there? She dreaded hearing his comments. He would tell her how foolish she was for going to the protest. For daring to question the king's authority. Part of her even thought he might be right to do so.

"I shall give you two a moment," said Willien, leaving Charlotte and her brother standing in the entry way.

"I received word that you were at the protests," Brondin said in an even tone, once they were alone. He looked her up and down, wincing at her dishevelled state.

Charlotte explained what had happened. How their protest gathered peacefully in the square. How they had been attacked by the royal family's griffins. How she had seen people, who just minutes before had been cheering and laughing, torn apart in front of her eyes. How she still did not know if her comrades had made it out alive. How she had not even been sure *she* would make it out alive.

As Charlotte told him what had happened, his expression softened. He hugged her. "Dear sister, it was pure barbarism from the king. It simply cannot stand!"

Charlotte squeezed him tightly. More tightly than she had ever before hugged him. For so long, they had been at odds, but as they embraced, there was a connection between them that Charlotte had not felt for some time, if ever. If even Brondin could come to see the wrongs of the king's actions, perhaps others could as well.

THE FOLLOWING DAY, Charlotte sought information on the massacre in the press. She was heartened to see an edition of Jackson's newspaper, *The Voice of the Working Man*. His associates must have rushed this issue to print before the king's forces closed down the shop.

A thick black line bordered the entire front page of the newspaper. It was the sign of mourning. A picture of Jackson adorned the centre of the page. He had been killed in the attack, she read, along with dozens of others. Her eyes frantically scanned the pages for news on Quinneas Raeil. At last, she was relieved to read a short section reporting that he had escaped with only minor injuries.

The radical papers naturally condemned the massacre, but even the *Goldhall Gazette* contained the headline "GRIFFINS MASSACRE PROTESTERS," and it described the brutality of the attacks. Perhaps the mood of the country was turning against the king.

The paper also reported that Kephalos had resigned his position as high priest out of disgust at the king's actions. Kephalos called for a meeting of priests, nobles, and other prominent leaders for the following day in order to discuss the king's leadership.

WITH BRONDIN, Charlotte attended the meeting, held in the city opera hall. Walking into the ornate auditorium, with its golden candelabras, velvet carpeting, and hand-painted designs upon every surface, she scanned the crowd. There must have been one hundred of them altogether, everyone dressed in their finest suits and dresses. They congregated in the main section of the theatre, even though on a typical night at the opera most of those who gathered would be sitting in their private boxes high above.

Charlotte's eyes were quickly drawn to Quinneas, who was across the room at the centre of a small group, standing taller than the others around him. Despite the easy way he talked with the others, he looked in poor shape. There were scrapes and scratches on his face – but this only made him more intriguing.

As Charlotte and her brother entered, she waved at Quinneas in order to catch his attention, yet she escaped his notice.

"At whom are you waving?" Brondin asked.

"Quinneas Raeil," she said. "A friend."

At last, he saw her and waved back. But before she could make her way through the crowd to speak with him, Kephalos brought the meeting to order.

Kephalos's white hair and beard signalled his status as elder statesman of the group. Surprisingly, he eschewed the usual blue robe of the priests and instead wore a simple dark grey suit that might more properly be found on a commoner.

"Friends," he said, standing at the podium, illuminated by the gaslights around and above them, "the past days have been extraordinary, with the decision by His Majesty to send griffins upon our own people. This was an action I could not accept, and, as I feared, it produced a great loss of life. I have called this meeting of the city's finest residents in order that we might discuss the future of the government."

The crowd moved restlessly in their seats, as Dario, Duke of Prencroft, was invited by Kephalos to come to the stage and speak. "My friends, I come to you as a representative of His Majesty, King Aramal. Many of you disagreed with His Majesty's actions two days ago. While it was a difficult decision, we believed, and we still believe, that it was a necessary step in order to prevent a complete overthrow of our nation by radicals."

Charlotte smirked at the chorus of disapproving murmurs

this statement produced. She was heartened to know that the other so-called prominent residents were at one with her views.

"Much blood was shed," Dario went on steadfastly in the face of the audience's discontent, "and this was indeed a tragedy. But we must remember those who bear the true responsibility for the event – some of whom are in this very room as we speak."

All eyes turned to Quinneas, who was the target of the remark. He shook his head gently at the mention. Charlotte could only see the back of his head from several rows behind, yet he said something to his neighbours, causing them to chuckle.

"Yes, it is with these democratic radicals that the blame lies," Dario continued. "They stir up the working people with their dangerous rhetoric and false promises. And look what occurred! His Majesty did what was right – what was necessary – and neither he, nor I, shall apologize for it."

With that, he exited the stage defiantly.

"A disappointing speech," Brondin whispered to Charlotte.

"Indeed," she responded.

Next to the podium was Richard, Duke of Saundley, one of the most prominent noblemen in the nation. "It is with great difficulty that I disagree with Lord Prencroft," said Richard. "I must register my concern with His Majesty's actions. I have no sympathy for these dastardly radicals who manipulate the masses for their own purposes. But the masses are angry, and not entirely without justification. I fear that if something is not done, their riotous violence will soon engulf us all. As a first step, we must ensure that the people are not again sent to be slaughtered needlessly by dragons."

"Hear, hear," shouted the crowd.

Charlotte could hardly believe it. Here the great Lord Saundley – who had more wealth and property than most of the others in the room combined, who was the very last person who could be considered a friend of the masses – was suddenly speaking on their side!

She was stunned as she realized Saundley was far from alone

in his views. Several other nobles, priests, and prominent leaders all rose to speak, echoing precisely the same sentiments.

Having heard a number of different voices, and realizing the mood of the room, Kephalos spoke again. "My friends, for much of our nation's history, the wisdom and benevolence of the monarch ensured the happiness and prosperity of all. However, there have been instances in our history in which the wisdom and benevolence of the monarch could not be assumed. In such cases, the most recent of which was in 1121, under the reign of King Sera, a Great Chamber was formed of representatives of the nobility, the priests, and the commoners. This chamber offered guidance to the monarch, to ensure that he governed justly."

The crowd murmured as they realized what Kephalos was suggesting. Charlotte turned to Brondin, whose face was locked in an expression of disbelief.

"Today," continued Kephalos, "I call for the formation once again of the Great Chamber."

27

SAMUEL

Samuel knew not how to feel as he strolled through Karazin Square. It was virtually empty today, but only yesterday it had been the scene of the massacre of civilians at the hands of King Aramal's griffins. Even though Samuel thought the draft a disastrous idea, he had refused to join the protests. He couldn't bear it. Whenever he thought of such a crowd, his mind shifted to the terrible executions of his two "noble" friends. It made him sick. As Samuel looked down at the square's stone bricks, which were stained red from the violence of yesterday, he realized he had made the right decision.

Samuel gazed up at the statue where Quinneas had given his speech. Quinneas! How had Samuel been so stupid as to listen to his advice? To turn himself in to the police? Utter foolishness.

In the days afterward, Quinneas had deserted Samuel, refusing to answer his calling cards. Samuel was all alone now. All his former allies had deserted him. Even Greta refused to answer his letters.

Samuel fixed his eyes upon those poor souls scrubbing the stones in the square. In a way he admired them. Yes, their clothes were dirty, their countenances ugly, their bodies warped from years of labour. And yet, he wished he could trade places with them. They had but one simple task to perform in the world. It required no thought, no ambition. It was true that they would never know the ecstasy of climbing to the heights of greatness, like he did. But at least they would never know the crushing misery of the fall either.

~

WITH THE DRAFT POSTPONED INDEFINITELY, and Samuel's career as a scientist in tatters – blacklisted from even the most menial scientific jobs – the question presented itself of how to earn his bread. He thus gathered, along with other shiftless men, outside the gates of the Goldhall docks at dawn. Just then, the bell rang and the gates opened. Samuel and the others swarmed through the entrance, raising their hands in desperate hope of being selected by one of the foremen for the day's work.

As he looked at the sorry state of his potential co-workers, Samuel knew he had a reasonable chance of being selected. Some reeked of alcohol and could barely stand straight; others appeared so withered and hunched over that more than a few minutes of manual labour would leave them incapacitated the remainder of the day.

The foreman passed through the crowd and pointed to those he wished to help unload the cargo ships. At last, he came to Samuel. He looked him up and down with indifference, before nodding with a grunt and pointing his finger over his shoulder to indicate he wanted Samuel's services.

"Thank you, sir," Samuel said, bowing – though inside he raged at the indignity.

Their task was to unload the ships from the overseas colonies in Otela and Ozenzal. Estenland's desire for plundered resources needed to be satiated, and fortunately for the nation's greedy inhabitants, there were always colonies from which to plunder.

The weather was nice enough on this warm summer day as he walked onto the docks alongside the other chosen ones, awaiting the first assignment. The sun had already risen, yet there were enough clouds to shield them from its rays. Seabirds squawked all around. And the smell of the River Elden was less pungent than usual. It was almost a pleasant atmosphere.

The foreman called over Samuel and another man, much younger than him and with a strong physique. He had the two work together to begin hauling crates off a ship – this from one of the colonies in Ozenzal. The two climbed on board and began to carry off a large crate of raw cotton, bound for processing in one of the city's textile mills.

The other man lifted his end with ease. Samuel struggled

with his side but managed well enough. Just as they were descending the ramp off the ship, Samuel felt an uncontrollable itch coming from his leg. "I… I need to set it down."

"We haven't much further," the man said.

"Please," Samuel panicked, shaking, "I need to set it down!"

Samuel nearly dropped the crate before, at last, the other man lowered his end.

"Dear Oqci! Are you a woman or something?" he shouted. The foreman and some of the other workers in earshot laughed at this remark. "Even my wife could lift this."

Your wife is a filthy ape, Samuel thought. Anger bubbled up inside him, though he had no choice but to silently endure the remark.

He scratched at the terrible itch once his hands were free. "I'm sorry," he said. "I… I have a skin ailment."

The man sighed and shook his head as they lifted the crate and carried it the remainder of the way to its position on the docks.

But the man was right, Samuel reluctantly accepted. He *was* much weaker than the others. The rest of the day, Samuel struggled to lift some of the heavier crates. It made him realize he was no longer as physically adept as in his youth. Two decades ago, when he had taken his first job as an assistant surgeon with the army in its campaigns in New Selver, he was the very model of fitness. On days of leisure, at dawn, he would ride on horseback into the wilderness to hunt native game. But working in a lab all these years had made him grow weak.

The babbling and guffawing of the brutish dockworkers interrupted his reminiscing and made him consider the present circumstances. Looking at these ignorant men, his mind could not help but turn to the democratic protests.

To think, men like that… having a say in government! Writing laws, managing the budget! What a cruel joke. If Oqci did exist, Samuel thought, he was surely enjoying watching him suffer these fools.

CHARLOTTE

Frantic murmuring filled the room after Kephalos announced the idea of forming the Great Chamber. It was brilliant, but Charlotte certainly had not expected it, least of all from a priest. And she wondered why she hadn't thought of it first.

Within moments, someone began to applaud, and soon the entire room was clapping and cheering. Charlotte looked over at Brondin, who was still stunned, but he quickly began to clap as well, not wishing to deviate from the rest of the crowd.

Dario rushed to the podium and had to shout to be heard above the noisy crowd. "This is not wise," he called out. "This is not wise." Slowly, the noise began to dissipate. "I have listened intently to your words, but I wish to warn against forming the Great Chamber. If the masses begin to think their disrespectful actions have an effect, they will only grow bolder. Soon," he sputtered, "soon they will be saying that there is no difference between them and the nobility!"

Charlotte suppressed a smile. Yes, she thought, that was exactly what *should* happen.

"Let us hear speakers on this proposal," said Kephalos.

Before Charlotte had time to think, she stood. "I wish to speak."

The heads of the crowd turned to her. Brondin, too, looked at her with a puzzled expression. Charlotte amused herself imaging their thoughts: What was this? A woman having the audacity to speak?

"My name is Charlotte of Evesbury. As a member of the noble class, I believe Lord Prencroft's warning of the dangers of the Great Chamber is well taken. But let us not forget that even greater dangers await us if we fail to act. This is why I join Priest Kephalos in calling for the formation of the Great Chamber."

This statement received loud applause. Her eyes met Quinneas's across the room. He smiled at her.

In quick succession, others rose to indicate their support, not least Brondin, who spoke as if he had supported democracy all along. He looked quite proud of himself for this statement, expecting to receive a thunderous ovation, but in its place only received a smattering of polite applause.

Quinneas stood next but paused before beginning and scanned the crowd. It was his opinion that everyone in the room, most of all Charlotte, wished to hear. "Friends, as a member of those who come from neither the noble nor priestly class, I thank you for your willingness to sacrifice for the good of the country. I, too, call for the formation of the Great Chamber. What is more, I call for us to select members at this very moment for an interim committee that will manage the elections for that body. Many of the most prominent representatives from all three classes are present in this very room. Today, we can begin to work with our friend Lord Prencroft on plans to hold elections."

One nobleman exclaimed, "Are we to trust this man? Quinneas Raeil is a well-known friend of the radicals. He led the very disrespectful protest several days ago! The blame for the sad scenes that day must fall at least partially, if not entirely, on him."

This statement elicited several cheers but a greater number of hisses.

"You are quite right that I was there," answered Quinneas, "but look at the scars upon my face from the griffins' attacks. I have experienced firsthand the cruelty of the king. It is true that I was one of the leaders of the protests, but I have always maintained that it was the wisest course to have the masses guided by a respectable leader, to ensure their worst tendencies are repressed. This is what I have always endeavoured to do."

"What did that guidance achieve at the protest?" the same nobleman asked Quinneas.

"It was undoubtedly a tragic event," he replied. "I believe the protesters acted respectfully toward King Aramal in expressing their displeasure, but it is true that some behaved poorly and, for that, I have considerable regret."

Charlotte had no time to be tickled at Quinneas's conciliatory rhetoric, even as she knew he did not completely believe his words. Instead, sensing he had done enough to quell the objections of the crowd, Charlotte sprang to her feet to second his call for the selection then and there of an interim committee. Others in the room also sensed that the time was right, perhaps calculating that they might have the greatest influence if they agreed and nominated themselves to be part of it.

Of course, Charlotte had made the same calculation. She asked to be considered as part of the noble section of the interim committee. This elicited some murmurs of dissent.

"While we appreciate the noble lady's enthusiasm," one priest said, "it would be highly unusual to consider a woman for this position. It is something entirely without precedent."

In the midst of further murmuring, Brondin stood as well. "I know not whether it is right for a lady to serve. That will be for others to decide. But I rise to signal my own intention to be considered for a seat on the committee."

"Thank you for your support, you fiend," Charlotte whispered as he sat.

Before Brondin could respond, Quinneas rose quickly: "Friends, some have raised questions about a woman's place on such a committee. They have said this is an unprecedented proposal. But are these not unprecedented times? Lady Evesbury has impressed us all with her courage and intellect, and she is a respected scholar of philosophy. I believe that we ought to consider her. The committee could benefit immensely by having someone of her brilliance."

Others, swayed by Quinneas, also indicated their support for Charlotte's ability to stand for the committee. A vote was hastily arranged. The interim committee was to contain fifteen members, five each from the three sections of nobles, priests, and commoners. Papers were soon distributed on which the attendees could write five names from their own section.

Charlotte considered her choices and wrote in her selections, naturally including her own name, before depositing the ballot with Kephalos.

~

CHARLOTTE WAITED in the lobby of the opera hall as the names were tallied. She stood alone at the edge of the room, awaiting the results. She was too nervous to engage in conversation with the others. Would she be one of the five selected? Or would she be humiliated and receive few votes? Perhaps she had been foolish even to put her name forward.

Out of the crowd emerged Quinneas with a smile, causing her doubts to cease at once.

"It is good to see you, Mr. Raeil," she said. "I must thank you for speaking on my behalf just then."

"Thanks is unnecessary, Lady Evesbury. You would make an excellent representative, and I thought it unfair to disqualify you on the basis of something so trivial as gender. I hope we shall be able to serve together."

"So do I hope."

"Whatever the results," he said, "I wonder if you would dine with me tomorrow evening?"

Charlotte's heart almost stopped as he asked, but before she could answer, a bell sounded from the main hall. The tallying was complete.

YANIS

"I have a surprise," said Nadeni with an amused smile on her face.

Yanis couldn't possibly imagine what this surprise might be, although he was curious to notice his mind wandering in lascivious directions trying to guess. "Well, what is it?"

She slowly revealed her hand that had been hidden behind her back. In it, she held a small jar. "Marmalade!" she said. "From the fruits of Umiri… Or at least from somewhere in Otela."

Yanis burst into laughter. It was not at all what he had expected. Nonetheless, he knew the marmalade would provide a welcome change from the bread and butter that they had eaten for the three days since his arrival.

She removed the lid and spread it upon the slices of bread.

"What is the occasion?" he asked.

"There is no occasion," she said. "Only that at the end of each month I have saved enough to afford it as an extravagance, and today is that time."

"Oh, Nadeni!" Yanis said, with his mouth still full just as he had taken a bite. "I can't accept this. It is yours alone!"

"I insist. In fact, I wish I could offer you more."

"It is an honour," he said. "I shall repay you once…"

Yanis did not know how to finish the sentence. He had no plan. His future still seemed impossible to imagine. They had heard of proposals for a Great Chamber, yet political change in the nation still seemed far away. And he remained a fugitive.

Yanis watched Nadeni as she carefully chewed her bread, savouring the taste of the marmalade. It raised a question he had been thinking since he met her, since the day he had made his speech and she had asked her question.

"Perhaps it is inappropriate of me to ask, but are you from New Selver – I mean, Umiri?"

"No, I am from Estenland," she said. "From Iron Town. Not far from here."

Yanis did not know how to proceed. "But…?"

Nadeni looked at him, a playful smile upon her lips. "But what?"

"Your question at my speech… Do you have a connection to that country?"

Nadeni chuckled. "My father was from there."

"And your mother?"

"From here."

"How did they meet?"

"Dear Oqci, Yanis! Is this some sort of investigation?"

"I'm sorry," he said. Her tone remained good-humoured, yet he realized he had been far from delicate in his questioning. "Let us change the subject."

~

NADENI HAD ALREADY GONE when Yanis awoke the next morning. Her day at the factory began at sunrise. She would not return until evening. Yanis dared not leave the flat. The only thing to read was yesterday's newspaper, another radical paper that explained the developing plans for elections to the Great Chamber.

With Nadeni gone, Yanis laid upon her cot. Nadeni had offered him a blanket, but it provided little reprieve from the harsh stone floor.

Yanis re-read the paper. By this point, he had read every word, even the readers' unfortunate poetry submissions. When he had worked with Jackson in his printshop, they would receive similar entries and though they were grateful for the material to fill column space, few could be described as eloquent.

He even read the advertisements, so desperate was he for diversion. "EVERY COUPLE'S FRIEND" read the top line: it was an instrument to prevent conception. If the political content of the newspaper did not attract the ire of government censors, this surely would.

Sexual gratification passed through his mind. It had not been since Calina… Yet being there in Nadeni's flat, safe for the moment from danger, Yanis's mind began to be filled with similar urges.

～

NADENI RETURNED THAT EVENING. With tea, they shared the last bit of marmalade.

"Yanis, I'm sorry for my evasion yesterday when you asked of my family. It is a sensitive subject, you understand. There are prejudices against those from mixed families…"

"Nadeni, please know that I hold no such prejudices!"

"I know," she said. "Many Estenlanders do, however, and so it is not something I discuss readily. But I can already tell that you are someone kind, someone who can be trusted." She looked deeply at him and smiled. "My father arrived as a young man to work. And here he met my mother. Then they had me."

"Have you siblings?"

"I am the only one," she said. "My father died when I was young. And my mother, she died in the great plague."

"Dear Oqci," he said. "I'm sorry."

"Yanis, there is something more. There is something much more."

"What is it?"

"This is not something to share with anyone, for if someone learns, I should be in grave danger. There is a greater reason the future of Umiri holds such importance to me, beyond just that I am descended from there." She paused and took a drink of tea. "You see, my great-grandfather was the Prince of Shadows."

Yanis's eyes grew wide at the mention.

"So you know who he was," said Nadeni, noting his reaction.

"Of course, I…" He hesitated to say more. He did not wish to mention how he had participated in some of the fighting against the rebellion during his exile, even as the Prince of Shadows had long been dead by then. Yanis had no choice but to participate in the fighting. Yet she might not understand.

"Estenland executed him and his only son – my grandfather – but his wife managed to flee," Nadeni continued. "And at that time, she was pregnant with my father, unbeknownst to the conquerors. She and her son lived in obscurity in Umiri. After her death, he came to Estenland as a teenager, searching for work, for redemption. He worked on railway construction but was killed in an accident while his team blasted through a mountain pass."

Yanis looked at Nadeni intently, realizing that she was descended from the most feared resistance leader in New Selver's history.

"You see now why the issue of Umiri's freedom means so much to me. But Yanis, you must not tell anyone of my ancestry. The Prince of Shadows remains a powerful symbol of resistance, for the Umirian people... and even for Estenlanders."

DELLIREA

ellirea's father rapped upon her bedroom door. She sat at her study, refusing to answer. She still could not bear his presence. People… ripped apart by the beautiful creatures. In front of Dellirea's very eyes.

The creatures were brought by Oqci to admire. They were intended to help create a connection with the divine, not to be treated as weapons of war! Especially against their own people, however badly behaved they might have been. And this blasphemous order had come from her own father.

Dellirea couldn't stand to speak to him. Or even look at him.

"Delli, darling, please open the door," he said, as he persisted in knocking. "You've been in there for days now. Please!"

She remained silent.

"I'm sorry that you disagreed with my decision," he said, "but… but you must understand… it was the only choice I had."

"That's bullshit!" she shouted abruptly.

Dellirea was shaking, so angry had she become, but her face quickly turned hot. Such foul language had never before crossed her lips, and she regretted it immediately. Was this not language frowned upon by Oqci? Was this not language used exclusively by the coarser classes?

She knew not what to say now, and evidently neither did her father. He lingered outside her room for some time before at last his footsteps retreated down the hall.

DELLIREA WAS ALWAYS close to her father. She was only a small child when her older brother had died in the great plague, alongside so many of their countrymen. Not even their royal ancestry could protect him. While others in the family, including Dellirea, fell ill, he alone had succumbed.

She remembered little about her brother and even less about her relationship with her father then. But in the time after her brother's death, she had helped her father exit the depths of his despair. After that, he had always treated her like she was older than she was, in part to prepare her for when she would assume the throne. And she felt a certain pride in knowing that he relied upon her.

But now she resented it. She never asked to be placed in such a situation. She never asked for such a weight to be placed upon her shoulders.

Her musing was interrupted by yet more knocks on her door. Could not these people just leave her in peace?

This time it was Dario, Duke of Prencroft. Again she refused to answer, but from the other side of the door, he told her it was urgent. A collection of prominent leaders had made the radical decision to re-form the Great Chamber.

Dellirea listened intently but said nothing. This was shocking news. Such a thing had not been done for centuries. Not since the reign of Sera the Terrible.

Her father, Dario continued, was furious with the decision. He was considering imprisoning some of the members for treason, as a warning to the others. "Your Highness," Dario said, "I believe this is the wrong course for your father to take. Would you speak with him? To convince him of its folly?"

It would indeed be unwise to try to imprison those who would organize elections for the Great Chamber. It would only heighten the tensions with the people. Even King Sera had known better than that. Perhaps she should speak out. Perhaps she should try to convince him that his approach was imprudent.

Just as she was about to open her mouth to express those words, the image of her father's stupid, emotionless face flowed back into her mind. That face, staring blankly as griffins massacred the people – tore them limb from limb – as blood flowed through Karazin Square.

Why did it fall to her to reason with him?

"Let him do it," she huffed finally. "I care not."

"Please, Your Highness, if he goes down this path, the situation will only grow more dire. I believe he would listen to you."

"As he listened to me when I begged him not to send the griffins on the people? Do you remember how well he listened to my counsel then? He will do as he wishes and neither you nor I can do anything to change his mind."

This elicited no response from Dario. Dellirea placed her ear to the door. She could hear him pacing the hallway. "I understand your decision," he said at last and walked away.

CHARLOTTE

Charlotte still could not believe her situation as she walked to Quinneas's door. Yesterday she had been formally elected one of the noble representatives to the interim committee of the Great Chamber. And tonight she dined with Quinneas.

"Welcome, Charlotte, if I may," he said, bidding her to enter.

She had never visited a commoner's home, and she observed the interior carefully as she walked inside. His home was similar to any noble's. The halls and the drawing room where Charlotte was first led were tastefully decorated with classical oil paintings and masks from the natives of Otela. A bachelor having such discernment in art!

It was unusual, Charlotte supposed, for a man and woman who were not married to each other to meet in such a fashion, but neither were conventional. Charlotte was still married – in name only. She doubted whether Willien had other women, but it wouldn't have bothered her if he had. And she assumed he felt the same. She had told him that she was dining with a colleague that evening, which was not technically untrue.

Glasses of wine were brought by one of Quinneas's servants as they awaited the service of dinner.

"It is a celebration," said Quinneas, as they clinked their glasses together. "Both of us elected. Together we shall bring about the change our nation needs."

Another reason for celebrating – although Charlotte did not say so for fear of sounding petty – was that Brondin had fallen pitifully short in his own attempt to win election.

Tomorrow they would all meet formally as a group. But tonight was entirely for pleasure.

Next, they were led to Quinneas's dining room. Courses of beet soup, Friezzian salad, a selection of cheeses, roast pork, and peach pie followed in succession, while the servants generously refilled their wine glasses throughout the meal.

"I don't always eat in such a fashion," said Quinneas, "but I wanted you to feel at home."

"The food is lovely," Charlotte said. "Thank you."

When the servants were out of sight, Charlotte whispered her surprise that a commoner would have so many.

"They are necessary to running the household," he explained. "Rest assured that I pay them handsomely."

After dinner, the servants removed themselves to their quarters, as Quinneas and Charlotte moved to a separate room to be alone. Quinneas opened a bottle of sweetberry wine as Charlotte sat down.

"How is it that a famous lawyer like yourself is not married?" she asked.

"It's a legitimate question," he said as he sat next to her on the sofa. For a moment, Charlotte's breath stopped as his leg brushed hers. "I suppose I have not yet had the urge to settle down."

"But someone at your age," she teased, "you must really begin to consider it."

He laughed. "I'm barely above forty! There is plenty of time for that."

Charlotte took a long drink from her glass. Her head was spinning slightly, but she enjoyed the feeling. Perhaps it was Quinneas. Perhaps it was the wine. Charlotte stretched out on the sofa and breathed in the smell of vanilla from the burning candles.

"In the meantime," she joked, feeling uninhibited, "you are inviting married women to your house for dinner? Have you no shame?"

He made a feigned gesture of protest. "Why, I would estimate you are the first married woman I've invited!"

"But have there been unmarried women?"

Quinneas laughed. "I suppose so." He refilled their glasses.

"I can imagine that." She moved closer to him on the sofa, drawn in by his jasmine-scented perfume.

"Can you?" he said as he placed his hand upon her thigh.

Electricity ran throughout Charlotte just when he did. A feeling she never once had with Willien.

"I can," she said.

His intense green eyes stared back at her in the flickering candlelight. Charlotte gently caressed his cheek, the wounds from the griffin attack still visible. She wanted him – needed him – so badly at that moment.

Charlotte leaned forward to kiss him. As she did, he grabbed hold of her and pulled her tight. Her lips locked around his. Charlotte tasted the sweet wine upon his lips as she kissed him, almost ravenously. He pushed her onto the sofa and climbed on top of her, the weight of his body pinning Charlotte, in a pleasurable manner. Charlotte's rationality, so prized to her, disappeared completely as she buried her face into his neck, kissing him there. She was entirely overtaken with lust.

THE NEXT DAY, walking with greater verve in her step despite the paucity of sleep the night before, Charlotte joined the other members of the interim committee of the Great Chamber to formally begin their work. They were to convene at first outside the palace, where the king had offered them the use of one of its chambers.

Thinking it prudent to arrive separately, Quinneas already waited outside at the front of the palace with the others as Charlotte approached. She greeted him cordially.

"It is nice to see you," she said.

"And you as well, Lady Evesbury."

A devious smile came to his lips at the formality of their conversation. Charlotte liked this secret between them.

She reflected upon their intimacy from last night as she watched Quinneas, standing tall and conversing easily with the other members of the committee. The few times when she and Willien attempted the act were unpleasant for both of them. But she now understood how it should feel.

Once the fifteen members had assembled, Dario beckoned them inside. It was to be a historic day. The pleasures of the previous evening needed to be set aside as the future of the nation became their focus.

Charlotte entered the palace near the back of the group. She was struck with awe as she walked down the intricately patterned red and gold floors of the hallways, lined on all sides with marble statues and crystal chandeliers above. No space upon the walls, no matter how small, was left unadorned. It all made her own noble upbringing seem like that of a pauper.

They were led to the Peace Room, so named to celebrate the victory over Friezzia thirty years ago in the Great War. Light poured in through the windows onto the paintings depicting General Karazin's heroism and King Andamar's brilliant leadership. Peace Room? Charlotte found it absurd to think of Estenland as the peacemaker of Ogard.

"This space will suit perfectly," Quinneas said to the group.

Everyone looked around the room, none of them saying anything. The weight of what they were to accomplish in the space became heavy upon them all.

Before they could settle, a flurry of footsteps came from the hall outside. As Charlotte spun to face the door, dozens of royal guards swarmed into the room. By the time she discerned what was happening, two of the guards held her arms behind her back.

"What is the meaning of this?" shouted Quinneas as both he and Kephalos were also seized by the guards.

"You three are under arrest for disobedience to His Majesty, King Aramal," said Dario. "Quinneas Raeil, you are under arrest for your role in organizing the protests. Priest Kephalos, you are under arrest for illegally calling for the formation of the Great Chamber. Lady Evesbury, you are under arrest for participating in the protests. And for authoring a treasonous work titled *The Downfall of the Monarchy*."

All eyes turned to Charlotte. Quinneas's mouth hung open.

She swallowed hard. She was too shocked for words. No one knew she had written the work. How did the police find out?

"You will be taken to the city prison at once to await trial," continued Dario.

"This is not right, Lord Prencroft," said Kephalos, as the police led him toward the door. "To imprison elected members of this committee? You will regret this decision."

The three of them were marched back through the palace, the same way they had entered only moments before, as the others watched, dumbfounded. Charlotte looked uneasily at Quinneas as she was forced into the back of one of the carriages waiting outside.

"We shall be all right," he shouted to her as he was placed in another carriage. "Worry not!"

Charlotte wished she shared his confidence.

YANIS

"Selver Bronn?" said Nadeni incredulously.

"He is the only member of the committee I know," Yanis said as the two of them sat in her flat. "And even then only barely, through Jackson." At the thought of Jackson, Yanis glanced down at his right arm, upon which he still wore a black armband for mourning.

"Selver Bronn is a pompous ass who cares nothing for the people," she shot back.

"That may be so, but he certainly hates the king. That makes him our ally."

She shook her head in resignation. She knew he was right, Yanis could tell. They needed to do something to protest the arrests of Quinneas, Charlotte, and Kephalos, but they could not do it themselves. They needed the help of the interim committee, which meant working with Selver Bronn.

Yanis felt a duty to Quinneas. He had represented Yanis, while asking nothing in return, when he was arrested for writing his pamphlet against the king. Quinneas was not successful in gaining Yanis's freedom, but without his help Yanis might have suffered a far worse fate than exile. It was true Yanis had saved Quinneas from the griffin's attack, yet now Yanis would once again have the opportunity to repay his debt.

Nadeni accompanied Yanis begrudgingly to Selver's palatial house after he agreed to a meeting. Selver adorned himself with a top hat and crisp black suit, which fit tightly on his wide frame. He welcomed Yanis, knowing he was a friend of Jackson and Quinneas, but Selver was colder toward Nadeni – perhaps out of prejudice, something all too common.

Selver's servant led them to his drawing room, where they spoke of the imprisonment of the members of the interim committee.

"Yes," he grumbled, as he twirled his moustache. "It is a grave injustice what has happened. A grave injustice indeed. Typical of this wretched monarch!"

Decorating his drawing room were various model trains, larger versions of which ran on the Bronn railway lines that criss-crossed the nation.

Yanis explained their plan to march upon the prison and ask for the release of the prisoners, to which Selver Bronn nodded. "Can you convince your colleagues to join us?" Yanis asked.

"I shall do my best to gain their support," he said, "but I can make no promises. The priests and nobles care little for anyone but themselves. They do not share the compassion for their fellow man that commoners like ourselves possess."

Nadeni snorted a laugh.

Selver raised his eyebrow. "Did something amuse you in what I said?"

Nadeni quickly regained her composure. "Not at all," she said.

"Very well," he said, rising from his chair. "We shall meet again soon."

"Compassion for their fellow man?" said Nadeni as she and Yanis made their way home. Her eyes burned with that fiery disposition of which Yanis was becoming fond. "What a load of rubbish!"

"But why do you say so?"

Nadeni stopped. She was silent for several moments. At last she turned to look at him with her thoughtful brown eyes. "My father... He was killed while building one of Bronn's cursed railways. Do you think Bronn gives a damn about the safety of his workers, let alone ones who came from the colonies to work?

He cares not if they work in dangerous conditions, so long as he earns his profits. Compassion for his fellow man indeed!"

"Dear Oqci," Yanis said, placing his hand gently on her shoulder. "I'm so sorry. If I had known, I wouldn't have –"

"It is fine," she said. "You are right that we need him as an ally, so I shall have to stomach him. For now."

Yanis regarded her carefully as they walked, her face still seething. He imagined this fierceness was inherited from her great-grandfather. The one who was reputed for single-handedly killing an entire company of Estenland soldiers in battle, and with none of the technology that the Estenlanders possessed. When Yanis was in New Selver, at night, the soldiers would keep careful watch at the outskirts of their camp. Still fresh were the memories, even decades later, of the Prince of Shadows sweeping into camps without a trace and slitting throats of half the men, their bodies only to be discovered in the morning.

The Prince of Shadows' capture dealt the fatal blow to the genuine possibility of resistance, even as scattered upheavals persisted. Yanis recalled these stories as he watched Nadeni determinedly marching forward.

Of course, he appreciated Nadeni's softer side as well, which he had discovered in the week and a half since the protest. Since he had nowhere to go, she had selflessly allowed him to stay with her, even if her apartment was hardly big enough for just her. Yanis risked arrest for his role in the protests while supposedly on medical leave. This made him a fugitive, if one of low priority. For sheltering him, Yanis owed Nadeni a great deal. He hoped he had not erred by forcing her to work with Selver Bronn.

CHARLOTTE

As the guards led Charlotte up the staircase to the top floor of the prison, she still could not understand how the police had discovered her. Was it Brondin who had turned her in? No, Charlotte reasoned, he wouldn't do such a thing. It would simply be too low. Even for him. And yet, the only other person she had told was Willien, and surely he would never turn her in. So it had to be Brondin. Either that, or the police discovered it on their own, through diligent investigative work… something Charlotte judged possible but unlikely.

"Right this way, my lady," said the guard, leading her around the corner.

Charlotte's shoes clacked on the ancient stone floors of the dim hallway. The guard opened the door to her cell – this one designated for nobles – and beckoned her inside.

As she examined the room, the guard locked the door behind her and walked away. It was nicer than she expected. A large rug covered the floor. A fireplace in the centre of the room would provide warmth for the evenings. A window looking to the north of the city illuminated the room. There were chairs, a desk, and a bed that were serviceable, if not luxurious. A bookcase on the wall was filled with a selection of dusty books, brought by previous prisoners.

Charlotte clutched the cool metal bars on the outside of her cell and looked into the hallway, lighted by gas lamps.

"Is anyone there?" she called out into the emptiness.

"Charlotte?" Quinneas's voice echoed from down the hall. "Worry not. They cannot keep us here long."

Their talk elicited hurried footsteps in the hallway. "Cease your talking at once," ordered a guard.

Charlotte slunk away and sat on the bed. She hoped Quinneas was right, that this would be but a temporary stay, that

King Aramal would soon realize what a catastrophic decision he had made and set them free.

To imprison members chosen by the people? No, it couldn't stand.

Could it?

~

TIME in the prison passed slowly. By the fourth day, Charlotte had lost hope for a swift release. Visions of execution flashed through her mind. To author such a scathing book... The harshest possible punishment would have to be inflicted. Aramal would do no less.

The stay was monotonous, interrupted only by restless sleep and meals of bread, cheese, and wine brought by the prison servants.

To take her mind from her captivity, Charlotte read whatever books were there. Their quality was typically low. Chivalrous adventure tales of knights in battle, or bawdy stories that previous nobles brought to satiate their loneliness.

Yet she found most instructive a history of Estenland written decades ago, during Andamar's reign. For her amusement, she opened to the section on King Sera the Terrible, a shameful moment for the Zendar dynasty. Sera's reign was marked by arbitrary cruelty and mental deficiencies. He had become king when he was only a teenager, following the untimely death of his father. Sera was already mentally unstable but grew more so with time. He believed he could convene directly with the spirit of Oqci. The priests thought this blasphemous, yet had no choice but to accept his ranting and raving. It was that, or face the gallows.

Sera imagined that Oqci commanded him to wage war against Estenland's neighbours, supposedly for straying from the divine path laid out by Oqci. In order to fund the futile wars, he raised taxes and for a time he even lost control of several of the nation's southeastern provinces as the people revolted.

Most absurd of all, Sera forced the nobles at court to perform plays about Oqci. These included the major events of Oqci's life: his descent with the sacred creatures from the clouds, the rejection of his message by the people of Otela, his travel across the Sea of Dreams to Ogard, the embrace of his doctrines by Ogard's inhabitants, his marriage to Mazir, and his return to the Cloud Kingdom following the fulfilment of his divine mission. The plays were meticulously scripted by Sera and would sometimes last hours. Those nobles who bungled their lines – or worse, fell asleep during the plays – suffered a grisly fate.

At last, the Great Chamber was called upon to restrain him. The Great Chamber ruled while Sera remained king in name only. He lived out the rest of his life confined to his palace, where he continued rambling about Oqci, this time with no one around to pay heed.

The Great Chamber had proved successful in its aims. When Sera died and his successor, a cousin, took power, the Chamber was disbanded and the Zendar dynasty continued its reign.

As Charlotte closed the book, she pondered whether – if it were ever allowed to convene – their own Great Chamber would preserve the monarchy, as it had in Sera's day, or whether it would signal the monarchy's death.

THE SOUND of the guard's footsteps disappeared down the hall. Charlotte looked through the bars. There were no guards in sight.

"Quinneas," she said, "are you there?"

"I'm here, Charlotte," he responded. "I'm thinking of you."

"I'm thinking of you, too."

"Don't lose hope."

She so wished that she could embrace him again. And to confess to him that she *was* beginning to lose hope.

"Charlotte," he said again after a period of silence, "is it true that you wrote that book? *The Downfall of the Monarchy?*"

"It is."

He was silent again for some time and Charlotte grew worried. Was he ashamed of her?

"Knowing that makes me admire you even more," he finally said.

YANIS

A small crowd of several dozen – armed with sticks, club, and rifles – milled about the Iron Town Commons waiting to begin the march on the prison on this overcast morning. Yanis and Nadeni had gathered the group from among those who had attended the protest against the draft, though the fresh memories of the griffin attack frightened others away.

At last, Selver Bronn appeared, along with some of the other members of the interim committee, mostly commoners, but surprisingly one noble as well.

"Welcome," Yanis said, greeting him and the others.

"Unfortunately," Selver said, "the other priests and nobles declined the invitation to join us. They possess not the shared purpose of commoners!"

Yanis winced inside at how Selver's lust for profits had led to Nadeni's father's death, yet now was not the time to raise that issue.

"I believe I speak for everyone," Yanis said, "when I say that we are glad you have come."

Nadeni nodded but her face showed no signs of sharing his sentiments.

Selver, content that he had won their admiration, turned to address the crowd. "Let us march to the prison and demand the release of the prisoners!" The crowd cheered and doffed their green caps. "We shall meet the governor of the prison. Your presence will show them that we represent the will of the people."

"What if the governor refuses?" asked someone in the crowd.

Selver hesitated for a moment. "Then we shall..."

"Then we shall take the prison by force," said Nadeni, stepping forward before he had a chance to speak and raising a dagger she told Yanis had been passed down to her from the Prince of Shadows. Wild cheers followed her statement, with other members of the crowd hoisting their weapons in the air. Yanis turned toward Nadeni and she winked at him, but he was unsure if hers was the best course.

"I don't believe that is a wise recommendation," stammered Selver. "And I don't think we should be taking advice from a descendant of the deniers of Oqci."

Nadeni's mouth dropped open at this insult. Yanis's eyes met hers and he saw her anger, but she decided not to rebuke him.

"No," continued Selver, stepping in front of Nadeni, "if the governor refuses, we shall turn back and think of a new plan."

"What say you, Dragon Slayer?" asked a voice in the crowd. "Will you lead us to take the prison if necessary?"

All eyes in the crowd fell upon Yanis. He stared back at them, struggling to know what to do. Nadeni's proposal was too bold, while Selver's too timid.

"Let us hope it does not come to that," he said, avoiding the question. "Now, let us march!"

Selver Bronn and the other members of the interim committee joined uneasily. From their faces, it seemed they were already second-guessing their decision to join this fool-hardy march. As was Yanis.

YANIS MARCHED at the head of their ragtag group, alongside Nadeni. Selver Bronn and the other members of the interim committee followed close behind. As they marched, they gained more followers, swelling their numbers to over a hundred.

Yanis turned to Nadeni and gave her the most confident look he could manage, even if he did not feel so in his heart. He prayed that Selver and the others would be successful in their negotiations. Yanis and some of the others carried arms, but this was hardly enough to do battle with the professionals guarding the prison.

"Let us begin a rendition of 'Justice for All'," called out

Nadeni to the group behind them. She was in a jubilant mood. She evidently shared none of Yanis's worries.

As the marchers belted out the opening lyrics, he wondered if this plan was not foolish.

Why did Nadeni ever suggest such a thing? Taking the prison? Did she fancy herself the Prince of Shadows resurrected? She had told Yanis that growing up in Iron Town, she was no stranger to confrontations, but a fight against professionals was hardly the same. As he watched her singing, he feared for her safety. And his own.

They drew ever closer to the prison and Yanis gazed at the parapets atop the three-story structure. Memories of his time there as a young man filled his mind. The prison had been his last stop before exile in New Selver. That he knew the layout of the prison would, he hoped, be an advantage. The entrance was surrounded by a walled courtyard and a moat encircled the prison itself, accessible only by drawbridge. Bringing down the drawbridge would be essential, if it came to a fight.

As they neared the courtyard walls, he caught sight of a group of five sentries, some pimply faced, probably barely older than teenagers, standing atop the parapets.

"As members of the interim committee of the Great Chamber," Selver Bronn said, stepping in front of the group to address the guards, "we demand to speak with the governor of the prison to discuss the immediate release of the prisoners."

The guards nervously exchanged words and looked down at Yanis and the others. The oldest said, "We shall let you and one other person in to speak with the governor, but the rest must remain outside."

"That is satisfactory," said Selver, who selected another commoner from the interim committee to join him.

"We would like to wait in the courtyard," said Nadeni, as the guards descended to open the gate. "We cannot very well wait here in the street."

The guards hesitated at this suggestion. Selver looked surprised at Nadeni's boldness, though by this point Yanis was not.

The guards conferred once more and decided this was permissible. Yanis and the rest of the group filed through the gate and into the courtyard. The drawbridge was lowered for Selver and his colleague to enter the prison, then raised again. The iron gate slammed shut behind Yanis and the others, locking them inside the courtyard.

THE GROUP STOOD around the courtyard for over an hour awaiting Selver's return. The commoner members of the interim committee chatted with the people as they waited. Yanis was surprised that the young nobleman, Koralo, Count of Ulsted – the lone representative of his class – had no hesitations in mixing with the working people. A small but vivacious man, he talked eagerly to those waiting as if there were no distinctions between them.

"What do you reckon Mr. Bronn's chances of success?" Yanis asked him.

Koralo ran his hand through his blonde hair as he considered the question. He tilted his head to look up at Yanis, who stood more than a full head taller than Koralo. "Let it be known that I fear the chances are decidedly scanty. But he may well surprise us yet."

They turned their gazes toward the prison and imagined what might be taking place behind the closed doors. The people in the courtyard were growing restless.

"Tell us again about the dragons," said someone in the crowd.

"I declare that I, too, wish to hear the enchanting tales of this celebrated Dragon Slayer," Koralo said.

"Go on, Dragon Slayer," said Nadeni, grinning.

Yanis recounted it as close to the truth as he could. When he explained about the second expedition to the island, where they shot at the dragons, the people grew excited and applauded. It was uncertain, Yanis explained, whether one of his shots had even hit the dragon.

"He is only being modest," Nadeni added, drawing laughter and cheers from the crowd.

The creaking of the drawbridge interrupted them. Everyone turned to Selver and his colleague, who marched across the bridge with sullen expressions.

"The governor has refused us," said Selver. "Even with the threat of the people, he would give no ground. He said it was not his decision to release the prisoners, but rather the king's."

The people, already agitated, were in no mood to hear this news. "It's an outrage!" someone shouted. "We shall take the prison!"

"We must not act hastily," said Selver. "We shall make a formal protest through the courts."

This only caused hissing from the crowd. The guards at the top of the courtyard walls looked down with concern.

"We have the Dragon Slayer on our side," said a voice in the crowd. "Let them try to stop us!"

Raucous cheering greeted this statement. The people in the crowd prodded Yanis to say something. Nadeni turned to look at him expectantly.

For a moment, Yanis was frozen. Mismatched memories flooded his mind. The expeditions to the Dragon Isles. The griffins at the protest. Jackson. Dear old Jackson.

Yanis felt as though he were being carried along by he knew not what, when he suddenly shouted, "I have slayed dragons!" The crowd cheered wildly. Pumping his fist in the air, he shouted, "Do you think this prison will be any match for me?"

"No! No!" shouted the crowd.

"We shall follow you wherever you will lead us," said another in the crowd. Enthusiastic cries of agreement filled the air.

Selver tried to interrupt, looking quickly back and forth among the other members for support. "This... this is not wise!" he shouted.

But the people would not be deterred. They gripped their weapons and readied for battle as Selver and the other members of the interim committee rushed to seek shelter in the corner of the courtyard.

"We order you to cease your actions," shouted one of the guards from the wall of the courtyard.

A large rock was hurled at him, sailing just past his head. The battle was underway.

The guards readied to fire as the group pelted them with stones from around the courtyard. A bugle sounded from the prison's roof and soldiers there began to take their positions on the battlements. Yanis scrambled for cover in the open courtyard as bullets rained down from above.

Nadeni led some of the others in breaking down the door leading to the staircase to the top of the courtyard walls. Yanis fired at the guards on the roof of the prison and hastened to reload.

They could not hope to win in a pitched battle with the soldiers on the roof, Yanis knew, and it would only be a matter of time before the king's forces arrived. "The drawbridge," he shouted, "we need to get it down!"

A handful of their group dove into the moat and swam across. They climbed to the drawbridge as gunfire from the roof continued.

Yanis returned fire while watching Nadeni from the corner of his eye. Wielding her dagger, she squared off against one of the guards. The man fumbled with his gun while Nadeni lunged toward him. He edged back and jumped over the wall, perhaps wagering the long drop below was preferable to facing her. She turned to assist the others in clearing the prison walls.

The cannons above fired closely-packed projectiles, causing havoc below as the shots sprayed out, ripping through the group. With others, Yanis grabbed what he could – rocks, pieces of wood – to construct a barricade to protect themselves.

He glanced back to the courtyard walls. There was no sign of Nadeni. Where was she?

Several of the attackers took axes and clubs to the chains on the drawbridge. They clanged away in the face of more shots from the roof.

From behind the hastily made barricade, Yanis and the others continued firing on the prison, unsure whether they were gaining any ground against the defenders. Dead bodies of their comrades grew numerous around the courtyard while others writhed about following injury.

"We have more ammunition here!" Nadeni shouted down to Yanis as her head poked above the parapets on the courtyard walls. Praise Oqci, Yanis thought. She was safe. For now.

More of the attackers climbed to join her to fire at the roof of the prison. But the situation appeared hopeless.

From the south of the prison came soldiers' footsteps marching in unison: the king's troops. This would surely be the end of them, Yanis knew.

The red uniforms and white trousers crashing through the courtyard door revealed it was indeed the Estenland army. There had to be about two hundred of them. Yanis and his forces were beaten.

"Hold your fire," Yanis shouted to his comrades. He raised his arms in surrender and walked from his barricade. Firing from atop the prison ceased.

It was futile to resist. They were already fighting a losing battle against the forces defending the prison, and now reinforcements had arrived. They had failed. Yanis had failed.

The red soldiers marched into the courtyard in an orderly formation, but then Yanis saw a familiar face.

Vinzent?

"If it isn't Yanis the Dragon Slayer," said Vinzent of Highfalls, Yanis's commander from New Selver. "I see you could use some help."

Yanis could not believe it. His unit? He knew they had been stationed in Goldhall after the second dragon expedition. Vinzent must have got word of the march and led his soldiers there.

Vinzent raised a speaking trumpet to his lips and turned to the prison. "Surrender the prison now," he said, "or we shall take it by force."

Everyone waited in silence for an answer from above.

Nothing. Nothing.

At last, their answer arrived: The firing from above began anew.

Yanis nodded to those at the top of the drawbridge to continue hammering away. Vinzent's soldiers moved expertly into position and fired orderly volleys. Others manned their cannons and launched artillery, battering the prison walls.

At once, one of the drawbridge chains gave way, causing one side of the door to begin to open. The weight snapped the other chain and the drawbridge came crashing down, leaving the entrance to the prison open.

Nadeni and her group rushed down from the courtyard walls as Yanis and the others stormed across the bridge. A line of soldiers guarded the entrance in formation. They launched a volley at the onrushing attackers. The shots brought the first wave down, but there were too many. They continued pushing toward the entrance. The defenders had no time to reload and came out onto the bridge, using their bayonets to attack.

One soldier stabbed his gun wildly toward Yanis, missing and leaving himself vulnerable. Yanis swung the butt of his gun, hitting the soldier in the temple and sending him to the ground. Another blow ensured he stayed there.

At the edge of Yanis's vision, on the other side of the bridge, Nadeni grappled with one of the guards. Just then, another guard came from behind and clubbed her in the head.

"Nadeni!" Yanis called out.

She tumbled down from the bridge and dropped into the water like a stone.

All around him was chaos. He needed to get into the water. He fought his way through the crowd to the edge of the bridge. Others on his side dove into the water to find Nadeni.

There was barely room to swing one's gun, so thick was the crowd. One of the guards lunged toward Yanis with his bayonet. He dodged the attack, grasping the soldier's forearm with one hand and the long gun with the other. The man tried to yank the gun away, but Yanis maintained his grip. He pulled him close, aimed at the man's nose, and jerked his head forward. The direct hit knocked the soldier backward.

Yanis spun toward the edge of the bridge.

Others on his side treaded water to stay afloat. "We cannot find her," one said. "She has sunk too deep."

Yanis took in a lungful of air and dove into the water, plunging as deep as he could.

Water rushed into his nostrils as he descended into the moat. He pried his eyes open but could see little in the murky water.

He swam ever deeper, not yet reaching the bottom, and frantically searched. Where was she? Thoughts of losing Calina swirled around his mind. Not again. Not again!

A flash of a green scale reflected the faint sun from high above. The fish swam toward him.

But it was no fish. No fish was so large. And no fish Yanis knew possessed hooves.

A… sea goat?

Behind him swam another, then another. Their thoughtful goat faces watched Yanis for a moment and then swam away. He tightened his chest to conserve his air and followed them. Followed them to where Nadeni lay, at the bottom of the moat.

He grasped her and, with the help of the three sea goats, lifted her toward the surface.

The dim impression of the sun shone through, far above Yanis. Rapidly, they ascended ever closer to it. At once the brightness of the day filled his eyes as they splashed into the open air. Yanis gasped for breath as the sea goats held Nadeni afloat on the surface.

A plank of wood was lowered toward them. Yanis grabbed it with one hand and with the other carried Nadeni along. The crowd hoisted them from the water.

Nadeni was placed upon the bridge as the fighting continued in the entrance of the prison. She coughed out several mouthfuls of water and slowly opened her eyes.

Thank Oqci, Yanis thought. Thank the mysterious sea goats.

Yanis turned back to look at them. Three horned goat heads bobbed above the water before they dove back down again, revealing for an instant their green tails above the surface. It was said that sea goats inhabited many waters around Goldhall, but Yanis had no idea they swam in this moat.

Yanis bent down and hugged Nadeni tightly as she regained consciousness. "I… I thought you had surely drowned."

"What happened?" she said groggily, rubbing the back of her head where she had been hit.

"Someone struck you with their gun and you crashed into the water," he said. "I dove in to save you, but… but I thought you had sunk too deep. Then… sea goats appeared!" He squeezed her tightly again and she weakly hugged him back.

They embraced for several moments before Nadeni pulled away. She looked at him intently. "You must continue the fight."

Yanis hesitated and looked back toward the prison. The hand-to-hand fighting had now moved inside its walls.

"Go," she said. "Go!"

Still dripping wet, Yanis made his way to the entrance, joining the throng of Vinzent's soldiers and his own side's irregular troops, as others tended to Nadeni.

At the back of the pack, some wearing the red Estenland uniform, others wearing mismatched threadbare trousers and shirts of various shades of grey, Yanis pushed into the prison, sure to overwhelm the remaining defenders. The guards ran for their lives as they approached. Others dropped to their knees in surrender.

Meeting no resistance, they advanced up the flights of stairs to the rooftop where the governor awaited. Yanis and the others burst through the doors. Vinzent was at the front of the charge, but a path was cleared for Yanis to join him. The governor and his closest allies glared at them. They knew they had been defeated.

"Traitors!" the governor spat. "Miserable traitors."

"You are the true traitor," said Vinzent. "Imprisoning innocent people like this."

The governor meekly submitted to Vinzent's troops.

"Let us release the prisoners," Yanis called out.

By this time, the members of the interim committee had ascended to meet them. Koralo bounded toward Yanis and enthusiastically shook his hand. Selver Bronn, however, was bent over with his forearms braced against his knees, panting, after climbing the three flights. They all descended to the level below and began unlocking the cells.

"Yanis!" Quinneas said in disbelief as his cell door was opened. He looked Yanis up and down, no doubt perplexed by the fact that he was soaking wet. "First, you rescued me from the griffin," he continued, "and now this!"

Before Yanis could respond, Quinneas looked over Yanis's shoulder and called out, "Charlotte!" He stepped around Yanis as the freed noblewoman ran toward him and wrapped her arms around him. "Yanis has saved us," Quinneas said to Charlotte as the embrace ceased.

She bowed. "Thank you… but what shall we do now?"

It was a question Yanis had not considered. He brushed back his wet hair from his forehead as he contemplated what had happened. Would the king's soldiers soon descend upon them?

"Let us return to the palace," Quinneas said. "We must confront the king!"

~

As they exited the prison, Yanis found Nadeni in better spirits and better health. She clasped his hand and whispered, "Well done, Dragon Slayer."

The shock, however, of exiting and seeing dozens of his dead comrades laying on the bridge and in the courtyard made Yanis realize the enormous cost they had paid.

Before he had time to think further, Quinneas took his hand and raised it in front of the crowd. "All hail the Dragon Slayer!" Everyone cheered, including Yanis's former commander. But it was hardly a victory won by him alone, Yanis knew. The arrival of Vinzent's soldiers was the true decisive factor.

"All hail the ruler of the sea goats!" added Nadeni to further cheering. As she spoke, Yanis realized how strongly his feelings toward her had become these past days.

DELLIREA

"It's some kind of revolt?" Dellirea asked Dario after he told her the news.

"Your Highness," he said through the door, "some are saying it is a revolution."

A revolution? This was enough to draw Dellirea out of the exile in her room. How had they reached a point where the people were responding to the decisions of their king with violence? While Dellirea deplored such disobedience, she wondered if her family did not share at least some of the blame for their actions.

A council meeting was hastily arranged. She would attend, Dellirea told Dario.

Dellirea's entrance was greeted with surprised looks. Her father wore a sheepish expression, yet no one said anything. Dellirea silently took her seat. It was better not to acknowledge the reason for her previous absence but to focus on the matter at hand.

Dario warned that the members of the interim committee were marching toward the palace and would soon arrive with a group of soldiers and other ruffians accompanying them. "We need to meet with them," Dario urged, "or they could well storm the palace. Further violence cannot be the answer."

Aramal rose from his chair and wandered the room in thought, glancing up at the portraits of past kings and queens. "What are our other options?" he asked in a defeated tone.

"We can try to arrest them again," said Dario, "but such an action would only provoke further violence. And I worry whether we can depend on the loyalty of our own soldiers, given the actions of one of the other units earlier today."

Dellirea's father sighed and looked to the ceiling. "How did we get here? Oqci, have you forsaken me? Is it because I sent the creatures on the people?"

No response was forthcoming. Everyone remained silent.

At last, he looked toward Dellirea. "What do you think we should do?"

She took a deep breath. She still felt considerable anger toward her father, but she believed he was beginning to recognize his grievous errors and would make amends with the Creator and Oqci. "I can see no other way," she said, "than to allow the imprisoned members to return to make preparations for forming the Great Chamber. It is the right course."

"Then that is what we shall do."

THE MEMBERS of the interim committee of the Great Chamber arrived at the palace an hour later, in front of a parade of uniformed soldiers and radicals brandishing guns and sticks. The contrast between the two groups was striking, yet they marched in unison. Dellirea felt conflicted watching them. They *had* been disobedient. But was their bravery not admirable?

She joined Dario and the other members of the king's council outside; her father remained in the palace.

Kephalos, looking steadfast yet wearied from his days of imprisonment, stood at the centre of the other committee members, flanked by their accompanying mob. Dellirea and the others faced off with them, neither side saying a word.

At last, Dario looked at the rest of the council, then turned to Kephalos. "We welcome you to the palace. Today we shall discuss how we can work together to oversee elections to the Great Chamber. Please enter."

The fifteen members filed through the palace gates, leaving the small army of radicals behind to stew.

Dellirea and the other council members greeted the fifteen as they entered. Naturally, the priests and nobles correctly followed protocol by bowing and waiting for Dellirea to speak before they addressed her. Whatever changes might have occurred, protocol must remain, Dellirea knew.

Last among the group of nobles came the noblewoman who was said to have written that treasonous book against her family, although of course Dellirea dared not read it. Yet as the woman approached, Dellirea was struck by her great beauty. She had flowing light brown hair and piercing blue eyes. As the noblewoman bowed before her, Dellirea found herself struck with nervousness.

"Greetings," Dellirea said, suddenly unsure of what to say. "I am Princess Dellirea of Estenland."

"Hello, Your Highness," the woman said, revealing a small grin at Dellirea's awkwardness. "I am Charlotte of Evesbury."

Charlotte of Evesbury. Dellirea rolled around the name in her head and found that she rather liked it. As the others walked into the palace, she found it difficult to take her eyes away from the noblewoman. How could someone like her have written such a horrid book?

Next came the commoners, in particular Quinneas Raeil, that notorious radical. Dellirea watched him carefully, not wishing to show that she was repulsed by him and everything for which he stood. He bowed before her correctly, and she greeted him as cordially as she could.

As the last of the commoners entered, Dellirea took one final look at the hundreds of people amassed at the gates before turning and entering the palace.

DELLIREA WALKED at the front of the procession to one of the palace drawing rooms, where her father waited.

"Greetings," he said simply, careful to make no reference to the fact that some of them had just spent several days in prison.

Kephalos exchanged looks with the other fourteen members before beginning, "Your Majesty, I thank you for your welcome and I hope that we can work amicably together. There are many issues that our great nation faces and I believe that we must face them together."

"Hear, hear," said the others.

Dellirea stood tensely, fearing a wrong word from either side could dissolve the unstable peace. From Dario's expression, she could see he shared her worries. Yet Dellirea was glad that wise Kephalos acted as the leader of the group. He appeared willing, for now, to overlook his past treatment at the hands of her father.

"Yes," Aramal said stiffly. "I... too... believe that we must work together."

"Before we begin, I must insist," continued Kephalos, "that henceforth none of the committee members face danger of arrest for any criticism, actual or alleged, of His Majesty or his government."

This phrase "actual or alleged" gave Dellirea hope that perhaps Charlotte of Evesbury had not truly written that horrid book after all. Perhaps it was all a great misunderstanding.

Dellirea's father considered Kephalos's demand. He looked to Dario, who nodded. "The members will face no such dangers," he said at last, and motioned for them to sit.

YANIS

anis's jubilation at the day's events gave way to exhaustion as he returned with Nadeni to her tiny basement flat. The sun had set several hours ago and Yanis had been awake since dawn. He had not slept well the previous night, fretting about what was to come. His eyelids were heavy. His body ached. His head pounded.

How he wished Jackson were there. How he wished Calina were there. The pain of losing them hurt more than all of the other physical injuries he had sustained. He felt suddenly alone, even as he sat next to someone who was a friend. But how reckless she had been earlier! She could have gotten them both killed. Fortunately, Nadeni appeared to have recovered from her fall, aside from a bump on the head.

"Let us have some of this bread," she said, as she placed upon the table a half loaf that was growing ever staler. "Could you believe the looks on the faces of the king's council as we marched to the gates of the palace?" she asked, then took a bite.

Her tone was much too happy for Yanis's taste, as if she had not nearly plunged to her death hours ago. He had nearly lost her, just as he had lost Calina. Had she no understanding of the gravity of what occurred?

"Some of them looked almost as if they were going to piss themselves," she said with a laugh.

"Nadeni," Yanis said, unable to stifle his growing frustration at her frivolity, "why did you feel the need to interject about taking the prison today? And then about us entering the courtyard? It felt as though you were stoking the conflict the whole time."

"I *was* stoking the conflict," she said. "And it was the correct decision."

Yanis's stomach growled as he tore away a piece from the

meagre loaf. "If the soldiers hadn't arrived just then to save us, we'd have all been killed," he said. "And if the sea goats hadn't miraculously appeared, you'd have surely drowned! Have you any idea of the danger you put me in? The danger you put yourself in?"

"I care about justice," she shot back. She set down her bread and frowned. "Justice requires boldness. If you truly care about justice, you must know that the powerful never relinquish their power without a fight."

Angry thoughts swirled uncontrollably in Yanis's head. "Of course I care about justice!" he said, his voice rising, thinking of all he had lost. "How could you even question that? I've sacrificed so much for my principles. I've sacrificed more than you could ever know. More than you could possibly understand!"

"Are you serious? Do you not realize that I have lost people too?"

"It's not the same!"

Nadeni's face froze in an expression of fury. She stood from the table abruptly, saying nothing. She stared at the kitchen wall with her back to Yanis, breathing heavily. After several moments of silence, she turned to face him. "Yanis, I have been very generous in allowing you to stay with me. You may sleep here for one more night, but I believe it best if tomorrow you go elsewhere."

Yanis was stunned. But he refused to let his anger show. "If you wish it," he said evenly, "then I shall go."

Nadeni said nothing more as she walked into the private section of the apartment that contained her cot. Yanis was furious with her. He had nowhere to go, and what was more, he still faced danger of arrest. He had been granted leave from his post in New Selver and had never returned. To the government, he was still a fugitive.

Yanis had saved her life – and this was his repayment!

~

ALL NIGHT YANIS tossed and turned on the harsh stone floor. After several hours of restless sleep, he rose and poked his head into the hallway. From the window of the apartment door, the first signs of dawn were appearing. Yanis gathered his few possessions and slipped away before Nadeni awoke. He walked the streets for some time, waiting for the sun to arise.

Once it was a reasonable hour, he sought out Quinneas. He would surely help. It was true that Yanis had owed Quinneas a great debt for defending him when he was arrested for his pamphlet against the king. But had he not already paid that back, and more?

Yanis called upon his house and was escorted inside by one of the servants, where he awaited Quinneas's arrival in the drawing room.

"If it isn't the Dragon Slayer," Quinneas said warmly upon entering. He moved close to examine the scrapes on Yanis's face from yesterday's battle. "Are you feeling well?"

"The injuries are minor," Yanis said curtly. He had not time for pleasantries. He explained that he had no place to stay and that he feared arrest.

Quinneas listened carefully. "Of course, Yanis. You should have come sooner. Myself and Charlotte and the other members owe you tremendous gratitude for all you have done." He ordered one of his servants to bring a small pouch filled with dozens of coins, which would provide enough money for a temporary stay in a boarding house. "And worry not about your legal status. I shall see to it that you are pardoned for your past crimes."

"Thank you, Quinneas."

"Don't forget, Yanis," he said as Yanis turned to go, "you will always have an ally in me."

CHARLOTTE

"Who was that?" Charlotte asked Quinneas upon his return to the bedroom. She still lay in bed, even as the morning sun peeked through the curtains.

"It was Yanis Haller, the Dragon Slayer."

"At this hour?"

"Why, it is nearly eight thirty!"

She rolled over and groaned. She curled herself amongst the silk sheets. She did not yet wish to contemplate arising from bed. They had only just gained their freedom. And she felt that if she left the bed, she would be thrust back into reality, back into danger.

"What was his call regarding? Was there a problem?"

"No problem. Only that he needed money for somewhere to stay, which I readily supplied him."

"Very good," she said, raising her head from the pillow. "We owe him a great debt. But do you believe those stories about him slaying dragons?"

"Perhaps the stories are exaggerated a touch, but the people seem to enjoy them. Just look at how he gathered the crowd yesterday! Besides, Yanis is an honest, decent fellow. I helped him many years ago, you know. I represented him when he was tried for treason. I wish I could have done more for him then."

This talk of treason elicited a strange feeling in the pit of Charlotte's stomach.

"But there was no possibility his pamphlet could have escaped the king's wrath," Quinneas continued. "To be frank, Yanis was lucky he was only exiled."

"Please, Quinneas, stop talking about this," Charlotte said, her face back in the pillow, terrible memories, still fresh, circling in her mind of the time in the prison. "It causes me such anxiety."

Everyone now knew she had written *The Downfall of the Monarchy* – or at least they must suspect there was some truth to the government's charges. All of the interim committee members were technically safe from prosecution, yet she could not forget the great worries of the past months. And the thought continued to linger in her mind that Brondin or Willien had betrayed her.

"I'm sorry, Charlotte," he said, stroking her hair as he sat down on the bed. "There is no need to worry now."

She pulled him close so he too lay down on the bed, even though he was fully dressed. "Let us remain here a while longer."

Quinneas opened his arms and Charlotte curled into a ball, burying her head in his chest. He wrapped his arms around her, holding her close.

"Please don't let me go," she said softly.

"I won't."

DUTY EVENTUALLY FORCED Charlotte to remove herself from bed. No more time could be spared as preparations for elections to the Great Chamber were to begin that day.

As she and Quinneas travelled by carriage to the palace, Quinneas turned to her. "Before anything else, we must ensure that Yanis is pardoned. And everyone else involved in the attack on the prison."

"Before anything else?"

"Of course," he said. "We owe it to Yanis. To the people who saved us."

"I agree, naturally," she said, "but do we risk alienating allies by pursuing such a measure?"

"It must be done," he said. "Even if we must make concessions on other issues, so be it. Yanis can be an important ally for us. You see the command he has over the people."

Charlotte conceded the point and said no more. Yet she wondered about the wisdom of tying themselves too closely to him.

38

SAMUEL

Samuel slunk through the quiet hallways of Iron Town College. In these times, slinking had become his principal mode of movement, so accustomed was he to his status as a pariah. To think, just a half a year ago, this was his home! Now he was the very last person anyone would wish to see.

Greta had refused to answer the calling cards Samuel had left for her. His only hope of speaking to her again was to *accidentally* run into her.

He was prepared to wait the day, if he had to. Nay, he was prepared to wait the year! Of course, he still remembered the lab schedules and with correct timing, no such waiting would truly be necessary.

Samuel paced outside the lab, turning to engross himself in a notice posted on the wall whenever someone passed.

At last, the door to the lab opened, and several students exited, Greta among them. She walked next to another student. Samuel slunk behind them, watching as they made their way to the exit. She continued walking next to the student. When he turned, it was, Samuel realized, Robert Grim, another former student of his.

Samuel followed several paces behind them until they exited the building, but he knew he could not pursue them forever. He needed to act.

"Greta!" he called out.

She and Robert spun around. Her eyes widened as Samuel approached.

"Greta," he said again. Then, hastily, "Robert, nice to see you."

"Dr. Nox," she said, "I… what are you doing here?"

"I was only out for a walk when I thought I spotted you."

Robert and Greta looked at one another uneasily.

"Nox!" cried out a man's voice from behind him. Samuel

turned: Professor Kelson. "What in Oqci's name do you think you're doing on our grounds?"

"It's none of your business what I am doing," he shot back. "If I wish to walk out in public, I have every right."

"You do not have the right to taint our college's students any further. Have you not harmed our reputation enough already?"

"If these two students wish to speak to me, then they have every right. You do not get to control every aspect of their lives, however much you might wish." Samuel turned to face Robert and Greta who stood awkwardly, their eyes glancing between him and Kelson.

"If you get your foul odour on them," spat Kelson, "they'll be unemployable in the scientific community, just as you are."

"I only wish to converse with them, to inquire as to their well-being."

"They are both very well," said Kelson, moving between Samuel and them, "and you need know no more than that."

"I should like to hear from them, and not you." Samuel moved so that they once more appeared in his field of vision. "Well, well, how are you?" he stammered.

Greta and Robert both stayed silent, trading glances between each other, Kelson, and Samuel.

A furious need to scratch all over presented itself, but Samuel resisted.

"Perhaps Professor Kelson is right," Robert said to Greta. "Perhaps it is best that we should be going."

Robert nodded to Kelson, then turned. Greta hesitated for a moment as Robert began his walk. She looked at Samuel and gave a weak smile. "Good day, Dr. Nox," she said, and turned to follow Robert.

"I... Greta, please..." he said quietly.

But she could not hear him. His world crumbled as she walked away. She was everything – yet she was lost to him now! Samuel felt like falling to his knees and damning Oqci for all he had suffered.

"What bloody nerve you have," Kelson said, interrupting his anguish. "Is it not enough to destroy your own life with your...

misadventures? You must destroy those of our students as well? Shame on you, Nox. Have you no decency?"

Samuel's fists clenched tightly. He glared at Kelson.

Kelson looked him up and down, and his nose squinched. "Do you bathe, Nox? You smell like sea water and rotten eggs. It's repulsive to the nose."

Without thinking, Samuel shoved Kelson so hard that he fell to the ground. Samuel bent down and grabbed Kelson by the collar. "I ought to throttle you! You... you..."

"Help!" shouted Kelson, as he held up his hands to shield himself, his face full of fear. "Help!"

Samuel's gaze shot back to where Greta and Robert had been walking. They were further down the path but close enough to hear the cries. They turned back and began to approach. Samuel released his grasp on Kelson and hastened away before they could pursue him.

39

CHARLOTTE

Today the fifteen members met once again, alongside the Duke of Prencroft, to discuss the elections. Yanis's pardon had been achieved earlier in the week. Yet it had come at a high cost. To secure a unanimous agreement, Charlotte and Quinneas relinquished their demand for no property thresholds and no restrictions whatsoever related to status in the elections.

As Richard, Duke of Saundley, stood to make an argument for the need for a restrictive wealth threshold, Charlotte wondered whether they had agreed too quickly. The only question remained as to what the threshold should be. Richard spoke in pompous tones. Charlotte glanced at Quinneas across the chamber. She wished to squeeze his hand, yet he was too far.

Polite applause greeted Richard as he took his seat. Koralo, Count of Ulsted, rose next to speak. "My friends –"

Just then, the door burst open. One of the Duke of Prencroft's aides rushed into the room. "My lord, I must speak to you immediately."

"What is the meaning of this flagrant breach of decorum?" cried Koralo.

They were meant to be a closed chamber, without outside interference. How dare the king's men meddle like this, thought Charlotte.

"Forgive me, my lord," said the embarrassed aide. "There is terrible news." He was flustered, but he gathered himself and addressed the entire room. "We have just received a telegram from Mariesand. The Friezzian navy have amassed at our shores and threaten the city's defences."

"What? Is this some sort of trick?" asked Quinneas, standing abruptly from his seat. "More subterfuge from the king?"

"It is no trick," said the messenger. "The Friezzians appear to be preparing an attack upon our great nation."

This could not be right, could it? Was this yet another deception to undermine their work?

Dario rose to exit with his aide. Kephalos called behind him, "We shall join you."

"What do you mean?"

"If our nation is under attack as this man says it is, then we have the right to learn about it as well."

Dario and the messenger traded glances. "Very well."

"How is this possible?" said Aramal. The fifteen members stood crammed in the king's chamber, while the king and his council sat around the table.

Not only was the port city of Mariesand under attack, Charlotte and the others learned, Estenland's fortress at Winterbridge on the Friezzian border, too, was being ravaged. "We have the strongest navy!" the king continued. "The strongest army!"

"Your Majesty," Dario began uneasily, "our armed forces have suffered setbacks in recent weeks, as you know. The mission to the Dragon Isles, the plans to build the war machines... All of these have diverted our resources and left us vulnerable, I'm afraid."

The king shook his head in embarrassment. He refused to look any of the others in the eyes. All of the interim committee members looked at each other, but they were too polite to say aloud what Charlotte knew they all thought: Curse this incompetent king. Curse his foolish actions.

More information continued to pour in, too fast for anyone to fully comprehend. Telegraph reports from various sites along the western border and northern ports informed them of further attacks. The nation's principal defences in Mariesand and Winterbridge had fallen. Multiple Friezzian units were converging upon the capital. They were expected to arrive within days.

Charlotte quickly performed calculations in her mind, imagining all the different scenarios of what this situation meant for the revolution. And she saw an opportunity.

"Elections for the Great Chamber cannot be held in such an environment," she said to the assembled group, looking particularly at Quinneas, whom she hoped would understand her meaning.

"Yes," he said slowly. "Yes, the elections must be postponed."

"Given this situation," Charlotte continued, "I do not believe it unreasonable to suggest that our interim committee be granted the full powers of the Great Chamber until such time as elections can be safely held."

Other members of the committee were stunned for a moment, but they quickly nodded their agreement. Some, like Selver Bronn, salivated at the prospect of increasing their own authority, but even the principled ones, like Kephalos, understood this was the right decision.

"Your Majesty," said Kephalos, "do you agree with this proposal?"

The king sighed and looked at Dario, whose expression indicated his assent. The muscles in Aramal's face tightened. His nation was under attack, and he could see his power trickling away before his eyes. Worse still, he would forever be remembered in the history books alongside Sera the Terrible. But what choice had he?

"If the elections cannot take place," he said at last, "then it seems proper that you fifteen act as the temporary Great Chamber."

YANIS

"You the Dragon Slayer?" one of the soldiers grunted to Yanis. An unkempt bearded man, several years Yanis's senior, stood before him.

"I… some have called me that."

The man's hardened expression gave way to a smile. He turned back to his comrades sitting around the camp. "Some of the others wanted me to ask if you could tell them about your adventures."

It was embarrassing, but Yanis remembered what Jackson had said to him. If it did others good to think that he possessed some kind of special power, he should embrace it. Yanis motioned for them to join him.

"I looked up at that horrid, scowling dragon," he recounted, the two dozen men hanging on his every word, "flying high above us, puffs of smoke coming from its nostrils. I readied my rifle, aimed, and with a single, well-placed bullet, it came crashing down."

The men cheered and hollered at the story. The man, who told Yanis his name was Clem Lake, clapped him on the back. "Very good," he said.

They probably knew he was embellishing his achievements. But it was all toward the noble goal of inspiring his fellow soldiers, who awaited the arrival of the Friezzian army atop a bastion fortress on the edge of Goldhall.

When the Friezzians had attacked, Yanis felt a duty to return to the army. He had no obligation to do so, thanks to Quinneas and the other Great Chamber members, but he wished to defend his country and to have a place to stay after having roomed at a boarding house for a week. At his request, Yanis was reunited with Vinzent of Highfalls, who commanded a battalion of five hundred men.

As they waited in the late afternoon for the imminent arrival of the enemy, the quarrel with Nadeni continued to weigh on him. He had let his emotions get the better of him that evening and he had been insensitive in his remarks to her. Yanis hoped that, when the conflict with the Friezzians ended, he would have a chance to see her once more.

～

THE ENEMY APPROACHED AT DUSK. From his vantage point on the bastion, Yanis could see the mass of blue uniforms steadily marching toward them. It was hard to make them out in the growing darkness, but a sense of dread filled him, as they moved, almost as one giant organism, toward his unit's position.

Aside from the attack on the prison, he had only ever been in minor skirmishes with the rebellious natives in New Selver. They possessed inferior firearms, some decades old, if they had any at all, and their troops were no match for the Estenlanders' technology or their firing discipline. But the soldiers from Friezzia were equals of the Estenlanders, or close to it. The Friezzians had long nursed their defeat three decades ago at Estenland's hands. They had spent those years training and building their army in preparation for this moment.

The enemy began to establish their cannons as the Estenlanders launched preliminary artillery fire of their own. But there was no serious attempt on either side to begin a battle. Such a battle was exactly what the Friezzians hoped for, but rather than being drawn in, it was thought better to amass the army for the defence of the city and to then strangle the Friezzians' over-stretched supply lines.

Overnight, the Friezzians battered the city's fortress, with little effect. They were content to wait as they fully encircled the city, hoping they could cut off the city's supplies, Yanis knew. It could take months to starve the Estenlanders into surrender and it would then become a matter of which side could hold out longer.

Yanis thought of Nadeni again. That day at the prison.

Hadn't she been correct after all to call for the attack? To be bold? A voice in his head told him the time to strike was now. His rational brain said this was foolish, but his heart told him otherwise. Just like at the prison – just like Nadeni had said – this was a time for boldness. Yanis knew he needed to speak with Vinzent right away. He walked through the camp in the twilight to the officers' tent.

"We should push into their lines," Yanis urged him. "If we wait, the Friezzians will only gain strength. They will dig trenches and fortify themselves. Let us hit them now before they have a chance to get settled."

"That would be foolish," Vinzent said.

"Conventional military strategy tells the Friezzians we shall not be drawn into a battle. They will not expect it!" he insisted, feeling almost prophetic.

Other officers in the tent listened closely. "Yes," one said, "let us listen to the Dragon Slayer!" More and more men were now agreeing that they must carry out the plan.

Vinzent agreed that Yanis could propose the idea to his superior. With Vinzent and a collection of other officers, Yanis approached the general of the army, a white-haired nobleman, and explained the plan. They would attack tomorrow at dawn, Yanis said, catching the Friezzians by surprise.

Vinzent explained to the general that Yanis had the support of the soldiers. Yanis had, he said, quite a following among the men.

"Yes," said the general. "I too have heard the rumours about the so-called Dragon Slayer in our ranks." He stood to examine a map of the battlefield. "Lord Highfalls, I am a religious man. I have always been able to sense the presence of Oqci." He turned to look at Yanis. "Perhaps he is working through this one they call the Dragon Slayer. Yes, the attack will take place. We shall have the divine on our side."

Yanis only nodded, yet inside, he was horrified. Seeing the credulity of this general suddenly made him question himself. Was this plan not foolhardy? But it was too late now.

A surprise attack would be launched in the morning, but as

Yanis lay on his rough bed of straw, he couldn't sleep. Some of the men were spoiling for a fight, even with the threat of injury or death looming over them. They wanted action. It was a certainty that some of the men that lay beside him would be dead within the day. Yanis hoped he was not among them.

As the sun rose, the men from the neighbouring bastions along the city readied for attack. Not a cloud darkened the sky.

The Friezzians had no idea what was coming for them.

The men gathered around Yanis as they assembled in formation. He tried to nourish himself with the confidence they had in him. Yanis told himself that he was the Dragon Slayer. Yet an anxious feeling ran throughout his body. Not even fear, but a desire to get on with the battle… with whatever was to come.

Yanis was arranged in one of the back rows of a column that guarded the right flank of the line. They marched, several thousand strong, down the clear slope from the bastion.

Friezzian skirmishers raced back to their lines, sounding the alarm for their attack. Yanis prayed they would not have enough time to rally. These would be a far cry from the native armies in New Selver. Yanis's heart beat frantically, but there was no time for second thoughts and there was nowhere to run.

"Stay strong, Dragon Slayer," said Clem, who marched beside Yanis, perhaps sensing his nerves.

Bugles sounded from the Friezzian lines. Their soldiers began to appear, hurrying into formation.

"Forward. Don't fire," urged Vinzent as they marched closer to the enemy.

Several hundred paces away stood the Friezzians, frantically ordering themselves into a line. They raised their muskets, but, like the Estenlanders, held fire.

Yanis and his unit continued marching. Closer now. Closer. Vinzent implored them to hold their fire.

At last, the signal came. Yanis's group hurried into a line

formation and those at the front launched the first volley. They stepped back to reload as the next row took their shot.

Yanis's turn came. He fired and stepped back to reload. He did his best to ignore the bullets whizzing overhead and all around them, and to ignore the unlucky comrades in the line dropping to the ground.

The smoke from the guns soon filled Yanis's eyes and nose and hung in the air, obscuring the enemy.

After several rounds of orderly volley fire, discipline on both sides broke down. It became fire-at-will whenever one reloaded. Take a shot, begin reloading, all the while the cracks of muskets sounded out. Yanis continued firing in the general direction of the enemy, but through the cloud of smoke he had not the faintest idea where any of his shots landed.

A cavalry charge on the Friezzians' left flank was repulsed. Soon, one was coming at the Estenlander flank.

"Form square!" Vinzent shouted.

Yanis and the others hastily shaped themselves into a square, sticking out their bayonets, preparing for the charge.

"Hold!"

Bearing down in front of their side of the square were a dozen riders, galloping at a furious pace.

"Don't fire! Hold! Hold!"

Yanis was shaking, kneeling down at the outside of the square, pressing the butt of his musket with all his might into the ground, the bayonet sticking outward. Clem and Yanis's other comrades knelt next to him, maintaining their stillness. Behind him were three more rows of standing soldiers.

"Come on you, bastards," said Clem, under his breath.

"Hold!" Vinzent shouted again.

The riders stampeded toward them but halted so close that Yanis could feel the gust. They lost their nerve. The riders fired their pistols as they came near, but then they turned back and rode away.

"Typical Friezzians," said Clem, rising again. "Lacking conviction!"

Yanis and the others raced back to their line formation as the cavalry charge was repelled. Their unit had mostly held together, though some had succumbed to the Friezzian firepower.

Yanis's unit resumed their organized volley firing. Mechanical shooting, followed by mechanical reloading. His shoulder was growing sore from the kickback of the musket, his ears ringing from the explosions all around. After thirty minutes, some of the men retreated from his column, out of ammunition – or at least claiming so – and rushing back to the rear.

As reserves filled the gaps, the signal was given for a bayonet charge. From Yanis's position, the shape of the battle was impossible to gauge, and he could only trust the officers that this was the correct timing. He gripped his musket tightly and began sprinting toward the Friezzian line, some hundred paces away.

A wall of bullets from the Friezzians cut down many of his onrushing comrades. Yanis could barely see, the smoke was so thick. Chaos was all around. Red-uniformed bodies lay scattered next to him on the field, below the cover of smoke. Some writhed and screamed in anguish, others lay lifeless.

The signal came to retreat. Yanis turned and sprinted back to the original line. It was a mad scramble among the men. Yanis tripped and fell in the mud, yet Clem appeared from the chaos to help him up. Rearguards stepped forward to halt the Friezzian pursuit.

Yanis made it to the safety of their lines and collapsed to the ground. Exhausted, bloodied soldiers lingered around the camp. Their attack had been an utter failure. Yanis looked up to see Vinzent's body, limply draped over a stretcher, being rushed from the battlefield toward the surgeons. He did not get a close look, but the expressions of the faces of the bearers looked dire. Yanis held his head in his hands.

Other soldiers looked at him as he lay on the ground, still catching his breath, but they quickly turned away when he tried to return their glances. Yanis's head spun. He was responsible for this blunder.

What was he thinking? How could he have been so stupid as to believe those myths about himself?

SAMUEL

Samuel was at the docks, surrounded by those imbecilic men with their imbecilic bleating, prying open crates filled with unicorn carcasses.

Then… Greta appeared. All of the other men disappeared. Samuel and Greta were alone. At last. It seemed unusual that she would be there at the docks, but at once perfectly natural. The gentle wind blew her hair across her face.

The two stood suddenly in his lab, in the dissection room, surrounded by cadavers of more sacred creatures.

"I'm sorry for not standing by you," she said. "What happened was unjust."

"I'm sorry too." He clasped her hand. "I wished terrible things upon you when you rebuffed me that day at the college. But I was wrong to do so. I knew your heart was pure."

Bang. Bang.

"What is that sound?" she asked.

"It is nothing," he said. "Construction in the lab above, perhaps."

They embraced. Happiness coursed through Samuel. A happiness that he had not felt in some time.

Bang. Bang.

"What is that sound?" asked Michael of Highstaff who now stood beside them.

Whence did he come?

"It sounds as though it is getting closer," Greta said, as Adar of Winslough joined them in the room.

Bang. Bang.

What was that infernal sound? It was ruining his long-awaited reconciliation with Greta!

∼

SOMEONE WAS SHAKING HIM. "Eston, wake up. We are under attack!"

Samuel half-opened his eyes. Where was he? Who was Eston?

Men scrambled all around him, stuffing their belongings into suitcases upon their cots.

Now he remembered. Eston was him. His false name in this boarding house.

"The Friezzians are shelling us, Eston! Get your things. We need to go to the basement!"

Sleep still weighed heavily upon his eyes. He pulled his feet down to the cold floor and sat up. He forced open his eyes. All around him was chaos. Men gathered what meagre possessions they had before racing toward the staircase.

Another crashing sound from close by jolted Samuel's brain to reality. He needed to move quickly. He crammed some clothes and valuables and most importantly his research notes into the suitcase he had pulled from under his bed and joined the line of men who hurried down the flights of stairs to reach the basement.

Huddled there, dozens of them, most still in their sleeping wear, they listened to the booming and crashing of the shells close by. Their neighbourhood, on the edge of the city, was an easy target for the Friezzians.

People shrieked as the ground shook. A direct hit on the building. In that moment, Samuel instinctively gripped his suitcase tightly as if it would somehow help.

One man gathered his things and rose to leave. "We can't stay here! We shall surely be killed if we stay."

Another crash came from nearby.

"Don't be foolish," Samuel said. "We are as safe here as anywhere else."

The others muttered their agreement. As booms and bangs rang out from near and far, the man sheepishly sat back down.

"Perhaps a prayer?" someone suggested. Some of the group brought their hands together as the man mumbled incantations to Oqci. Samuel did not partake.

Samuel queued for the second round of daily rations, where a server would plop some barely edible goop into bowls as the people bowed gratefully. His boarding house had been severely damaged in the shelling two weeks ago, so Samuel and the others were relocated to one of the many hastily assembled shelters organized by the leaders of the Great Chamber – this in a temple of all places. Rows of cots lined the temple's stone floor and they slept under the watchful eye of a statue of Oqci.

"Hey, mate," one of Samuel's fellow vagrants said to him. "Guess what?"

"Oqci's descended from the clouds and told us to stop stinking up his temple?"

The man frowned at this. "No," he said. But his smile quickly returned. "The princess will serve our meal today!"

Samuel rolled his eyes. How lucky they were that dear Princess Dellirea decided to grace them with her presence!

"I've never seen a royal up close," the man continued.

Samuel sighed. What a simpleton!

With the Friezzians blockading all entryways to the city, including the ports, there was no more work at the docks for Samuel. He had lost even that meagre salary and now had no choice but to receive charity. To think, someone of his stature, receiving hand-outs! But one day, Samuel thought, one day he would be vindicated.

First, however, was the matter of obtaining the basic necessities of life. Yet as Samuel stood in line, the stench of the others in front nearly made him lose his appetite. Regular bathing was one of the luxuries that had fallen away during the siege, assuming that any of these people practiced hygiene even in good times. Samuel's stomach rumbled nonetheless.

He watched the front of the line as the princess and various other helpers doled out the meals. The princess – a small, blonde, innocent girl – beamed at the hungry people and talked eagerly, her smile never waning. She wore a modest dress, evidently not wishing to flaunt her immense wealth during these times.

At last, it was Samuel's turn to bask in the glow of the lovely princess as he received his rations. He walked to the front of the line and held out his bowl. The princess filled it with a thin, greyish soup and handed him a piece of bread.

"Here you are," she said happily.

He turned to go, but before he could, she continued, "Before you eat, I wished to ask if you know about the doctrines of Oqci?"

Samuel was taken aback by this shameless attempt to win a convert. "They're a load of rubbish. That's what I know."

"Oh dear, please don't say that," she said, her cheer not at all affected, which only agitated Samuel further. "Have you read the Book of Oqci?"

He hesitated and sighed. He knew not what to say to such stupidity.

"My apologies," she said, misunderstanding the reason for his hesitation. "We also have an edition with pictures if you are unable to read."

"I can read just fine, princess. I used to be a professor, for Oqci's sake!"

"I see." She narrowed her eyes at him, and just then he knew he had said too much. "Wait a second. Do I know you? You're Samuel Nox, aren't you?"

"I..." He knew not what to say. He only hoped no one heard her.

"I followed your case every day in the press. I recognize you from your portrait."

He leaned in and said quietly, "I suppose I have gone by that name, but no one else needs to know that."

"You did a terrible thing, but it's not too late to repent. You can still embrace the teachings of Oqci."

Samuel was in no mood for these attempts to convert him. Had he not suffered enough without having to deal with this proselytizing too? But an idea suddenly came to him.

"Is that right, princess? And what about your mother? Is it too late for her?"

Her smile gave way to concern. "What... what are you speaking about?"

"That private residence of your mother's? Didn't you ever wonder about that?"

"What do you mean?"

"Well, I've heard she has been whoring around the palace grounds while your father pretends not to notice. Does the Book of Oqci say anything about that?"

Dellirea's face grew red. She was silent now. Clearly she hadn't considered it before, but Samuel could see all sorts of horrible thoughts swirling around her head about the reason her parents shared separated residences.

"That's right," he continued. "She's probably fucked half the men of our great city. And maybe even some of these stinking wretches in our very midst," he added, motioning to the lines of grubby, dishevelled men waiting for their soup.

"You are a disgusting, despicable man!" she cried. "Disgusting! Shame on you!"

"Such strong language, princess," he said. "What would Oqci think of that?"

"You should've been hanged like the others, you vile man. You should've had your neck snapped like the scoundrel you are!"

Quickly realizing the danger Samuel had put himself in, he hurried away.

"Your Highness! Whatever is the matter?" one of her helpers called, as Samuel disappeared back into the crowd before anyone could catch a glimpse of him.

At a safe distance, Samuel ate his bland soup and reflected that the visit of the princess had brought him cheer after all.

CHARLOTTE

Charlotte and Quinneas picked at their food. There was no joy in eating as their fellow citizens starved. Even though she and Quinneas were wealthy, they too had suffered through these past weeks of the siege. They rationed their food now that the city's supply from the countryside was cut off. It was a paltry meal that evening of bread and thin vegetable stew, yet they knew that things could be much worse.

"That poor unicorn..." Charlotte said, thinking of the story they had read in the papers that morning.

"The people are forced to eat cats and rats to survive," Quinneas said. "Why not a unicorn?"

The perpetrators had been caught and were certain to be executed. Charlotte sympathized with the starving people, of course... but the thought of them stealing a noble's unicorn for food deeply unsettled her. Her mind could not help but turn to her own beloved winged horse, Silver Justice, and the two creatures at her estate that had been murdered and mutilated by the scientist Nox.

"Besides," Quinneas continued, "haven't you ever wondered how sacred creatures taste?"

"Of course not! You shouldn't joke about such things."

"Who is joking?" he said. "What difference is there, really, between eating a cow or a horse and eating a unicorn or a griffin?"

"Well," Charlotte said, stumbling to find a rational response, "the creatures are just not meant to be eaten!"

Quinneas smiled dismissively. "So said Oqci, right?"

"No, of course not... but... it just isn't right," Charlotte retorted, even as she recognized the irrationality of her position.

"Let us change the topic. It's not pleasant to discuss while eating."

"I'm sorry, darling," said Quinneas. "I didn't mean to upset you."

"I'm sorry, too." She regarded her stew as she swished it about her bowl. "It feels as though this cursed siege will never end. Winter quickly approaches. How will the city survive when it does?" She hesitated. She dared not speak the words aloud, but before she knew it, they were already flowing past her lips. "Our only option may be surrender."

Quinneas reached his hand across the table to caress her cheek. "We shall find a way through this, Charlotte. I'm sure of it."

She pushed his hand away. She was in no mood for vague promises. "It is very well to make promises, but we're in charge now. *We* must think of a plan. Certainly the king will not."

Quinneas sighed and shook his head. His eyes moved down to gaze into his bowl.

"If only the attempt to break the siege had been successful," Charlotte continued. "Ha, I suppose the so-called Dragon Slayer is not as great as we were told."

Quinneas's eyes darted back up. He frowned. "What a strange thing to say! It's hardly fair to Yanis. The responsibility for the failure of the attack cannot rest on his shoulders alone."

"I suppose you're right," she said, slouching in her chair. She tore off a piece of the bread, which was growing ever staler, and dunked it in the stew. The food provided sustenance. But no more than that.

She examined Quinneas's weary face, the wounds from the attack by the griffin nearly invisible now. This called to mind the horrible day of the protest. The day she began to fall for him. It seemed so long ago now.

As Charlotte thought of the protest, an idea flashed into her mind. She winced at everything it would mean. First their citizens ate helpless unicorns, and now she was going to propose this! But it seemed the only way.

"The sacred creatures," she said. "What if we used them

against Friezzia's forces? The same way the king used them against our protest?"

Quinneas narrowed his eyes. "Are you being serious?" he asked cautiously.

"When I was younger," she said, "I rode Silver Justice every day. Many other nobles have done the same. I think the creatures could be used effectively."

Quinneas nodded enthusiastically. "There are surely hundreds of griffins, winged horses, and winged lions in our city, all of which could be used against the Friezzians."

"This might be a solution," she said. "But is the taboo against it too great?"

"The king himself broke the taboo," said Quinneas, "when he deployed them against his own people! Surely to use them against our enemies would be far more legitimate." Quinneas stared into his stew in thought. "We need only eight votes for a majority in the Chamber. I shall talk with the commoners. I believe they will all agree with the measure. This leaves us needing three more votes – two with yours. Could we gain two more? Perhaps the priests are a lost cause, but if you spoke with some of the other nobles, they will recognize that you are making a sacrifice. We can attain a majority, even if a slim one."

"Am I the right person to convince the others?" she asked. "Surely one who wrote such a book might not win favour with the rest of the Chamber?"

"That is true, but it was never determined that you were the author. And many suspect that it was just a fabricated story to justify your imprisonment."

"Very well," she said. "But even if we gain the numbers, surely the king will veto it."

"He may, but the other chamber members may see such a veto as a repudiation of the chamber's power. Through a unanimous vote, we can then override the veto. But let us hope it does not come to that."

～

THE NEXT DAY, Charlotte visited the Duke of Saundley's estate. If she could win the support of the most prominent noble in the Great Chamber, others would surely follow.

His wife, Solorina, bid Charlotte to enter and led her upstairs to a spacious drawing room, where her husband sat waiting. Once seated, Charlotte proposed the idea. She explained that Quinneas and the other commoners also supported the measure.

"I have reservations," he said, biting into one of the chocolate biscuits that a servant had brought. Evidently, Richard was not suffering from lack of food. "I see your logic, but once we allow this, a fundamental barrier is broken in society. Having the creatures on the same battlefield as the commoners, even if they were commanded by nobles or priests? I believe this would simply be too much."

Solorina shook her head in agreement.

"But what choice have we?" Charlotte said. She felt that he could be swayed, even if it meant playing to his sympathies. "Our supplies are running low, and the masses are becoming desperate. Just think about the poor unicorn that was slaughtered by those brutes!"

"A horror," said Solorina, who stood behind her husband's chair.

Richard sighed, but perhaps the thought made him hungry as he popped the final piece of biscuit into his mouth.

"We must not only think about the consequences of allowing the creatures in battle," Charlotte continued, "we must also think about the consequences of not acting." Richard listened, nodding. "We must be prepared to anticipate the worst impulses of the people. Think of what kind of chaos might result if we fail to act! By acting now, we can prevent something far worse in the future."

"You make a convincing case, Lady Evesbury," he said, "but I would prefer such a measure to be voluntary. If a noble or priest wishes to send their creatures into battle, they can do so."

"But what if none agrees?"

Richard shrugged.

"Then it means that the nobles care more for preserving the sanctity of the creatures than earthly squabbles," added Solorina.

"I am prepared to volunteer my own creatures," Charlotte said. "Will you two volunteer yours?"

Richard and Solorina exchanged looks. "We would need to consider it further," grunted Richard. With this, he and Solorina rose to see Charlotte out. His compromise was preferable to nothing, but Charlotte doubted whether a voluntary order would be sufficient.

HAVING FAILED WITH LORD SAUNDLEY, she next called upon Koralo, Count of Ulsted. He was the closest to Charlotte's age in the chamber, being only a few years older.

She felt much more his equal than Lord Saundley, not to mention that they stood at approximately the same height. In fact, she was perhaps even several hairs taller than him. And she was not a tall woman.

After she arrived at his estate, Koralo listened carefully to her proposal. He agreed with the premise but also expressed hesitation. However, when she told him of Richard's unwillingness to contribute his own creatures, Koralo became more animated.

"Typical of the great Lord Saundley," he huffed, standing up in annoyance. He cut an amusing figure as he stamped around the room, waving his arms wildly as he spoke. "Typical! No, let it be known that the great Lord Saundley cannot be made to suffer the slightest inconvenience in his life. The rest of the population is starving, their stomachs groan with the pain of hunger. But no, Oqci forbid that Lord Saundley be made to feel even a fraction of the discomfort of his fellow people!"

The famous feud between the Ulsted and Saundley families remained very much alive, Charlotte was pleased to observe.

Coming to a stop at last, Koralo turned to her, his cheeks red. "Yes, let it be known that I shall support the measure."

Even if Koralo's support for the idea was more about casting

Saundley in an unfavourable light than for higher motives, Charlotte hardly minded. She thanked him and rose to leave.

Before she could, Koralo clasped her arm to stop her. "Lady Evesbury, before you go, I wished to ask you something."

Charlotte nodded.

He looked at her seriously. "Is it true that you wrote that book against the monarchy?"

She hesitated. She wasn't yet sure she could trust him.

"Because," he continued, "if it is true, let it be known that I admire greatly your boldness, from the depths of my spirit. I have criticisms of the monarchy myself, but I have always been too timid to give them voice."

Was this a trap? Charlotte looked into his kind blue eyes but couldn't be sure. "Well," she said at last, "the government would surely not arrest someone on fabricated charges, now would they?" She winked.

He burst out laughing. "A sufficiently ambiguous answer. Lady Evesbury," he said, as he walked her to the door. "Just give our friend Lord Saundley enough rope to hang himself. You need do no more than that."

In the meeting the following day, Charlotte introduced the motion. As expected – as planned – Richard rose to say that he wished the measure to be voluntary. She gave a knowing glance to Quinneas, who had agreed with her plan.

Selver Bronn, one of the representatives from the commoners, stood in anger. "The noble and priestly classes have for too long failed to sacrifice for our country. The common people have sacrificed. I have sacrificed!" As he grew increasingly animated, his eyes bulged from his head. He turned to address the nobles and priests. "When will it be your turn to sacrifice? It is very well and good to talk about the use of the sacred creatures being voluntary, but who among you will volunteer? Lady Evesbury, our noble friend, is willing to sacrifice. Will the rest of you?"

Koralo rose next. "Let it be known that I, too, am willing to sacrifice. But I must also register my deepest, most fervent conviction that the measure be mandatory. Unfortunately, my friends, I believe there are some who sit among us who cannot be trusted to sacrifice for the good of our entire nation."

It was plain for everyone that all of this was directed toward poor Lord Saundley, whose face was growing red as he looked nervously around the chamber.

Selver Bronn looked at Richard and raised an eyebrow. "Well?"

Richard frowned: "'Well' what? As if a commoner has the right to address me in such a tone."

Selver retorted, "I shall address you in any tone I please as we are both equal members of this chamber!"

Charlotte's eyes briefly met Quinneas's. It was all going to plan.

"Equal? You aren't fit to wash my boots."

Koralo entered the fray, suppressing his glee. "Lord Saundley, please. Distinguished noblemen such as ourselves should always behave with the utmost decorum and grace. Let it be known that I, for one, think Mr. Bronn is a fine man."

"Yes," Charlotte added delicately, "I think Mr. Bronn is a fine man who has sacrificed much for our country."

Richard looked sheepish as the other nobles cast their gazes toward him. He recognized his blunder.

One noble after another stood to express support for the measure, so it would easily pass with the support of the commoners. Some of the more conservative priests expressed their objections, but Kephalos too supported the measure. However, he said he wished to ensure that the creatures always be under the command of a noble or priest on the battlefield, that only fifty percent of the creatures be drafted, and that after the end of the fighting, they be returned to their owners.

This idea, with Kephalos's compromises, was agreed upon with a 12–3 vote, with Lord Saundley and two priests voting against. They now awaited the king's approval.

DELLIREA

Dellirea returned to the palace in a foul mood as she thought of that hideous man, Nox, and his horrible comments to her. She tried to remind herself that it was her duty, being from royal birth, to take the comments of a lower-class man in stride.

But part of her wished to see him strung up like the common criminal that he was. It brought her great pleasure, excitement even, to imagine his final moments on the gallows, desperately crying and pleading for her mercy – which she then refused to grant.

No, no, she told herself. She mustn't think such terrible things!

But was it true what he said about her mother? That she had been unfaithful to her father? This thought too disturbed her, but she tried to block it from her mind.

DELLIREA WAS TOO embarrassed to tell anyone else, least of all her parents, about the vile comments Samuel Nox had made, but they continued to weigh on her mind.

When she returned to the palace, she learned of the Great Chamber's request to commandeer half of the sacred creatures for use in battle. She despaired to think of it. Things were changing too quickly. The dragons! The protest! The Friezzian attack! Her life before seemed so much simpler. And now everything was out of balance.

At a meeting of the king's council, her father expressed his anger at the Great Chamber's request. To think, their magnificent creatures being sent to be slaughtered on the battlefield as creatures of war! An anger welled up inside Dellirea too.

"If we reject the proposal," her father said at the council meeting, holding up the formal notice from the chamber, "only a unanimous vote in the Great Chamber could enforce the measure."

"Achieving unanimity would be difficult," said Dario, "but, Your Majesty, I recommend that we think not only of politics. It is indeed possible that we could prevent the measure from taking effect. But we cannot survive much longer and we risk Goldhall falling to Friezzia, or being forced to surrender."

Her father shuddered at the thought, as did Dellirea. When Estenland had defeated Friezzia thirty years ago in the Great War, Estenland punished them with harsh terms of surrender. The Friezzians would not have forgotten.

"What of our war machines?" Aramal asked.

"We have only four in total that could be used in combat," Dario replied. "Not nearly enough to be useful on the battlefield."

"Four is better than nothing," he said. "They have been built to take on dragons, surely they can also take on an army of men." He turned to his daughter. "What do you think, Dellirea?"

Her thoughts turned to that horrible man Nox. How he had mutilated those innocent creatures. How he had dared to speak to her in such a manner! And now this? Use the creatures in battle? It needed to be stopped. Somewhere, they had to make a stand against the further erosion of their system. They needed to demonstrate to the people that there were lines that could never be crossed.

"I think you ought to veto the measure."

Her father thought on this for several moments, his eyes trained on the formal paper from the Great Chamber still clasped in his hand. "Then I shall veto it."

WITH ARAMAL'S VETO, the issue was once more before the Great Chamber. Would they have the audacity to overturn his decision?

As Dellirea sat in her room, waiting to hear the Chamber's response, a steady clanging noise from outside the palace drew her out. She walked to the balcony and looked upon Karazin Square. Dozens and dozens of the poor – mostly women – paraded through the square, banging on empty pots with wooden spoons as a sign of their hunger. They were thin and sickly, their hair stringy and dirty. Some of the women dragged along emaciated children, dressed all in rags.

She had seen poverty before, but it was rising to new levels during the siege. Her heart went out to these poor, simple women who only wished to feed their families and to be respectable followers of Oqci. Part of her wondered if they had made a mistake in vetoing the measure for the creatures.

The women filled the square in front of the palace, just as the protesters had done many weeks ago. That day seemed almost an eternity ago. That day... The memories still sickened her. People torn apart by griffins!

But women were the more peaceful sex, Dellirea knew. They would not pose such a problem as the protesters that day. Yet as more and more women seeped into the square, they began to shake the gates of the palace and a feeling of dread filled Dellirea's stomach.

"Get back! Get back!" the guards shouted as they tried to push the women away. But there were too many.

Desperate shouts from the guards and the constant clattering of the pots made Dellirea's head hurt. She recoiled from the balcony, then looked once more.

Some of the women had started to climb the gates around the palace. Her eyes darted back and forth. In some places, the guards fought the women off. In others, some managed to breach the gates.

Dear Oqci. They were getting inside the palace!

Frightened, Dellirea ran to find her mother and father. Where were they? Where was everyone?

Her heart beat quickly as she hurried through the halls, fearful that she might come upon one of the crazy women before she found her parents.

The palace suddenly seemed deserted. She peeked her head into one of the banquet rooms, and she saw three young women – one brunette, two blondes – their faces buried in leftover dishes like animals at a trough.

The floor creaked as Dellirea backed away from the door. The sound alerted the women to her presence.

"The princess!" the brunette cried. They removed themselves from their food and chased after her.

Dellirea struggled to run in her dress. The women ran much faster than she did.

"Help! Help!" she called out as they drew closer and closer.

At last, Dellirea saw her mother along with Yuvela and another noblewoman. "In here," said Yuvela quietly. The four of them slipped inside one of the rooms and locked the door. They huddled together and stayed deathly quiet. The only sound was their heavy breathing.

Seconds later, six fists pounding on the door caused Dellirea to shriek with fear.

"Where are the bloody guards?" her mother whispered, pulling Dellirea close.

The sound of the pounding on the door suddenly stopped. Silence.

Dellirea breathed a sigh of relief. Perhaps they had gone away. Please. Please let them have gone away.

But then.

A loud thump against the door made the hinges strain. Then another thump. They were using something to break down the door.

Dellirea could hear their crazed laughter outside with every thump. She gripped her mother's hand and prayed to Oqci.

Thump. Thump.

Suddenly, the door swung open and the three women swarmed in, their mouths ringed with food. They dropped the bench they had used to break through the door, and with their filthy hands picked up the wine bottles they had taken from the banquet rooms. They laughed merrily at their great fortune to encounter the queen and the princess. One of the blondes carried a rifle. Dellirea prayed she knew not how to use it.

Dellirea and the others huddled in the corner of the room, gripping one another closely. The women came over and pulled her mother from the group. Dellirea's heart was pounding.

"Hello, Your Highness," said the brunette, laughing and guzzling from the bottle of wine. She bowed in a false gesture of respect.

"Get out of our palace at once, you nasty brutes!" Dellirea's mother commanded in a shaky voice.

The women paid her no heed. It only made them laugh more. They forced Bravala into the centre of the room. When Yuvela stood to protest, the blonde raised her rifle.

"Citizen Bravala," said the brunette, baring her purple-stained teeth, "we knew you were a friend of the revolution. Won't you announce it to the world?"

Dellirea's mother, trying to summon bravery, said, "I... I shall do no such –"

Before she could finish, the brunette held Bravala's arms behind her back while the other blonde forced upon her head one of those green caps that all the revolutionaries wore. The women threw back their heads in laughter.

Dellirea's mother shook from fright – from anger – at the humiliation. For a brief moment, they made eye contact. Terror filled Dellirea's mother's eyes as the brunette ran her greasy fingers over the fine silk of her mother's dress and up to the jewelry on her neck. Her mother stood with her arms stiffly at her side, not daring to move, as the brunette lifted the aletolium necklace from her skin to examine it. Her fist tightened around the necklace and with one motion yanked it away, sending some scattered gems to the ground.

The blonde kept the rifle carefully trained on Bravala, who could only look on with horror. A tear dripped from her eye.

"Cheer up, Citizen Bravala," said the brunette, forcing the wine bottle to Dellirea's mother's lips. "This is a celebration. Let us be merry." She cradled her with one hand and tilted the bottle upward, forcing her to drink. Dellirea's mother coughed and jerked her head away, spitting out the wine and causing most of it to run down her chin and onto her dress and the carpet. The women doubled over with laughter.

"Halt!"

Dellirea's eyes darted toward the door. At last!

Two guards appeared. The women loosened their grip on Dellirea's mother and swung their gaze around.

Dellirea's mother rushed to safety in the corner of the room as one of the guards drew his pistol. He fired upon the blonde woman holding the gun before she could react. Dellirea shrieked as the shot rang out. Blood splashed upon the carpet. The other two women stood, frozen. Two more gunshots. The women fell to the ground.

Dellirea and the others rushed to escort her mother from the room, without having time to remove the horrid green cap that still sat upon her head. As they moved down the hallway, her mother turned back to the guards and shouted, "Where in Oqci's name were you? We could've been killed!" She paused. "And clean up their wretched bodies. They are going to ruin the carpets!"

44

CHARLOTTE

"Friends," Quinneas said, addressing the Great Chamber, "the king has done what we feared. By vetoing our measure to draft the sacred creatures into the armed forces, he has directly challenged our authority. *We* represent the collective will of the people, and, even if some among us personally disagree with the proposed action, surely, we must not allow the king's will to suppress that of the people!"

There were only three holdouts preventing a unanimous decision: Richard, Duke of Saundley, and the two priests.

Kephalos spoke next, addressing his priestly brethren. His voice was thin, yet his words were uttered with conviction. "Friends, it is true that Oqci's scriptures tell us that the creatures are not to be used as weapons, but this is an unprecedented time. Our entire society is under threat. You all know how much I cherish my faith. I resigned my position as high priest to protest His Majesty's use of the creatures. I believed that was wrong and I still do."

As Kephalos spoke, the sound of banging grew ever louder outside. Charlotte had heard that a small gathering was planned to express discontent with the siege, and she supposed this was whence the noise originated.

"His Majesty used the creatures for violent and immoral purposes," Kephalos continued. "But to use the creatures to defend ourselves? I believe that it is just, that it is no offense against Oqci's doctrines. You know that I would never endorse such a measure lightly. But I believe that it is necessary."

Even though Charlotte disagreed with his religious views, no one could question Kephalos's principles. The two remaining priests were swayed by Kephalos's words and signalled their intention to vote with Charlotte's side.

She turned her eyes to Richard, the last holdout. "What say you, Lord Saundley?"

"No, I cannot allow it," he said, sitting back in his chair and folding his arms across his chest. "I refuse to grant my vote. That's final."

"You will stand with the very king who turned these creatures against his own people?" she shot back.

"I stand by my own convictions," he said. "It is wrong to take this step. I have made my decision, and I see no reason to further discuss the matter."

Charlotte sighed. Quinneas shook his head. It seemed there was to be no convincing him.

Suddenly, a flustered guard burst into the room. Some of the women had breached the palace, he explained.

"Let us talk to the crowd," said Quinneas confidently. "We shall tell them that a solution is at hand."

"There is no solution at hand!" said Richard. "I've already told you my decision."

Just then, another guard entered. "It is not safe here! The queen and the princess have been attacked by the women."

"Dear Oqci!" said Kephalos. "Have they been harmed?"

"We believe not," said the guard, "and fortunately those intruders have been apprehended. But we must go now. There may be more women yet."

A pack of guards led the members along a series of winding corridors. They came to a nondescript candle holder upon the wall. The guard twisted it and slid open a door, revealing a secret passageway. "Here," he said.

They filed down a narrow stairway that descended deep below the palace. As they marched, Quinneas looked at Richard. "See what is happening? The people are starving. There is no end in sight. We need to act now!"

"I shall not be held hostage by such animals," spat Richard.

At last, they reached the bottom, where a doorway took them into a large, well-lit sitting room. It was there Charlotte saw the queen and princess, along with two other noble-women. Dellirea's face was still wet with tears, while Queen

Bravala had a stony look on her face as she stared straight ahead. They all seemed too shaken by the attack to pay the members any mind.

As Charlotte and the others settled at the opposite end of the bunker, Quinneas leaned toward Richard. "Let us make a deal. All of your creatures will be exempt from the draft if you agree to support the motion."

"What is the meaning of this?" Koralo cried. "An exceptional deal for Lord Saundley? Let it be known that I find such an agreement most deeply unfair!"

"Please, Lord Ulsted," Charlotte said, reaching out and gently touching his forearm, "if this is the only way we can pass the measure, I fear we must."

Koralo shook his head slightly but protested no further. The others indicated their support for this deal, however unfair it might be.

All eyes were now on Lord Saundley. "Fine," he grumbled. "Fine." With that, they had a unanimous agreement – if an imperfect one – to pass the motion and override the king's veto.

~

KING ARAMAL, alongside Dario and Aramal's brother, was brought into the bunker soon after. When he entered, he ran toward his wife and daughter. The three hugged tearfully.

"It was horrible! Horrible!" sobbed Dellirea.

After comforting his family, the king turned to the members.

"Your Majesty," said Kephalos, "I'm afraid that the Great Chamber has voted to overturn your veto. We shall draft the sacred creatures into the army."

The king put his head in his hands for several moments. "Delightful," he said, raising his head. "What is one more indignity we have to endure? My wife and daughter, attacked by those... those... those animals! Of course," he continued sarcastically, "let us be sure to save the precious lives of these brutes at all costs." Staring at the floor, he muttered, "I would be just as happy to see the Friezzian army invade the city. Let us see these women begging for my rule after the Friezzians get through with them."

"Please, Your Majesty," said Dario quietly. "Let us not say such things."

Aramal simply shook his head in frustration, saying no more.

Dario came to Charlotte and the other members. "In the coming hours," he said gravely, "we shall draw up the notices mandating the nobles and priests relinquish their creatures for the nation's service. May Oqci help us."

There was little mood for celebration, considering how dire the situation was. Yet a deal was now struck.

"Let us go and speak to the people," Quinneas said, loud enough for Aramal to hear. "We shall tell them that a resolution is close at hand."

"I am in no mood for it," said Aramal, refusing to move from his place. "After everything my family has been through today, I can't bear to look upon such rude people."

"Is that wise, Your Majesty?" Dario said. "The people may begin to think that the Great Chamber is in control and not you."

Suppressing the urge to say that the crowd would be correct in thinking that, Charlotte said instead, "Your Majesty, our only goal would be to calm the protests, not to undermine your authority."

Dario and the king reluctantly agreed and, with that, a group of guards led Charlotte, Quinneas, and Kephalos back up the staircase and through the palace.

They stepped through the door and onto the palace balcony. The cool air refreshed Charlotte after her time in the stuffy bunker underground.

The crowd of mostly women milled about restlessly outside. It seemed as though they were growing cold and weary as the sun was beginning to set. The number of guards had increased around the palace to prevent any further breaches.

Charlotte stood between Kephalos and Quinneas. It was agreed that she would address the protesters. Perhaps, it was decided, they might find it more agreeable to listen to another woman. As Charlotte held the speaking trumpet to her mouth, the crowd quieted to listen to her speech. A flutter of nervousness danced in her stomach as hundreds of eyes stared expectantly at her.

"Friends," she began shakily, "we have understood your plight and the hardships you have experienced. The siege has taken an immense toll on our fair city, has it not? And we recognize the tremendous sacrifices you have all made."

The crowd remained silent, unmoved by her words.

She continued, "The Great Chamber has just voted on a solution that will break the siege. His Majesty King Aramal has agreed to it. We cannot reveal our plans at this time, but be assured that an end to this misery is in sight!"

"Can we trust a noble?" shouted one of the women below.

"You can trust me," Charlotte said. "I too have sacrificed. I have been locked in prison for my principles. You can trust me!"

There was some scattered applause, but Charlotte was unsure if she was reaching them. She looked over at Quinneas who gestured for her to continue. "Friends, there have been many rumours about the identity of the author of *The Downfall of the Monarchy*. The king imprisoned me, saying that I was the author. Friends..." She looked once more back at Quinneas whose reassuring expression gave her strength. "Friends, today I tell you that it was true. I wrote it. I risked my life standing up to the king. Standing up for you. I beg you now: please trust me!"

With this, the crowd began to cheer furiously. She had won them over.

"The siege will soon be over," she continued, "but, please, I ask you to disperse so that we can begin our preparations. I promise that your misery is soon to be relieved."

Quinneas smiled at Charlotte as he placed a hand gently on her forearm. Kephalos looked at her with the slightest curl of a smile on the corners of his lips. She swelled with pride as the women began to trickle out of the square.

45

YANIS

The arrival of a letter offered a rare reprieve from the monotony of army life, from patiently standing guard at the edge of the city since the disastrous battle with the Friezzians. Since then, it was a seemingly endless stretch of tedium, not to mention hunger.

Yanis scrambled to open the letter, praying it was from Nadeni. Throughout the siege, he had missed her greatly and wondered of her well-being. At last, he had decided to pen her a letter, apologizing for their quarrel that night before he left. More importantly, he had asked, was she safe? Was she well?

Hurrah! The letter was from her!

Yanis read it over three times fully, admiring the loops in her handwriting. She was well! But things were difficult during the siege, she explained. She had been part of a women's protest. Yanis was shocked as she told him that some of the women even managed to breach the palace, although Nadeni was not among them. She accepted his apology and said that she too bore some of the blame for their quarrel.

How Yanis missed her. How he wished to see her again!

He started immediately on another letter. In this one, he confessed that he was eager to see her again – eager in a way that went beyond mere friendship.

He only prayed to survive the siege, to turn such a hope into reality.

THE NEWS CAME of the Great Chamber's decision to allow the use of the sacred creatures in battle. Soon they would join the lines for an attack on the Friezzians. The thought of another battle filled Yanis with dread – but also excitement. It would be a chance to redeem himself from the foolhardy attempt to break the siege weeks ago that he had done much to engineer. His reputation had been dealt a serious blow that day. He had cost many men their lives, not least Vinzent.

Clem tried to reassure him that he must not blame himself, but there was no doubt that the men's confidence in Yanis had lessened. Justifiably so. The failure made Yanis see the folly of his delusions of grandeur. In the coming battle, he only hoped that he might perform competently. Or even make it out alive.

Two days before the battle, Yanis and the others were graced by the presence of His Majesty, King Aramal, who, with the rest of his royal party, rode on horseback through their camp to inspect the soldiers. He mostly looked above them, carefully avoiding eye contact with any of the soldiers. He had been worn down from the revolution and then the siege, Yanis discerned.

The king stopped briefly in front of Yanis's battalion and inspected them. "Very good," he said. "Very good. The fate of Estenland rests on your shoulders."

"For the glory of the king!" called out Dario.

"For the glory of the king!" the battalion said at once. But it was half-hearted. To a man, they blamed Aramal the Incompetent for dragging his feet over the use of the sacred creatures.

Clem turned to Yanis and grinned at the tepid response from the soldiers. "You think Andamar the Great would have given such a limp address?" he said. "Never! Now that was a man you could proudly serve."

Yanis nodded at Clem's comments, but did not wish to let on that, to him, there were no kings or queens worth serving.

Having given an uninspired performance, the king and his party rode on. But, following in his wake, the procession of the sacred creatures destined for Yanis's battalion filled the men with cheer. Nobles and priests, wearing turquoise aletolium amulets around their necks, slowly led out fifteen unicorns. Looks of awe appeared on the men's faces as fifteen winged horses, then five winged lions, arrived. At last, the soldiers erupted in applause as three griffins joined their lines.

Yanis watched the griffins carefully. The last time he had

seen one was that fateful day at the protest. But these were magnificent. Their stunning white heads and piercing eyes gave the appearance of royalty. Massive wings, surely each the length of his body, remained folded behind them as they marched. Yanis's eyes turned to their yellow front legs, with talons sharp enough to cut through flesh with ease. Their back legs and paws, too, he was sure, could do equal damage. The griffins' tails swayed casually behind them, as if to say that they feared neither the Friezzians nor anyone. Having faced the griffins as enemies, Yanis now looked forward to fighting alongside them as allies.

Yanis was already in a jubilant mood, sitting with the other soldiers on the eve of the battle, when the mail was delivered. Anticipation filled his heart as the postman called out his name and handed him a letter.

It was Nadeni once more!

He opened it and scanned the words as quickly as he could to discover her response to his admission of feelings for her. She reciprocated them! Once he knew that her answer was positive, he read the letter again, slowly, enjoying each word she wrote.

She too had been smitten with him since the very day he gave his speech so many weeks ago. She had sensed a connection between them right then and there.

Yanis concealed his emotions from the other men in the camp. But, inside, his heart exploded with joy. How he loved her!

Nadeni's letter gave him something greater than himself to fight for. That night, he closed his eyes and dreamed only of her. The siege, the coming battle, the revolution – all seemed to be taking place in another world.

At dawn, Yanis woke to reality. His unit advanced in column to meet the Friezzians for battle. There was much more confidence in their marching, knowing that at their rear were the sacred creatures. They would be the crucial element that, Yanis hoped, the Friezzians would not see coming.

The creatures, they were reminded again and again, were only to be commanded by nobles and priests. This was part of the deal that was struck to authorize their use.

Enemy scouts raced back to their lines to inform the Friezzians of the Estenlanders' approach. To the untrained eye, it would seem as though nothing had changed since the previous battle. Several hundred paces ahead, the Friezzian lines began forming, waiting for the Estenlanders' assault. Yanis and the others marched confidently toward them, holding their fire.

"It's a shame we can't make out the expressions on their faces," Yanis said to Clem. "I wish I could see them when they catch a glimpse of the creatures!"

"They're going to be filling their trousers when they realize," said Clem with a laugh.

As they drew nearly to within firing range, they heard the signal behind them. Overhead flew the noble commanders on the winged horses, alongside the winged lions. Yanis and the others broke into a dash behind them.

The creatures flew down into the Friezzian lines. The Friezzians were late to realize what was happening. One poor soldier raised his musket to fire, but it was too late. A flying lion landed upon him with full force and began mauling him. His horrified screams were audible even to Yanis some distance away.

The Friezzian line was already in chaos. The horses and lions trampled the helpless Friezzian soldiers. Just as quickly as they landed, the creatures flew back up again. Yanis's unit formed a line and began firing in volley at the disorganized Friezzians. Their reserves moved forward to plug the gaps in their lines, but they only walked into a wall of fire.

The Estenlanders' line spread out and through their ranks, the unicorns, ridden by nobles, charged with the griffins flying overhead. Yanis and the others sprinted behind them. One of the griffins grabbed a Friezzian soldier with its beak and bit down, nearly severing him in two. Another Friezzian soldier stabbed the griffin with his bayonet in its side in an attempt to rescue his comrade. It recoiled in pain. Yanis fired his musket at the man, missing, but enough to scare him away from the griffin as Yanis and the others ran closer and the griffin hobbled back to safety.

Yanis looked down at the soldier who had been bitten by the griffin. A gash extended over halfway across his torso as blood and innards spilled out. Yet the man was still half-conscious. His eyes flittered open and he stared at the sky, glassy-eyed, muttering something weakly in his foreign tongue, which Yanis could not comprehend. He stood over this man, barely more than a boy, barely old enough to shave. These men had no choice in the fight, Yanis understood. They too were victims of a cruel monarchical regime.

Yanis plunged his bayonet into the soldier's heart, ending his misery.

Commotion was in front of Yanis as the charge of unicorns and griffins had shattered the Friezzian lines. Most of the soldiers ran for their lives back to their fortifications. Yanis hurried to catch up with the rest of the line as they continued their furious pursuit. As they ran, more and more Friezzian soldiers threw down their arms and surrendered. It was becoming a rout. The back ranks of the Friezzians launched artillery fire toward the Estenlander charge, but the gunners were quickly forced to flee when the winged lions and horses descended upon them.

Yanis looked back, now thousands of paces from their fortress. On the ground lay dead or wounded soldiers, most wearing the Friezzian blue. Scattered here and there were the bodies of fallen unicorns or lions. The Estenlander surgeons dispersed to help their own soldiers and creatures. Smoke from the guns hung over the terrain like fog.

"We must keep pushing forward!" Clem shouted.

Yanis regained his focus and rushed ahead to join Clem and the rest of the advance. The Friezzians could be finished right here. As they pushed forward there were fewer and fewer Friezzians to find, since so many had already surrendered or been killed. Groups of Friezzians raised white flags as the advance continued.

One of the griffins, lusting for more blood and finding no Friezzian enemies to attack, turned toward Clem. Its noble commander was nowhere in sight.

"Clem, look out!" Yanis called.

Before Clem could recognize the danger, the griffin charged and launched him into the air with a butt of its head. Clem landed and lay on his back as the griffin approached. Its noble commander ran from a distance and called for it to cease.

But Yanis was closer.

He sprinted toward the griffin and waved his hands. "Halt!" he shouted.

The griffin's intense yellow eyes turned from Clem to him. It stepped away and slowly approached Yanis. Clem climbed to his feet tenuously and darted to safety.

The griffin, a dozen paces away, stared Yanis down. "Halt!" he said again, extending his arm out, his knees shaking.

Its sharp beak, Yanis knew, could tear him in half before he would have a chance to react. But he remained steadfast.

The griffin stopped its movement, seeming to obey his command even as it continued eyeing him.

At last, its noble commander reached the griffin and motioned for it to return to the Estenlander lines.

The commander glared at Yanis. "Soldier, you were ordered not to command the creatures."

Yanis stifled his anger. "I had no choice, my lord. The griffin was attacking one of ours!"

"Even so," he said, "you must remember your place."

The commander turned to follow the griffin back to their lines. Clem shouted to him as he left, "That's the Dragon Slayer! If anything, he should be commanding you."

The noble turned back, stunned by this insubordination and unable to find words to reprimand him.

"Let us press on," Clem said to Yanis. They ran ahead to join the pursuit deep into the Friezzian lines.

By NIGHTFALL, they were far outside the edge of the city. They had routed the Friezzians and more Estenlander soldiers had arrived to solidify the gains. Hundreds of enemy soldiers lay dead on the battlefield and hundreds more were held as prisoners in the fortresses around the city border. The end was in sight, Yanis knew. The Friezzians were in disarray and would be forced to return to their territory.

Yanis and some other soldiers gathered around a fire drinking beer and eating food plundered from the enemy camp, still too energized from the battle to sleep.

Clem came to Yanis and placed his hand upon his shoulder. "The men never should have doubted you, Dragon Slayer," he said. Turning to the rest of the soldiers gathered around the fire, he cried, "This man saved my life!"

Yanis chuckled. This was Ronar all over again. "I only did what I had to do," he said, standing tall to address the group. "Any one of you would have done the same."

CHARLOTTE

A crowd of hundreds gazed upon them as they stood on the top of the stage in Karazin Square. The king was presenting medallions to those who performed heroically in defeating the Friezzians and pushing them back to their territory.

All fifteen members of the Great Chamber were there, yet they were relegated to the far corner. It was the last time they would be together as a group, as new elections would soon be held now that the country was safe once again.

The generals were at centre stage, but Charlotte believed that the people recognized it was the Great Chamber, particularly her and Quinneas, who were the true heroes. If it had not been for them, Charlotte reasoned, the idea of using the sacred creatures would never have been proposed.

As the ceremony concluded, Koralo walked toward Charlotte. "Lady Evesbury," he said, with a slight grin, "I remember what you said about your book. That the government had never wrongly imprisoned someone. And let it be known that you were right!"

"Of course, I would never lie!" she said, pretending offense. "Although," with a wink, "I might sometimes be purposefully vague."

"Indeed," he said. "That is most prudent. Oqci forbid lying, but I cannot recall, even in my deepest memories, that he ever forbade purposeful vagueness!"

They both laughed.

Talk of the book, however, brought her mind back to the question of how the government had discovered she was its author. Her suspicions remained centred on Brondin.

CHARLOTTE RESOLVED to confront him about the issue. She had not spoken to her brother since the siege began, but she needed to learn the truth at last. When she arrived at his estate, one of the servants led her inside to where Brondin waited in the drawing room.

Brondin looked much older than when she had last seen him, even though it had been only a matter of months. "I'm surprised you would show your face around here," he began, without any greeting. "Mother has practically forgotten who you are, which is probably for the best anyhow. She would be horrified to learn her own daughter wrote such trash about the monarchy."

"You were the one who insisted I not come here," Charlotte said, "so do not pretend as though it were my decision. Besides, I shall not stay long. I need only to know whether it was you who alerted the government that I authored *The Downfall of the Monarchy*. You and Willien were the only people who knew."

"Ha!" he said. "What kind of person do you take me for? I heard, like everyone else, that you had been arrested, but I had no idea how the police discovered it. And it is still a mystery to me."

She wasn't sure if she accepted this explanation, yet he seemed genuine.

"I thought you might have been jealous of me after I upstaged you at the meeting of the prominent leaders," she said. "I wouldn't blame you if you told the police. All is forgiven. I just need to know the truth."

"Ha!" he said again, much to her annoyance. "Upstaged me? You hardly upstaged me at that meeting. Is it any surprise you were elected instead of me? Many of those noblemen: They see a pretty face, then they lose all sense of rationality. They begin to think with another organ instead of their brain."

"How dare you," she said. "My accomplishments have nothing to do with something superficial like my appearance!"

Brondin simply laughed condescendingly. "Charlotte, there is another matter I wished to discuss with you," he continued. "To be frank, you can do as you please, but I have read these stories about you spending so much time with that radical, Quinneas Raeil. You are married, remember? And not to him."

"Brondin, I appreciate your worry, but really my personal life is none of your concern."

"It is my concern insofar as it drags our family name through the mud."

Charlotte shook her head. "Not that I need to tell you, but I am going to see Willien about that very issue later today."

Brondin looked to the sky. "Dear Oqci. It's a wonder mother hasn't died from the stress of your... your escapades."

CHARLOTTE HAD WISHED to visit her mother, but she was apparently resting and feeling too weak for visitors. Charlotte therefore ventured next to Willien's estate.

When she arrived, his servant led her to his glasshouse in the back gardens. The hot climate within warmed her from the cool winter air. There she found Willien bent over a table, in deep concentration examining one of his specimens, such that he did not even hear her enter.

Charlotte stood for a moment watching him. She respected the diligent research that he had undertaken for years, but part of her wondered whether it was truly leading somewhere. What importance could there be in studying the shape of pea plants' leaves or some such? But it was true that many people could say the same for her own philosophical writing.

At last, she cleared her throat to alert him to her presence.

Willien looked up in surprise. "Oh, Charlotte. Why, it is nice to see you." He paused. "It seems much has happened to you since we last spoke."

"Merely leading a revolution against the king and defeating the Friezzians," she said. "Other than that, my life has been mostly uneventful."

He frowned at her tone. "This isn't a joke," he said. "Your actions affect me too. My name has been in the papers too. I am your husband, don't forget."

"I haven't forgotten, believe me. In fact, that's what I wished to speak to you about." She took a breath. She reached down to run her fingers over the leaves of one of Willien's plants. "I wish us to divorce."

Willien's eyes shot wide open. He looked oddly hurt by this news.

"I spoke with Kephalos," she continued, "and he agreed to authorize the divorce, so there is no need to worry on that account. Yes, it would create a minor scandal, but I believe it better to do this now so we can both continue on with our lives. There has already been enough speculation in the press about Quinneas and me."

He stared down at his flowers. "Ah yes," he said, lifting his head back up. "Raeil... You know, I had taken you as someone who was not governed merely by animal instincts, like so many others. But now I see I was wrong about that."

Charlotte cared not for his statement, but she held her tongue. Was he suddenly jealous? But there was no object in exploring the issue further. It would only lead to one or both of them becoming hurt.

"Will you agree to the divorce, or won't you?"

"Very well," he said. "Send me anything I need to sign, and I shall see that it is resolved." With that, he turned back to his work and said nothing more as she departed.

Quinneas shook his head. "Do not let their ignorant remarks affect you, my treasure."

"You're right, dear," Charlotte said. She forced herself to cease brooding from the previous day's discouraging meetings.

He smiled warmly. "Today is a day for happiness."

She and Quinneas prepared to speak to the people today. And there were more important matters than her personal travails.

They had come to a radical meeting hall in the Palace District in advance of the Great Chamber elections. Of course, they both sought election again, although this time there were to be no divisions in the Great Chamber between nobles, commoners, and priests.

The two stood on the stage flanked by some other radical leaders, including Yanis Haller. Quinneas insisted that the Dragon Slayer's endorsement would be useful for winning popular support, although their own election chances were hardly in doubt.

"Friends," Quinneas said, "the coming vote is critical for the future of our country. The representatives of the new Great Chamber will draft a constitution for Estenland. We must ensure that the true representatives of your will are returned. I call on those who meet the property thresholds to vote for us. We shall ensure that the new constitution allows for absolute equality for all. In our new constitution, there will be no more property requirements for voting. No accidents of birth should determine one's rights! All divisions must be stripped away!"

"Hurrah!" shouted the crowd.

Quinneas handed Charlotte his speaking trumpet. "Friends, I believe, as with Mr. Quinneas Raeil, that our new constitution must protect the equality of all. What is more, this new constitution must also consider the most important question: Ought we to be ruled by a king or by the people? Let us not forget, that while King Aramal dithered, it was the Great Chamber who helped to defeat the Friezzians by deploying the sacred creatures!

"What is more," Charlotte continued, "our entire system of nobility must be abolished. This is why that, today, before the people, I formally renounce my noble titles. I no longer wish to be considered a noble. I no longer wish to possess the unearned privileges of a noble. Rather I wish to be placed on an equal basis with all of my fellow citizens."

Wild cheers greeted her speech and the crowd began a rendition of "Justice for All" as she and Quinneas stood in the centre of the stage.

47

YANIS

The first thing Yanis did once freed from his commitments in the army was see Nadeni. The month and a half of the siege made him realize how much he had missed her. How much he had longed to hold her in his arms.

They met outside her familiar apartment in Iron Town. Yanis hurried toward her as soon as he saw her, restless with anticipation. As he wrapped his arms around her, he could feel the effects of the siege on her slender frame.

"I was unsure whether I would ever see you again," he said, restraining tears.

"I felt so too," she said. "I thought of you every night."

"And I of you. Let us take a walk."

Yanis planned that they would stroll the banks of Hope Stream, which wound its way through Iron Town before connecting to the River Elden. He had spent many days of his childhood there, catching minnows or skipping stones. There was a spot he knew that would be perfect.

As they walked the stony path, Yanis told her of the horrors of battle and the ecstasy of victory. She told him about life in Goldhall during the siege: the ever-present threat of shelling from outside the city, the days where there was nothing to eat, the uncertainty and dread about the future.

But all that was behind them now.

The water flowed gently beside them as they walked. The sunlight speckled through the trees onto the stream. For a moment, the beauty of the scene masked how polluted the water had become since Yanis's youth. But no matter.

At last they came to the spot Yanis wished, where the path jutted into the stream. He held her hand as they walked onto the point. He stopped and turned to her. His heart was racing. He looked into her eyes and clasped her hands. "Nadeni, on a dark night during the siege, when things seemed so bleak, I made a promise to myself that if, somehow, I managed to survive, I would ask you something."

A smile formed on her lips.

"Nadeni," Yanis said, "you are the most amazing woman I have ever known. And I know not how I could have endured the siege without the hope of seeing you again. You inspire me. And you make me wish to become a better person. I know not what the future holds, but whatever it does, I wish to experience it with you. Would you do me the honour of becoming my wife?"

"Of course! Of course, I would, Yanis," she said, as she threw her arms around him.

As Yanis clutched Nadeni close, a terrible, unwanted thought intruded into his mind for just a moment: She was the second-most amazing woman he had ever known.

YANIS HAD RETURNED from the front lines a hero. That he had saved a fellow soldier from a griffin was just another of the stories to add to the myths about him. Why not, therefore, use his status as somewhat of a celebrity to support his friends?

Yanis spoke at election rallies for Quinneas and Charlotte. Whether his presence made a difference was unclear, but Quinneas and Charlotte were both successful in their respective campaigns. They were among the three hundred members elected to the new Great Chamber. The moderates and conservatives, however, were the majority, led by those like Kephalos and Richard, Duke of Saundley. There was considerable anger toward the king because of his action, or rather inaction, during the siege, but not enough for people to wish to end the monarchy altogether. Even so, the Great Chamber now held the true power.

After the election, Quinneas invited Yanis to his home, saying there was a pressing matter he wished to discuss.

When Yanis arrived, Quinneas and Charlotte sat close

together on the sofa in the drawing room. Yanis sat in an armchair across from them, feeling somewhat out of place. Quinneas's home was much closer to that of the nobility than of the commoners. And to be sitting across from a noblewoman was something to which Yanis was unaccustomed.

"I hear that you intend to wed?" began Quinneas.

"Indeed," he said. "I plan to marry Nadeni Lichenxu."

"Terrific news," said Quinneas. "That is the lady from New Selver?"

"She was born here in Estenland," Yanis said. "But New Selver is where her father is from." He hesitated. On the walls hung masks and artwork that must have come from New Selver or other nearby nations. Yanis felt a strong urge to tell them of Nadeni's famous ancestry. Part of him thought that if they knew, they would see him as more than just another commoner. Instead, he said simply, "She too was involved in the capture of the prison."

"Yes," said Quinneas, "I heard talk about a so-called 'Denier of Oqci' when the prison was taken."

"I think Selver Bronn was babbling something about that," added Charlotte with a smirk.

Quinneas let out a dismissive laugh. "Such a silly prejudice. Once we gain power in the Great Chamber, we shall build a new society in which all such arbitrary divisions of birth will disappear."

"A glorious vision," Yanis said. "I hope it becomes reality."

"Let us come to our main focus," Quinneas said. "Charlotte and I owe a great deal to you. For helping with our election campaigns, but more importantly for helping to liberate us from prison those many months ago. Without you, the revolution might have been crushed before it could even begin. Then to display such heroism against the Friezzians…"

"Thank you," Yanis said, slightly embarrassed by such praise.

"During the battle for the prison, you showed yourself a shrewd leader," he continued. "The new Great Chamber members will soon be seated, but our revolution remains fragile.

We need to entrench the revolution and ensure it can never again be threatened by the king."

Charlotte nodded at this, as did Yanis.

"This is why," Quinneas went on, "I propose the creation of a separate force to defend the Great Chamber and its members. The police and the army are still made up of the king's men. They are loyal to him first, rather than to the revolution. This new force would be for the people. It would have the people's interests at heart. It would be made up of the people. And it would be led by the people."

"Yes," Yanis said, "that is a wise idea."

"Indeed," said Quinneas. "But why I have asked you here is to propose that *you* organize and lead this Revolutionary Defence Force."

Yanis leaned forward in his chair. "Me? Are you sure I am the right choice?"

"Naturally Charlotte and I both think so, and I have already spoken with Kephalos about the idea. He too is in agreement, and the idea is sure to pass in the Chamber. You have already displayed considerable ability in your military career. And, importantly, the people know you and they trust your leadership. In truth, you are the only person who could do this."

Yanis reclined, contemplating the proposal and the enormous responsibility it would place upon his shoulders. "It will be the greatest challenge of my life," he said, "but it is one I shall embrace."

"We shall discuss it in more detail later, but importantly the position will also come with an ample salary and a house," Quinneas said. "It will be a considerable upgrade from what you have had before, but it is certainly what you have earned. This will allow you and Ms. Lichenxu to settle into a happy and comfortable life."

"I am grateful for your trust," Yanis said. "I shall not let you down."

~

THE PROPOSAL TO create the Revolutionary Defence Force passed in the Great Chamber, just as Quinneas said it would. Not all of the Great Chamber members voted in favour, however. Richard, Duke of Saundley thought it was an affront to the monarchy to have a parallel force, but enough of the moderates joined with the radicals to pass the measure. The RDF would consist of one hundred soldiers, with Yanis at the top and several officers below. Its sole task would be to protect the Great Chamber and its members.

Yanis chose Clem Lake, his companion from the siege, as one of the chief officers. Clem knew little about politics, but he had served in the army for almost two decades. His experience would be critical. And like Yanis, he came from Iron Town.

To announce the creation of the RDF, Quinneas arranged for Yanis to speak to a large gathering in Iron Town, which would be one of the main recruiting grounds for the force. The air was chilly on this winter day, but they desired a large crowd and no building could accommodate it.

Nadeni stood next to Yanis on the podium, as did Quinneas and Charlotte, along with other members of the Great Chamber. All of the members shook Yanis's hand, as well as Nadeni's.

Except for Selver Bronn. After he shook Yanis's hand, he passed on to Nadeni. She did not extend her hand and neither did he. He looked at her for a moment before walking to his seat on the podium. Nadeni turned to Yanis and rolled her eyes, yet Yanis wondered if she was not equally responsible for the frigid encounter. He trusted that his relationship with Nadeni would not cause a rift with the other Great Chamber members. That would be something to discuss with her later.

Quinneas introduced Yanis to the gathered crowd that packed the square. He recalled the speech at the democratic meeting he had given soon after returning from the Dragon Isles, and how nervous he had been. So much had changed since that time. Rather than nervousness, he was now eager to speak to the people.

"I suppose I have had a great many adventures," he said at the start of his speech, knowing what the people wanted to hear. "It all began when I was sentenced to serve as a soldier in New Selver, after having been convicted for writing treasonous material against the king."

The crowd was silent, their faces staring intently at him.

"It was when I was a soldier there, sent on an expedition to a chain of uninhabited islands, that I first encountered the dragons."

The crowd hung on his every word as he recounted the two expeditions against the dragons. How he had participated in the protest against the king when he had returned to Estenland. How he had led the attack on the prison. How the sea goats had helped him to save Nadeni. How he had fought side by side with griffins, winged lions, and other sacred creatures against the Friezzian army. There was much tragedy in his adventures, but Yanis did not dwell on that. He looked over at Nadeni and the members of the Great Chamber, and he reflected on his newfound good fortune.

"All of that," he concluded, "has led me here. To ask for your support in the creation of the Revolutionary Defence Force. Long live the revolution!"

"Hurrah!" the crowd cheered.

As he stepped away from the podium, his mind turned to the job of recruiting and training this new force. It would be a difficult task... but Yanis told himself that he was the Dragon Slayer, after all.

48

CHARLOTTE

"What did you think of Yanis's speech?" Quinneas asked as he and Charlotte returned home from the slums of Iron Town. Their carriage bounced along the uneven roads as a light drizzle began to fall.

"It was better than I expected."

Quinneas cocked his head. "How do you mean?"

"You know that I had doubts about whether Yanis was right for the position. But he clearly has the support of the people. They will do whatever he says, it seems."

As they continued their journey through Iron Town, nearly all the people they spotted wore the dark green caps of the revolution.

"For such a position," Quinneas said, "the most important thing is ensuring that he has the trust of the people. The Great Chamber can only be successful if the people recognize its authority. But, if I may say, it is not necessarily a disadvantage from our perspective that Yanis lacks experience. This way, his loyalty to the Great Chamber is assured."

Charlotte nodded. Quinneas's reasoning made sense. Perhaps there was a deeper wisdom in the choice than even she had realized.

~

YANIS AND NADENI stood atop the platform of a local democratic association's banquet hall, in front of a congratulatory banner and several vases of flowers placed about the stage.

The traditional way to marry was of course in a temple, blessed in the eyes of Oqci. All marriage ceremonies, it was supposed, took after the holy wedding of Oqci and Mazir, his earthly bride from one of the primitive tribes he first encountered in Ogard. But neither Yanis nor Nadeni were believers.

Charlotte and Quinneas attended; indeed, they paid for the entire wedding, even though Yanis and Nadeni insisted it be a modest affair. Friends, well-wishers from the democratic movement, and some members from the Great Chamber attended in place of family members, of whom Yanis and Nadeni had none – or at least none with whom they were on cordial terms.

Yanis looked even more handsome than usual in a finely tailored black suit, which Quinneas had gifted him. Nadeni was adorned in a simple white lace dress. She had told Charlotte that she would dye it later so that it might be worn again. Charlotte smiled at this, for her thrift was no longer necessary now that Yanis had accepted the position as the head of the RDF. Yet Charlotte supposed such habits did not die easily.

As Yanis and Nadeni made their declarations of love at the front of the room, Charlotte's own thoughts drifted to marriage with Quinneas. Her divorce with Willien had at last become final. Inevitably, there was the usual gossip in the press, which was sometimes cruel – particularly to Willien – but it was nothing they had not expected. What was more, the process of forswearing her noble privileges had also been completed.

Freed from those hindrances, Charlotte wondered if Quinneas would ask her for marriage. She hoped he would, in fact. It was true that she now had no sources of wealth and none of the privileges that came with being a noble, like her tax exemption. But these material concerns were unimportant. For her, it was about love and companionship. She looked over at Quinneas as he watched the ceremony. As usual she could not discern what was going on inside his mind. Whenever they had talked about marriage, he often acted as if she were joking.

But they had been living together for months. This was hardly typical for unmarried people and the conservative press gave them great difficulties about this. She had no doubt that Quinneas loved her, but his innermost feelings were shrouded by an exterior she could not quite penetrate. She wondered if this was not the result of his difficult childhood.

~

"IT WAS A BEAUTIFUL CEREMONY," Charlotte said, as Yanis clumsily sat down at the table next to her and Quinneas.

The ceremony had ended and guests chattered away as they feasted and imbibed alcohol – Yanis and Quinneas especially so for the latter.

"I've never been so happy. She is very special," Yanis said, holding a glass of beer and splashing it around as he gesticulated toward Nadeni, who stood at the other end of the room. "Very special indeed. Even more than meets the eye."

"So she is, my dear friend!" said Quinneas, clapping him on the shoulder. "You two make a perfect match."

"How do you mean special?" Charlotte asked, since Yanis made the remark as if he wished to say more.

Yanis leaned close and looked around to ensure no one else could hear. In a low voice, he said, "She is descended from the Prince of Shadows. He is her great-grandfather. That is whence she gets her fighting spirit."

"That is surprising news," Charlotte said. "I'm quite sure that he left no descendants after Estenland executed him and his family. Our nation, to its shame, made sure that none remained alive."

"No, no," sputtered Yanis, perhaps embarrassed by Charlotte questioning his news, "her grandmother was spared." He looked wistfully over at Nadeni again. "A real fighter."

"Well said!" said Quinneas, glassy-eyed from the alcohol and perhaps not even fully paying attention to what Yanis was saying. "Truly well said!"

49

SAMUEL

A poster with a picture of Yanis Haller, the so-called Dragon Slayer, advertised the Revolutionary Defence Force. This force, the poster explained, would protect the Great Chamber and the revolution. And you too, it read, could be part of it.

No doubt this poster, and others like it, were hung around the docks to target the shiftless men like Samuel. With the siege lifted, work at the docks was plentiful again, but it brought him no joy. The poster, however, caught Samuel's eye.

He decided to attend one of the screenings for a lark. He had no experience in combat, but he had been a hunter in his days in New Selver. He certainly was proficient with a firearm, even if it had been many years since he had fired one.

At the Iron Town Commons, a group of men – of much the same calibre of those Samuel saw at the docks, which was to say, not good – as well as some women gathered in the grassy field for the recruitment. The weather was overcast and misty and the grass was slick. As they waited, the people talked excitedly about the great Yanis Haller as if they were school children babbling about Oqci's descent from the clouds.

"I've seen him speak before," gushed one of the men to his neighbour in line. "There is something special about the Dragon Slayer."

"I hope we shall have a chance to meet him," said the other, with a slack-jawed expression.

Samuel shook his head at their credulity.

At last, a hush fell over the crowd as Yanis ascended the creaky wooden stage and stepped toward the podium. He was handsomely dressed in the Revolutionary Defence Force's uniform of green with white and yellow trim. He was surrounded by colleagues dressed in the same uniform, as well as a lady. Samuel heard that Yanis had been shacking up with a "Denier of Oqci." That must have been her.

"Friends," Yanis said, "I am happy to see you all. Serving on the Revolutionary Defence Force is one of the most important contributions men and women like yourselves can make to our revolution. Our goal is to protect the Great Chamber from any foes and to preserve the gains of the revolution. Today, you will undertake a series of cognitive and physical tests that will help us to select suitable candidates for the RDF."

How fast could they run a thousand paces, how many push-ups could they do, how many sit-ups, and so on. Their height and weight. All of this was measured by Yanis's underlings. They were also asked their experience with firearms.

Samuel performed tolerably well at the physical tests, better than expected in fact, though his stamina and strength were not what they used to be. But the cognitive tests were where he expected to excel. A written exam tested basic skills like arithmetic and literacy, as well as more complex cognitive tasks. Additionally, there were questions about their loyalty to the revolution. Samuel finished his well before any of the others and stood to deliver the test. He looked back at the astonished faces of his fellow test-takers. "But... but... how did he finish so quickly?" they thought – or so he imagined.

SAMUEL HAD COME ONLY for a bit of fun, but by the end of the testing, he grew hopeful of being selected. To his delight, one of the officers summoned him to speak with the legendary Dragon Slayer personally.

"Eston Miller," Yanis said, eyeing Samuel's results and sitting in his chair while the officer stood behind him, "I was very impressed with your scores and would like to consider you for an officer position in the RDF, something which will require further screening. Is this something that would interest you?"

Samuel was stunned. An officer position? That was even better than he had hoped!

"Absolutely," he said quickly. "It would be an honour to serve."

Visions of being part of this elite force filled his mind. This could yet be his path to redemption. Perhaps even to becoming a hero.

Yanis's colleague, standing behind his right shoulder, narrowed his eyes at Samuel. "Is Eston Miller your real name?" Yanis looked back at his colleague with surprise.

Samuel hesitated and sputtered, "I… I don't understand…"

"It was a simple question," the man replied. "Given the results on your written test, I should have thought you could grasp it."

Yanis turned back in his chair to again look at his colleague. "State your meaning. Do you think this man is misleading us?"

"I do. I think this is Samuel Nox, the disgraced scientist. I attended several of his public lectures in Iron Town and cannot forget the face."

A chill ran through Samuel's body. His past… coming to haunt him once again! Samuel had trimmed back his side whiskers; evidently he was still recognizable.

"Is this true?" asked Yanis.

Samuel flushed as he considered his answer. "It is true," he said slowly, realizing there was no alternative. "I have gone by that name before. But there was no intent to deceive."

"No intent…!" said Yanis's exasperated colleague.

Before he could finish his thought, Yanis interrupted him. "Dr. Nox, I read about your story in the press. It seemed as though you made a grave error then, but whatever happened in your past should be no barrier to you serving in the RDF. Everyone is deserving of a second chance. Who among us can claim to be without flaws?"

Samuel's mouth dropped open as if he were one of those men he had mocked earlier. He couldn't believe his good fortune. He had underestimated Yanis. He had been too hard on those who idolized him. Maybe the stories of his greatness *were* true after all. Samuel's eyes almost welled up, thinking of his kindness. The only person who had shown him any since his fall.

"Of course," Yanis continued, "I shall need to consult with the Great Chamber leadership, but I expect no problems."

"I understand," Samuel said. "Thank you."

He shook Yanis's hand and smiled at him, though Yanis's colleague was less happy. Samuel walked away gratified for the first time in a long time. Perhaps there was an end in sight to his ordeal.

DELLIREA

It seemed like an eternity ago when Dellirea's country had discovered the dragons and was ready to begin study of the aletolium blocks that had been taken from the island. Now they languished in crates in the palace basement. After everything – the siege by the Friezzians, those awful women who had invaded the palace, the new constitution – whatever mysteries the blocks contained seemed trivial now.

Dellirea's whole world had been turned upside down. A constitution gave the people new rights never before imagined. Her noble and priestly friends lost much of their land, appropriated by the state and redistributed to the poor. She had long been a great friend of poor people, but she had to admit that she was unsure whether they were capable of the great responsibility of possessing these new rights.

But today was a special day, the celebration of Victory Day. Set in Karazin Square, a large stage had been assembled. The royal family, the high priest, the king's council, members of the Great Chamber, as well as soldiers from the Estenland army and the so-called Revolutionary Defence Force gathered there. Despite the steady drizzle, a large crowd gathered in the square, many holding umbrellas to shield themselves.

As they awaited the start of the festivities, Dellirea exchanged pleasantries with Kephalos, who by now acted as leader of the Great Chamber. "Priest Kephalos," she said, "I hope it is not inappropriate to ask you a substantive question."

"Of course not, Your Highness."

"I wish to ask why you supported extending the right to own sacred creatures to everyone, even commoners. It seems to me that this was an affront to our holy doctrines, and I must confess my surprise that you supported it. The ownership of the creatures is a strict barrier between the common people and the nobles and priests. And in breaking it, the Great Chamber has undermined one of the foundations of our society."

Kephalos contemplated her words before speaking. "Your Highness, this was a difficult decision, but my reading of Oqci's words in the original language of the holy scriptures is that when he said the sacred creatures belong to the best of us, to those with the purest hearts, he was not only referring to those from the noble classes."

"Well," Dellirea said, slightly confused, "I have also studied the ancient tongue. Even though I am not as expert as you in these matters, I find this a very unusual reading of the texts."

He did not say anything, but turned his gaze – in a condescending way – to the growing crowd in the square.

"Did you know," Dellirea continued, "that some nobles who had mismanaged their finances have decided to sell their creatures to commoners, as if they were not divine at all, but just like any other kind of property? What do you think of this?"

"I believe that the importance of the creatures is not in themselves, but the way in which they remind us of our connection to the Creator."

She was puzzled by this statement. "Are you suggesting that the creatures are not divine?"

"Not at all," he said. "Just that we must think differently about what it means for them to be divine."

Dellirea did not fully understand what he meant, but she did not like it. "Well," she said, "I think we should be careful about how this change will affect the common people. Some of them already behave no better than animals. And now we seem to be suggesting there are no differences in ranks?"

"Your Highness," Kephalos said, "I believe that the difference of ranks should be in the content of our hearts, not in any earthly titles."

Dellirea swallowed hard upon hearing this. It was deeply disturbing for her to listen to this kind of talk. And by a holy man no less! Kephalos was someone she deeply respected, yet she could hardly believe he shared the same faith as her. These were quite warped views of the doctrines of Oqci, as she understood them.

~

KEPHALOS, as the representative of the Great Chamber, began the Victory Day proceedings. In his speech, he lauded the new constitution that marked a new era in Estenland. Representatives of the rest of the Great Chamber listened, some of them donning green caps, supposedly a sign of the revolution, although they only reminded Dellirea of the hideous women who had attacked her and her family in the palace.

Dellirea's eyes fixed upon Charlotte of Evesbury, no longer a noblewoman, she had learned. Dellirea watched her closely but was careful not to stare. Charlotte was dressed very beautifully for the occasion, even if she too wore one of the green caps. Dellirea was, however, discomforted about the way she sat next to the radical, Quinneas Raeil. Charlotte seemed to be very familiar with him, yet, as far as Dellirea knew, they were unmarried.

Another speech was given by the new high priest, Omephas, before Dellirea's father addressed the audience in the final speech of the day.

"Subjects," Aramal began, "we meet today to remember our heroic victory against Friezzia three decades ago."

"I am not your subject, I am a citizen," some boorish person called out from the crowd.

Dellirea's father ignored this remark and pressed on with his speech. "My father, Andamar the Great, led our nation to victory then, just as I have led us to victory against the same foe only a short time ago."

"You didn't lead us to victory at all," another voice cried out.

"It was the Dragon Slayer!" someone else shouted. This prompted scattered cheers but also some jeers.

Dellirea could not believe such disobedience. She grew nervous as she looked at her father. His breathing became heavier, and she could tell he was struggling to remain composed in the face of this insolence. Dellirea noticed that Charlotte whispered something to Quinneas. Even they looked uneasy with the boldness of the crowd, some of whom waved flags of green, white, and yellow.

"Yes," her father resumed, ignoring the interruptions, "it was a great victory. And demonstrated the value of wise leadership."

"Of the Great Chamber," someone in the crowd remarked. Laughter followed.

Aramal's face grew red. He appeared ready to explode. Kephalos, however, quickly made his way to the podium. "Friends, you must respect His Majesty King Aramal and remain silent during his speech."

The audience quieted and Dellirea's father hurried to finish before he could be undermined once again. But his voice wavered during the rest of the speech. His confidence was clearly sapped by the great disrespect shown by the people.

It made Dellirea think about her conversation with Kephalos earlier. All these changes – in the government, in the ideas about the holy doctrines – were beginning to have bad effects on the people. They were losing respect for their betters.

But a voice inside her said that it was unfair to prohibit the people from having a say. They had legitimate grievances, it was true, and sometimes as the result of her father's own policies. Sometimes she regretted that her father ever pursued that silly adventure with the dragons.

THAT EVENING, Dellirea ate dinner with her mother and father, alone. Her father insisted that he could not bear to eat under the watchful gaze of nobles and others at court, as was common. His head was downcast as he moved his food about his plate.

"Bring more wine," he ordered one of the servants. When his glass was filled, he glugged it down. "How dare they treat me like that? How dare they?"

Dellirea and her mother looked at one another, unsure of how to respond.

"The people were very disrespectful today," Dellirea said evenly, avoiding eye contact.

"I was so embarrassed," added her mother.

Her father raised his eyebrow at her. "You were embarrassed? You? Think about what I had to endure, giving a speech while these brutes guffaw and babble!"

"Perhaps you need to be more assertive in your speeches," she responded. "To command the people's respect."

Her father huffed. "Bravala, frankly, I blame you." Pointing his fork toward her, he continued, "You haven't taken your duties seriously since the day you became queen! You have done nothing but bring gossip and rumours upon us with your behaviour. Is it any wonder the idea of royalty has been cheapened?"

"Father, please," Dellirea said, "that is not fair to mother."

Neither her mother nor father paid Dellirea any mind. "Me?" her mother said, holding her glass of wine and sloshing it around as she spoke. "Are you serious? Don't pretend as though your stupid decisions did not lead us here. You and your obsession with those dragons! If you hadn't been so stupid –"

"I was only looking out for the glory of our country!" her father thundered. "I did what any king would have done. It is not my fault these ungrateful fools cannot see that!"

"Please, mother and father!" Dellirea interjected. "Stop it! It does no good to talk about who is to blame."

"Glory of the country? Please!" her mother fired back, completely ignoring Dellirea. "It was your own selfishness. Your own ego!"

"I'm sorry I ever married you. I should have left you to rot in Esbeck with the rest of your inbred family."

"I would've been much happier there than in this shithole, believe me!"

A fire was growing inside Dellirea. She was almost shaking with anger. Suddenly, without thinking, she yelled, as loudly as she could, "You're both fucking wretches!"

Her mother and father became silent and darted their heads toward Dellirea, their eyes wide with disbelief.

Dellirea was shocked at herself. She looked back at them, embarrassed. She knew not whence that outburst had come. The servants slunk quietly to the edge of the room.

"I… I'm sorry," she said, "mother and father… for uttering such profanity. For such disrespect."

"Well…" her father said, stunned, "that's… that's alright."

"Yes… we should not have been quarrelling," said her mother. "We're… we're sorry about that."

"Yes, we're sorry," her father said. "This new situation has placed a great strain upon us all."

SAMUEL

Two days after the trials for the RDF, Samuel received a letter from Yanis. This would undoubtedly inform him of the next stage in the officer recruitment process. He tried not to get ahead of himself, but it was difficult to resist the thought that if he managed to redeem himself, perhaps... perhaps he might yet win the love of Greta. He would not be a famed scientist after all, and he was hardly attractive. Yet he thought of how sharp he would look in his green officer's uniform. She would surely respect him then!

Samuel hurried to recover his letter opener and cut open the seal. His eyes scanned the letter eagerly.

But his heart sank as he read the words.

Dear Dr. Nox,

After discussion with the leadership of the Great Chamber, I regret that we have decided against considering you for a position as officer. The decision is final and was made with careful deliberation. I wish you well and thank you again for your willingness to serve the people.

Long live the revolution!

Yours,

High Commander Haller, RDF

Samuel crumpled up the piece of paper and threw it to the ground as hard as he could. He shook with rage. His mind raced through the scenarios. Who had betrayed him? Who? Not Yanis. But what of the other members of the Great Chamber?

Samuel scratched furiously at his right forearm. Then his left buttock. Then everywhere. He needed to get the sulfur.

Wait.

He froze in the middle of the room.

Quinneas! No, Quinneas could never let Samuel gain such a position, he realized. To have helped one of the most infamous scoundrels in Goldhall avoid prosecution for his crimes! Then to have him serving as an officer. No, that would draw too much controversy to him. It had to be Quinneas.

Samuel paced around his apartment, scratching, hot with anger.

~

EVERYTHING SAMUEL HAD HOPED for but never thought possible when he was a young man was now happening: a revolution had taken away the king's power and given it to the people. But now that he had seen it come to pass, now that he understood more about human nature, he realized how stupid he had been.

These thoughts had danced around his mind all night, interrupting his sleep. He had been awake for some time and he slowly emerged from bed as the sun rose.

Samuel prepared for another day at the docks, however much he despised it. He dreaded seeing once more these groups of poor workers strutting around with an unearned sense of superiority. They thought they were as good as nobles just because some document said so? What a fate!

As he opened the morning newspaper, however, the headline immediately drew his attention: "QUINNEAS RAEIL QUESTIONED ABOUT CONNECTION TO SAMUEL NOX."

Samuel read the article gleefully as it recounted how Quinneas had acted as his lawyer and how he had helped Samuel avoid prosecution in the case. Now Quinneas would know how it felt to be ruined!

Samuel's blood, however, began to boil as the article quoted Quinneas: "I helped Dr. Nox as a favour to someone who was reputed to be an able scientist. Dr. Nox told me that he had information on the identity of the men but did not say that he had received the bodies to dissect. I did not inquire into the information that Mr. Nox possessed, but had I known the full details, I never would have represented him. I deeply regret that my involvement meant Dr. Nox was never prosecuted. I believe his fate should have been the same as the men who were hanged."

The liar! The miserable liar! Samuel fumed. Quinneas knew exactly what information Samuel had when he agreed to represent him.

❧

THAT EVENING, Samuel lay in bed, sore from the day's work. Itches developed in new places just as soon as he scratched one away, and thoughts kept spinning through his mind. Thoughts about the supposed revolution. And he needed to get them out.

He left his bed, put on his robe, lit a candle, and sat down at his desk. Over the course of several hours, he scrawled out dozens of pages. His wrist was cramped from the long session of writing as the first signs of daylight streamed through the openings in the curtains.

It was called, simply, *A Revolution of Dirt*.

"Human beings are equal," he wrote on the first page. "We are all equally dirt. We were no better than dirt before the revolution, and we shall be no better than dirt after it."

The book allowed him to express his opinions on all the leading figures of the revolution. Yanis, the so-called "Dragon Slayer," Kephalos, Charlotte, the king and queen, and the beloved princess. Frauds! All of them!

But he reserved his strongest condemnation for Quinneas Raeil, a lying, two-faced, opportunist hack with delusions of grandeur. Many had even forgotten that he was born a bastard. And that his real name was not Quinneas at all, but simply "Quin." He only adopted the longer version to differentiate himself from the lower classes. Completely lacking in principles, he would sell out anyone to get what he wanted.

Samuel knew all this from firsthand experience. Quinneas knew exactly what Samuel had done when he agreed to help, then abandoned him when he was no longer useful. And, not content with ruining Samuel once, Quinneas next denied him the chance to serve his country in the RDF.

Raeil, the great fraud, was the perfect representation of the revolution.

~

IN THE COMING DAYS, Samuel revised the manuscript, polishing it to a state he was happy with. But who would ever agree to print such a thing? No publisher would dare question the great revolution. Every publisher Samuel approached rejected it.

After weeks of futility, an idea came to him. He was going about it all wrong.

He contacted someone who was no friend of his, but who was no friend of the revolution either. This, Samuel supposed, made them allies.

Samuel sent a calling card to Richard, Duke of Saundley, along with the manuscript pages, and received an invitation to Richard's estate to discuss the matter.

He arrived at the appointed time and Richard hastened to welcome him inside.

"Well, Dr. Nox," he said, as the two of them took their seats, "you have authored quite a book. Your dissection of the revolutionary leaders is masterful."

"I suppose I do have some experience with dissections," Samuel said.

Richard grimaced, perhaps regretting his choice of words. "To the matter at hand," he pressed on, "I know of a publisher who would be suitable. I must insist on one condition, however."

"Name it."

"There are some offending passages about myself that I wish you to excise. I need not be praised, but I do not wish to be besmirched either, especially if I am arranging the publication."

It was true that Samuel skewered Richard in the book as well. But could he compromise his artistic vision? His genius?

"What say you, Nox?"

If it was his only hope to see the work published, then Samuel had no choice.

"I shall see that the offending passages are removed."

MUCH TO SAMUEL'S DELIGHT – much to his surprise – the book sold out its initial print run. Bookshops could not keep it on the shelves and soon another printing was ordered. Then another.

Publicly, many denied having read it, or they protested that they read it merely out of curiosity, to see the ramblings of a bitter and mentally unstable man. But Samuel thought many secretly enjoyed it. And maybe some even agreed with him.

All of those critiqued in the book refused a comment to the press, including Quinneas, except to deny again that he knew anything of Samuel's crimes. To see the humourless leaders of the revolution squirming around, trying to deal with his criticisms, brought Samuel great joy.

And his skin ailment even seemed to be improving.

DELLIREA

"Remember your great aunt falling asleep during the speeches?" Dellirea's father laughed.

"I was mortified!" her mother replied. "She had drunk at least two bottles of sweetberry wine herself by then."

Dellirea could hardly believe the change in her parents. Her mother and father laughing at the dinner table. Actually *smiling* at one another!

"And," her father said, barely able to contain himself, "when she woke up in the middle of the Duke of Hornbeck's speech and began clapping, then collapsed back onto the table." Her father pantomimed the actions as the two guffawed.

"Oh please, stop it!" her mother protested, though it was clear she enjoyed reminiscing about their wedding.

Dellirea could not help but laugh at the absurdity of the scene, though the abuse of alcohol so described was hardly something to be celebrated.

"Did this not create a scandal?" she asked, wishing to contribute to the conversation.

"After the ceremony," her father said, "everyone was in a pleasant mood, so no one paid her any mind. Though I suppose the Duke of Hornbeck was rather ruffled by this breach of decorum." Her father took a drink of his coffee and rested back in his chair. "Dear Oqci, it will be twenty years in a few months."

"So it will," her mother said, reaching across the table to rest her hand on her husband's.

Dellirea was heartened to see such tenderness between them. In the weeks since their awkward conversation over dinner, the two were getting on better. Her mother spent less time at her private residence and more time in the palace with her father. The difficulties of the past year had clearly put a great strain upon their relationship, yet they were finally adjusting to the new situation. The more Dellirea thought of it, there was nothing to stop the family leading a happy life, governing in partnership with the Great Chamber.

And maybe it was even for the best to work together with the people.

∼

ON A BRIGHT MORNING that signalled the first signs of spring, Dellirea had her servants dress her in modest clothing. She was to attend the urban charity centre to feed the poor, as she did once per week. Poverty in the city was not so bad since the siege, but the poor would always be with them, Dellirea knew.

As she exited her room to leave, however, her father was there waiting.

"Delli, you are not to attend that charity centre today."

"Why not?" she said uneasily.

"Or any other day, I'm afraid. I have some important news for you, and I am worried that you are not going to like it. But we have no choice."

Dellirea grew worried. "What is it?"

He led her back inside her room and bid the servants to exit. He slowly shut the door behind them. When he was certain no one lingered outside, he said, "Tonight, our family will leave for Friezzia."

"Whatever do you mean? For a vacation?"

"It will be no vacation, Delli. We will be staying there for quite some time."

So overwhelmed and confused was Dellirea that she could muster no response.

"Our situation here has become intolerable," her father continued. "I cannot live like a prisoner here, subject to the rule of our inferiors. Treated as a laughingstock by the people. No, I cannot do it."

"I don't understand." Her head was suddenly spinning. "How can we leave? And to go to Friezzia?"

"You must mention this to no one else, but since the elections to the Great Chamber, we have been corresponding with the Friezzian royal family. King Hyazaral sympathizes with our situation. In the past, we have been enemies, but he recognizes that a threat to monarchy in one country is a threat to monarchy everywhere. He has already sheltered some noble families from Estenland, and he has promised us safe passage across the border. Once there, we shall live in exile and his government will help us take back our rightful rule."

"But this is illogical," Dellirea said. "Why would the Friezzians help us?"

"Once we are back on the throne of Estenland and can reign without interference," he said, "we shall ensure that our country is a close ally of Friezzia, and we shall share our resources with them."

Dellirea could not believe what she was hearing. "In other words, we shall be their pawns?"

"Never mind what we shall be. The important thing is that we shall have our rightful rule. My birthright… and yours!"

"I shall not go!"

"It is not an option," he said. "Listen to me, Dellirea. I know that you are a very charming, kind-hearted girl, but I am your father and I am telling you – not asking you – what will be done. My decision is final. Pack your belongings and do not leave your room until I summon you."

With that, he marched off.

Dellirea's world had fallen apart. Her future, previously so certain, now seemed impossible to imagine.

What would Friezzia be like? She had studied the country in detail and could speak their language… but to live there? And she could hardly believe they would be treated well. Friezzia had just attacked them months ago! It was incredibly naïve to think that the Friezzian royal family would be happy to see them. After their victory against them in the Great War, Estenland had denuded the country of as many resources, not to mention sacred creatures, as they could take. And how could they possibly make it to Friezzia without being noticed?

~

JUST BEFORE SUNSET, Dellirea was summoned by her father to meet the rest of the family in the menagerie behind the palace. There awaited her mother, aunts, uncles, and cousins.

The air was cool outside and Dellirea wrapped her arms around herself for warmth. She still knew not how they would be travelling. But then appeared Rodnel, the one who had designed the war machine. He grinned widely, although how he could be smiling at a time like this, Dellirea knew not.

"Everyone's here," Rodnel said. "Do not move a muscle!" He hurried into one of the stables in the menagerie.

Seconds later, a regal purple-and-gold carriage emerged, pulled by six winged horses, with Rodnel in the driver's seat. The carriage, he explained, climbing down, was equipped with a kind of fin on either side. This would allow the carriage to remain airborne as the horses flew. The Friezzian border would take days to reach on horseback, but it would be much quicker by air.

Some of the other family members, who had also been kept uninformed about the plans, expressed their disbelief, but Rodnel assured them it was perfectly safe.

"The horses will need to land several times before we reach the border, for rest," he continued, "but I have selected the six fastest flyers in our stables and we shall thus arrive in Friezzia by morning."

Dellirea was skeptical, but Rodnel seemed confident his idea would work, and her father had absolute faith in him.

They all wedged their belongings into the rear of the carriage and climbed in. It was cramped with all ten of them there, but comfort was the least of their concerns.

Rodnel sat outside the carriage in the driver's seat. "Hang on tight," he called back to the passengers.

At a straightaway on the palace grounds, he gave the signal and the winged horses began galloping furiously. The clap of their hooves on the ground grew ever more rapid. Faster and faster now their carriage moved along the ground. The trees and gardens rushed past in a blur.

Faster, faster, and the sound of clopping hooves dissipated as the horses rose two-by-two. The wheels of their carriage lifted from the ground, with the air whipping underneath the fins, pushing it up in line with the horses. Wind flew inside the carriage, blowing around Dellirea's hair. She could not believe it: Rodnel's idea had worked!

Her father smiled widely and clapped his hands together triumphantly. "We've done it!"

They all laughed joyously and looked at one another with anticipation.

Dellirea peeked out the window. They were now high above the city. Scattered lights dotted the urban landscape. Smoke billowed from a few of the factories in Iron Town.

Ahead, their horses' wings beat steadily as the carriage glided along with them. The thrill and magic of the ride had taken away all of Dellirea's worries about Friezzia. Anything seemed possible now.

THEY DESCENDED several hours later on a deserted road outside a small village. The horses slowed the beating of their wings as they got nearer to the ground. Then nearer still. *Crash!* Dellirea clutched her seat as the wheels hit the ground. Their carriage bounced up and down before it regained its balance. The horses ran ever more slowly as they came to a stop. A bumpier landing than Dellirea had imagined, but a landing all the same.

They exited the carriage to stretch their legs. The sleepy village was illuminated only by moonlight, but soon a gas torch was lit.

The horses rested and drank some water while Dellirea's father and the other men gathered around Rodnel's unfurled map. They were about a third of the way to the border, Dellirea overheard them saying. If everything went according to schedule, they would land once more before reaching Friezzia, this time just before dawn. The last portion of the trip would take place in daylight, but they would be so close to Friezzia that they need not worry.

While they waited, Dellirea's father brought out a bottle of liquor and passed it around to the other members of the family. "Delli, here, have some."

She had never drunk alcohol before. It was, she knew, a source of great malady in the world. It weakened the impulses of men and women, who went on to commit evil acts under its influence.

"I shall decline," she said, "but thank you."

"Come," he insisted, "we're celebrating."

He thrust it into her hands and she looked at the bottle uneasily. At last she relented and took a sip. The liquid burned her throat as she swallowed. Her eyes watered slightly. It was deeply unpleasant. Its warmth spread through her and she became a little dizzy. She wanted no more.

Following their rest, they rose once more into the air. Their carriage was considerably merrier after the alcohol. The adults broke into song. Dellirea looked over at her three younger cousins. They were the only sober ones. Dellirea felt a strange sensation from the drink and found herself laughing at jokes which she usually would not find amusing. She resolved, however, not to descend to the silliness of the others.

Endless stretches of darkened forest and farmland were all she saw for hours, until at last, the slightest hues of purple began to appear in the sky.

THEY TOOK to the land for the final rest stop at the first signs of morning. Dellirea and the others exited the carriage and stepped down onto the empty road. She was growing ever more tired, having been unable to sleep with the wind rushing all around her in the carriage.

As they talked by the roadside, giving their horses time to

rest, Dellirea suddenly heard the clip-clopping of hooves approaching, and voices.

"Are those winged horses?" a woman said.

Dellirea panicked. How did they not notice anyone else here?

Nearing them were two peasants, a man and a woman, riding on donkeys who pulled carts behind them. Dellirea and the rest of the family tried to scramble into the carriage before the pair saw them, but Dellirea's aunt and uncle and cousins did not enter in time.

"Are you nobles?" the man said in a tone of stupefied awe.

"We are," said Uncle Lochmar. "But we need to be going now."

"Wow," the woman said, "they're so beautiful! I've never seen anything like these before. Can I touch them, my lord? Only for a moment."

These were simple, honest people, pure-hearted and uncorrupted by city life, Dellirea realized. Sitting across from her in the carriage was her father, and from their talk, his expression softened.

"I'm sorry," said Lochmar, "we are in a rush and must be going."

"We're so pleased to meet you, my lord," the peasant man said. "Where are you travelling from?"

"We must be going," Dellirea's uncle said again.

Dellirea's father suddenly stepped from the carriage, even as her mother tried to stop him.

"Brother, we can spare a few minutes to talk," Aramal said, climbing to the ground. "We are from the capital. And of course you may pet the horses."

"Oh my," said the woman, with an astonished look on her face, "I'd sure like to visit the capital someday." She walked past the carriage window and put her hand gently on one of the horses, stroking its mane. The peasants clearly had no idea of their identity.

The rest of the family exited the carriage, realizing it was safe.

"Let us have a drink together!" Dellirea's father said, hoisting up a new bottle of liquor.

Rodnel whispered, "Your Majesty, we really must be going."

Dellirea's father waved aside Rodnel as he opened the bottle. Glasses were quickly procured. The sky was growing ever bluer as the sun rose.

"What great fortune," said the man, "to meet kind nobles such as yourselves!"

As the drink was poured into the glasses, Aramal said, "Dellirea, come, you too."

"Dellirea?" the woman said. Her head tilted as she looked at Dellirea. "Why, that's the princess's name!"

Dellirea's face grew hot as the two peasants looked at her admiringly. Their heads darted back and forth at the family members. "If that's the princess, then…" the man said, trailing off as he looked at Dellirea's mother and father.

Quickly making the connection, the two dropped to their knees and bowed at her father's feet. "Your Majesty," the woman said, "we're not worthy of you."

"Yes, Your Majesty," said the man, "we're not worthy."

"Please, please," Dellirea's father said. "On your feet. It is always nice to meet some of my subjects."

They slowly stood. Drinks were poured as the group laughed and conversed. From the conversation, it seemed they had little idea about the revolution. The peasants never considered why the entire royal family might be passing through their small village in the early hours of the day. It was, to them, just a miracle that was not to be examined too deeply.

"Your Majesty," said the woman, "my mother is dying. She is sick in bed. Might you take a few minutes to visit her and lay your hands upon her? Our cabin is not far."

Before anyone could stop him, Dellirea's father said, "Of course, we can take a few minutes."

Dellirea and the rest of the family followed them to a shabby cabin at the end of a field. They could not all fit into the house at the same time. Dellirea's aunts and uncles and cousins waited outside while Dellirea and her parents entered.

An ancient woman lay in bed covered in blankets. "Wake up, ma," said the woman. The old woman half-opened her eyes. She was groggy and confused. "Look, ma, it's the king and the queen and the princess."

"Really?" the old woman said in a wispy voice, barely audible. "Really? Oh, isn't that wonderful? Just wonderful."

She might not have understood what she was looking at, but she certainly knew that whatever she was supposed to be seeing was indeed amazing. Dellirea's father approached and placed his hand upon the woman's cheek as she lay still.

"Thank you, Your Majesty," said the woman's daughter, bowing once more. "Her health will surely improve now."

Dellirea's father nodded seriously. "It is my duty as king. I wish you all good fortune."

The peasant couple said "thank you" over and over as Dellirea and her parents exited the cabin. Stepping out into the open air, the sun beat down upon them.

"Your Majesty," said Rodnel, with an anxious tone, "we must depart now. We still have a considerable distance to travel."

They said their goodbyes to the peasant couple before entering the carriage. They soon galloped away, back into the air. There would be no further stops until Friezzia.

Dellirea noticed that her father wiped away a small tear as he looked back down at the two humble peasants waving goodbye to the flying carriage.

YANIS

The sound of frantic rapping upon Yanis's bedroom door jolted him awake.

He forced open his eyes. The room was still dark. Nadeni rustled beside him. "What is it?"

More pounding.

"I know not."

Yanis put on his robe and hurried to the door, behind which he found one of his RDF officers. Yanis needed to come to the palace right away, the officer explained. It was an emergency: The king and queen and the entire royal family had gone missing!

Yanis quickly dressed. With the officer, he travelled by carriage to the palace. The driver urged on the horse as it galloped through the quiet city streets, the sun just beginning to rise.

Yanis rushed inside the palace and was led into the king's council room, where he found Kephalos and Quinneas seated; Dario paced the room nervously.

Quinneas explained the situation. One of the palace guards had become suspicious when the king's young niece, who always woke during the night, did not make a peep. Worried that something was amiss, he checked her room, only to discover her missing. Searches to discover her whereabouts revealed that the entire family too was missing.

Yanis eyed Dario, a small, weaselly man, with suspicion as Quinneas told him all this.

"He claims no knowledge of their location," said Quinneas, sensing Yanis's thoughts.

"I am just as disturbed by their disappearance as all of you," Dario said. "I have arranged for a full search of the palace, and for all of the palace guards on duty yesterday and overnight to speak with us."

Throughout the early hours of the morning, a parade of witnesses came through the council room for questioning. One guard told them that he was instructed to keep watch on Dellirea for the entire day to ensure that she packed her things and did not leave her room for any reason. He insisted he knew not the reason for these instructions, only that they came from Aramal himself.

Other guards claimed that they saw flying horses pulling a carriage through the sky in the evening. This sounded absurd to Yanis, but three different guards claimed to have seen it, and six winged horses were missing from the menagerie. All the guards confirmed the carriage was flying west.

Yanis tried to make sense of the situation. "Where could they possibly be going? And for what purpose?"

Quinneas walked angrily around the room. "Wherever they are going, they are plainly up to no good." His striking green eyes bore down on Dario. Quinneas walked slowly toward him as Dario backed away. "Where are they?"

"I know not!" said Dario, cowering in the corner as Quinneas loomed over him. "I swear it. I swear on the Book of Oqci that I know not!"

Quinneas stepped back from Dario and shook his head in anger.

"We must telegraph our posts around the country making it known that the royal family is unaccounted for," Yanis said, as Kephalos nodded his agreement.

Quinneas turned back to Dario. "See that it is done!"

Quinneas was not technically in charge, nor was Kephalos, nor was Yanis. It was not clear exactly *who* was in charge with the king missing. But Dario meekly obeyed the order.

THAT MORNING, telegrams arrived from across the country, responding to the requests for information. Some claimed that the royal family visited with a group of peasants in a village in the west of the country. As Yanis and the others placed markers upon the map of every location a flying carriage had been spotted, a pattern became clear to all of them.

"They are heading toward Friezzia," Quinneas said, putting into words what they were all realizing. "They surely intend to undermine the revolution from abroad. They must be colluding with the Friezzians!" Turning to Dario, he shouted, "Did you have anything to do with this? Did you have any knowledge?"

"No! No!" Dario protested. "Please!"

Even Yanis felt sympathy for poor Dario as Quinneas berated him. "Please, Quinneas," Yanis said, stepping forward and clasping his shoulder, "I believe he is telling the truth."

"They must be stopped at all costs," Quinneas said, brushing him away. "We cannot allow their carriage to cross the border into the territory of our enemy. If they must be shot down, then so be it."

"Shoot at the king?" Dario said. "This is not right."

"If they are trying to flee to our enemy, this is treason," exclaimed Quinneas.

Quinneas was right, of course. Yanis turned to Dario. "They are nearing the border. And we must act quickly. If they are crossing into Friezzia, they will certainly pass over Winterbridge. The carriage must not be allowed to cross! Any means necessary must be used to stop it."

"I can't," Dario said, almost pleading with himself as much as anyone else. "I can't."

He turned to look at Kephalos, who offered no help. "Mr. Raeil and Mr. Haller are correct, I'm afraid."

"Send the message that the carriage must be shot down if necessary," Yanis said, "or, as High Commander of the Revolutionary Defence Force, I shall."

Dario swallowed hard. Yanis reasoned that Dario knew he must act now if he wished to preserve whatever scrap of authority he still had. "Very well," Dario said weakly. "I shall send the order to our fortress at Winterbridge: Shoot down the carriage."

He wrote out the message and sent it to be telegraphed. Dario looked up at Yanis and the others after he handed away the message. "May Oqci forgive me."

DELLIREA

The family took much too long visiting the peasants, Dellirea realized, even if it had been an agreeable visit. It was now late in the morning. They should have been in Friezzia by now.

Dellirea was exhausted, confused, panicked. She had barely slept at all, except perhaps for a few moments. And the lingering feeling of the alcoholic drink made her perception of time unclear. Was it only last night that they had made their escape?

But soon they would be in Friezzia. They would need not touch down again. Rodnel assured them the horses had gotten plenty of rest with the long stop in the village.

The bright sun gave an excellent view of the green countryside below, carved out into neat squares. Dellirea thought of the simple peasants down below and the way in which they adored the royal family. Did not their honest, unconditional love for them show the value of the holy doctrines and the need for a monarch to guide the people? She imagined that someday, her father would be back on the throne, ruling unchallenged. And she, too, would one day rule.

Her mind's wandering was stopped by a terrible, loud cracking sound from below.

"What was that?" someone said.

"It sounded like… gunfire?" said another.

They all crowded at the windows to get a look. At ground level, a detachment of soldiers were grouped in formation, raising their guns at the carriage.

Crack. Crack. Crack.

A clang came from the outside of the carriage as a bullet careened off it. Everyone shrieked in terror.

"Dear Oqci, fly away from them!" Dellirea's father shouted to Rodnel.

"What do you think I'm doing?" Rodnel shouted back.

Another crack. One of the flying horses whinnied in pain. Rivulets of blood danced through the air, splashing on the front window of the carriage.

Dellirea's heart pounded so hard that it felt like it was going to come right out of her chest.

Crack. Crack. Crack.

The horse went limp. The others flapped their wings harder to keep their comrade afloat. Their carriage wobbled to the side and continued its flight crooked. The carriage dipped quickly down, and all the passengers shrieked before the horses steadied them.

"Get us out of here!" Aramal commanded Rodnel.

More cracks came from below. Another of the horses cried out and went limp. They were dipping up and down, struggling to remain airborne.

"We can't make it!" Rodnel shouted back to the passengers. "We need to land."

Crack. Crack. Crack. More bullets whizzed past.

They descended rapidly and uneasily. A clearing down below seemed a suitable landing spot. Dellirea peeked out the window to the ground, where the soldiers mounted their horses and rode to where they were making their descent.

No one in the carriage said anything. Dellirea's father and mother gripped her sweaty hands tightly. The colour had disappeared from their faces.

"Hang on!" Rodnel shouted as they approached the ground. "Hang on!"

Closer, closer, closer. Crash! They hit the ground. Screams of terror filled the carriage. The bodies of the dead horses hit first. And hard. The other horses struggled not to trip over them as they were dragged along the grassy terrain, but they all collapsed into a heap. The carriage bounced wildly as it landed, throwing the family about. It tipped onto its side, scraping across the grass, before at last it came to a stop.

Dellirea lay in a pile of her relatives on one side of the carriage. Her younger cousins were wailing. Rodnel yanked open the carriage door and helped them out one by one. Dellirea was sore from the crash but not seriously hurt, nor were any of the other members of their party. Three of the horses, however, had been badly injured on the landing. They writhed on the ground, their legs broken.

"What are we going to do?" Dellirea's father demanded. The carriage was clearly unusable now. And they had only one good horse left.

Not far away, Dellirea could hear the soldiers' horses galloping toward them. They would soon be captured and taken back to Goldhall, Dellirea realized. Dear Oqci. What would they do to them?

"Take Dellirea," her mother said to Rodnel. "Fly her to safety in Friezzia!"

"Yes," said her father. "Take her!"

"No! No! I can't leave you two," Dellirea said, tears suddenly rolling down her cheeks. "I can't!"

"There is only one horse left!" Aramal said. "Only Rodnel knows how to ride it and only he knows the route to Friezzia. We shall stay here and appeal for mercy. Hurry!"

Dellirea didn't wish to go. She couldn't! But she feared what would happen if she stayed… And there was no time to wait.

She hugged her mother and father. The two squeezed her hard and told her how much they loved her.

"I love you both," she said, breaking away to wipe the tears from her face.

Rodnel unharnessed the horse and began putting a saddle on it, as she said goodbyes to the rest of her family.

"Let us hurry, princess," he said.

She raced back to Rodnel who helped her climb up. As the soldiers' horses trotted into the clearing, Rodnel gave the signal. At once, the horse galloped ever faster in the open field and soon they were airborne. Dellirea looked back behind her to the earth below.

"It will be all right, Delli!" her mother called out.

"We love you!" shouted her father. He ran to the soldiers as they raised their rifles. He motioned for them to stop and indicated his surrender.

From high in the air, Dellirea tilted her gaze back down to the earth. There the soldiers gathered around her family and led them away as prisoners.

Ahead of her, Dellirea could see across the border into Friezzia, her new home.

CHARLOTTE

From the balcony of the palace, Charlotte and Quinneas watched a procession of the Revolutionary Defence Force, led by Yanis, escorting the king and the rest of the royal family through the city streets. Yanis sat in the lead carriage, next to the driver; the one behind contained the royal family. The carriage was closed, so Charlotte and Quinneas could only imagine what they looked like inside.

The crowd that lined the streets heckled and threw refuse at the king's carriage. The RDF soldiers who walked alongside the procession pushed the crowd from the carriage's pathway. Yanis waved to his supporters in the crowd. From his proud expression, he looked to Charlotte as if he had personally caught the king.

"That scoundrel," said Quinneas, leaning upon the balcony and glaring at the procession. "How dare he? He thought he could slip away? Now he will see justice awaits him. And his family."

Charlotte placed her hand on Quinneas's forearm. "They will face justice, Quin. Not to worry."

He brushed away her hand and turned to her, annoyed. "Haven't I told you not to call me Quin? It reminds me too much of my childhood."

"I'm sorry," she said, and softly added, "I think Quin is a nice name."

Quinneas said nothing more as he continued to stare at the royal family's carriage.

THE GREAT CHAMBER, with ascending rows of benches on either side, was filled with raucous members. The royal family was being held elsewhere in the palace, under close surveillance. Alongside Quinneas and other radicals, who sat on the left benches of the chamber, Charlotte rose to speak. "Friends, the actions of the king and queen and the rest of the royal family have placed us in turmoil. The question presents itself: what is to be done with them? All evidence indicates that the royal family was colluding with the Friezzians and planned to escape there. Friends, the king and queen have committed treason. They must be tried, publicly, in front of the eyes of the people, in front of the Great Chamber."

Shouts of "hear, hear" rang out throughout the chamber, even from the more conservative members.

The chamber secretary asked for a roll-call vote to decide on the matter, though there was little doubt of the outcome.

Each member stood, one-by-one, to signal yes or no to the public trial. The parade of yeses was such that a rare no vote elicited considerable surprise and momentarily hushed the chamber before the next yes vote again boosted the room's mood. Even the moderates like Koralo and Richard, Duke of Saundley, voted yes.

At the end of the vote, the yeses took it 290–10, with only a handful of the king's most loyal supporters opposing.

Quinneas spoke next. "Surely," he said, "we cannot allow the king to have any further powers while we decide upon his fate. I propose, therefore, that we immediately suspend the monarchy's powers and make the Great Chamber the sole government in the country."

Lord Saundley rose amidst murmuring in the chamber. "Have we the power to do this?"

"Our constitution allows for such a measure to be taken," said Quinneas.

He was right, Charlotte knew. It was a provision in the constitution that no one thought would be used so soon, but one that was carefully inserted by Quinneas in the event of treason. Charlotte marvelled at his foresight on this matter which, at the time, even she had overlooked.

The members talked amongst themselves. Taking such a vote

would make the country a monarchy without a monarch. But what choice was there? They could not allow the king to have power while he and the rest of the royal family faced trial.

The vote was closer this time, but it still passed handily: 196–104. As the votes were read out, Charlotte and the others on the left side stood from the benches and shook hands, congratulating one another. Charlotte could barely believe it: The monarchy was, for all intents and purposes, no more.

SAMUEL

Samuel had an extra measure of verve in each step he took on the way to the docks this morning. The thought of what was to come filled him with pleasure.

Since writing his little screed about the revolution, things had improved for him. The book had become something of a sensation, and even though most of the profits were gobbled up by the publisher, they provided him with more than enough to be comfortable.

And with the upcoming trial of the king and queen, there would soon be need for a second edition of the book. Already it had been revealed that the king and queen had been corresponding with the Friezzian ruler. Letters were discovered detailing the whole conspiracy. But of course Samuel had seen the whole thing coming. Aramal was at once too weak and too proud to be able to govern.

Not that it mattered what happened with the king and queen. Whether the king ruled, or the people, humans were only fated for hardship and misery, Samuel knew. If anything, the people needed a strong ruler to command them, to dominate them, to shape their miserable lives into something valuable.

When Samuel arrived that morning to the docks, observing the men there only confirmed his opinion. Those men who laughed at him. Who mocked him. Who looked down their noses at him. To talk about equality was a sick joke. As if these men were somehow equal to their social betters!

As the masses assembled to fight over the table scraps of work, Samuel climbed atop a crate. The men all gawked at him. The curiosity of the bosses was also piqued.

"You," he said. Some of their heads turned toward him. "That's right, you!" Confused stares greeted him. "You ignorant louts. For many months I have worked beside you, enduring your sneers at what you imagined my own shortcomings. But all the while you had no idea that I had more intellect in my pinky finger than you had in your entire brains!"

"Who is this man?" said one of the foremen. The audience chatted away, trying to determine who this mysterious man was, as if they had never seen him before.

"Who am I? Who... who am I?" Samuel said, his anger giving way to confusion. "Have you not realized I have been working alongside you all these months?"

Puzzled conversations continued. Some seemed to have a vague recollection of him, others insisted they had never seen him before.

This was not at all like what Samuel had planned.

"Well," he said, the conviction in his voice deflating, "what I wished to say is... I wished to say... well... never mind."

What Samuel imagined as a triumphant statement of his resignation was only met with looks of bewilderment. He stepped down from the crate, realizing that these imbeciles were not worth his trouble.

FOLLOWING THAT FAILURE, Samuel walked along the banks of the River Elden, where booksellers installed their carts to hock their wares to passers-by. He stopped at one that had several copies of *A Revolution of Dirt* displayed at the front. He picked one up and absent-mindedly flipped the pages.

What must Greta think of him? She would have heard by now about his book. Perhaps she was intrigued. Was Samuel not the talk of Goldhall? Or, at least, he reasoned, he was before the royal family's escape captured everyone's attention.

"You buying that?" said the bookseller. "Or just reading the whole thing for free?"

Samuel gave the middle-aged woman an annoyed glance and returned the book to the cart.

Greta had always been a supporter of democracy, of equality. She would not understand Samuel's new views. But who could blame her? After all, he fell for the same bunk for much of his life. In time, perhaps she would mature, like he had. Greta would soon complete her degree at Iron Town College. What would be next for her? It would be a shame if her talents were wasted on such idealism.

"A wise choice," said the woman, interrupting his thoughts again. "The book is a load of rubbish anyway."

"Is that so?"

"That is so," she said. "If it were up to me, I wouldn't have it on my cart. But the people seem to demand it."

Samuel let out a laugh. He thought better of revealing his identity, however satisfying it might be.

"I wonder what Nox thinks of Quinneas," the woman yammered, "now that he will lead the prosecution of the king and queen."

"What?" Samuel said, suddenly much more interested in what she had to say. "I didn't know that."

"Yes, indeed," she said. "It was just announced today. It would appear that Citizen Aramal and Bravala have finally met their match."

"Hmmph," Samuel said, and walked away.

Quinneas! Blast him! Thoughts of Greta were now mixed with thoughts of Quinneas. Samuel's research, his promising career... his downfall.

It all made Samuel wonder if he could return to his old research someday. He still had all his notes. And restrictions on the ownership of the creatures had been relaxed, so procuring specimens would pose no difficulty. Perhaps it was still possible.

But then the anger returned. After everything that had happened to him? No! The people didn't deserve to know his insights.

57

CHARLOTTE

"Good luck, darling," Charlotte whispered to Quinneas.

"This is what I was born to do," said Quinneas, with a prophetic look in his eyes. "I have been preparing for this all my life."

His response left Charlotte somewhat cold. A simple thank you would have sufficed.

The other members began taking their seats as the secretary of the Great Chamber called the session to order. A week had passed since the vote. The king and the rest of the royal family were to stand trial today in front of the Great Chamber. It could wait no longer than that.

Electricity pulsed through the room. Everyone knew that the eyes of history were upon them. In the balconies sat prominent figures, including the other members of the royal family who would be questioned later in the day. But this morning the king and queen would face justice.

Members talked to their neighbours, but the room went silent as the secretary banged the gavel. "Great Chamber members," he said, "we call before us His Majesty, King Aramal, and Her Majesty, Queen Bravala, to stand trial for treason."

The two entered with their heads down and solemnly walked down the centre aisle toward the front of the room. The king wore a brilliant red coat, intricately decorated with frills and jewels, and the queen an equally ornate red dress. The royal colours. Colours purposely chosen to insult the revolution, Charlotte knew. Yet their sullen expressions clashed with their ostentatious outfits. In attempting to project confidence and power with their clothing, they only showed how superficial were their claims to authority.

The only sound in the entire chamber was the footsteps of

the royal couple, then the squeaking of the chairs as the two pulled them out from the oak table at the far end of the room. Legal counsel for each sat by their sides.

One of the members coughed and it echoed through the entire chamber.

Quinneas stepped to the centre aisle and walked toward the king and queen. This time, the only sound was *his* footsteps.

"Mr. and Mrs. Aramal Zendar," Quinneas said, using their dynastic name in a demonstration of their powerlessness, "you have been brought here to stand trial for the charge of treason. How do you plead?"

The king looked surprised and then hurt by the use of anything other than "Your Majesty." He looked over at his defence counsel. His main lawyer rose to indicate that they pleaded "not guilty."

Quinneas delivered an opening statement, making clear the charges. He would lay out the evidence, the letters from Friezzia, the conspiracy, the escape. Charlotte was impressed with Quinneas's poise given the enormity of the task that stood in front of him.

The first witnesses were the king and queen themselves. The king moved from his chair to the witness box.

Quinneas began the questioning. "Why were you and the rest of the royal family travelling in a flying carriage to Friezzia?"

Aramal sat silently in thought for several seconds before responding: "We were not travelling to Friezzia," he said. "We were visiting our subjects around our country. After the recent turmoil, I wished to make a royal tour."

"Which places did you visit and for what purposes?"

"We visited the common people in their countryside villages. We met a charming peasant couple. They requested I visit their sick mother and I happily obliged."

"I wish to remind you, Mr. Zendar, that you have sworn on the Book of Oqci to tell the truth," Quinneas said. "Why was your entire family with you, including all your belongings?"

"It was important for all of my family members to visit with the people. It has been a difficult time for our great nation, which is why I thought it appropriate and welcome to do such a thing. As to why our belongings were with us, we were unsure how long our trip would take."

"Did you tell anyone else about your plans, such as the Duke of Prencroft?"

"No."

"Why not?"

"It was a divine spark of inspiration that day."

"A divine spark of inspiration in which you packed all of your belongings and had a special carriage designed?"

"The carriage had been designed by Rodnel, Count of Summerstone, some time ago, for purposes of travel and of delighting the common people. And it was no trouble at all for us to pack a few of our possessions that day."

The temerity of the king stunned Charlotte. His lies were not convincing in the slightest. At least not to her. Yet she noticed some of the other members nodding as he told his story.

"Mr. Zendar, we have discovered several letters from King Hyazaral of Friezzia, in which he explains the price of harbouring you and your family. They would help you overthrow this democratic body and place you back on the throne to rule alone. It is as plain as day. You agreed to betray your fellow citizens for your own selfish gains, did you not?"

"It was a clever piece of negotiating," said Aramal, seeming to gain confidence. "To make the Friezzians think we were weak. It was but a ploy. I never had any intention of acting upon it. When you have been in my position long enough, you learn such tactics."

Charlotte stifled a laugh at this, but other members appeared to find this convincing. How could they be so gullible? At the start of the day, she was certain the others would find him guilty. Now she was becoming less sure.

Quinneas next questioned Queen Bravala. "Mrs. Zendar, why did you bring your daughter Dellirea along on this voyage?"

The queen sat silently, as if she did not hear the question.

"Mrs. Zendar?"

"Were you speaking to me?" she said. "I only respond to 'Your Highness.'"

Quinneas looked as though he might explode then and there. Charlotte almost felt an urge to rush into the aisle to restrain him. But he took a breath to compose himself. "I do not respect that title. You are no different than any other citizen as far as this body is concerned, hence I will address you as Mrs. Zendar. Shall I repeat the question?"

Bravala pretended once again not to hear.

"Mrs. Zendar?"

She continued to remain silent. Murmurs grew louder in the chamber.

"Mrs. Zendar, if you refuse to answer, you will be held in contempt of the Great Chamber."

With a haughty expression, Bravala looked around the room, again saying nothing even as the murmurs became even louder.

The secretary of the chamber intervened. "Your Highness, I find you in contempt of the Great Chamber for refusing to answer. Your punishment will be determined following the trial."

"Very well," she said.

Quinneas smiled at this, although Charlotte understood not how he could find it amusing. The king's testimony appeared to leave enough doubt in the minds of the Great Chamber members of his innocence, and the queen gave no testimony at all.

With that the queen stood and returned to her place next to the king.

"IT IS SHAMEFUL," Charlotte said to Quinneas as the two stood outside the palace, the trial in recess. "Even if the king and queen disgraced themselves, you are performing admirably."

"Thank you," he said.

That was a more appropriate response, she thought.

"But do you not worry that the king and queen are swaying the chamber?"

Quinneas snorted. "The Zendar couple can say whatever they wish," he said. "It will make no difference soon enough."

Before Charlotte could discover his meaning, they were called to return inside for the trial to resume.

58

DELLIREA

A giant skull stared back at Dellirea and Rodnel. The skull, carved into the massive stone wall of Fortress Gul, caused her to pull herself more tightly to Rodnel. They flew over the wall, perhaps the height of ten of their palaces stacked upon one another, and into Friezzian territory. Waiting for them on the other side was a group of King Hyazaral's royal guard, who greeted them passably in the Estenlander language upon their landing. The royal guard were shocked and disturbed when Dellirea told them what had happened. How their carriage had been shot down, how her mother and father had been apprehended.

The group huddled together and spoke to each other in their own tongue. Dellirea had studied their language and so she could pick out some of their words. They seemed to be wondering whether or not her father had deceived them and whether this was not some kind of trap.

"It is no trap," Dellirea said to them in Friezzian, as she stepped toward the group. "What we told you is the truth."

They turned to her in surprise.

"She can speak Friezzian," said one of them.

The group huddled together once more before determining they had no choice but to believe her.

"Come," one of the soldiers said, "we shall travel to Freless where you will meet His Majesty. It will be several hours before we reach the capital. Climb in."

He motioned for Dellirea and Rodnel to get into a carriage, while their winged horse, as exhausted from the trip as Dellirea, was pulled along in a cart at the rear of the convoy.

Dellirea still had not slept in what seemed like forever. She was shaking as she stared out at the Friezzian countryside. The grass seemed to be a different shade of green. Even the air smelled different. Aside from several brief visits to Esbeck, she had never left Estenland before, and now it seemed as though she might never see her home again. Or her family.

The significance of what had happened began to hit Dellirea all at once. Tears came to her eyes. Rodnel, sitting next to her in the carriage, clasped her hand and gave her a reassuring look. But she could tell that beneath his confident expression, he too was worried.

~

DELLIREA DRIFTED to sleep on the carriage ride but was startled awake when they arrived at the royal palace in Freless. She was struck by how it was at once so similar to her own palace in Estenland, yet completely different. It was a large, imposing structure, surrounded by elegant gardens, but while her palace had smooth, rounded edges, the Friezzian palace had sharp, pointed towers. The stone of the palace was a greyish black and the impression of it all made her despair.

A handful of unicorns and winged horses walked about the palace gardens. But there were far fewer creatures than at her family's palace. The Estenlanders had taken so much from the Friezzians after the Great War. Their sacred creatures, their resources, chunks of their territory, their overseas colonies in Otela and Ozenzal. What might they do in revenge? Dellirea shuddered at the thought.

She and Rodnel were escorted through the palace and into the king's chamber. It was a dim, spacious room with a high ceiling. The clacks from Dellirea's shoes echoed on the stone floor as she walked toward the throne at the other end of the room. There sat King Hyazaral VII, an ancient man with a long flowing beard who looked as though a strong wind would knock him over. Yet, when he spoke, his voice seemed like that of a much younger man.

"Princess Dellirea," he said, inspecting her. "Your grandfather gave our country quite a lot of trouble many years ago. Quite a lot of trouble."

His tone was friendly, but underneath it was a hint of menace. She was unsure how she should react to his words, so she remained silent.

"A quiet girl. That's good. That's as it should be," he said. He smiled and revealed yellow-stained teeth. "You are our guest here for now. We shall provide accommodation to you and your companion, and you both will want for nothing."

"Thank you, Your Majesty," Dellirea said.

"Yes, thank you, Your Majesty," said Rodnel.

"I was expecting your father and mother, but I think you can still be useful to me," Hyazaral said. Turning to the guards, he concluded, "Please show them to their accommodations."

With that, they were swept away to another building located on the palace grounds. An opulent bedroom connecting with a sitting room awaited her. Dellirea was exhausted from the trip and soon collapsed upon her bed. As sleep approached, she could only contemplate what awful fate awaited her parents back in Estenland.

59

CHARLOTTE

As the trial resumed in the afternoon, questioning of the queen's sister Meritoria led to similar obstructions. Just like Bravala, Meritoria refused to answer any questions.For the first time, Charlotte began to wonder whether the royal family might actually get away with it, whether the fall of the monarchy was but a mirage.

It was so clear what they had done. How could the others not see it? Yet the royal family seemed to be sowing enough seeds of doubt in the minds of her colleagues. But, somehow, in the midst of Meritoria's denials, Charlotte knew not how, Quinneas remained calm.

As Meritoria exited the witness box, next came Lochmar, the king's brother. More of the same obfuscations, denials, and misdirections were to come, she was sure.

Lochmar walked uneasily to the front of the room, his head down, refusing to look over at his brother and sister-in-law.

"Mr. Zendar, thank you for agreeing to testify," said Quinneas once Lochmar was seated.

Thank you? Charlotte was confused. Quinneas had not been so kind with the other members of the royal family.

"Now," Quinneas continued, "please tell me the purpose of your recent carriage ride."

Lochmar sat silently, fidgeting with his hands, not making eye contact with Quinneas, and carefully avoiding even turning his head in the direction of the king and queen. He cleared his throat. "Our plan…" he began, before stopping to clear his throat again. "Our plan was not simply to visit peasants as has been previously claimed. It was rather to escape to Friezzia."

There were gasps throughout the chamber.

"Order," shouted the chamber secretary as the room filled with chatter. "Order!"

Lochmar continued, hurriedly, even as the Great Chamber was still in a frenzy. "The plan was devised by my brother and his wife, in conjunction with Rodnel, Count of Summerstone, who built the flying carriage. But we were all fully aware of the plans when we took the voyage."

"He is a liar and a snake!" the king shouted as he stood from his chair.

"Please remain quiet, Mr. Zendar," said Quinneas. The din of the chatter of the Great Chamber members drowned out Aramal's continued protests.

"Order! Order!" the secretary continued shouting, seemingly in vain.

"Having said this," Lochmar went on, "and agreeing to take any further questions, I ask the Great Chamber to show mercy to my wife and me, and our children."

"I can corroborate his story," a voice called down from the balcony. It was Meritoria. "I would like to change my earlier testimony."

This produced yet more shock in the Great Chamber, as everyone realized the king and queen's story was crumbling before their eyes.

"Very well," said Quinneas.

She hurriedly walked from the balcony to the floor of the Great Chamber, also avoiding looking at her sister and brother-in-law.

Bravala stood up. "Meri?" she called in disbelief, fighting back tears. "How could you? How could you?"

But Meritoria pretended not to hear as she continued walking, while Quinneas admonished the queen to remain silent.

YANIS

The king and queen merely slouched along, their heads down, saying nothing. With a dozen other soldiers of the RDF, Yanis led them from the Great Chamber through the palace to their temporary rooms, converted into holding cells.

"Permit absolutely no communication between them," Yanis told one of the RDF soldiers standing guard, as the king and queen each entered their own separate room. Yanis knew that they could take no chances with the regular army, so the cells were guarded by his RDF soldiers until the vote on their guilt was taken the next day.

Content that the king and queen – or rather, Mr. and Mrs. Zendar – were accounted for, Yanis exited the palace to return home. A crowd of people waited outside the palace gates, stewing angrily, even as the sun was soon to set. By now they had learned that Lochmar and Meritoria had betrayed their siblings, implicating them in the treason. The conspiracy was now plain for all to see.

The enormity of the day was beginning to hit Yanis as he made the trek home. The Zendars were sure to be found guilty. And what then? He dared not even think it.

~

NADENI HAD ALREADY ARRIVED home when Yanis returned. She had watched the trial unfold from the balcony above. She knew what was to come, just as he did.

Nadeni was waiting with glasses of sweetberry wine. "It is a celebration, is it not?"

Yanis removed his uniform and sat beside her in their sitting room.

"Here is to the end of the monarchy," she said, as they touched their glasses together.

"Cheers."

It was everything Yanis had always hoped for, yet somehow it felt hollow. Perhaps it was simply the exhaustion from the past weeks that clouded his judgment. He took a sip of the wine.

"I wish to join the RDF," said Nadeni.

Yanis nearly spit out the wine from laughter.

She narrowed her eyes at him. "I'm serious."

His cheeks grew hot. "Join the RDF? But are you sure?"

"After the treason of the king and queen, I feel even more strongly the need to contribute to defending our revolution. Part of my ancestry is from Umiri, but I will always be an Estenlander at heart. This is my country, and I wish to fight for it, just as my great-grandfather fought for his."

Yanis nodded. He admired her fighting spirit. But the thought of her joining made him uneasy. It was a dangerous business, and they had already seen the lengths the king would go to defend himself. Yanis willingly accepted the risk, but to see Nadeni in danger? The thought of losing her in the same way as… No, he couldn't do it.

Yanis took another sip of wine as he thought more. "But… have you combat experience?"

"I was involved in the capture of the prison alongside you, was I not?" she said. "Did I not fight bravely then?"

Yanis sighed. "Of course you did."

"Then what say you, High Commander Haller?"

"I… well, perhaps it would pose a conflict of interest," he said. "The other soldiers might worry I would favour you. And they would be right. How could I do otherwise?"

"We would find a way," she said and took another drink. "Perhaps I could primarily recruit other soldiers. My connections in Iron Town could be valuable."

Yanis shook his head. "I don't think it is a good idea."

"Consider Charlotte and Quinneas. Do you think Charlotte simply sits at home, twiddling her thumbs, while Quinneas serves his country? No! She is equally involved in leadership. That is what I wish for myself."

It was futile to argue against her. Curse Nadeni! Yanis could not say no to her, however much he might wish to.

"So then it is settled," she continued. "I shall join the force."

She set down her wine and wrapped her arms around him. He returned her embrace, even as he felt ambivalent.

But perhaps he *could* use the help. Quinneas had already denied his selection of the scientist Nox as an officer. It was too controversial, he had said. It would bring out too many uncomfortable associations. And Yanis could not deny his wishes.

But talented men and women did not grow on trees. And Nadeni was right, she knew Iron Town better than Yanis did. She could find good people. With the Zendar's treason, the pressure on the revolution would only grow…

CHARLOTTE

One by one, Great Chamber members rose to cast their votes on the guilt of the king and queen. One by one, the members voted "guilty." It was a unanimous decision, never in doubt.

The closing statement from the defence had denied the king and queen's guilt while simultaneously rejecting the authority of the Great Chamber to decide upon their fate. But this did nothing to sway the body. The king and queen's siblings were found to have been complicit in their treason as well, but they would be spared a harsher penalty because of their cooperation.

The question before Charlotte and the others now was to decide on the punishment for the king and queen. The two sat in shock, staring blankly, as speeches were given on either side. There were passionate defences of the injustice of sending them to their deaths, and equally passionate defences of the need to ensure they were suitably punished.

Charlotte stood before the raucous chamber to signal her own support for the death penalty. "The king and queen have conspired against our nation," she said, almost shouting to ensure she was heard above the cheering and jeering. "They would have made our country the pawn of Friezzia. They have committed the most egregious offense against our nation. Friends," she concluded, "it gives me no pleasure, but we must vote for the highest penalty that our nation possesses."

Quinneas and the others on their side of the chamber argued similarly. Kephalos, for his part, pleaded for lifetime imprisonment, as did conservatives like Lord Saundley.

With debate closed, the chamber secretary called for a vote by roll. It would surely be a much closer vote than the one on their guilt. Each vote would be critical, Charlotte knew.

The secretary called out each member alphabetically by surname to state their vote aloud.

The king and queen watched nervously as each member rose. The first several voted "no," save Selver Bronn. Charlotte's name was called and she voted "yes." After her was a string of "yeses." More "noes," more "yeses." Charlotte counted the numbers in her head as each vote was cast. It would be close.

With only a dozen members left, the vote was tied. "Yes," "no," "no," "yes." Every vote caused Charlotte's heart to vacillate between joy and despair.

One more "yes" vote brought them to 149 to 148 in favour of death, with three votes remaining.

"Lord Wallington," called out the secretary.

The obscure earl rose slowly. "Yes."

150.

"Mr. Yeller."

A lawyer from the western provinces. He too rose and paused for a moment. "Yes."

Horrified screams and ecstatic cheers filled the chamber.

The secretary pressed on to call the remaining member, who also voted yes, but by then it did not matter. They had won it!

"The final vote," called out the secretary over the cacophony of the chamber, "is 152 in favour, 148 opposed."

The meaning of what had happened hit people in waves. One member fainted and needed to be revived. Others cheered and congratulated one another. Quinneas hugged Charlotte.

Lord Saundley stood and addressed the rest of the chamber. "You are all regicides! Oqci will have vengeance upon you yet!" All the while the chamber secretary tried desperately to maintain order in the midst of the chaos.

Charlotte observed that the only ones silent in the entire room were the king and queen, who had seemingly already made peace with their fate. Aramal the Incompetent absent-mindedly drummed his fingers upon the table, no doubt imagining what was soon to come.

SAMUEL

"We must take a stand against these revolutionaries," called out the great Richard, Duke of Saundley. "We must take a stand for our traditions."

The others at the solemn banquet mumbled their agreement. Samuel nodded his head too, not wishing to seem out of place, even if he felt so.

How stupid Richard was to invite him, thought Samuel. After having arranged to publish Samuel's book, did he think they were now best friends, or that Samuel shared his fondness for the monarchy and for the system of religion? Wrong on all counts.

"We are delighted to be joined by Samuel Nox, one of the finest, most able critics of the revolution," Richard continued, flanked by his wife, his siblings, and his children – three sons and two daughters.

A smattering of applause greeted Samuel's name. Richard's wife, Solorina, applauded as well. She was several years Samuel's senior, but even so, Samuel had to say that he would not kick her out of bed.

Richard was at least wise enough to explain to Samuel beforehand that he was not to be heard, only seen. It was useful to have someone who was not of noble birth, someone from the commoner class, to at least give the appearance of widespread disapproval of the revolutionaries.

"We do not agree on everything," said Richard, "but Dr. Nox and I agree on the evil of this terrible revolution."

Samuel raised his glass and nodded his head.

More applause. He glanced over at Solorina. Did he catch a seductive smile from her? Ha, what would Lord Saundley think if he knew?

But the thought of intimacy made Samuel wince. Greta. Oh,

sweet Greta. It seemed wrong to think of someone other than her… Almost as if he were being unfaithful.

Samuel had renown, he had money – well, *some* money – but he did not have what he truly wanted. He did not have her.

He took a long glug of wine to quiet those troubling thoughts.

"They may take away our king," thundered Richard at the podium, when Samuel decided to pay him notice once more, "but they will never take away our traditions. Our religion. Our lands! Never. I would sooner die than give them up!"

Other crusty old men rose to speak. One after another. Duke of this, Earl of that. All spoke of the terrible injustice of what was soon to happen to the beloved king and queen. Of course, no one dared raise the uncomfortable fact that the king's own brother had sealed his fate. So much for the wisdom, honour, and integrity of the Zendar family to act as the guide for the nation, Samuel thought.

It all made no difference to him. As Richard and the others droned on, he could only smile to himself. Keep sending more food and drink, you fools.

Saundley's eldest son, Aldred, spoke next. At last, someone who was neither fat nor bald nor grey-haired.

"Gentlemen, we have seen great strife in our nation these past months, have we not?"

"Hear, hear."

Samuel downed the last bit of wine and signalled to one of the nearby servants to refill his glass. He needed to be drunker if he was going to sit through yet another of these speeches.

"But, gentlemen," continued Aldred, "while I share your views of the revolution, we must recognize that there is some legitimacy to the grievances of the common people."

This caused some murmuring among the crowd. Perhaps Aldred had bigger balls than Samuel imagined.

"If we act wisely," he continued to ever louder mumbling, "perhaps we might be able to create a better society for all, even the lower orders."

Saundley the elder sprang from his chair with a vigour

Samuel did not know he possessed. "That will be quite enough, *boy*," he said, as he confronted Aldred at the podium. "Quite enough."

For a brief moment, the two locked eyes and it appeared Aldred might challenge his father. The room went silent. But Aldred quickly relented and slunk back to his seat.

"I apologize for my son's behaviour," said Richard, taking Aldred's spot at the podium. "I know not how such poisonous ideas made their way into his simple head. But I assure you it was not from me!" He looked down at Aldred, who stared helplessly at his dinner plate as his father scolded him in front of Goldhall's finest citizens. "No son of mine would utter such tripe! Such foolishness!"

A small part of Samuel felt bad for poor Aldred as he received this tongue-lashing. His short speech reminded Samuel of his own past idealism.

He took another sip of wine.

Once Aldred grew older, Samuel was sure he would come to realize everything he believed was a load of rubbish. But it was still charming to see such idealism in the world, however fleeting.

63

DELLIREA

The sun pouring through the curtains awakened Dellirea. She lay in bed with her eyes open, staring at the ceiling.

A knock on the door made her arise.

It was that miserable old woman, Lady Fondyrel, of course.

On Dellirea's first day in Friezzia, it was her who had explained the rules. She would come to Dellirea's room each day to help her dress and bathe, and to escort her to meals or if she wished to walk around the palace grounds. But Dellirea was not to go anywhere without her or see anyone, even Rodnel.

After these past weeks, Dellirea had become accustomed to Lady Fondyrel's presence and no longer even noticed the uneven gait from her two wooden legs.

Unthinkingly, Dellirea followed the routine of bathing then dressing. Lady Fondyrel said nothing, as ever, as she mechanically went about her tasks of readying the bathwater and setting out Dellirea's clothes.

Dellirea could not guess how old Lady Fondyrel was – much older than her parents, she imagined – but she dared not ask. And she dared not inquire how she lost her legs.

LIFE in the palace was monotonous. Dellirea was a captive there. She could not move without Lady Fondyrel's watchful eyes upon her. Everywhere she went, Lady Fondyrel was there. Aside from the two of them, the palace might as well have been empty. Sometimes, while walking in the palace grounds, Dellirea saw others walking in the distance, but Lady Fondyrel ensured she stayed well away from them.

Lady Fondyrel said nothing to Dellirea aside from what was

necessary. She did not ask how she was doing, nor did she tell her anything about her own life.

"Might I ask if you have any information about my family?" Dellirea asked her, as she did every day while Lady Fondyrel helped her dress.

She usually responded with a curt "no," but today she hesitated before answering. "Do not think of such things," she snarled. "For your own sake. Your life is here in Friezzia now. You will only become mad thinking of anything else."

But Dellirea was already becoming mad. Mad with worry over the fate of her family. Over *her* fate.

Thinking that perhaps she was in a talkative mood today, Dellirea continued, "What are His Majesty's plans for me?"

"I know not," Lady Fondyrel said with frustration. "It is fruitless to guess His Majesty's plans. Give your attention to living your life one day at a time. To eating your meals. To sleeping. Block everything else from your mind." She paused and looked down. More softly, she said, "That is what I do. That is how I keep from going mad."

Dellirea turned sharply toward her. For the briefest moment, she had revealed something of herself.

But Lady Fondyrel looked embarrassed. "I should have said nothing. But please, just follow my advice."

64

CHARLOTTE

Charlotte had never been to a public execution before. But it was her duty to attend the king and queen's and not avert her eyes at the critical moment, since it was her who had voted to send them there just one week ago.

As was custom, the execution would take place publicly. Karazin Square, in front of the palace, was the only place large enough to accommodate the crowd of spectators.

Charlotte had been there just two months ago at the Victory Day celebrations. Just as then, they stood atop a large stage, erected for the occasion. Yanis and the rest of the Revolutionary Defence Force stood guard.

Among the radicals, it was decided that Quinneas should address the crowd, where most people wore the green cap of the revolution.

"Friends," he said, "today we are joined here for a solemn occasion. This is not a time for celebration, but for contemplation about how fragile our revolution is, and what is necessary to secure its gains. We should take no pleasure in what will occur today but face it with solemnity and with the principles of our revolution in mind."

The crowd rustled throughout his speech. They were in no mood for speeches, Charlotte surmised. They were eager for action.

The king and queen were brought to the gallows, dressed only in simple white garb, the colour of justice. As they appeared, the crowd began to jeer loudly. The queen looked composed as she was marched out, but the king wiped a tear from his eyes. The crowd pelted them with rotting vegetables and rubbish as they assumed their position on the stage. A tomato hit the king squarely between the eyes before he could dodge it. The tomato guts dripped down his face. The crowd burst into laughter and applause. More and more refuse was thrown, with the king and queen trying in vain to contort their bodies out of the way.

"This is disgusting," Charlotte whispered to Quinneas. "The people are acting in an undignified manner."

"It is to be expected," he said evenly. "The people have much repressed anger at this family of criminals."

Bravala remained defiant in the face of the taunting and made an obscene gesture toward the crowd, which only caused them to throw more debris. The king, his face and clothing stained in the juices of the projectiles, looked to the sky and called out, "Have mercy upon me, O Creator!"

It was a sad sight. This man who aspired to greatness, mocked and humiliated in the final moments before his death. But Charlotte tried to bring to mind all the pain his actions had caused. She looked over at Quinneas's face to see if he shared her ambivalence. A blank, determined stare showed her that he did not.

The crowd grew quiet with anticipation as the nooses were placed over the queen's neck first, then the king's. There were to be no hoods placed over their heads to preserve their dignity. Thousands of their fellow citizens, from the highest nobles down to the lowest paupers, stretched as far as the eye could see across Karazin Square. The nooses were tightened.

Not a sound was heard among these thousands.

Crack.

The two trap doors opened and the king and queen dropped.

In an instant, it was over. It all seemed too simple. Too easy. These two – once the most powerful, the most feared, in all of Estenland – now hung limply. The crowd remained silent.

But for just a moment. Someone far out in the crowd began the first lines of "Justice For All." More and more soon joined in, then the entire crowd was arm-in-arm, singing merrily as the two dead bodies, covered in the debris thrown by the crowd, swayed pathetically at the end of each rope.

It took everything Charlotte had not to be sick.

~

THAT NIGHT, Charlotte could not eat. She merely picked at the special meal Quinneas had his chef prepare them. It was a rare cut of meat, Quinneas had said, alongside boiled potatoes and colourful root vegetables. But the horrible images of the execution in her mind limited her appetite.

Quinneas's plate was already nearly empty, however, as he shovelled another chunk of the meat into his mouth.

"Quin… Quinneas, I must say that I feel conflicted over what we have done," she said.

Quinneas set down his fork and looked at her with surprise.

"I try to think of the injustices perpetrated by the king and queen," Charlotte continued, "and how they were willing to betray our country for their own personal power. Still, a part of me looks at the brutal, bloodthirsty crowd – how they cheered their deaths – and wonders what we might have unleashed."

Quinneas swallowed his mouthful of food. "I too have thought of this and it is true that the behaviour of the people was less than dignified," he conceded. "But let us remember all of the terrible things for which they are responsible. Aramal sent his griffins upon us! I was nearly killed. And you might have been too. And then to imprison us. It would not have troubled his conscience for us to suffer the precise same fate."

"That is all true."

Quinneas's green eyes stared into Charlotte, trying to touch her soul. "You do not doubt the righteousness of the Zendars' execution, do you?"

"Of course not."

"I think the reaction of the crowd shows that we have more work to do to build a new society," Quinneas continued. He leaned back in his chair and wiped his mouth with a handkerchief. "This is only the beginning of the revolution. Not the end."

"Yes," Charlotte said unconvincingly, "this is what we have spent our whole lives working toward. We must not cease now."

It was what Quinneas wanted to hear, she knew. Yet she did not fully believe her words.

"Charlotte, this is meant to be a celebration," he said, looking at her plate, still full of food. "I have had a special meal prepared for the occasion. Don't you enjoy it?"

She cut a piece of the meat and placed it in her mouth. It was chewy with an unusual flavour.

He watched her hopefully. "I didn't wish to tell you what it was at first, for fear of prejudicing you." He grinned. "We are dining on unicorn tonight."

Charlotte had already swallowed the morsel, though she instantly wished she could spit it back up. "Unicorn...! What were you thinking?"

"Charlotte, I feared you wouldn't want to eat it if you knew. I imagined once you tasted it..."

She felt even sicker than before. "It's disgusting!"

"I... I'm sorry," he said. "I thought you would be happy. It's meant to symbolize the end of monarchy, the end of super-stition..."

"You have misjudged me," she said coldly.

Quinneas rose quickly from his chair to comfort her. "Oh dear, I have made a terrible mistake," he said. "I only wished to serve you something novel for this event. But I shall have the chef dispose of it at once."

YANIS

"That bastard!" cried Clem. "We shall have his head!"

Dozens of RDF soldiers stewed around and cursed the Duke of Saundley with every expletive known. With Nadeni and this group, Yanis prepared to make the departure to the Saundley estate.

The elections following the execution of Aramal and Bravala had swept the radicals to power in the Great Chamber. The newly expanded Revolutionary Defence Force was tasked with carrying out the land redistribution ordered by the new Great Chamber. The RDF saw to it that there was no mischief as noble titles were abolished and their lands were redistributed to the poor. Some nobles reluctantly gave in and stayed on their reduced estates, while others took their wealth and fled to Friezzia.

Richard, Duke of Saundley, who had lost his seat in the election, refused to part with his lands. In an open letter published in the *Goldhall Gazette*, he explained that these were historic lands held for generations by his ancestors. He had armed the peasants who worked his estate and said that any intruders who stepped onto the property would be treated as hostile.

"He sacrificed nothing during the siege while we suffered!" called out Clem, as the other soldiers paced about angrily.

Quinneas had happily leaked to the press that Richard had demanded a personal exemption to the draft of sacred creatures into the armed forces, all the while stuffing his face with gourmet food as if his fellow citizens were not starving. This did nothing to endear him to the masses of Goldhall.

Next to Yanis stood Nadeni, armed with a musket and her trusty dagger, recovered from the moat that day at the prison. He was reluctant for Nadeni to join them in combat, and he would have otherwise forbade it, but Richard's forces would prove no match for theirs, so there was little chance of danger.

"Saundley will soon face the justice of the revolution," shouted Devon Black, one of the officers recruited by Nadeni.

"Hurrah!" the others responded.

Devon too had come from Iron Town and had been active in the democratic underground, like Yanis had. They needed those hardened professional soldiers, like Clem, but also those idealists, like Devon.

As they marched close to the edge of Richard's lands, through binoculars Yanis could see his small peasant army, clad in ragtag uniforms and numbering several dozen, holding their muskets uneasily. Some were positioned by cannons atop the battlements of Richard's manor house walls. But their faces betrayed that they wanted no part in the conflict. They were hardly experienced soldiers and would present little challenge for the RDF in battle. Yanis just hoped that there would be no needless bloodshed. On their side, or his.

"Lord Saundley," Yanis said into a speaking trumpet, "you are commanded to surrender your lands now or face justice."

Dressed in a striking red military uniform, Richard rode out on a unicorn. Into a speaking trumpet of his own, he responded, "I shall kill anyone who steps foot onto my lands."

Reasoning him with was hopeless, so Yanis addressed the peasant army directly. "To Lord Saundley's workers, our quarrel is not with you. We wish you no harm. Surrender now and you will not be held responsible for your lord's actions."

Do not be fools, Yanis pleaded in his head, as he glanced down the line at Nadeni, clad in the green and yellow of the RDF. Do not be fools and risk the lives of good people.

In the distance, Yanis could hear Richard barking instructions at his sons and relatives, who in turn urged on his peasants. None of the peasants budged from their position, perhaps more terrified of their lord than of Yanis's force.

"This is your last warning," Yanis said. "We shall advance unless you surrender now."

He waited for several seconds. No movement. He ordered his

army to advance in three columns. Yanis joined his unit in charging into Richard's fields. Cannon fire sailed toward them as they advanced.

Yanis jogged behind his soldiers, commanding from the rear. They stopped and assembled into line formation. Orderly firing commenced, just as he and Clem had drilled them. Nadeni stood strong and capable next to the others.

Richard's peasant army fired some feeble volleys of their own, but under steady waves of bullets from Yanis's side, their line quickly broke. Scattered peasants threw down their muskets and sprinted toward the RDF line in surrender.

One of Richard's noble commanders pulled out his pistol and shot a fleeing peasant before he had a chance to escape. A warning to any other deserters. But it was too late. Resistance was broken.

"Press ahead!" Yanis shouted. Fire continued from atop the battlements of Richard's manor house. But only Richard and his noble officers remained as the rest of his army fled.

Up ahead, Yanis's soldiers burst through the doors of the estate, abandoning their orderly marching. Yanis rushed to catch up with them and urged his officers to maintain discipline. Upon reaching the outside of the house, Yanis could already hear commotion coming from inside. He entered, the door broken off its hinges, and looked around in shock.

Soldiers ran through the hallways, tearing down paintings and smashing furniture. Vases and platters were thrown against the ground in joyous celebration. The sounds of shattering porcelain, cracking wood, and boisterous laughter echoed through the hallways.

All order was lost.

Richard and his family were nowhere to be seen, but everywhere was chaos as Yanis's soldiers ransacked the place. "Halt!" Yanis called through his speaking trumpet. "Halt!"

"Halt, you fools!" cried Nadeni, who appeared beside him.

No one was listening. Yanis was becoming panicked. All around him, RDF soldiers were running through the estate in a frenzy. The previous discipline had descended into an orgy of destruction.

"Cease at once!" he called out again.

"This is no justice," shouted Devon at a pair of passing soldiers. "Stop this instant."

Sheepishly, the two ceased their rampaging. In time, Clem, Devon, Nadeni, and Yanis managed to calm some of the other soldiers, but more were still wreaking havoc upon Richard's house.

"Stay here," Yanis urged his officers. "Maintain calm. I must find Richard and his family."

As he raced through the estate, a pool of dark red blood on the white floor stopped him. Following its trail, he found a girl's body, lifeless on the ground, stabbed numerous times with a bayonet. It was, Yanis quickly realized, Richard's teenage daughter.

Everything was spinning. This could be a bloodbath if he could not restore order. Richard's other children and his wife, Solorina, remained unaccounted for.

Why did Richard force them to stay at his estate when he knew violence was possible? How could he have been so reckless?

Again, Yanis spoke through the trumpet and commanded the rioting to stop. Clem and Devon had located the rest of Richard's children and guarded them, but Richard and his wife were still missing.

At last, Nadeni located Solorina and led her to Yanis. She wore a defiant expression on her face.

"Lady Saundley," he said, "it is my sad duty to report that your daughter was killed during the combat."

At once, the hardened look fell away as she collapsed to her knees and screamed in anguish.

"We have yet to account for your husband," Yanis continued, over her screams.

Nadeni reached out to gently touch Solorina's shoulder.

But Solorina flailed her arms as Nadeni drew near. "Get away from me, you awful brute!"

Nadeni's expression turned to ice, and she stepped away.

Yanis looked out into the fields beyond the estate walls and saw a unicorn approaching. Was that Richard coming to surrender? As the unicorn came closer, Yanis realized it was not Richard. The green uniform told him it was a soldier from the RDF.

But as the soldier rode the unwilling unicorn closer, Yanis was horrified: atop its head was Richard's severed head, the unicorn's horn acting as a pike. Grotesque red lines drizzled down the unicorn's white head. The soldier was grinning as the unicorn trotted to a halt. Some of the other soldiers pointed and laughed at the spectacle.

Solorina, still on the ground, glanced up and let out a deafening shriek as she collapsed once more. She screamed again and again as she pounded her fists on the ground in agony. Nadeni and the others could only watch. Consoling her would be impossible.

"You there," Yanis ordered the man on the unicorn, "get down!" The man jumped off with a smirk. "Arrest him," Yanis ordered Devon and two others, who quickly restrained the soldier, seemingly surprised that he had done anything wrong.

"Soldiers," Yanis said, "we are not animals."

His men hung their heads.

"We have let you down, Dragon Slayer," said Devon, looking out at the others. "We have let down the revolution."

"You have been selected for the Revolutionary Defence Force to uphold order," Yanis continued, "not to create chaos! I shall not have such brutality and disobedience in my ranks."

Solorina remained crouched on the ground, quiet and staring down. She raised her head to look at Yanis. "You monster! Look what you have done. Oqci will see that you get what you deserve."

66

DELLIREA

Dellirea gazed up at the panelled ceiling of the library reading room. Giant murals on each of the panels depicting various scenes from Oqci's life looked back at her. These were some of Mikazal's finest works, painted centuries ago. This was a place she could contemplate Oqci's doctrines more closely and become more connected to her faith. This was a place she could almost forget about her current life.

Until she noticed Lady Fondyrel keeping careful watch on her from the edge of the room. Then it all returned.

As Dellirea stared up at Mikazal's murals, she reminded herself, begrudgingly, that Estenland did not have a monopoly on cultural achievements.

All around the edge of the spiral room were shelves and shelves of books in every language. She pulled down a work that Kephalos had recommended to her after their conversation at the Victory Day celebration. If she wanted to better understand his views, he had said, she should read this book. *The Book of Oqci Critically Examined*, as it was called, was written twenty-five years ago by a priest named Phantos. He came from Estenland but spent much of his life in New Selver, where he devoted himself to teaching the native inhabitants the ways of Oqci.

It was a noble calling to teach the holy doctrines to those less civilized than themselves – and it was something Dellirea had thought of doing herself from time to time – so she knew she would find the book agreeable. Yet the more she read, the more disturbed she grew. Phantos explained that the natives of New Selver asked him penetrating questions about the Book of Oqci as they noticed inconsistencies in the texts. Did Oqci's crossing of the Sea of Dreams take thirty days, or fifty? Where was the exact site of Oqci's landing in Ogard? Was Oqci's skin colour light or dark? Was Mazir with Oqci when he ascended to the

Cloud Kingdom, or was she not? Did Oqci ascend on a winged lion or a winged horse?

Oqci himself never wrote anything, so all of the details of his life came from various accounts by his followers, written sometimes decades after Oqci's return to the clouds, and cobbled together into the Book of Oqci. Phantos said that all the inconsistencies in the text meant that the Book of Oqci could not be an accurate record of what actually happened.

No, no, these were only minor issues, Dellirea told herself. Trivial concerns! And yet... if these basic facts were not right, could she be sure about anything written there?

Phantos raised other issues too. Why had Oqci never mentioned the existence of Ozenzal? How could he leave out an entire continent? And furthermore, Phantos mentioned the ambiguities of the ancient term, *arxequb*. The doctrines stated that Oqci claimed the sacred creatures should only belong to the *arxequb*, and the Estenlanders had long translated this as "noble." But Phantos said that the primitive tribes of Ogard had no such concept as "noble." In their language, the word only meant those with pure, good hearts. Dellirea now understood whence Kephalos acquired his strange views.

All of these ideas made Dellirea's head spin. She felt a strange sensation in the pit of her stomach as she read on. Phantos said that they could still find value in the messages of Oqci, even if the stories might not have literally happened the way they were described. This is what Kephalos said too. But everything in Dellirea's life was already changing so much. And now she couldn't even count on the stories of Oqci to be true!

She slammed the book shut and tried to find a more congenial text to read. Something written by a *proper* follower of Oqci.

67

YANIS

"This is an absolute disaster," Charlotte said to Yanis. "How could you lose control of your men like that?"

Yanis sat uneasily opposite Quinneas and Charlotte in Quinneas's office at the palace. Yanis had explained to them what had happened at Richard's estate yesterday and how things had gone so wrong. Richard and his youngest daughter were both brutally murdered. His eldest son Aldred was also killed in the fighting, they learned later that day, but, small mercy, his other three children had survived.

"It was a difficult situation," Yanis said, trying to remain calm. "I... I did my best as commander of the RDF."

"If that was your best, I shudder to imagine your worst," said Charlotte.

Anger boiled up inside of Yanis, but he had to remain composed. Had to remain professional. "I shall ensure that all the men responsible for the violence will be brought to justice. I shall do a full review of the Revolutionary Defence Force to ensure that any other unstable individuals are removed."

"I told you this would happen," Charlotte said to Quinneas, as if Yanis were no longer in the room. "It was to be expected. Did I not warn you?"

Furious at the way she spoke, Yanis retorted, "You should lead the force if you suppose you can perform better."

Charlotte glared at him. "I'm smart enough to realize my lack of experience in those matters. And therefore, I would find someone who could do the job properly."

"Calm down," said Quinneas. "Let us all calm down."

Yanis seethed. There was always condescension in the way Charlotte spoke to those she considered her inferiors. Deep down, she would always be a noble.

"Yanis said he would see that all is sorted," Quinneas said to Charlotte, "and I trust him to do so."

"That's right," Yanis said.

Charlotte's expression softened. "I suppose ever since I watched the mobs at the execution of the king and queen, I've worried about what we might have unleashed. Such animalistic violence should be no part of our revolution."

"Are you doubting the revolution?" Yanis said.

"Do not dare question my support for the revolution," Charlotte fired back, her intensity returned. "Do you know what kind of risk I ran supporting democracy when I didn't need to? Writing the most famous book on the subject! Perhaps you've heard of it?"

"You're right, you 'didn't need to.' You could always retreat back to your noble lifestyle if things ever became too difficult – just as you're trying to do now."

Charlotte bolted from her chair and stormed from the room, slamming the door as she went.

Yanis and Quinneas looked at each other silently, trying to determine the right thing to say. Quinneas looked annoyed with Yanis for agitating his lover, but Yanis could tell Quinneas agreed with him.

"The reaction of the people at the executions deeply affected her," said Quinneas, leaning back in his chair. "I know that Charlotte supports the revolution. There can be no doubt of that. But we mustn't flinch when things become difficult. Even when they become unpleasant. I know that deep down Charlotte realizes this too."

Yanis nodded his head.

"The RDF is vital to carrying out the revolution," he continued. "And you are vital to leading it. There might be anger in the Great Chamber over what happened at the Saundley estate, but I shall always protect you and ensure your position is safe."

~

AFTER THE MEETING, Yanis returned to his house. The larger house that he had earned as the head of the RDF. The house that he *deserved*. With the wife that he *deserved*.

Charlotte's remarks swirled around his mind as he walked to the door. Samuel Nox's book was full of lies and mistruths, but he at least captured Charlotte's essence perfectly. She *was* obnoxious… arrogant… entitled!

Worst of all, Yanis thought, she was right. Right about him. That's what made her criticism sting so much.

As Nadeni greeted Yanis, he was still hot with anger. He did not return her greeting. He couldn't bear to tell her about the embarrassment Charlotte had caused him. Instead he walked up to her and kissed her tightly.

How dare Charlotte talk to him like that!

Lust overcame him as he kissed her more. He grabbed Nadeni's behind and squeezed her close.

She kissed him back before pulling away, smiling. "What has come over you?"

"I want you so badly."

A devious expression came to her face. "I want you too, Dragon Slayer."

Yanis kissed her again. He imagined for a moment that Nadeni was Charlotte. He imagined everything he would do to her as they scrambled to undress right there in the hallway.

SAMUEL

The long-awaited, second edition of Samuel's book sold like moonberry pies. The people clamoured to know his thoughts about the deaths of the ill-fated Zendar couple. Of course, he had to rely on reports for the gory details of their executions. Samuel had avoided the spectacle. Witnessing his two supposedly noble co-conspirators meet their deaths had been too unsettling. He never wished to relive such an experience. Yet he was glad to see the king and queen go, and he wondered what fate awaited poor Dellirea in Friezzia.

The revolutionary government was already in chaos, just as Samuel predicted. Lochmar had sold out his brother, thinking he would soon be sitting on the throne. But instead he was sitting in prison.

And nobles, with their lands depleted and their privileges taken away, suddenly had to find a way to earn their bread. They could no longer rely on the peasants to work on their behalf while they loafed about. The poor dears! They were practically losing their heads over it – apologies to Lord Saundley.

"This is the most trustworthy and graceful unicorn you will ever find," said the unicorn's handler as Samuel passed its pen.

Samuel had always fancied sacred creatures, and he had earned enough money from his book to afford one. With restrictions on the ownership of the creatures loosened, and nobles struggling to make ends meet, small auctions around the city began to spring up.

A large griffin, confined to a cage far too small for it to be comfortable, screeched in frustration. Its right talon was shackled to the bars. It could barely stretch its wings. It made

Samuel think about those nights, working in his lab, dissecting the creatures. On the brink of becoming a scientific legend. It seemed a lifetime ago.

He wished to be able to give these creatures a decent life. No other commoners could appreciate the creatures the way he could. Yet that griffin would be outside his price range. Samuel could surely bid on a unicorn though.

He saw one he fancied and made note of its number. In his head, he debated how high he would go to obtain it. While looking at the other wealthy commoners – the way they dressed so nicely, in their suits and dresses, as if they were as good as any nobles – an anger stormed inside him; he knew he must outbid anyone who dared challenge him.

From nervousness, from anticipation, Samuel scratched at his midsection, then his left arm. It was a rare thing these days to feel the urge to scratch. It was, he supposed, the intensity of the coming auction.

At last the auctioneer stepped to the stage. "Fellow citizens," the man said, wearing a showy top hat, "we shall have an exciting time today, shall we not? And some of you will be going home with your very own sacred creatures... if the price is right, that is!"

This called forth applause and chatter from the crowd.

"We shall first begin by going over the rules."

The auctioneer stopped abruptly as a group of five individuals dressed in black cloaks and wearing black masks walked onto the stage. Before the auctioneer could react, one of the masked figures grabbed him, twisting his arms behind his back.

"Help! Help!"

Frantic, confused murmurs came from all around. At the edge of the crowd, more masked figures arrived. They stood around the crowd, menacingly holding long guns. The black triangular masks had golden borders and left only a slit for the eyes and mouth.

One of them moved to the podium. A cry of "silence!" from the figure quieted the audience. The figure, a woman, said, "We are the Soldiers of Oqci. We have come to purge the world of your blasphemy. To allow sacred creatures to be owned by common trash such as yourselves? This is disobedience to Oqci's teachings. We cannot allow it!"

The crowd hissed.

"Quiet!" she shouted as her companions raised their guns and pointed them toward the crowd. "We must never allow the creatures to fall into your grubby hands."

The auctioneer's face was full of fear. "Please don't hurt me!"

"See what awaits those who make a mockery of our faith," said the woman.

Samuel's legs grew shaky. The others in the crowd stood helpless. They were completely surrounded by the masked figures.

The main figure stood behind the auctioneer and drew a dagger across his throat. He coughed out blood, then crumpled to the stage in a heap.

"The creatures will never belong to you," the leader shouted. "Now go! Tell everyone what we have done here."

A few members of the crowd began to slowly leave. Others broke into a run. Samuel stood frozen. Could he be a hero? Could he rush the stage and fight?

Who was he kidding? He needed to get as far from there as possible. He joined the stream of panicked onlookers flowing from the square.

69

CHARLOTTE

"It is necessary and just," Quinneas said before a meeting of the Great Chamber, "for us to take immediate emergency measures against these so-called Soldiers of Oqci who wish to thwart our revolution!"

"Hear, hear," shouted the other members of the Chamber.

Charlotte, along with everyone else, was horrified by the attacks at markets for the sacred creatures. Fourteen men and women had been captured – all from minor noble families whose lands had been expropriated. They were interrogated, but they refused to give up the leaders who were still on the loose.

Were they supporters of Lochmar? He languished in prison and would for some time. But he was technically the rightful heir to the throne with Dellirea in Friezzia, even as the powers of the monarch were indefinitely suspended. Would the Soldiers of Oqci wish to place him back on the throne?

And how deep did their influence extend? Could they have infiltrated the police? No one knew. This was why, despite Charlotte's reservations about Yanis's leadership, it was necessary for the Revolutionary Defence Force to be given the power to search and arrest suspects without need for a warrant.

"Friends," said Kephalos, looking wearied from the events of the past months, "let us be careful of extending too many powers to the RDF. We must respect the rights of the citizens, as enumerated in our constitution. We must stop the Soldiers of Oqci, but we must not be dragged down to their level while doing so."

"The time of those like Kephalos has passed," thundered Tressa Smith, a radical member from Iron Town elected at the most recent election. "They do not understand how fragile our revolution is. How precious it is. If they did, they would know why we must stop at nothing to protect it from its enemies!"

Kephalos shook his head, but Tressa continued, "I fear that even some of my colleagues on this side of the chamber have not fully recognized the gravity of the situation. With Dellirea Zendar and other exiled nobles in Friezzia, who is to say that they have not been sending support to this terrorist group? All measures must be at our disposal. Even torture, if the captured terrorists refuse to speak."

Scattered cheers were drowned out by cries of "shame!"

Torture! Members from all sides looked at one another uneasily. Who could be trusted?

Quinneas's expression, as ever, betrayed neither support nor disapproval, but Charlotte knew that his views on torture were at one with her own.

The day was unusually hot for the late spring, and the chamber was sweltering from the heat and the high emotions. Charlotte wiped away sweat from her forehead as she rose to speak. "Friends, our constitution prohibits torture because we know too well how the king employed it against us. We cannot turn our backs on our values, even in the face of a grave threat. The added powers of the emergency declaration will be sufficient, without resorting to such measures as torture."

The emergency measure passed easily in the chamber, 241–58. There was one abstention: Tressa. Her abstention, she said, was a protest that the measure did not go far enough against the Soldiers of Oqci.

THAT EVENING, as Charlotte rode in the carriage with Quinneas back to his home – their home, rather – she could not escape the feeling that everything was all happening so quickly. Horrible bloodshed everywhere. First the execution of the king and queen. Then the Soldiers of Oqci. And now talk of torture. Their revolution was spinning out of control, and Charlotte knew not where it would stop.

Everything she had hoped for when she wrote her book seemed to be happening. They had a democracy. The monarchy was finished. Yet she felt no happier because of it. Part of her wished to return to how things were. Even before the revolution. To feel safe and secure again.

But this was exactly what Yanis had alleged of her. Charlotte could not very well prove him correct. Going back was not an option. The only choice was to push forward with the revolution. To see it through.

"Is everything alright?" Quinneas asked once they returned home.

"Yes," Charlotte said glumly.

"You were terribly quiet on the ride home."

"It is nothing."

"Charlotte, I know things have been difficult, but we shall get through this together." He clasped her hand. "In addition to everything, there is something else that has been weighing on my mind."

She grew worried from his tone. "Dear Oqci, what is it?"

"It is awful timing," he said, his voice unusually unsteady, "but it seems as though we shall never be able to find a time that is suitable. Therefore, I wish to know whether you would marry me."

Charlotte laughed with relief and extended her arms to embrace him. "Of course! Of course, I would."

She felt the clouds begin to lift as she buried her head in his chest. The sun would soon come out. They would move past this present crisis, and she and Quinneas would build a happy life together in the new society that they were helping to create.

70

DELLIREA

Today was Descent Day, the happiest day of the year. The time to celebrate Oqci's descent from the clouds and the arrival of the cherished holy doctrines. Yet Dellirea could not stop the poisonous ideas from Phantos's book from entering her brain.

Did Oqci's descent from the clouds even happen? No, it must have, Dellirea reassured herself. How else would they have the sacred creatures if the stories were untrue?

It was just before the last Descent Day when they had learned that the dragon mission had failed. Dellirea was overwhelmed by the thought of how much had happened since then.

The holy day made Dellirea miss home even more than usual. It made her miss the traditional roasted duck for dinner, the moonberry pie for dessert, the Otela ferns, the singing... And it made her miss her family.

When Lady Fondyrel informed Dellirea that she was invited to attend a banquet with the king and his family, she nearly cried in joy. For weeks she had seen not a soul aside from Lady Fondyrel. It would be a great feast, Lady Fondyrel said, and Dellirea was to dress in her finest clothes. As Lady Fondyrel helped her dress, happy thoughts filled Dellirea's mind. Maybe they would have some of the same foods as back home. Maybe some of the other exiled nobles from Estenland would be in attendance. And maybe she would even see Rodnel.

~

THAT EVENING, Lady Fondyrel led Dellirea to a grand dining room, intricately decorated with the ferns, where she met the rest of Hyazaral's family. His wife, his two sons and two daughters, and all their spouses and grandchildren. Dellirea's face grew tired from all the forced smiles, but she was happy at last to converse with others again.

As she took her seat, she glanced back at Lady Fondyrel, who stood patiently at the edge of the room. She had a resigned expression. Evidently, Hyazaral did not permit her to join them for the meal.

Dellirea was seated next to the king's eldest grandson, Yunolarol. He was one or two years older than her, she guessed. He had dark hair and dark eyes that some would say were handsome, though his face was marked with pimples.

"Hello, it is a pleasure to meet you," she said to him in her best Friezzian, but he did not reply. Instead, he looked over at his siblings and cousins, grinning. He mimicked her accent as he repeated her words to them.

Dellirea deflated with embarrassment. How stupid she was to think she had mastered their language!

"Ha," said Yunolarol's father, the prince, "you should try speaking her tongue and see what she thinks of *your* accent."

Yunolarol's mouth gaped open as if he were about to offer a rebuttal, but instead it only hung open, stupidly, which filled Dellirea with delight. Perhaps not everyone in Friezzia was horrible. The prince smiled at her.

They were to have wine with dinner and one of the servants poured her a glass. Politeness dictated that she not refuse, so she took a sip. The only other time she had drunk alcohol was on their voyage to Friezzia. The warm feeling as the wine slid down her throat brought the memories of that fateful night back. She drank another mouthful in hopes of stifling them.

Servants rushed in and out of the dining room, bringing them course after course of elaborate dishes. Salads, roasted vegetables, soups of all descriptions, cheeses and cured meats of every kind. Naturally she preferred Estenland's cuisine, yet Friezzian food was not wholly bad. Dellirea's stomach was becoming full even before the main course.

At last, a covered dish was brought to her table and the servant removed the lid, revealing an elaborate beefsteak wrapped in a kind of pastry and covered in brown gravy. It was not the traditional roasted duck that they would have on Descent Day back in Estenland, but the aroma wafted into her nostrils, and she knew she would enjoy it all the same.

After Dellirea had taken a few bites, Yunolarol said, "Are you enjoying that beef?"

"I am indeed," she said, "thank you."

"It is our special dish for Descent Day. Does it taste good?"

"Yes, excellent. Thank you."

"Very good," he said. A quizzical expression appeared on his face. "Where is your friend Rodnel, I wonder?"

"What do you mean?" Dellirea said. Yunolarol grinned at her question, but she understood not why. "Are you making some sort of joke? Where is he? I would like to see him. I have not had word from him since we arrived."

"I think you're closer to him than you think," he said, a toothy smile coming to his face as he lowered his eyes to the meat on Dellirea's plate. "Yes, I would say you're very close to him right now."

Her gaze darted down to her plate. Dear Oqci. It couldn't be true! Could it?

Yunolarol burst out laughing. "It is only a joke! Calm yourself! We are not animals here. Indeed, one might even say we are more civilized than you Estenlanders."

Rage bubbled up inside Dellirea. She leaned in close to Yunolarol so that none of the others would hear her. "Fuck you," she whispered. "And fuck this country."

Yunolarol's mouth gaped open in the same stupid expression as earlier, but after this he remained quiet and she ate the rest of her meal in peace.

Dessert was moonberry pie, just as they had back home, but the moonberries here were a touch too sour for Dellirea's tastes. As she finished the final bites, the king walked from far away down at the other end of the table and approached her and Yunolarol.

"How did you get on with Yunolarol?" he asked Dellirea as Yunolarol eyed her anxiously.

"We got on well," she said, not wishing to create a scene.

"Excellent. And Yunolarol, how did you get on with Dellirea?"

"Very well indeed," he replied. "She is a lovely girl."

Girl? Why, she was almost the same age as him!

"You know," Hyazaral said, "I placed you together in hopes you would get on well. You two would make an excellent couple. Think of it… a marriage to unite our two nations!"

Dellirea's heart sank at this idea. She must have had the same stupid look on her face as Yunolarol had before, she thought. She knew not if she were even interested in boys. She never thought about them much. And most certainly not Yunolarol.

Neither Dellirea nor Yunolarol said anything, and so Hyazaral continued, "It is something that we shall think about more in the coming days."

~

DELLIREA WENT to bed feeling awful. Terrible thoughts swirled around her mind. About her captivity. About the fate of her family back home. About Yunolarol. Everything was so confusing.

As she drifted to sleep, she dreamt about those horrible women who had tormented them at the palace. She felt frightened as they swarmed around her, but soon, the women disappeared. Everyone disappeared.

All except for one.

It was Charlotte of Evesbury, the beautiful noblewoman from the Great Chamber. What was she doing there?

Charlotte stood in front of Dellirea at the other end of the room. Nervousness and excitement mingled together inside her as she and Charlotte were all alone.

Charlotte approached Dellirea slowly, and Dellirea backed away toward the wall until she could move back no further. Charlotte pressed her up against the wall and ran her fingers through Dellirea's hair.

Dellirea was breathing heavily now. She looked at Charlotte but could say nothing.

Charlotte caressed her cheek and, as she moved her hand gently down Dellirea's neck, Dellirea moaned with pleasure.

She woke up sweaty and tangled amidst her bed sheets. The holy doctrines of Oqci did not permit such thoughts, but she closed her eyes and continued her fantasy.

71

YANIS

Yanis and Nadeni walked hand-in-hand through the bustling city centre on their way to the palace. They were both dressed in the freshly pressed green uniforms of the RDF. As they walked, the crowds parted to both sides of the street, giving him and Nadeni unimpeded access. The crowd stood stiffly, looking respectfully – with a hint of fear – at the couple, not saying a word as they strode past. Yanis nodded his greetings to the people and Nadeni waved.

"Look how the people revere us," whispered Nadeni.

"The people respect us for our role in the revolution," Yanis said, not wishing to seem as though he relished the treatment – even as he did.

After the debacle at the Saundley estate and the attacks by the Soldiers of Oqci, Yanis ensured those responsible for the murder of Richard and his daughter were identified and would face justice. He spoke personally with each soldier in the force – which now numbered over five hundred – to weed out any bad seeds. Anyone who expressed any sympathy with the violence was removed. The force was strong now and there would be no further problems, Yanis knew.

As he and Nadeni entered the palace, they took the familiar route to Quinneas's office, where they met with Quinneas, Charlotte, and Kephalos.

"These attacks from the Soldiers of Oqci could not have come at a more dreadful time," Quinneas said, "just days before Descent Day. It will be the first Descent Day without the monarchy. Kephalos wishes to ensure the tradition is maintained, and Charlotte and I agree. It is important to provide continuity to the people in these changing times."

"That is wise," Yanis said, although of course he thought that the descent of Oqci and the sacred creatures from the clouds was no more than a silly story. But the common people loved the holiday. His own memories were less fond. His parents could neither afford moonberry pie nor the gifts that purported to come from Oqci's winged lion.

"The role of the RDF will be critical," said Charlotte, addressing Yanis and Nadeni. "We need absolute security in the Great Temple on the day. The Soldiers of Oqci will wish to target the crowds, but we cannot allow that."

"Of course," Yanis said. "I shall have my best men and women patrolling the outside of the temple and the surrounding area. Everyone who enters will be thoroughly searched. We shall allow no breaches, you have my word."

"And you are confident that the men and women of the RDF can be trusted?" Charlotte asked.

Yanis bristled at this expression of doubt in his leadership, but he said, as evenly as possible, "I told you I would straighten out the force, and I have. I have absolute trust in the soldiers."

Nadeni nodded and squeezed his hand tenderly under the table.

"Very good," said Quinneas, before Charlotte could say more.

"The plan is for High Priest Omephas to preside over the service," said Kephalos, "but I shall make a speech to represent the Great Chamber."

"Yes," added Quinneas, "it is important to ensure that the people do not forget about the revolution, even on this holy day."

"Worry not, Dragon Slayer," said Devon, standing alongside Clem, who nodded his head in agreement. "We have left nothing to chance. The temple is impenetrable."

Yanis had to smile at Clem, who had even trimmed his unwieldy beard for the occasion. Devon and Clem had grown to become his most trusted officers. But despite their preparations, doubts continued to enter Yanis's mind. Had he done enough to ensure the loyalty of the force? He could not have another deba-cle. It would ruin him.

On the day, the dignitaries were allowed in first – the Great Chamber members, Omephas and the rest of his priestly under-lings, as well as Nadeni, who wore her RDF uniform.

Clem and Devon saw to it that all those who entered the Great Temple, even the dignitaries, were carefully searched for any weapons or anything that could possibly be used as one. The temple could hold nearly a thousand people and thus a long line stretched from the temple as they searched each person individ-ually. The worship would be delayed, but it was the only possible way to ensure safety.

Yanis stood outside, watching every detail, trying to spot anything unusual. But nothing caught his eye. As everyone at last filed in, he looked around one last time at the outside of the temple, carefully guarded by dozens of the RDF. All would be well. They had done everything necessary. He nodded to Clem and Devon and stepped inside, where he took his seat next to Nadeni. Placed around the inside of the temple at various points were the green-uniformed soldiers who would provide addi-tional security.

"Friends," said Omephas as the crowd quieted, "we gather today to mark the anniversary of Oqci's descent from the Cloud Kingdom. We thank the Creator. We thank Oqci."

He led the crowd in prayer. Yanis bowed his head but did not speak the words aloud.

The end of Omephas's speech meant the service was halfway complete. Yanis began to relax. Everything was happening without incident.

Kephalos spoke next. In his speech, he defended the goals of the revolution. "Some have disagreed with our practice of extending ownership of the creatures, but I believe that the true meaning of Oqci's doctrines is that the best of us should own the creatures, not just those who happened to be born into noble families. Oqci opposed artificial divisions created by humans. What mattered to him was having good and pure hearts. I believe this is also the central message of the revolution. Friends, our revolution would be welcomed by Oqci!"

Kephalos stepped down from the pulpit as applause filled the temple. Omephas walked to meet him at the centre of the altar and the two bowed to one another.

As Kephalos walked back to his seat, Omephas reached under the central table on the altar. What was he doing? A flash of metal glittered in his hand. It all happened so quickly.

"For the Soldiers of Oqci," he cried as he drove the dagger into Kephalos's back, causing both of them to fall to the ground. Omephas pulled it out and drove it in again. Shrieks of horror filled the room. "For dishonouring the teachings of Oqci," he shouted as blood splashed upon himself and across the altar.

Yanis froze. No. No. It was all happening again.

Nadeni rose from her seat and pulled Yanis up as well. She ran toward the altar as Yanis followed. "Drop the weapon," she cried.

No. No.

She ran onto the altar, Yanis close behind. She had no weapons with her. She could not face Omephas unarmed.

"Nadeni!" Yanis cried. But he was too far away from her.

Omephas rose from Kephalos's body with a crazed look in his eyes. He held the dagger out, ready to strike.

Nadeni balled her fists as she approached, preparing for a fight.

"No!" He was going to be too late.

As Nadeni got within several paces of Omephas, he raised the dagger toward her. But then, he brought it to his throat. In one motion, without hesitation, he drew it across. The red dripped down upon his blue robe. He collapsed to the ground just before Nadeni could reach him, with Yanis following moments later.

Yanis turned to Kephalos, who lay sprawled on the marble floor, a pool of blood forming around him. More of the RDF raced onto the stage and those from the Great Chamber gathered in a circle around Kephalos as the worshippers streamed toward the exits. Blood poured from the wounds in Kephalos's back. It was clear that he could not be revived.

Yanis screamed in frustration as Nadeni grabbed hold of him.

"It's not your fault, Yanis," she urged. "It's not your fault."

But she was wrong. How could he not have examined the altar for weapons? How could he have been so slow to react? Yanis had failed once again.

CHARLOTTE

"Yanis," Charlotte said, kneeling beside him, "this was not your fault."

He crouched upon the floor next to Kephalos's body, his head hanging down.

"We need the RDF now more than ever," she continued, putting her hand on his forearm. He turned to her, and she looked him in the eyes. "We need strength now. Strength from you."

The temple had nearly emptied now, save for the Great Chamber members and the RDF soldiers who stood around the altar. Perhaps Charlotte was numb to the situation. Kephalos's death had not yet hit her. Quinneas too simply stared at the two bodies and kept shaking his head, unable to summon words.

Yanis slowly nodded. "You are right. Thank you, Charlotte." He rose to his feet to collect his RDF soldiers and gave instructions in a soft voice.

Nadeni approached Charlotte. "Thank you," she said. "I know you and Yanis have quarrelled. But I appreciate your kind words."

Charlotte nodded. She still felt nothing, yet she looked down at her hands and saw they were trembling.

Instinctively, she climbed to the pulpit to address those still gathered. "We have lost a great man," she said. "The revolution would not have happened without gentle Kephalos. It was he who proposed the formation of the Great Chamber. It was he who provided strength even when the king imprisoned us. It was he who inspired us by his great integrity, by refusing to be bound by narrow class or religious interests. Kephalos will go down in history as a martyr for equality and justice. He always acted in the interests of all humanity, not just believers. His faith, which transcended class lines, should serve as an example to us all. Friends, we have lost a great man today."

The loss was finally beginning to hit her as Charlotte reached the end of her impromptu speech. "But friends, we must carry on his work. We cannot allow our revolution to be destroyed by the work of these terrorists. We must be strong. Long live the revolution!"

"Hear, hear!" shouted the crowd. Quinneas nodded to her as she descended. It was exactly what the people needed to hear.

"THE SITUATION CANNOT STAND!" Quinneas seethed once he and Charlotte returned home. "I've had enough of this Oqci bullshit!"

Charlotte held his arm in a bid to calm him as they sat next to one another on his sofa. His pulse pounded. "You're right," she said. "The situation is untenable. We must do everything in our power to stop them."

There was to be no traditional Descent Day meal this evening after the earlier horrors. Who could possibly have had an appetite at such a time?

"Yes," he said, growing calmer. "But this nonsense just shows how deep the rot in our society runs." He broke free from her and stood. "Charlotte, I have been thinking about something. Since the first attacks by these Soldiers of Oqci. Even before."

"What is it?"

He paced around the room slowly. "When we were the interim committee... there were fifteen of us. We were able to govern so much more effectively. We could make decisions much more quickly."

"That is true," she said. "But what are you suggesting?"

"In normal times, the Great Chamber and its large member-ship is valuable. But now, during these times of crisis, what is needed is a smaller, more nimble body," he said. "One that can take decisions rapidly in the face of this grave threat."

"But, Quinneas, the Great Chamber and the constitution are the triumphs of our revolution, are they not?"

"Indeed, but did not today prove how fragile the revolution is? How enemies lurk all around us, even among those we considered friends?"

Charlotte sighed. His words were logical. No one knew how far the influence of the Soldiers of Oqci extended. Those they thought were allies could actually be working against the revolution. "What you are proposing would only be a temporary body, would it not?"

"Of course," he said. "Once the situation with the Soldiers of Oqci is brought under control, the body will be disbanded."

THE NEXT DAY, an emergency meeting of the Great Chamber was called. A surge of pain jolted through Charlotte when her eyes fell upon the empty seat that once belonged to Kephalos. His body would be laid to rest the following day.

Quinneas paid tribute to their late colleague in a speech and proposed the idea he and Charlotte discussed the previous evening. The situation with the Soldiers of Oqci was too grave. It was therefore necessary, he said, to create an Emergency Committee, a small body that could act quickly without needing to pass legislation in the full chamber.

Recognizing the importance of the situation, the Great Chamber passed the proposal overwhelmingly. There was much wrangling about who should compose the committee. Selver Bronn demanded a position, but this was refused. In the end, the committee included just five members. Quinneas and Charlotte, naturally, were on the committee. Additionally, Quinneas had suggested two radical members, Tressa Smith and Aran Potter. Tressa, from Iron Town, was from the working classes and had organized strikes by women factory workers. Aran was also a radical, a cobbler from the rural south of Estenland. But they should, Charlotte suggested to Quinneas, at least have a representative from the moderates, so they appointed Charlotte's friend, the former nobleman Koralo, Count of Ulsted, as the final member.

The five met later that day for the first session in the former king's council room. Quinneas entered and walked toward the end of the room, where a portrait of Aramal hung on the centre of the wall. He immediately pulled down the painting before anyone could even sit down.

"Let us store this painting somewhere," he said. "It is a relic of the past that might interest future generations."

Tressa and Aran snickered. The other paintings of the past monarchs were also removed.

With the king's eyes no longer looking down upon them, they sat around the table – much too big for just the five of them – and began their work.

Quinneas's voice echoed in the room as he suggested that, for matters of national security, it would be necessary for the Emergency Committee to have the power to interrogate and try those accused of crimes against the revolution. Petty crimes could be dealt with in the usual fashion, but the terrorism of the Soldiers of Oqci was too urgent to wait for the courts. It could take months for a case to wind its way through the legal system. Once the threat had passed, they would restore the normal laws.

This was agreed 5–0.

It was necessary as well to expand the role of the Revolutionary Defence Force. Tressa suggested that it be renamed the People's Army to better reflect that it was by the people and for the people. This proposal too passed 5–0 without concern, and the force was accordingly increased to five thousand soldiers.

Proposal after proposal came and went so quickly in their committee that Charlotte barely had time to contemplate them before they voted.

Tressa spoke next. "Some among us had previously expressed hesitation about reinstituting torture. But have not the terrible actions of the Soldiers of Oqci shown its necessity?"

Before Charlotte could even think, Quinneas signalled his agreement. "Yes, while there should be no formal laws allowing torture, in individual cases it may be necessary. I propose that in such cases, its use be voted on in the committee. I trust in all of us to ensure it is only used in exceptional cases."

With that, he called for a vote. The four other members voted in favour. The committee waited upon Charlotte. All their eyes were trained upon her. Quinneas furrowed his brow at her hesitation.

But his proposal was reasonable, she told herself. "I too vote in favour."

"Next," Quinneas said, "I believe it necessary to temporarily prohibit religious gatherings at temples in the capital. High Commander Haller, the Dragon Slayer, has warned that these temples are recruiting grounds for the Soldiers of Oqci. The group's leadership preys upon these simple-minded worshippers."

"Let it be known that I cannot lend my support to such a measure," said Koralo. "The people have a deep yearning for their faith. The holy doctrines signify so much to so many of our fellow countrymen, and it would simply not do for us to curtail their worship."

Quinneas shook his head. "No, no, Mr. Ulsted. We need to begin weaning the people off this Oqci nonsense. We have seen where it leads. Look at what happened to those killed at the sacred creature markets. And now Kephalos!"

"It is only a temporary measure, Mr. Ulsted," Charlotte added, more softly, in hopes of mollifying him. "Our constitution guarantees freedom of religion, and once the Soldiers of Oqci have been defeated, worship will be restored."

Koralo shrugged his shoulders. "Very well then. But let it be known that I object."

The vote passed 4–1 on Koralo's objection, the only non-unanimous vote the entire day.

As the day ended, Charlotte felt the spinning feeling again. All of this seemed to be happening so quickly. But her mind flashed back to the image of Kephalos's body, surrounded by a pool of blood, and she reassured herself that the measures were necessary to ensure the safety of the revolution.

SAMUEL

What did people think would happen after this so-called revolution? If only people understood human nature, like Samuel did, they would've known that it would end in disaster. First, the Soldiers of Oqci and now Quinneas using the crisis to further his own power. Samuel had seen it all coming. He had predicted it all in his book.

Yet few recognized it, even now. Still people wrote to him, cursing him as a miserable delinquent for daring to question the great revolution. But there was also the occasional letter that congratulated him for saying what they were thinking but were too scared to express publicly.

Samuel also received a calling card from Brondin, Earl of Evesbury, in the day's mail. The card spoke positively of Samuel's book and invited him to Brondin's estate. Brondin did not indicate the purpose of the visit, only that it was to discuss a personal matter. What could he want? After insulting Brondin's sister in his book, Samuel worried that Brondin wanted to enact some kind of revenge against him. But his curiosity was piqued.

THE NEXT DAY, Samuel took a carriage to Brondin's estate, just outside the city limits. One needed to travel along a road surrounded on all sides by fields and forest, up the snaking driveway until, at last, one reached the palatial house. Samuel could see that the land confiscations of the revolution had not seriously dented the Evesbury family wealth.

As one of the servants opened the giant wooden doors to the house and led Samuel inside, he thought of all the cramped, squalid apartments he had lived in – some of them smaller than the opulent drawing room in which he currently waited.

"Greetings, Dr. Nox," Brondin said upon entering. He wore a sparkling red coat, waistcoat, and breeches, all patterned with gold, a frilled white neck cloth, and an aletolium pendant. A simple black suit would not do for a great lord like him.

Brondin extended his hand. Samuel remained still as Brondin continued to hold it out awkwardly. He looked down with a grimace, then over at his waiting servant. Samuel paused several more seconds before at last he returned the handshake.

With the awkwardness broken, Brondin motioned Samuel to sit down, while he did the same. "Dr. Nox, let me begin by saying that I believe you have been responsible for a great wrong. In fact, two of the murdered creatures which you dissected belonged to my family."

"If the goal is to berate me for that affair," Samuel said, "I am uninterested."

"No, no," Brondin said. "I don't wish that. It was an unfortunate thing, but it is in the past." He stood and made his way to the one of the bookcases on the edge of the room. "No, I wished to discuss a different issue." He pulled down *A Revolution of Dirt* from the shelf. "I was very interested in this little book," Brondin said, holding it up. "I shall ignore the disrespectful things you said about my sister, but I believe the rest is spot on. Particularly what you wrote about Quinneas Raeil. He is a fraud and a deeply dangerous man."

"Indeed."

"He is dangerous for our nation," he said, returning to his seat on the sofa, "but I believe he also has a dangerous hold over my sister."

"In other words, he is performing such acts with her that would offend Oqci and the Creator?"

Brondin flushed. "I shall ignore that crude remark. But I believe he has had a very bad influence on her and I would like to remove him from her life." He paused. "Maybe I would like to remove him altogether. I understand you are no great admirer of his either. Perhaps we might together work on a plan to deal with him."

"So I should do your dirty work for you?"

"Don't look at it as doing something for me. Look at it as each of us helping the other to gain something we both desire. Come and walk with me."

They descended to the ground floor and exited at the back of the manor, which opened onto a lush garden. They walked down a path through trees and shrubs of every variety. Samuel saw empty pens that had once held sacred creatures. Samuel wondered if they were perhaps killed in the battle with the Friezzians or sold off to cover lost expenses.

"Here is my idea. I shall host Quinneas and Charlotte for dinner one night," Brondin said as they walked further from the house into ever denser gardens. "At the appointed time, I shall bring Quinneas here, into the gardens, while my wife entertains Charlotte inside. Once Quinneas is here, I shall tell him I need to retrieve something from the house, leaving him alone. As you can see, there is considerable cover for you to hide. No one will notice you in the darkness of the trees. Once Quinneas is alone, you can do as you please. The less I know the better. Just ensure you disappear promptly after the job is done. The blame will inevitably fall upon the Soldiers of Oqci and neither of us shall be implicated."

Samuel scratched his chin. "It is an intriguing plan."

Brondin was right, Samuel reasoned. It would be easy to conceal oneself in the trees and to disappear just as easily as one appeared. And as Brondin said, everyone's suspicion would immediately fall upon the Soldiers of Oqci.

The thought of seeing Quinneas, that arrogant fraud, whimper like a baby before departing this earth filled Samuel with a sick pleasure. Samuel would make him suffer just as he had made Samuel suffer.

But there was simply too much that could go wrong. Too many uncertainties. And was he not already becoming somewhat of a celebrity with his book?

"What do you think?" Brondin asked, as they continued walking in the gardens. "I shall of course compensate you financially."

Samuel shook his head. "It is tempting," he said. "Truly it is. But I must decline."

He bid Brondin well and departed his estate. Yet his proposal continued to bound around in Samuel's mind as he returned to his flat. Should he turn Brondin in for conspiracy to assassinate the leader of the Great Chamber? Ha! The idea of it. Samuel would be praised as a national hero!

But Samuel thought better of it. Let them have their family quarrel. He had no need to participate. And Quinneas would get his justice in time. Was that not the nature of things?

In Samuel's mail several days later came a bulletin from the King's Biological Society. (They had yet to change the name. Someone must tell them that the king was no more!) Scanning the table of contents, Samuel's eyes jumped immediately to the name "Greta." A flurry of excitement came over him. But her last name was different! The article, on plant anatomy, was co-authored by Robert Grim and... Greta Grim! But that wasn't right. Her name was Greta Esant.

Did she marry Robert? Or could this be a different Greta? Or a printing error? No, that would be impossible.

No! No! No!

Samuel's chest tightened and he struggled to breathe. The itching. Oh, the itching! He staggered toward his chair. He needed to sit down and scratch.

His mind turned to horrible thoughts. Robert Grim! He too had been a promising student. He had, Samuel imagined, won Greta's heart through his good looks and his scientific genius. The two must have worked in the lab long hours together and had fallen in love and married. No! This must be a terrible dream.

Samuel picked up the bulletin and hurled it as hard as he could across the room. No! This was meant to be his life!

Samuel returned the next day to Brondin's estate.

"Why the change of heart?" he asked.

"Never mind why," Samuel said. But he explained he wanted monetary compensation for his trouble, enough so that he could travel to New Selver or some far-flung place and never have to think about his miserable life in Estenland again.

Brondin agreed. Half the money would be paid beforehand; the other half to come after Samuel had completed the deed. The deal was done.

CHARLOTTE

A letter from Brondin? Whatever could he want?

To Charlotte's surprise, the letter was cordial. He had heard news of her engagement to Quinneas, he said, and wished to reconcile before the wedding. With this end in mind, he invited Charlotte and Quinneas to dine at his estate.

"We can hardly be dining out and enjoying ourselves whilst in the midst of a national crisis," said Quinneas sternly when she told him of the invitation. "And with your brother? The one who publicly undermined you? The one who gave you over to the police? No. We simply cannot go."

"Please, Quinneas," she said. "Brondin and I have a difficult relationship, but I don't wish us to remain on bad terms. Especially before our wedding. Let us to try to put old grudges aside."

"I don't trust the nobility," he said, shaking his head. "No, I never have. And I never shall. Being brought up in such wealth, such privilege. They cannot be trusted!"

A strange feeling came upon Charlotte as he said this. Did he not remember that she was from the nobility?

"But don't you trust me?" she said.

His expression softened when he realized what he had implied. "I... Of course I do."

"Then trust me that it will be fine. I promise." With that, he had no choice but to agree to attend.

As the two arrived at Charlotte's old home, anxieties filled her mind. Could Brondin and Quinneas manage to get along for several hours without descending into argument? More importantly, could she and Brondin? Charlotte prepared for the worst.

A disagreement that descended into a shouting match, with her and Quinneas storming off. But Charlotte had lectured Quinneas beforehand that he mustn't be baited by any of Brondin's remarks, and she told herself the same.

They were greeted by Brondin and Allegrette upon arrival. The dinner was to be the four of them, as their son had been put to bed. Charlotte's mother was, as ever, too unwell to join them.

They began with appetizers and discussion.

"I am so pleased that we could all be together," said Brondin, placing a small piece of cheese on a cracker. "There is no reason for us to be on bad terms."

"You're right," Charlotte said. "There is no reason we cannot be friendly with one another."

She looked over at Quinneas, who had a skeptical look on his face. Charlotte's eyes caught his. He realized this was his cue. "Yes," he said, a forced smile coming to his face. "Yes, I agree."

"You two seem a lovely couple," said Allegrette. "Have you set a date for your wedding?"

"Not yet," Charlotte said. "Once the threat of the Soldiers of Oqci has dissipated, we can begin to plan. The important thing is that we are committed to one another."

She expected Brondin to make a crack at this, but instead he said, "It is a dreadful thing, the Soldiers of Oqci. Simply dreadful."

"Our government is doing all it can do stop them," said Quinneas. "They must be defeated."

Brondin nodded his head. "Quite right."

Brondin led the guests into the dining room where the meal was served. As they dined and drank, Charlotte began to forget all the tension between them. Much to her surprise, everyone, even Quinneas, was having a pleasant time. Brondin was acting like a decent person for a change. Avoiding politics, their conversation addressed philosophy and literature and family life. Her fears of an argument were unfounded.

After dinner, they moved into the drawing room for a game of cards. "Let us have a drink while we play," said Brondin. He left and returned from his kitchen holding a bottle of liquor. It was very rare and expensive, Brondin explained. Charlotte worried that Quinneas, already slightly intoxicated from the wine at dinner, would make a scene about the pretensions of the nobles and their need for "rare and expensive" things, yet he simply said he was happy to imbibe.

She was pleased to see Quinneas in such a good mood. The alcohol had certainly enlivened him. The last months had been trying, but he seemed to be genuinely enjoying himself. At one point, he tried to stand from his armchair, but stumbled slightly and could barely walk straight, which caused everyone to burst into laughter.

"Let us get some air, my friend," said Brondin, who was none too steady himself. "Let us walk in the gardens and gaze at the stars. Here in the countryside they are more beautiful than what you are used to seeing in the city."

"Yes," said Quinneas, putting his hand on Brondin's shoulder, "I should like to see it."

They stumbled to the back gardens, arm-in-arm, while Charlotte made small talk with Allegrette, whom Charlotte found charming and intelligent.

Brondin returned alone soon afterward, saying he needed to retrieve his telescope from his study.

"Perhaps I shall join Quinneas outside whilst you retrieve it," Charlotte said. "Besides, he does not usually drink so much and I should keep him company in the garden."

"No, he'll be fine," Brondin said. "Worry not!"

"I'd feel better to see him."

"I said it was fine."

"Maybe Charlotte is right," Allegrette said. "It would do no harm for her to check on him."

Charlotte stood, but Brondin moved to block her path. "Just stay here."

"Excuse me," she said, "you don't have the right to determine where I go." She walked around him and toward the door, but he grabbed her arm. "Let go of me!" she shouted.

"Brondin, what on earth are you doing?" cried Allegrette.

"I told you to wait here," Brondin said angrily as he tried to pull Charlotte back to the drawing room.

"Stop it!" she screamed. "Stop it!" She shoved him away and ran downstairs toward the door.

SAMUEL

Samuel arrived before the scheduled time to camp in the gardens. The carriage dropped him some distance from the house and he walked the rest of the way, slipping through the back fence just as Brondin had instructed. The sun was already beginning to set as he found his way into the shrubbery off the path. The perfect hiding place.

The problem before him was that it could well be hours until Brondin brought Quinneas outside. But Samuel must remain there, even as insects buzzed all around and bit him. Curse them! Samuel brushed them away as he leaned against a tree and set his knapsack on the ground.

Perhaps this was all a mistake.

Samuel reached into his knapsack where he kept his pistol. And the pile of banknotes that Brondin had given him, in case things went awry and he needed to make his escape. Samuel pulled out a flask of liquor that he had brought to keep him occupied.

He considered the plan in his mind. Shoot Quinneas, disappear into the night, and wait for Brondin to send him the rest of the money. From there, Samuel would depart for his new life as the police searched in vain for the Soldiers of Oqci who would be presumed responsible. It all seemed reasonable.

But should he go through with it? Samuel took a large gulp to quiet his doubts, then another.

His mind flashed to Greta. And to that fucking Robert Grim. And to his ruined career. Why should Quinneas get to be happy? Why should he get to be the hero? After everything he did to Samuel!

Samuel took another swig. He sat now in growing darkness, breathing in the freshness of the country air and the scent of the trees' needles. From his hiding spot, he could see the house. He could discern light coming from the windows, but nothing more. Quinneas should enjoy himself now, Samuel thought. It will be his last night alive.

Another sip.

When would he come out? What time was it? How long had Samuel been waiting?

The effects of the drink lowered his willpower to resist the urge to scratch. Why not? He scratched so hard at a spot on his arm that he drew blood.

Maybe this was all a mistake.

Another sip.

Samuel's head spun. The darkness was disorienting, but at least the insects seemed to have quieted. Doubts crept into his mind, disappeared as quickly as they came, and returned quicker still.

Better take another drink. Samuel brought the flask to his lips but nothing came out. He tipped it upright and shook. A few measly drops splashed upon his face. He had drunk the whole thing without even realizing it.

Where was Quinneas?

Samuel pulled out his pistol and ran his hands over it, fiddling with the trigger. Soon justice would be done. Soon!

He needed to piss. He stood but tipped to one side and nearly toppled over. He braced himself against the tree trunk for stability. Keeping balanced required considerable effort. The world spun around him as he relieved himself for what seemed like several minutes, creating a small puddle in the dirt.

The door cracked open. At last!

Samuel straightened his trousers and quickly grabbed his pistol.

Two men's voices. Talking and laughing together. Two shadowy figures came into view under the moonlight. Quinneas and Brondin, just as promised. They stumbled together as Brondin led Quinneas into the gardens, only a dozen paces from Samuel. Brondin returned inside, just as they planned, while Quinneas stood outside in the fresh air.

Quinneas had no idea Samuel was there, lurking in the trees, waiting, watching him. He stood there, looking innocently up at the stars. Samuel quite enjoyed watching him, completely unsuspecting of what was to come.

Samuel stepped from the bushes, taking care not to lose his balance.

Quinneas looked over, groggily, rubbing his eyes to figure out who the figure was. He jumped back when he realized.

"Hello, dear friend," Samuel said, revealing the pistol and raising it toward him.

This seemed to sober Quinneas – and Samuel.

"Nox? What are you doing here?"

"You ruined my career. You ruined everything! You ruined my career as a scientist, then you kept me from serving in the RDF. If I had never met you, I wouldn't be in this mess. You cost me everything!"

"I did no such thing," Quinneas said, slowly backing away from Samuel. "I… I tried to help you when you were in trouble."

"Liar!" Samuel shouted as he walked toward him. "You lie to me now, just like you lied to the press. You think I should have the same fate as those men who were hanged, do you? Maybe *you* should have that fate!"

A noise from behind Quinneas distracted Samuel. The door!

"Quinneas?" a woman's voice called out.

Samuel looked toward the door, squinting to see who it was. Charlotte? His eyes moved back to Quinneas.

Too slowly.

Quinneas lunged toward him. Samuel aimed and fired, hitting him. A mist of blood in the darkness.

The kickback nearly toppled Samuel over. He struggled to regain his balance, but before he knew what was happening he was tackled to the ground. His pistol went flying. Charlotte flailed her fists at him.

The door creaked open. "Charlotte!" a man's voice said.

Samuel raised his hands to defend himself, but she was on top of him, pummelling him. Blows landing against his face and chest. He reached out to grab her arms, but she swung them away, out of his grasp.

"What is happening?" a woman's voice shrieked in the distance.

Suddenly, Brondin was on top of Samuel too, weighing down his chest while Charlotte grabbed his legs. Samuel squirmed on the ground to escape their grasp, but it was no use.

"Stop moving!" shouted Charlotte, as she exerted her whole weight upon his legs.

The door creaked opened again. Someone else exited. The two turned to look.

A weak woman's voice: "I... heard... shouting. What... is happening?"

"Mother!" cried Charlotte. She and Brondin both stood, relinquishing their grip on Samuel.

"What... is...?" the voice said, breathing heavily. A dull thud filled the night air as she collapsed to the ground.

"Mother!" Charlotte shouted again. She and Brondin raced toward her.

Samuel slowly rose to his feet. Everything was spinning. Charlotte and Brondin and another woman knelt over the mother, while Quinneas lay motionless on his back. Samuel looked for his pistol, but the ground was too dark. Blast it! He started running as fast as he could along the garden path.

DELLIREA

"If you care about me, you will tell me what happened to them," Dellirea said to Yunolarol.

"You know I am not able to talk about that," he said, as the two walked along a garden path near the palace on this warm summer day.

The restrictions on Dellirea's movement persisted, but if she agreed to spend time with Yunolarol, she was allowed to leave her room and get time apart from Lady Fondyrel – even if she still watched them from afar.

"But we shall one day wed," Dellirea said. "Then we shall have no secrets between us. Don't you trust me?"

Yunolarol sighed. "You can never tell anyone I told you. You must promise."

"I promise."

"It's a difficult thing," he said, looking down toward the ground, his foot awkwardly pushing about the stones on the path. From his tone, Dellirea braced herself for the worst. "I… I know not how to say it. But… they both… passed away."

Dellirea had long been sure of their fate, but to have it confirmed was more horrible than she could have imagined. She knew from his tone precisely what had happened. Yunolarol tried to put his arm around her, but she pushed him away.

"What about Rodnel?" she said. "Is he alive?"

Yunolarol sighed. "I've already said too much!"

"Please," she said, flashing her tearful eyes, "I would be forever grateful."

He sighed again. "This is the last thing I shall tell you. Yes, he is alive. He is safe and living on the palace grounds, but he is not to have any contact with you and vice versa."

Dellirea was cheered to learn that Rodnel lived. Other exiled nobles from Estenland lived in Friezzia as well, yet it was nice having one other Estenlander nearby in this strange land, even if she was not permitted to speak with him.

∼

"WHAT WERE you talking about with Yunolarol earlier?" said Lady Fondyrel as she led Dellirea back to her room.

"Nothing important," she said. "We were simply comparing Friezzian and Estenlander customs."

"Is that so?" she said. "It seemed as though the discussion was much more animated than it might be for a subject such as that."

Lady Fondyrel frightened Dellirea a little, but she did her best to persist in lying. "I suppose it did become rather animated for a topic so trivial."

"Do you wish to know how I lost my legs?" she said as they entered Dellirea's room.

At this Dellirea grew even more frightened. The question had certainly crossed her mind, but she really did not wish to know. It could be nothing good.

"It was when I crossed His Majesty."

Dellirea swallowed hard. She did not wish to look into Lady Fondyrel's eyes.

"Do you wish to know what I did?"

"No," Dellirea said weakly.

"I am going to tell you anyway," she said. "And you are going to listen. So you will not do anything so stupid."

Dellirea was shaking slightly as Lady Fondyrel talked. Dellirea knew there was to be no disobeying her. She knew she would have to listen.

"After the Great War, after your cursed country defeated ours, my husband and I attempted to overthrow Hyazaral. We gained the support of some of the other nobles at court. But Hyazaral discovered the plot just before it took place."

"Dear Oqci," Dellirea muttered. Her mouth had gone dry.

"He killed all those involved. Except my husband and I. He said he would spare us both. If only I could successfully run through the Hall of Blades. Do you know what that is?"

"No," Dellirea said, barely loud enough to be audible.

"It is a passage of a dozen swinging circular blades, each twice as tall as me. My task would simply be to cross through. If I escaped unharmed, the king promised to spare our lives and exile us."

Dellirea already imagined how the story would end, though Lady Fondyrel continued.

"In the gallery, my husband watched helplessly next to the king and his sons and the other nobles at court who joked and laughed, as if they were at a sporting match. 'Go on,' said Hyazaral. I gazed at the massive blades swinging in an alternating pattern. It would need to be a straight dash to make it through."

"Dear Oqci…"

"I studied the pattern of the blades closely and prayed for Oqci to grant me his favour. When the first blade was in the centre, I knew it was the time go. I could tell there was an opening that if I just ran fast enough, I could do it. I took a deep breath. I dashed forward, running with all my might. I cleared the first, then the second, then the third… It all happened in a blur. I pumped my legs as hard as I could and dove past the final one. I landed hard on my stomach. But I had done it. We were safe!"

"But…?"

"The king and the nobles started laughing. My husband shouted, 'No! No!' I tried to lift myself up but noticed I couldn't. I turned onto my back and looked down. There I saw two bloody stumps where my legs had once been. The severed legs lay there upon the floor, just below the final swinging blade, my blood still dripping off it. I had come so close. So, so close to winning both of us our lives. But not close enough.

"Hyazaral taunted me from up in the gallery. 'The deal was that you had to make it through *unharmed.*' I looked in horror at my husband. He began to say, 'I love…' when one of the king's guards grabbed him and slit his throat right there. I screamed and pounded my fists upon the floor. I couldn't even feel the blood pouring from me.

"The rest I don't remember. For my punishment, the king ordered his doctors to spare my life. So I could live forever in the palace, thinking about my failures." Lady Fondyrel stopped and stared at the floor. "But how I wished he had just killed me, too."

Dellirea felt like crying, or vomiting, but she was too weak for either. "I'm sorry," she said quietly, shaking from the story. "Dear Oqci, I am sorry."

"Lady Zendar, awful things await you if you are not careful," Lady Fondyrel said. "Hyazaral may not care for you. But, against my better judgment, I do. This is why I beg you, please, learn from my mistakes and do not cross him. Good night."

HAVING to spend her seventeenth birthday, alone, in Friezzia was a terrible fate. The king had asked what she wished for her birthday. Would she like, he suggested, to dine with Yunolarol? To this, Dellirea politely declined. But what she really wished to say was that of all the things that she could possibly imagine doing for her birthday, dining with Yunolarol would fall at the very bottom of the list.

She dined alone that evening instead, as she requested, before Lady Fondyrel escorted her back to her bedroom. She gave Dellirea a weak smile as she wished her happy birthday and shut the door for the night. The terrible story of her fate continued to run through Dellirea's mind. She could hardly imagine such cruelty.

She tried to efface all these thoughts from her mind – about Lady Fondyrel, about Yunolarol, about everything. She tried to think happier thoughts, like about Charlotte, the noblewoman. But this, too, was a vexed subject.

Dellirea had had similar dreams in the nights since the first one, but she was not sure that they were right. The doctrine of Oqci taught clearly that one man was supposed to be with one woman, just as he had married Mazir. Yet, Dellirea wasn't sure she wanted to be a Mazir to some man. Perhaps she wanted a

Mazir for herself. But if she did, she wondered, would she be able to enter the Cloud Kingdom when she died? Would she be able to see her father and mother and brother again?

But then, she thought of Kephalos's words and the book by Phantos. All the inconsistencies in the holy scriptures. Maybe there was a true core, beyond the stories themselves. Maybe the message of Oqci was simply about love, and if this were true, Dellirea reasoned, she could still go to the Cloud Kingdom.

The sun had now gone down. Before she went to sleep, she lay in bed reading the Book of Oqci by candlelight, even as she could hardly focus.

Just as her eyes were becoming heavy, a loud streaming sound followed by an explosion jolted her to reality. It sounded like a rocket flying through the air and exploding. The palace was under attack!

Dellirea raced to her window and drew back the curtains as her heart pounded. Bright flashes from the explosions illuminated her room and made her shield her eyes.

Wait… These were not rockets at all!

Explosions of every colour dotted the sky outside Dellirea's window. Fireworks!

The whirring and booming and crackling continued as her room turned the most brilliant shades of green, red, purple, orange, and blue.

Dellirea pressed her face against the window and looked to the ground. Why, it was Rodnel! He was lighting them for her.

She waved down to him. He looked up and waved back, before lighting another firework.

Happiness filled Dellirea's heart, and tears came to her eyes. Rodnel was a true friend.

YANIS

anging upon Yanis's door startled him awake in the middle of the night. He stumbled out of bed and to the door. It was an aide from the People's Army.

"High Commander, I have terrible news," he said. "Quinneas Raeil has been shot."

"Dear Oqci!"

"But he is alive."

Yanis and Nadeni quickly dressed and rushed to the hospital. They rode in a carriage with the aide. Along the way, he told them what was known so far. Samuel Nox, the disgraced scientist, had shot Quinneas then disappeared. It had taken place outside the Evesbury estate, where Charlotte and Quinneas were meeting Charlotte's brother for dinner. There was no indication yet whether this was connected to the Soldiers of Oqci.

Yanis's mind hurried through the scenarios. Nox had enough of his own motives to hate Quinneas. For his role in the end of his scientific career and for denying him the position in the RDF, but it couldn't be ruled out that he was working with the Soldiers.

"We need to search the area around Brondin's estate," Yanis ordered the aide as they rode to the hospital. "Learn where Nox lives and post a team there. We must find him!"

When they arrived, Yanis and Nadeni were led down a series of corridors to Quinneas's room. A team of doctors and nurses surrounded Quinneas, while Charlotte and another man – quickly introduced as Brondin – sat next to him. Guarding the door were some of Yanis's soldiers from the People's Army.

Charlotte rose to greet them while her brother stayed seated. She had bags under her red, puffy eyes.

"How is he?" Yanis asked.

"He was hit in the shoulder, but he lost a great deal of blood," she said. "The doctor gave him an experimental gas in order to ease his pain. He is now asleep."

Yanis looked over at Quinneas, his face bone white and his eyes closed. "I'm so sorry, Charlotte."

"And my mother…" she said. "My mother passed. When she heard shouting and the gunshots, she rushed outside and collapsed from the stress. It was all too much for her in her weakened state."

"Dear Oqci," Yanis said, clutching her hand. "That's horrible." Turning to Brondin, "Lord Evesbury, I'm deeply sorry for your loss."

Charlotte's brother nodded, but he was clearly still in shock. Charlotte fought back tears.

"We shall find Nox and bring him to justice," Yanis said. "I pledge that to both of you. No resources will be spared."

"Thank you," said Brondin.

"Yanis," Charlotte said, suddenly more composed, "might I speak to you in private?"

He nodded and the two found an unoccupied room in the hospital as Nadeni stayed with Quinneas and Brondin.

"What is it?" Yanis asked once they were alone.

"I believe that Brondin orchestrated Nox's actions."

"What? How could that be?"

She described Brondin's dinner party, how Brondin led Quinneas outside and tried to restrain her from exiting, just at the time Nox confronted him. It could not be a coincidence, she said.

"But what did Brondin say afterward?" Yanis asked.

"He said it must have been the Soldiers of Oqci. I feared for my life since, with Quinneas incapacitated, I was all alone with Brondin and his wife. I made no accusations against him. I said nothing so that we could take Quinneas and my mother to the hospital and to alert the People's Army. But I know he was behind it all."

Yanis reflected on her words. What she said made considerable sense. "It was wise not to let him know of your suspicions. I shall question him."

YANIS RETURNED to the People's Army headquarters – the old police station – with Brondin while Nadeni remained with Charlotte. Brondin complained the entire way that he needed to remain at the hospital to support Charlotte, which only led Yanis to suspect him more. But he assured Brondin it was merely a common procedure to begin the investigation.

Once they arrived at the headquarters, Yanis brought Brondin into one of the interrogation rooms. "Did you have any role in this?"

"Me? I had no part in this. How could you even suggest such a thing? I have no idea how that... that maniac got onto my lands! For my part, I believe it was the Soldiers of Oqci."

"Charlotte told me that you took Quinneas outside into the gardens and came back inside at precisely the time Nox confronted Quinneas. When Charlotte tried to go outside, you attempted to restrain her. How can you explain that?"

"Charlotte said that?" he said, becoming increasingly erratic. "She had too much to drink that night! She is hardly reliable. And my mother has just died! Have you no decency, dragging me here and asking me these kinds of questions?"

"Were you working with Nox? Were you working with the Soldiers of Oqci?"

Brondin let out a laugh and shook his head. Yanis grabbed him by his collar and pushed him against the wall. He screamed. Yanis pulled him close, their faces inches apart. "Were you working with them?"

"No!" he cried. "No!"

He was lying. Yanis wanted so badly to make him talk, yet he stopped himself. He had always opposed torture. It was a tool of the king, and Yanis was lucky to have escaped it himself. Still, the Emergency Committee could authorize its use in specific cases. The thought entered Yanis's mind. However, one of the members was on the edge of death and another was in no shape to make such a decision. Yanis resolved that the investigation would continue as they held Brondin.

There was no time to waste. Yanis communicated with the other branches of the People's Army across the country. All were to be looking for Nox. Yanis's soldiers scoured the city and searched all trains and carriages leaving the city limits. He must be found!

SAMUEL

"Wake up," a woman's voice said. "Wake up."

Samuel forced his eyes open a crack, but the blinding sun made him shut them tightly again. Everything was hot. The ground was hard, and his clothes were drenched in sweat. His head felt like it was being pounded with a hammer over and over. Samuel let out a groan of pain as he opened his eyes again.

"The poor fellow," a man's voice said. "He's had too much to drink."

Finally, Samuel propped himself up on his elbows and reluctantly looked around. He was in a village, on the side of a dirt road. A middle-aged couple helped him to his feet and led him on a short walk to their small house.

Scattered memories of the previous night flashed through his mind, though he wasn't sure which were real and which dreams. Waiting in the bushes. Shooting Quinneas. Running in the darkness for what seemed like hours. His head continued pulsing as he thought about it.

Inside the couple's modest thatch-roofed house, Samuel saw some unicorn trinkets on their mantle. Religious fools!

"Where am I?" Samuel asked.

"Why, you're in Farnestead," said the woman pleasantly.

Farnestead? That was even further outside the city than Brondin's estate. Samuel must have been running in the exact wrong direction.

"Please sit," the man said, leading Samuel into the kitchen to a small wooden table. The couple, called Will and Olive Hunt, brought him some water and bread with jam. Suddenly he realized how hungry and thirsty he was. Samuel guzzled three glasses of water and crammed the bread into his mouth much too quickly, to the couple's bemusement.

They asked who he was and where he came from. He told them he was Eston Miller, a dock worker from Iron Town who had gotten lost while walking outside the city. Perhaps they didn't believe him, but they listened without cynicism.

A bath was prepared for him; he reeked of sweat and alcohol. He took off his damp clothes and noticed there were scratch marks all over his body. Blast!

Samuel lowered himself into the small tub full of lukewarm water. It felt nice. Refreshing. He laid back in the tub as best as possible, his knees sticking out of the water, and began to get his mind around his situation. The police would surely be on his trail now.

What happened last night? Samuel shot Quinneas... but did he kill him? And what about the mother?

Samuel leaned further into the tub and submerged his head under the water for several seconds.

He couldn't go back to his apartment in the capital. The police would be waiting there. An alternative plan began to form in his mind. He would travel to the port and use the money from Brondin to book a voyage overseas to one of Estenland's colonies on whichever ship had a place for him.

Dear Oqci! The money! The knapsack! Did he take it with him when he left? Where was it?

Samuel exited the bath and hastily dried himself before throwing on the fresh pair of clothes Will had provided for him. Samuel asked the couple if they had seen his knapsack when they had found him. They both looked at him confusedly.

"You didn't have anything with you," said Olive.

"No," said Will, "just the clothes on your back."

"There is something very important in that knapsack," Samuel explained frantically, as he dashed outside to look for it. "Something very important!"

The village was small and peaceful. Modest stone houses dotted the roads that cut across the fields. As puzzled villagers stood outside their little houses watching Samuel, he ran down every road, searching for it.

Nothing!

"I'm ruined!" Samuel shouted, falling to his knees. "I'm ruined!"

Olive and Will rushed behind and stood watching over him. "The poor man," said Olive. "He's gone mad."

YANIS

Quinneas's condition improved over the next several days, and Yanis and Charlotte agreed he was now well enough to learn the news.

"We have discovered Samuel Nox's knapsack, filled with a stack of banknotes, amongst the trees in Brondin's gardens," Yanis explained. "The notes were clearly payment from Brondin to Nox."

Quinneas looked agitated as he sat up in bed, but said nothing.

"What was more," Yanis continued, "one of Brondin's servants recalled Nox meeting with Brondin just days before. When we presented the evidence to him, Brondin confessed to engineering the whole thing. He has begged for mercy and promised to do everything to help find Nox."

Neither Yanis nor Charlotte were in the mood for mercy. Brondin had nearly killed her fiancé and caused the death of her mother. From Quinneas's expression of fury, Yanis could see he had the same opinion.

"I wish to speak with Brondin," Quinneas said.

"Are you sure that is wise?" asked Charlotte. "Your health is still fragile."

"Charlotte is correct, my friend," Yanis said. "You must rest. Brondin has confessed and we shall soon have captured Nox."

"No, the country is in crisis," Quinneas said, struggling out of bed. "It needs its leader."

Yanis caught a hint of confusion from Charlotte as he made that remark, since the country had no single leader. The five members of the Emergency Committee were supposed to be equal, and even then, they ruled with the consent of the Great Chamber.

"Hand me my clothes," he said to Charlotte.

When she hesitated, Quinneas charged past her and began gathering his clothes to get dressed right then and there.

~

Yanis accompanied Quinneas and Charlotte to the familiar prison where they had been held some months ago.

"My friend, slow down," Yanis pleaded, as Quinneas marched ahead of him and Charlotte across the bridge and into the prison's entryway.

He ignored Yanis as he strode down the hallways. Yanis and Charlotte struggled to keep pace with him even though it was he who had spent nearly a week in hospital.

At last, they reached the cell where Brondin sat meekly on his bed. Brondin turned to look at his visitors, and his face went white when he saw Quinneas.

Brondin rose to speak, but before he could, Quinneas shouted, "You wished me dead? You coward! Nox at least had the fortitude to do the deed. But you, you fiend, you acted so nicely to Charlotte and me, knowing the whole time you would soon be sending me to my death!"

Brondin put his head down, saying nothing.

"Pathetic," Quinneas said, shaking his head. "Pathetic. You will pay for your crimes. You will face the justice of the people!"

"Please," Brondin whimpered at last. "Please. I have a wife and son. They need me."

This only enraged Quinneas more. "You should've considered that before you plotted my death!"

"Quinneas," Charlotte said, placing her hand on his forearm, "this stress is not good for your health. Let us go."

"Yes," he said, "I can't stand to be in the presence of this vile excuse for a man any longer."

Quinneas walked furiously through the halls of the prison.

"Please, Quinneas," Yanis called out. "Please, my friend. Calm yourself."

He turned to Yanis, but his face was like stone.

CHARLOTTE

Charlotte busied herself at home during the day, awaiting news of the committee's decision. With the state of emergency in effect, the Emergency Committee had the sole ability to try cases. Brondin had already confessed so the only question was punishment. Charlotte was forced to withdraw – it would, the other four members agreed, surely be a conflict of interest – leaving the others to decide on Brondin's fate.

Attempts to divert herself were unsuccessful. She checked the clock impulsively, and she imagined that every sound outside was Quinneas's carriage returning. She tried to read a book to pass the time, but she could not focus. She managed to read only a paragraph, but by the time she reached its end, she realized she had no recollection what she had just read. Thoughts of Brondin, thoughts of the Soldiers of Oqci, thoughts of the revolution clouded her mind. How simple life used to be!

Just before sunset, the clopping of horse hooves outside indicated Quinneas's arrival. Charlotte raced to the window to watch him, attempting to gain a hint of the decision. He exited the carriage slowly and with considerable difficulty. He walked with an uneven gait, but Charlotte could gain no indication from his facial expression. By the time he arrived inside, he was already out of breath.

"Well?" Charlotte asked.

Quinneas raised a finger, signalling he needed a moment. He nearly collapsed into his chair.

Charlotte stood anxiously before him as he caught his breath.

"The committee… has decided unanimously… for the death penalty," said Quinneas, still huffing.

"Dear Oqci" was all she could say. She had expected the news, but it finally felt real hearing Quinneas say it aloud.

Brondin was still her brother, still her blood. How had it come to this? She could not disagree, and yet...

"I know that he is your brother, Charlotte. But this was not just a murder attempt. It was an attempt to overthrow the entire revolution. This was treason. It is the right decision, however difficult it may be personally. You must know we had no other course."

She wanted to plead for him to reverse the decision. To exile Brondin. To imprison him. To spare his life somehow. But she knew Quinneas was right. "I understand."

"The execution will be tomorrow," continued Quinneas.

"So soon?"

"It cannot wait."

Charlotte feared the answer to the question but she knew she must ask. "And the execution will be public?"

"It will."

That, too, she knew would be inevitable. She felt sick nevertheless. "Is there not some way to conduct the execution privately? Just think of the behaviour of the people at the execution of the king and queen... I'm not sure I can bear to see Brondin treated that way."

Quinneas lifted himself from his chair with difficulty. He stood over Charlotte with a frightening lack of emotion in his eyes and grasped her by the shoulders. "You know that would be inappropriate. We cannot show weakness to anyone who dares to challenge the revolution, even if they are family. You must understand that, Charlotte. You must understand that Brondin cannot escape justice."

That night Charlotte slept fitfully. Quinneas was so exhausted from his injury that he did not stir throughout the night, even as she tossed and turned.

She could not efface the images of the king and queen's execution from her mind. To think of poor Brondin up there on the gallows made her sick. Yet what choice did they have?

Brondin was guilty and his fate could be no other. Even so, Charlotte dreaded it just the same. She only hoped that the crowd showed some solemnity out of respect for her and all she had done for the revolution. She was owed that much, surely.

❧

ONE OF THE servants woke them at dawn. Charlotte had thought she had been awake all night, yet just then she realized she must have drifted off. But she was far from rested.

The execution would be taking place shortly.

"Quinneas, I wish to speak to Brondin before his execution," she said, as they dressed. "I understand that there is no delaying the execution, but let me say goodbye."

"I'm sorry, Charlotte. It is not possible," Quinneas said. He appeared more refreshed following his long sleep. "The execution has already been carefully planned, and a meeting would not be appropriate."

"Even for two minutes?" she said.

"It is not possible."

"Be reasonable, Quinneas," she shot back. "Two minutes will cause no harm to your preparations."

"You are letting sentimentality overcome you," he said coldly. "The answer is no."

They sat in silence as Quinneas ate oats and strawberries for breakfast. Charlotte had no appetite. Quinneas carefully avoided eye contact as he ate slowly but industriously, fuelling himself for the day ahead.

As Charlotte watched him, she tried to console herself that the decision had been made just as it would have been if Brondin were no relation to her. Yet at that moment she despised Quinneas.

❧

CHARLOTTE AND QUINNEAS walked to Karazin Square, still not

speaking. Along the route were signs all around that read, "PUNISHMENT FOR TRAITORS."

As they walked to the stage, Quinneas was already almost out of breath and Charlotte was wearied from lack of sleep. She was so delirious from the exhaustion and the strangeness of the event that she belatedly realized things were much different than when the king and queen had been executed. Where were the gallows? Instead, the stage faced out upon an enclosed pen with walls too high for anyone to climb, surrounded by hastily constructed bleachers. An eager crowd had already been packed into the seats.

"What is happening?" she said to Quinneas, her heart beating rapidly. She looked all around and began to feel dizzy. This was not right at all.

"Brondin is going to be punished in a manner suitable for his crime," said Quinneas.

"What does that mean?"

"You will soon see what it means. Everyone here will see what it means. I could not tell you beforehand, for I knew you would try to stop it."

Before Charlotte could protest, Quinneas left her seated as he walked to the podium. He used a speaking trumpet to address the assembled crowd. "Fellow citizens," he said, still struggling to gain his breath, "what you are about to see may disturb you, but it is important that you not look away. You must see what awaits all those who oppose the revolution." He took a deep breath and seemed to gain new energy. "Long live the revolution! Long live the revolution!"

The crowd cheered furiously as Brondin, wearing all white and bound at his hands and feet, was brought into the centre of the pen by two guards. Quinneas returned to sit next to Charlotte, though he did not dare look at her.

"Unchain him," Quinneas shouted from his seat.

Brondin's chains were removed. He looked around frantically.

Dear Oqci, what was happening?

"Release the griffin," Quinneas ordered.

The door of the pen was opened and several guards led out one of the royal griffins.

"Quinneas, what in the name of Oqci are you doing?" Charlotte said. "Have you gone mad?"

"Just watch," he said, his eyes never moving from Brondin. "Witness the justice of the revolution."

The griffin towered above Brondin and slowly circled him. It unfolded its massive wings, nearly covering the entire pen in shadow.

"Please, don't do this!" cried Brondin, looking up at the stage toward Quinneas. "Please!"

The griffin screeched, and the crotch of Brondin's trousers grew dark.

"Look," a voice in the crowd shouted, "he's pissed himself!" The audience erupted in laughter.

Cheers of anticipation filled the square as the griffin continued pacing around Brondin, eyeing him as if he were prey. Some people had even brought their children, whose innocent faces wore eager grins.

Charlotte gripped the arms of her seat tightly, feeling like if she didn't, she would tumble away from the dizziness.

The griffin's talons, each nearly twice the size of Brondin's head, dug into the dirt in the pen. The beast's tail swished back and forth as it crept ever closer.

Members of the crowd waved the tricolour flag of the revolution. Someone began the first lines of "Justice For All," and the rest of the crowd joined in, singing joyously. Charlotte suppressed the urge to vomit.

"Stop this!" she shouted to Quinneas.

"After he tried to have me killed?" said Quinneas angrily. "Charlotte, don't you love me?"

Helplessly, Charlotte watched in horror as the griffin drew closer and closer to Brondin, cornering him against the wall. It let out an ear-piercing screech.

"Please stop it!" she cried to Quinneas, who sat motionless, only staring at the ordeal taking place in front of him. She stood but could barely move. On wobbly legs, Charlotte staggered toward the pen, but several People's Army soldiers blocked her path.

The griffin swatted Brondin with its right talon, opening a gash across his face and sending him to the ground.

Charlotte shielded her eyes from the terrible sight, only looking at the ground below her.

As the singing continued, the griffin snarled, and Brondin let out a horrified scream from what must have been another blow.

"You maniac!" she shouted at Quinneas, who refused to look at her. "You fucking maniac!"

She needed to get out of there. She ran from the stage, hearing the tearing of flesh and Brondin's anguished screams above the din of the crowd. By the time she forced her way to the exit, his screams had stopped and the crowd's singing had only grown more vigorous.

SAMUEL

In the morning, as Samuel lay on the small cot the Hunt couple provided, he contemplated his plan. Except, without his knapsack, he had no plan. Without money, he couldn't leave the country. And he couldn't return to Goldhall, where everyone would be searching for him. He had not left the Hunt's small cottage for days. They agreed that he could stay until he was well enough to travel. They were exceedingly kind and generous to him, but their patience must eventually wear thin.

Samuel rose from bed to join the couple, but he lingered as he overheard the two discussing the news from the capital. Quinneas had lived. Brondin had been executed in a grisly fashion. Nox, the vile assailant, had still not been located and was the subject of a national search.

The Hunts weren't the sharpest tools on the farm, but even *they* would soon realize the man they were sheltering was the one who had shot Quinneas.

But, as Samuel continued listening at the edge of the doorway, their conversation gave him hope.

"Quinneas deserved it," Olive said. "Perhaps Nox was a swine, but I believe it was a message from the Creator that Quinneas's actions were blasphemous."

"Indeed," said Will, "Quinneas offended the Creator through his actions."

Their unicorn figures. Of course. They were a pair of religious fools!

The couple noticed Samuel waiting at the edge of the room. "Ah, Mr. Miller," Will said, "please join us for breakfast!"

As he sat down, a plan quickly began to take shape in his mind.

"I wish to thank both of you for your generosity in letting me stay," Samuel said.

"Please," said Olive, as Will nodded along, "it is our pleasure to have you in our humble home."

"Yes," Samuel said, "but I have not been completely truthful to you."

Their smiles turned to looks of suspicion.

"I needed to know whether you were allies first," he continued. "My name is not Eston Miller. In fact, it is Samuel Nox."

The couple let out gasps of surprise. Will stood, perhaps ready to throw him out.

"I know that you might wish to turn me over to the police right away, but before you do, please let me explain."

Will looked at Olive, and she nodded for Samuel to continue as Will returned to his seat.

"I have done horrible things in my life. But several days ago, I felt the presence of Oqci within me. I had never felt such a thing before. I had never believed. Yet I almost felt like Oqci was calling to me."

Their expressions softened. Will stroked his chin in intense thought. The couple seemed to be believing it.

"When Quinneas ordered the execution of the king and queen, and especially when he prohibited religious gatherings in the capital, I believe this offended the Creator deeply. Then Lord Evesbury, the nobleman, told me about his plan to kill Quinneas. I almost felt that it was Oqci talking to me directly, that the divine presence was guiding me!"

They stared at Samuel, engrossed by his story.

"I wanted to resist. And I'm ashamed to admit that I attempted to quell my doubts with alcohol, but I trusted Oqci was leading me. When I took the shot, I felt like Oqci was the one pulling the trigger. But I believe that Oqci guided the bullet into Quinneas's shoulder. Almost as if to offer a warning about his behaviour."

The couple nodded as if to agree that Oqci *would* do something like that.

"From there, I began running, and once more Oqci guided

me, here, to your happy home." The Hunts continued to stare at him. "I have done terrible things, but I want to atone for them. And I hope that you can help me. I believe it is the Creator's plan."

"Oh, Mr. Miller… err, Mr. Nox," said Olive excitedly, "if you wish to atone for your actions and become a better man, we shall help you."

"Yes," Will said, "it was the Creator's plan to bring you to us!"

They bought it, the fools!

"I need you to hide me," Samuel said. "The police may come looking for me."

"Of course," Olive said. "And henceforth we shall only call you Eston Miller."

"Yes," said Will, looking at him. "And you will need to change your appearance. Perhaps you should grow out your beard. I can lend you an old pair of spectacles to wear as well. We shall ensure no one recognizes you."

It was brilliant! Samuel's plan had worked better than he could have imagined. But what next? Live out the rest of his days as Eston Miller with these bumpkins?

CHARLOTTE

As Charlotte hurried from the scene of the brutal execution, she knew she could no longer marry Quinneas. Nor could she be with him any longer. But where could she go?

Sheepishly, she found herself once again at Willien's doors. Like most other former nobles, his property had been reduced, but he was lacking for neither money nor space. Charlotte had not seen him for many months, since the time she had asked for the divorce. This had hurt him, and she feared he might still be bitter toward her.

When she arrived, he looked surprised to see her. He had heard, of course, that Quinneas had been shot and that Brondin was to be executed, but when she explained what had just happened to Brondin and how she needed to get away from Quinneas, he was sympathetic and allowed her to stay.

He could no longer afford so many servants, he told Charlotte, so he helped her carry her things to the room in which she had stayed many months ago.

"Charlotte," he said, after she had settled into her room, "there is something I need to tell you."

"What is it?"

"Several weeks ago, one of my former servants came to speak to me privately. She told me that another of my servants had overhead you and I speaking a year ago when we assumed that we were alone."

"Go on."

He sighed. "She told me that this servant overheard you when you said that you were the author of *The Downfall of the Monarchy*. Having heard this, the servant believed it was necessary to tell the police. They must have held the information then decided to arrest you once you joined the Great Chamber."

Brondin! Charlotte had thought it was him who had betrayed her this whole time. But it was not true! And now he was gone…

"I fired that servant from my employ as soon as I found out, of course," Willien continued. "But it was too late."

"Thank you for telling me," Charlotte said. "But why didn't you tell me earlier?"

"Well," he said, "I supposed you wished not to hear from me, but rather to only spend time with Quinneas…"

"I understand," she said. Perhaps it was Willien's way of punishing her. And perhaps she deserved it.

Yet however inscrutable his desires were, she appreciated his friendship now more than ever.

QUINNEAS ALIGHTED from his carriage as Charlotte and Willien stood at the front of the house the next morning.

"Shall I stop him from entering?" said Willien.

"I shall be fine," she said, and went outside to meet Quinneas.

Quinneas hung his head low as he approached the door. His eyes were red and his hair somewhat unkempt.

"How could you do that?" she said. "Are you mad?"

"Charlotte, I'm so sorry. I reflected on my actions last night as I lay alone in bed, and I realized I made a terrible mistake. My desire for vengeance outweighed my principles. It shall never happen again."

His words were delivered so convincingly that for a moment Charlotte believed him. But she now knew him too well.

"Please forgive me, Charlotte."

She quickly calculated her options. With his control of the Emergency Committee, he possessed far too much power. Charlotte needed to stop him before it was too late. But she could not let on just yet.

"Please," he said again.

She walked over and embraced him to signal her forgiveness. He clutched her tightly. It felt wrong, but it was necessary. For now.

"Thank you," he said. "Thank you. I shall never let you down again."

~

OVER THE FOLLOWING DAYS, Charlotte continued to stay at Willien's, telling Quinneas she needed time alone before returning. But in that time, she would form a plan. She needed to find someone whom she could trust.

The only ally she had on the Emergency Committee was Koralo. He had always been a sensible man with a large heart. And he had been the only one to stand up to Quinneas the first day they sat in the Emergency Committee.

She arranged for him to come to Willien's. Willien, as ever, was occupied in his gardens, so he paid them no mind.

Koralo had been present at Brondin's execution, along with the other members of the committee, though Charlotte had not the chance to talk to him then. He had seen her run off, and she prayed that he shared her revulsion at Quinneas's actions.

Nervous energy coursed through her body as she waited for him in Willien's foyer.

When Koralo arrived, before she could say anything, he raced toward her and clasped her hands. "Oh Charlotte, I am ever so sorry for the loss of your mother!" he said. "And... I'm sorry you had to witness... that... yesterday."

"It was a horrific sight," she said evenly.

"Yes," he replied. He relinquished his grip and brought his hand to his forehead with a sigh. "I voted for the execution. But the method was Quinneas's idea. I had no foreknowledge of what he planned."

Charlotte looked at him deeply to try to discern his feelings as they both sat down. "Koralo, can I trust you?"

"You can trust me with all your heart," he said without hesitation.

She took several breaths. "What I am about to say is very difficult. And it must be kept between us."

"You have my word. I swear it on the Ulsted family name. I shall not tell another soul whatever you confide to me."

"Even before Brondin's execution, I have been uneasy with the direction of the revolution. This is not what our revolution was supposed to be about. It was supposed to be about democracy, equality, justice! Not delighting in the execution of those we take to be our enemies! Koralo, I am afraid of what we might have unleashed. I am ashamed to admit it, but I am afraid of Quinneas. I am afraid of the man I am supposed to marry."

Koralo ran his fingers through his blonde locks as he thought. "Oh Charlotte. Let it be known that I share your sentiments. I too worry what Quinneas might do with his power. The gruesome manner in which he executed Brondin… Dear Oqci. I have considerable fear about what he could do next."

Charlotte was relieved by his answer and leaned back in her chair, more comfortable now. "But Koralo, we are only two. Any votes in the committee will be lost three to two. And what is more, if we vote against anything Quinneas proposes, we shall immediately put ourselves under suspicion."

"You are surely correct," he said. "And Tressa and Aran are unlikely to oppose Quinneas, such faithful followers of him as they are."

"For now," she said, "let us observe them and pray for cracks in their alliance."

With that, Koralo nodded and rose from his chair. He walked to the window and gazed for some time upon Willien's gardens. When he turned back, his eyes were watery.

"Are you okay?" Charlotte asked.

"Oh Charlotte," he said, wiping his eyes. "I was only contemplating the beauty of life! And its fragility."

With her pact with Koralo established, Charlotte agreed to return to live with Quinneas, even as she recognized the danger. Yet it was better that he not realize her suspicions of him, and it was better to keep watch over his actions.

As the search for Nox and the investigation of the Soldiers of Oqci continued, Quinneas spoke of increasingly radical measures. There would be, he told her, oaths of loyalty required for all the former nobles and the priests. He also planned to close all the temples in the country and prohibit the keeping of religious paraphernalia, like the icons of sacred creatures, in one's home.

"Didn't the terrorism of the Soldiers of Oqci show the pernicious influence of this religion?" he said as they reposed that evening in the sitting room. "It must be stamped out." Quinneas stood and paced alongside the wall, examining some of the carved wooden masks from Otela that he had purchased as decoration. They were said to be the faces of distant ancestors who watched over their tribesmen. "The natives had the right idea by rejecting Oqci in the first place," he said with a chuckle. "But it's a shame that in its place they substituted another kind of religious superstition."

His house was adorned with these kinds of artifacts from Otela and Ozenzal, as well as landscape paintings from their own continent. But he refused any religious artwork related to Oqci.

"I agree with you that the religion is a false and harmful superstition," Charlotte said, hoping to make her criticism sufficiently gentle, "but will this not inflame tensions within society?"

"It might at first," he said. He pulled one of the masks off the wall and distractedly ran his fingers over its features. "But in time the people will come to accept that these fantastical doctrines about sacred creatures are silly superstitions. It is for their own good and they will thank me one day. It is the same with children, is it not? Sometimes parents need to do things that the children find unpleasant. But once the children grow older, they come to see these things as necessary."

"Quinneas," she said, "I went to Willien's because I feared your judgment was skewed following Nox's attack, as you yourself admitted. I... I fear that your judgment may also be skewed on this issue."

He frowned at this suggestion. "Charlotte, you misunderstand me completely. You are right that after Nox attacked me, I made a terrible mistake. That was a judgment based on personal hatred and it is one I deeply regret. But this idea – to begin the process of removing religion – this comes from a place of love. Love for the people. My love for them is such that I can't stand to see them live in delusion."

This sent a chill through Charlotte. It frightened her to think that a twisted kind of love, rather than a more comprehensible hatred, guided his actions.

"But should it not be their choice?" she said. "If they want to follow the religion, can we stop them?"

"It has become too dangerous for that, and for our revolution," he said. "Don't you understand, Charlotte? Didn't you write about the absurdity of these ideas in your book? Now is the chance to enact the change that we have been waiting so long for!"

Charlotte weighed her options. She could continue debating him, but she would only expose herself as a potential saboteur of his plans. It was better to relent. "That is all true," she said. "I worry about us moving too fast, but I suppose you are right."

"Change cannot wait, Charlotte. Half-measures no longer suffice."

Ahead of the meeting of the Emergency Committee, Charlotte had told Koralo privately what was to come. They both voted in favour of Quinneas's proposals, thinking it was best not to raise suspicion. With the new laws, the People's Army would be empowered to raid houses to search for religious items.

Former nobles and priests and any others who seemed to question the revolution would be forced to swear an oath of loyalty before the Emergency Committee, who would judge their sincerity.

After the new proposals came into effect, a parade of nobles and priests passed through their committee each day. They had already judged various people – even poor Dario, Duke of Prencroft – as insufficiently loyal and sent them to their deaths.

But today she saw the name of Selver Bronn on the docket, much to her surprise.

"What am I doing here?" said Selver indignantly as he entered the room. "I am not a nobleman or a priest. You know I hate those bastards as much you do!"

The mention of "bastards" made Quinneas wince, but Charlotte had the same question. He had lost his seat in the previous election but was always supportive of the revolution, as far as she knew. How he had been classed as a potential traitor, she knew not.

"Mr. Bronn," Quinneas said, "you are here to stand trial for the death of Maandi Lichenxu."

"Maandi what? I haven't the faintest idea who that is!"

Quinneas shook his head. "I assumed you wouldn't. He was one of the many workers you employed building your railways. One of the many workers you condemned to death through your negligence."

Charlotte had heard nothing of this, but she couldn't raise the issue now. But the last name. She had heard it before... It was the same as Nadeni's. Charlotte looked over at Koralo who also appeared confused.

"I... I... It isn't true!" said Selver, his face growing sweaty. "I have always cared for my workers and done my utmost to ensure their safety."

"It's a lie!" shot back Tressa. "It is well known among the workers of Iron Town that you forced the workers into unsafe conditions to maximize your profits."

"I... this isn't right!" said Selver.

"How can you be expected to be loyal to the revolution and to the constitution," Quinneas said, "when you show such disregard for your fellow man?"

"Of course, I am loyal!"

"I don't believe him," said Aran.

"Nor do I," said Tressa.

"I, as well, do not believe him," said Quinneas. "Let us call a vote on his execution."

Charlotte turned frantically to Koralo, trying to ask with her eyes, what can we do?

"Please," said Selver, bringing his hands together to beg and looking toward her and Koralo. "Please!"

"I vote in favour," said Aran.

"I vote in favour as well," said Tressa.

Quinneas too signalled his support for execution.

Koralo looked at Charlotte nervously before saying that he also supported execution.

"Yes," Charlotte said. "I vote in favour as well." It couldn't be helped, Charlotte realized. To hesitate would've only raised suspicion.

YANIS

"Everything's in order," Yanis said, eager to move on from this simple peasant family's home. He and Devon were carrying out a search of some houses on the outskirts of the city for religious paraphernalia. Yanis didn't enjoy this job, but what choice had he? It was a decree from the Emergency Committee.

"Just a moment," said Devon. "Something doesn't seem right." He knelt down and ran his fingers over the wooden floor as the peasant family huddled nervously in the corner. He stopped his hand on a loose floorboard and flipped it over to reveal a treasure trove of figures of griffins, winged horses, and so on. He looked at Yanis with his eyebrow raised and a grin. "Isn't this interesting?"

"Please, don't take them," one of the peasant women cried as she stepped forward. "They've been in my family for generations."

A jolt of pain passed through Yanis. He had no desire to see this poor family suffer. Even though he thought their religion was false, it seemed wrong to deprive them of these simple things that brought them such joy.

"Go outside and check around the house for further contraband," Yanis said to Devon. "I shall gather these items."

"Very well, Dragon Slayer."

Once the door had swung shut, Yanis motioned the family to come close. In a low voice, he said, "You may keep one of the figures, but you mustn't tell anyone."

"Oh, thank –"

Yanis brought his forefinger to her lips. The walls of their cabin were thin, and he could not risk Devon overhearing.

The woman nodded. She understood. She knelt down and

pulled out a particular griffin figure. She held it in her hands and gazed at it lovingly.

Yanis gathered the rest of the figures, knowing Devon had already seen them. He would be surprised had Yanis returned with nothing. Devon was loyal to Yanis, but even more to the ideals of the revolution. If he knew that Yanis had hesitated even slightly, Yanis feared what he might do.

~

YANIS RETURNED HOME to Nadeni with the thought that the revolution had taken a wrong turn weighing upon his mind. She, too, had been involved in these searches for religious contraband. Yanis prayed she shared his sentiments.

"It is no justice to harass these simple peasant folk," he told her. "And I worry that Quinneas is becoming too –"

"You're not doubting the revolution, are you?"

"I… Of course not," he said. "But I fear that Quinneas may be gaining too much power. The revolution is spinning out of control."

"I have talked with Quinneas," she said. "He is a great ally. I told him some time ago about how Selver Bronn was responsible for my father's death. Quinneas promised that he would see justice done in the matter, as a favour to me. Quinneas is someone who supports us. He is a good man. Just think of all he has done for us."

"Selver Bronn? What do you mean Quinneas 'would see justice done'?"

"He will be brought before the Emergency Committee to answer for his crimes," Nadeni said. "If Quinneas and the others deem he does not sufficiently support the revolution, then…"

"Then he will be sent to his death?"

"It will be justice served, after a long time coming."

Yanis looked at Nadeni. He couldn't believe she was capable of such an action. Sending a man to his death! And with seemingly no regrets.

"Nadeni, this is not justice."

"Bronn's negligence and greed caused my father's death, and the deaths of countless other workers! Frankly, Yanis, are you in a position to talk about justice and injustice? After you were responsible for putting down rebellions in Umiri? How many deaths did *you* cause?"

"I… that is unfair!" Anger flashed through Yanis. He could hardly find the words to rebut such a terrible accusation. And one from someone he loved! "You… you know that I was forced into serving in the army there. You know that I had no choice in the matter. You know that I was forced into committing crimes. What my unit did in Umiri was a grave injustice – one which I acknowledge!"

Nadeni sighed. "You don't understand, Yanis," she said, her voice softening. "With Selver Bronn gone, I shall finally have closure. I shall finally have peace about my father's death after all these years."

Seeing the lingering pain in her eyes, Yanis tried to understand. He tried to square his love for her with the fact that she had brokered a deal with Quinneas to send Selver to his death. Was it not true that Selver's negligence caused many deaths? Perhaps, looked at from that perspective, what she did was not unjust, Yanis reasoned.

"Quinneas is our ally," she continued, squeezing Yanis's arm gently. "He has done me a tremendous favour. It is the first step toward healing."

Nadeni was right, Yanis told himself. He needed to believe she was right. Selver *was* guilty of the death of her father and countless others.

"Think of all Quinneas has done for us," she continued. "Everything the revolution has brought us."

Yanis nodded slowly, willing himself to see her side. Where would he be without the revolution? Without Quinneas? Quinneas had always supported him as the leader of the RDF and the People's Army, even when others doubted him. And he had even paid for his and Nadeni's wedding!

"I think I understand, Nadeni," Yanis said. "I'm sorry for my cruel words before. You know that I love you."

"And I love you too, Dragon Slayer."

~

"Interrogations of several suspects of the Soldiers of Oqci," Quinneas said, at a meeting of the Emergency Committee, "have revealed that the terrorist group has received funds and support from the exiles in Friezzia, including Dellirea Zendar."

It was rare for Yanis to be invited to attend a meeting of the Emergency Committee, and he now understood why he had been. The princess, colluding with the Soldiers of Oqci? It was the first he had heard of such a thing.

Quinneas stood tall at the far end of the long table, showing few signs of the grave injuries that nearly claimed his life several weeks ago. "What is more," he continued, "we have intercepted communications that only confirm these facts."

They were in Aramal's former council room, but nothing remained that might have indicated this fact. The room had been denuded of its paintings of the kings and queens of the Zendar dynasty. The lone decoration in the room was the revolution's tricolour flag of green, white, and yellow.

Yanis sat on one side of the table with other government functionaries, while across from them were the members of the Emergency Committee. The intense stare of Aran Potter, a skeletally thin, bespectacled man, was fixed on Quinneas. The slightest hint of a smile appeared on his lips as Quinneas relayed the news of Dellirea's treason, while Tressa Smith frowned and shook her head violently. Charlotte's eyes widened with surprise, but she quickly calmed her expression.

Koralo fidgeted in his chair as Quinneas spoke. When Quinneas at last paused, Koralo bounded up and raised his forefinger. "Let it be known that I wish to examine these seized communications."

Quinneas darted his head toward Koralo. He looked stunned that someone had questioned him. "Why, of course," he said evenly. He called into the hallway. Devon Black, Yanis's most trusted officer, entered and handed him a box full of papers. "All the evidence is here. All the communications." Quinneas picked up some of the papers and held them high above his head.

Why wasn't Yanis informed of this? Why didn't Devon tell him such evidence existed? Yanis lamented that his own officers appeared to have information he did not. But he knew he would only reveal himself a fool if he admitted this publicly. His leadership of the People's Army was questioned enough as it was.

Koralo rose to gain a closer look at the papers, but before he could, Quinneas said sharply, "There will plenty of time to inspect the evidence later. Let me continue." Koralo looked around at the others on the committee who seemed reluctant to challenge Quinneas. He sheepishly returned to his seat.

"Lochmar and the other surviving Zendars are imprisoned where they can do no more harm," Quinneas continued. "But the revolution will never be safe so long as Friezzia continues to harbour traitors to our nation. This is why today I wish us to prepare plans for an invasion of Friezzia. We must end their support for terrorism. We shall bring them the blessings of our revolution and allow our two nations to finally live peacefully together.

"High Commander Haller," he said, turning to Yanis, "your role will be essential. We need to mobilize the People's Army to a size never before seen. You will lead the invasion. Your men will be flanked by our sacred creatures and the war machines that remain from Aramal Zendar's reign. It will be a great undertaking, but I trust you to do it."

He continued before Yanis could object. Yanis slouched in his chair, reluctant to make eye contact with anyone lest they noticed the doubts circling in his mind. Could he lead such a force? Controlling the People's Army was a challenge at the best of times and apparently other officers already knew more than he did. And go to Friezzia? Why, he had never even stepped foot on their soil.

～

AFTER THE MEETING ended and the other members of the committee filed out, Quinneas asked to speak with Yanis. Shutting the door, Quinneas turned to him. "I sensed some apprehension from you about the proposed invasion, did I not?"

"I… it will be a tremendous undertaking," Yanis managed. He worried Quinneas could almost hear his heart pounding in such a quiet room.

"Indeed. But I have absolute faith in you, Yanis." Quinneas paced around the outside of the room, eyeing the box that purported to contain proof of the princess's collusion with the Soldiers of Oqci.

"I shall not disappoint you," Yanis said, trying to summon confidence but feeling slightly intimidated being alone with Quinneas.

"Very good," said Quinneas. "As further motivation, should you succeed in the invasion of Friezzia, we shall begin the transition to independence for New Selver – or Umiri, as the natives call it. I know this is a cause dear to your and Nadeni's hearts. As you may know, I have already done one favour for Nadeni. And would this not be a fitting destiny for the descendant of the Prince of Shadows?"

Yanis nodded and thought of his earlier conversation with Nadeni. Quinneas was an ally, was he not? Had he not already accomplished many great things during the revolution? And then to grant independence for New Selver? Would this not be the fulfilment of the principles of the revolution, to grant liberty to one of their most important colonies?

The invasion of Friezzia was correct, Yanis told himself. The revolution could not be allowed to be undermined from those abroad.

And to think that someone like him – someone born in poverty in Iron Town – would be the one leading such a force! And yet…

84

CHARLOTTE

Things were happening much too quickly. Charlotte barely had time to process Selver Bronn's execution – a favour to Nadeni, Quinneas told her, to ensure Yanis's loyalty – and now they were planning an invasion of Friezzia. The proposed invasion caught her and Koralo by surprise.

The two of them had long known that Quinneas feared the presence of the exiles in Friezzia, but they had not imagined he would act so soon. They needed to do something before the invasion began. Charlotte and Koralo agreed that she would approach Tressa and Aran to see if they had any doubts about Quinneas.

Ensuring Quinneas had no knowledge, she met first with Tressa to attempt to sway her vote on the committee. Charlotte met her at her simple apartment in Iron Town. The apartment was small and sparsely furnished, with only two chairs, a table, and a cot.

"Why should I live any better than the people I represent?" Tressa said when she noticed Charlotte's eyes lingering on the bare apartment.

Tressa was a short, chubby woman, whose hair and dress were decidedly plain. Evidently, she took the same approach to her appearance as to her living quarters, Charlotte thought.

As they sat down upon her two chairs, both scuffed and chipped from years of use, Charlotte said, "Ms. Smith, I come to you because I wish you to put my mind at ease over the proposed invasion. I wonder if we should not ensure the revolution is more firmly established at home before we attempt to fight wars abroad."

"The two are not in conflict," said Tressa. "The revolution is being undermined by the traitors from abroad. Keeping the revolution safe at home depends on keeping it safe from outside agitators. And what better way for the people to build loyalty to the revolution, and to each other, than by working together, arm-in-arm, to defeat the enemies of the revolution?"

This response did not make Charlotte optimistic. It was precisely the same argument that Quinneas would have made. "Of course, those are important points," she said. "But can we be certain that the exiles are truly helping the terrorists?"

Tressa looked puzzled at this, as if she had never before considered the proposition. "The exiles have been plotting against us since the very start. The Zendars have shown themselves to be a family of scoundrels. And now we have direct evidence of contacts between the exiles and the terrorists, as Quinneas showed us."

"That is true," Charlotte said. "That is very true."

The purported letters could be forgeries. In fact, they probably were. And the testimony obtained by the interrogation of suspects was questionable. But Charlotte was reluctant to put these arguments to Tressa. Tressa probably knew they were fraudulent as well, and she would only become suspicious if Charlotte pressed the issue too strongly.

"You have put my mind at ease," Charlotte told her at last. "You have made a compelling case in favour of the invasion."

Tressa nodded, satisfied that she had won her over. "The revolution requires difficult decisions, Ms. Evesbury," she said, as they began to part ways. "You know that more than anyone."

~

CHARLOTTE'S next visit was to Aran Potter's temporary apartment in Goldhall. His apartment was at least more comfortably furnished than Tressa's, yet Aran too struck Charlotte as an austere, pleasureless man.

She tried the same tactics as before, but, as with Tressa, she was met with the same arguments about the need to defend the revolution by engaging in war. It was clear he could not be swayed. Even if Charlotte and Koralo both voted against the war, they would be certain of defeat. Worse still, they would reveal themselves as traitors.

There was one option left, however. One final hope.

The Dragon Slayer.

Charlotte and Yanis had their differences. She had long held reservations about his leadership of the People's Army, but he *was* a man of integrity. The war could not go ahead without him. If he spoke out against it, the people would follow, no matter what Quinneas or anyone else might say.

Nadeni, Charlotte learned, was visiting Iron Town to recruit for the People's Army. Quinneas had already suggested bolstering the force for the coming war effort even if it had not been formally agreed upon. But Nadeni's absence meant that Charlotte could speak with Yanis privately at his home. There she raised the issue of the authenticity of the evidence of the collaboration between the exiles in Friezzia and the Soldiers of Oqci. Yanis tentatively agreed that some aspects of the evidence were questionable.

"Are we not making the same mistakes as King Aramal?" she asked.

Yanis thought on this for a time. "I too have wondered about the wisdom of pursuing this war..."

"I know at heart Quinneas is a good man," Charlotte continued, not fully believing that part. "Yet I question if the events of the last months have not distorted his judgment. He only wishes the best for our nation, yet sometimes I ask myself if the course he is pursuing is correct."

Yanis hesitated and picked at his nails. "As have I."

Yes! He might yet be an ally.

"Koralo and I have discussed the invasion," Charlotte said, "and we both would like to vote against the war in the Emergency Committee. However, Tressa and Aran remain supportive of Quinneas so we are destined to lose the vote."

Yanis looked at Charlotte thoughtfully. "That is true," he said. "So what shall we do?"

"The people listen to you," she said. "They are enchanted by the tales of your heroism. To them, you are the Dragon Slayer! If you spoke against the war, they would surely follow. The people are easily swayed. If the rest of the Emergency Committee realizes that the people do not support the war, they will vote against it too. With your voice, Yanis, you could prevent the war from taking place. You could prevent it all."

He leaned back in his chair, the importance of the decision clearly weighing on his mind. At last, he nodded. "Yes... yes, I believe you're right. I shall make a speech on this tomorrow in advance of the vote."

"Thank you, Yanis," Charlotte said. "Thank you." She almost rose from her chair to embrace him but stopped herself. It would be inappropriate. "But we must plan for the worst," she continued. "Quinneas punishes any dissent, and he could turn against you. The people will support you, I am sure. But there can be no guarantees, and, in the worst case, you might be forced into hiding."

"It is true," he said. "But it is a risk I must accept."

She could not believe it. They were going to stop Quinneas. They were going to stop all this madness.

"Yanis, if Quinneas does indeed turn against you, there might not be enough time for us to contact each other to devise a new plan. So let us determine a way for you to contact me in such a case."

"Yes, that is very wise."

In fact, Yanis said he knew a perfect place. Along Hope Stream, in Iron Town, he explained, there was a point that jutted out, where he had proposed marriage to Nadeni. Just before there was a large tree with a hole in the middle. Few people walked down that path now, so if it ever came to it, he could leave Charlotte a message there and they could be confident that it would not be disturbed.

With this plan made, Yanis agreed he would make the speech tomorrow. A sense of cautious optimism filled Charlotte. An end to Quinneas's power – an end to this nightmare – was in sight. She only hoped that Yanis would be able to sway the people before it was too late.

85

DELLIREA

"His Majesty wishes to speak with you," Lady Fondyrel said grimly, the day after Dellirea's birthday.

She had no need to ask what it was about. She already knew. Now that she was seventeen, Hyazaral would have her marry Yunolarol. The thought of marrying Yuno disgusted her. Or for that matter marrying any man.

It had not been a terrible birthday after all, with Rodnel's brilliant fireworks display. But those happy moments were quickly overtaken by Dellirea's worries of meeting the king.

Lady Fondyrel led her to Hyazaral's chamber. As they walked, she thought of the cruelties that Hyazaral had perpetrated against Lady Fondyrel. But Dellirea was ashamed to realize that her father was responsible for similar acts. If Dellirea had been born in another body, like a poor woman's, or a Friezzian's, her father might have just as easily put *her* to death if it served his purpose.

They arrived at the chamber door. Lady Fondyrel opened it for Dellirea and bid her to enter while she waited outside.

Hyazaral sat on his throne at the far end of the room. And Rodnel! Dellirea was delighted to see him standing there, and she quickened her pace. But her happiness disappeared when she noticed Rodnel wore a grave expression on his face.

"Lady Zendar," Hyazaral said, his voice echoing in the large empty room, "what did I say when you arrived about having contact with this man?"

"That... it was forbidden."

"And you, Lord Summerstone, what did I say about contact with the princess?"

"It was forbidden... but let me explain, Your Majesty. I only wished to entertain her for her birthday. And we had no contact. I only lit some fireworks for her amusement."

"It seems as though you two feel no shame about disobeying a direct order from the most powerful man in the country!" the king bellowed. "The most powerful man in the world!"

Dellirea and Rodnel looked at each other guiltily.

Thoughts of Lady Fondyrel and the cruel punishment she endured again flashed through Dellirea's mind. Dear Oqci.

"You two are guests here," he said. "Lady Zendar, first you seduced my grandson in order to glean news about your family's fate!"

Seduced? How absurd!

"And now this!" he continued. "Sometimes I wonder why I ever made such a deal with your father and mother. Not only are they not here, they are as dead as doornails, and now I am stuck with you two. Lady Zendar, you still have some value to me, as the heir to Estenland's throne, but Lord Summerstone, I struggle to see your purpose."

"Please, Your Majesty, I can be useful to you," said Rodnel. When Hyazaral appeared unimpressed, Rodnel dropped to his knees and brought his hands together to beg. "Please, Your Majesty!"

It hurt Dellirea to see a genius like Rodnel humiliate himself in such a way. But she knew he had no choice.

"I have built a great many things that could be useful to you and your army," continued Rodnel. "I have built what I call a war machine that could prove useful in battle, if it should ever come to that."

"Bah," said the king. "We have plenty of engineers already. And we hardly need a second-rate nobleman from Estenland to teach us Friezzians anything! I am afraid I see no use for you here, Lord Summerstone."

"You will not lay a finger on Lord Summerstone," Dellirea said suddenly, before she had a chance to think.

"Excuse me," Hyazaral said. "How dare you address your king in such a tone!'

Her eyes met his and she did not avert them. She was shaking slightly, but she hoped Hyazaral did not notice. She knew not whence this confidence came. But it felt good.

"You will not harm him," she said, her voice as firm as she could manage. All the people Hyazaral had harmed. All the cruelties he had inflicted. It stopped now.

"Lady Zendar, please, I'm not sure this is wise," said Rodnel.

Yet the king looked flustered. He had never had someone question him like this.

"Do you wish me to marry your stupid grandson or not?"

"Stupid?" the king repeated. "He's not stupid! And if I decide you will marry him, then you will marry him."

"Do you wish him to have a happy life with me, or a miserable one? If the former, then you will not harm Lord Summerstone."

The king looked at Dellirea, his mouth stupidly gaping open. She could see whence Yunolarol inherited the expression. At last, Hyazaral's look of confusion turned to a smile. He chuckled. "You are a very precocious girl. Perhaps smarter than I gave you credit for. Your friend Lord Summerstone will live a long life while he serves the great Friezzian army. And you, you will be a faithful wife to my grandson, and one day the queen of the great nation of Friezzia, which will stretch across all of Ogard."

"I shall," she vowed, knowing that she had kept Rodnel alive and that at a later time she would confront the issue of her marriage to Yunolarol.

YANIS

So many conflicted thoughts swirled in Yanis's head as Nadeni returned home.

"I met a great many people, Dragon Slayer," she said happily. "I wished so much to tell them about our coming fight with Friezzia, yet I knew it would be premature."

Yanis nodded along glumly, knowing that tomorrow he would put an end to the war. He could not tell her about his conversation with Charlotte earlier in the day. About what he planned. Not yet.

"Still," she continued, "the people are enthusiastic about joining the People's Army. I cannot sign them up quickly enough. To finally have a democratic force that fights *for* the people! That fights for our ideals!"

Yanis said nothing. He did not wish to puncture her happiness, even as he knew he would in time.

"Whatever is the matter?" she said, noticing he did not share her enthusiasm. She clasped his hand and her expression grew serious.

"It is nothing," Yanis said. "I am only thinking of the coming war effort, and what it will mean. I believe a walk would clear my head."

Nadeni stared at him, perplexed. "Shall I accompany you?"

"No, it is a walk I shall take alone."

AS YANIS STEPPED out into the warm summer evening, he knew not what to do. Charlotte was right, of course, to be concerned about Quinneas. He had gained great power, perhaps more than any one person should possess. And if Yanis spoke out, he had the ability to change things before it was too late.

But could he betray Quinneas? The one who had helped him when he was arrested those many years ago? Who defended him without asking anything in return? Who had put such trust in him? Who had done so much for him and Nadeni? Moreover, could he betray Nadeni? She supported the principles of the revolution with all her heart. And the principles *were* just.

As Yanis strolled the streets of the Palace District, he thought of growing up. His life was so far from what he had imagined when he was young. And the revolution had made it all possible. Had they gone too far in the application of their ideals? Maybe some of the decisions made by the government, particularly by Quinneas, were flawed – but there were so many which were right!

Yanis thought again of how excited Nadeni was for the invasion. He could not share her enthusiasm, but how he wished he could. Was that not his flaw, rather than hers? Could he really betray her by supporting Charlotte?

Was his allegiance not better placed with Nadeni and Quinneas, than with Charlotte? Charlotte had always questioned his leadership of the People's Army and undermined his decisions at every turn, while Quinneas was always steadfast in his support of Yanis.

Yanis cursed his situation. He knew not the right path!

Flooding through his mind were memories of those he had lost. Calina, Jackson, even his former commander Vinzent of Highfalls. How he wished he could somehow have this decision removed from him. Let someone else take it.

He sat on a bench to think things over, his mind a muddle. As he looked out at the street, pedestrians walking along under the streetlights, his eyes caught sight of a man who looked like a younger version of himself. A working man, perhaps. Yanis followed his brisk, confident walk.

The revolution had done so much for men such as this. No more would those of a higher class have a right to look down upon those who were lower born. When he thought of all the times wealthy people looked down upon him for his background

– how Charlotte looked down upon him – he only grew zealous with the righteousness of the revolution.

He kept running her words through his mind. "The people are easily swayed." But what had she meant by that? That the people were mindless sheep? And who were "the people"? Surely by that she meant the poor, unwashed masses. But didn't Yanis use to be one of them? Wasn't he *still* one of them?

While Charlotte sacrificed more than any other noble for the revolution, she would always be a noble at heart. She would never know what it was like to struggle. She could never understand what the revolution truly meant to those on the bottom. Those like Nadeni, like Yanis.

Yanis rose from the bench with his mind steadfast. Tomorrow he would meet with Quinneas privately to let him know of the challenge brewing to his leadership.

"Is everything alright, Dragon Slayer?" said Nadeni as Yanis returned home.

"Everything is perfect, darling," he said as he wrapped his arms around her and felt the comfortable warmth of her body.

His mind was at last clear. That night he slept soundly.

THE NEXT MORNING, Yanis awoke ready to do what he must. His meeting with Charlotte was not until later in the morning. He needed to tell Quinneas as soon as possible.

Yanis marched with purpose to the palace and then inside, on his way to Quinneas's office to warn him. At this time of the morning, there would be few people around the palace and no problems to encounter.

Charlotte?

No! What was she doing here?

She spotted him from down the hallway. She tilted her head when she saw him, clearly not expecting to see him there either. She raised her hand to wave hesitantly, her expression remaining one of concern.

Yanis panicked. He could not see her now. He averted his

gaze and marched away down the hall, almost jogging, not looking back to see if she pursued him.

He felt a sickening feeling, knowing that he was about to betray her, about to send her to her… No, no, he could not think of that. He needed to focus.

His heart pounded with every step down the hallway, until finally he came to Quinneas's office. He entered and slammed the door behind him.

"Yanis?" Quinneas said, rising from his chair. "Whatever is the matter? Your face is white as snow!"

"Quinneas," Yanis said, catching his breath, "I have some very concerning news to disclose to you."

Quinneas walked close to Yanis, his green eyes practically piercing him. "What is it?"

"It is difficult to tell you," Yanis said, "but yesterday, Charlotte came to me. She expressed doubts about your leadership."

"What?" Quinneas said, a look of disbelief on his face. He came even closer. He clasped Yanis tightly by the shoulders. "What did she say?"

Quinneas was an ally. Yet he also struck fear into Yanis's heart. Yanis looked up at him and tried to maintain his composure. "She… she believes you have become too powerful. She and Koralo have been attempting to undermine support for you in the Emergency Committee. But they have not been successful in winning over Tressa and Aran. This is why she asked for my help. I agreed initially to help her, but as I considered it further, I realized that the revolution is safer in your hands."

The colour ran from Quinneas's face as Yanis spoke. He simply stared at Yanis, still clutching him, squeezing his shoulders so hard they were becoming sore. At last, Quinneas relaxed his grip. "Thank you, Yanis. You are a true friend of the revolution. I shall see to it that these attempts to overthrow me – to overthrow our revolution – will not succeed."

SAMUEL

Before Samuel embraced his new identity as a religious man in Farnestead, he needed to send something to Greta Esant – or Greta Grim, as she was now known. He spent some time crafting the letter, ensuring it said all he wanted to say.

Dear Mrs. Grim,

I hope this letter finds you well. By now, you have probably heard that I have done another horrible thing. It seems to be in my nature. Maybe you hope I am caught. If you do, that would be understandable.

I write to tell you that I shall start a new life elsewhere. You won't hear from me again. But I have enclosed a key with this letter. It is to a safety box under the name Eston Miller located at Goldhall Central Post Office. Inside the box are my research notes and drawings from the dissections of the sacred creatures.

It is too late for me, but I hope that you might continue the research. You were always my most promising student. There are secrets to be uncovered, and I know that you have the gifts to uncover them.

With best wishes,
Dr. Samuel Nox

Samuel felt unburdened when he deposited the letter in the mailbox. For too long, he had deluded himself that they had a future together. However absurd it felt, he clung to those hopes. Now, at last, he was ready to renounce such childish thinking. Samuel knew they would never be together. But he had at last found closure.

With that deed completed, it was time to truly embrace the charade of his new life.

The Hunt couple invited him to attend their temple, to hear the wonderful doctrines of Oqci. The weekly worship service was the highlight of these bumpkins' dull lives, and it was to be Samuel's social debut.

Just as the Hunts suggested, he sported an old pair of spectacles, and his beard was becoming fuller. All of this served as enough of a disguise that he could appear in public with none of the villagers thinking twice. After all, they were too simple and naïve to imagine this new stranger among them was the infamous Samuel Nox.

As he entered, memories of his youth flooded into his mind, and surprisingly they were not all unpleasant. He had attended a temple then, like most other children, but ceased when he became a teenager. The transparent silliness of the whole Oqci story was too ridiculous for Samuel to bear, much to the displeasure of his parents and siblings, who were hopelessly devoted.

The friendly villagers cordially made his acquaintance as the Hunt couple explained that he was from Goldhall but had come to seek a new life there in Farnestead, free from the corruption of the city. They nodded earnestly and welcomed him, content to learn that he wanted to become a true follower of Oqci.

Maybe they were all deluded fools, but they *were* nice. Samuel gave them that.

The service began and they sang songs that reminded him of a simpler time in his life. The Hunts, without embarrassment, sang as loudly as they could, even as they were terribly out of tune. Samuel stood silently as everyone else in the temple sang their praises to Oqci and the Creator.

Olive leaned close to Samuel and whispered, "Eston, don't you wish to join the singing?"

"I don't possess much of a singing voice," he said.

She smiled. "Will and I are hardly the best singers, yet together, the whole village creates a beautiful medley. Give it a try."

Samuel quietly began to sing along to the next song, and by the end of the service, he forgot all his self-consciousness and was singing just about as loudly as everyone else.

88

CHARLOTTE

Yanis! What in Oqci's name was he doing here? He was supposed to be preparing his speech.

Charlotte needed only to collect a few papers from her office. Perhaps Yanis was merely doing the same.

Yet he darted his eyes away, pretending not to have seen her, then marched frantically down the hall. He could only be going to one place.

He was going to turn Charlotte in. That coward. How stupid she was to confide in him.

In a matter of seconds, Charlotte made the calculation. She could not remain there. She could not wait to discover if he would betray her. By then it would be too late.

At a brisk pace, but not enough to attract suspicion, she walked out of the palace and caught a carriage. She anxiously directed the driver to Willien's. She felt horrible for implicating him in all this again, when he didn't ask for any of it. But what choice had she?

On her way, she quickly scrawled a message to Koralo and told the driver to deliver it as soon as possible. She warned Koralo that their plan might have been revealed. She prayed it was for nothing, but she couldn't risk it.

~

"Calm down, calm down," said Willien as Charlotte bolted into his estate.

"Quinneas may have found out that I betrayed him. You need to hide me!"

Willien froze for a brief moment but then sprang into action. "Here, here," he said, guiding her into his gardens. "Hurry!"

They ran inside one of his glasshouses. There he flipped

open a panel on the floor, revealing a small storage space for pots and garden tools. They both knelt down and began pulling things out – pot after spade after pot – and throwing them haphazardly around the glasshouse.

"Careful," said Willien as Charlotte hurled a small rake across the room, nearly striking him. It clattered upon a shelf in the glasshouse.

"Sorry!" she shouted. "We need to hurry!"

Her pulse pounded as she pulled more and more tools from the space.

At last it was empty. Charlotte stepped inside and curled up. It was not even large enough to stretch her legs. But it was the only option.

"Just stay here," he said. "We shall find something more permanent soon." With that, Willien placed the top back on.

Above her, footsteps moved back and forth as Willien tidied the glasshouse.

Willien's footsteps soon disappeared. She was now all alone. Could she survive in here? She would surely go mad.

Slowly her eyes adjusted to the darkness. Only the slightest crack of light came in from above. The tiny hiding space was dusty and dirty. Each inhale sucked in more dust and Oqci knew what else.

Charlotte ran over scenarios in her mind, hoping it was all a misunderstanding and that Yanis had not betrayed her. But this was far from likely. He would have told Quinneas, who would have ordered the entire People's Army to search for her. Then she imagined the happy scenario that Yanis had not been at the palace to tell Quinneas of her plans. But she once again told herself that was illogical. That surely Yanis had betrayed her.

These thoughts cycled endlessly through her brain, such that she lost all track of time. How long had it been? Minutes? Hours?

She regretted everything she had done. Everything that had led her to be hiding in this filthy, cramped hole. Why hadn't she just lived a simple, normal life as a noblewoman? Why did she have to become a revolutionary?

She had no idea how much time had passed when footsteps once again clattered above her. There was more than one person there in the glasshouse. Muffled voices of several men talking. But she could not make out what was said. Surely these were members of the People's Army come to look for her.

Charlotte lay as silently as she could, her legs nearly numb in that posture. An ant creeped across her arm. But she needed to remain absolutely still. She breathed in slowly, quietly.

The footsteps shuffled over top of her for half a minute. Finally, they disappeared again. She was safe. For now.

AT LAST CAME a rapping upon the floorboard. "It is safe to come out," said Willien. He lifted off the cover.

Charlotte squinted at the brightness of the day. Her legs were numb from the awkward pose. She strained to lift herself from the hole. Her neck ached. She uncomfortably stood and brushed the dirt from her dress.

Her intuitions had been right. Three members of the People's Army had come soon after she had arrived, demanding to know her whereabouts. Willien assured them he knew not, but they searched the whole property for her, discovering nothing.

"They eyed me with suspicion," Willien said. "I fear it is not safe for you here, Charlotte. They will be back."

"You're right," she said. But what to do? She needed to make a plan. "Willien, have you any clothes I can take?"

"Let me see what I can find," he said. He led her inside the former servant quarters where some clothes were left behind. These simple dresses would provide some measure of disguise. Willien turned away as she undressed and put one on.

"And my hair," she said. "You will need to cut it off."

"Oh Charlotte," he said with a sigh. "I shall do it."

He led her into a shed where she slumped onto a chair. He grabbed handfuls of her hair and lopped them off with his garden scissors as if he were trimming a hedge. She watched despairingly as her brown locks dropped to the ground. Once her hair was short, he did his best to make it appear uniform. But Willien was not much of a barber.

"Do you want to look in a mirror?" he asked.

Charlotte ran her hands through her hair and felt how short and uneven it was. "Maybe it is better if I not look."

It was horrible, but it had to be done. And Charlotte reasoned that it would provide enough of a cover that she could pass without notice in the streets for a time.

"Willien, I cannot tell you where I am going. It is too dangerous."

"Of course," he said, "I understand."

She made her way to go – not sure where she was headed – but turned back. She wrapped her arms around his large frame and squeezed for some time. She pulled away. "Thank you, Willien, for everything you've done for me. I'm sorry for putting you through this. You're a gentle spirit who didn't deserve any of it."

He nodded and smiled weakly. "Be safe, Charlotte."

89

YANIS

So many thoughts circled in Yanis's mind as he prepared for his departure to Friezzia tomorrow. Had he done the right thing by betraying Charlotte? What would happen to her once she was caught? Probably best not to consider it too deeply. He needed to turn his attention to the invasion. With Koralo arrested and Charlotte on the run, the measure to invade passed unanimously in the Emergency Committee.

Nadeni stood beside him, each of them packing their things. She talked happily of the coming adventure. Yet he needed to have a difficult conversation with her. It would not be easy, but he had dithered too long and time was growing short.

"Nadeni," he said, pausing to find the right words, "I wish you to remain here."

"What?" she said. "What do you mean remain here?"

"I wish you to stay behind, to not accompany me in the invasion of Friezzia."

Nadeni dropped the shirt she was holding and turned to face him. "Am I not a member of the People's Army?"

"Of course you are," Yanis said with a sigh. He gripped absent-mindedly one of his own green People's Army uniforms. "But I have given it much thought. I believe it is too dangerous."

"Too dangerous?" Nadeni said angrily. "How many times must I fight alongside you before you recognize that I fear no danger?"

Yanis winced as the thought of Calina again entered his mind. All of the pain, all of the loss. The thought of losing Nadeni too… He couldn't bear it.

"Please, Nadeni," he said weakly. "Please. Stay behind for my sake. I…"

"What is it? Why must you always try to keep me out of things?"

"The day at the prison... I nearly lost you. I can't risk it again. The Friezzians are not like any foes you have faced before. Please. Just listen to me!"

She shook her head. "I accepted the risk when I signed up for the People's Army, just as you did."

Yanis sat down upon the bed and grasped her hands, pulling her down beside him. He looked into her eyes, his face inches from hers. "There was someone I lost once," he said. "Someone very close to me. It nearly destroyed me. And I'm still not recovered from it. To lose you? It would be the end of me. I can't let that happen."

"Jackson?"

"Someone else," he said, shifting his gaze to the floor.

"But you never mentioned them before?"

"It was too painful to speak about."

Both of them sat for some time in thought. Yanis knew that Nadeni wished to go, but he prayed she understood.

At last, she placed her arm around his back and pulled him close to her. Yanis looked up, back into her kind eyes. She gave him a weak smile. "If you truly wish me to stay here, I shall. I shall put my energies into guarding the home front."

"Thank you, my dear."

Yanis placed his head upon her shoulder and they embraced.

When Nadeni finally pulled away, she said, "And Yanis, one day I hope that you will tell me more about that person. When you are ready."

"I shall."

As Yanis stared out the window as the railcar passed through the Estenland countryside, he could only think of Nadeni's disappointment at staying behind. But he knew it was the right decision. Oqci only knew what awaited them in Friezzia.

"Those dastardly Friezzians," said Devon as they rode along. "To think of them harbouring the princess! Harbouring terrorists!"

Yanis and Clem listened and nodded, not able to match Devon's enthusiasm.

"They'll be in for quite a surprise when they see what the forces of democracy can do," Devon continued. "*Our* soldiers fight proudly for the revolution, not as before: pressed into service for the king's wars."

Yanis looked over at Clem, who had a sour expression but said nothing. Yanis knew that Clem felt proud of his years of service to the army, even if it *was* under the rule of kings.

But Devon was surely right. Their forces numbered twenty thousand, all volunteers who had eagerly joined the cause. Alongside their railroad convoy travelled a large contingent of sacred creatures as well as a fleet of the war machines. As Yanis thought of the coming battle with the Friezzians, he prayed it would be enough.

SAMUEL

Samuel was almost happy in his new country life. And his skin ailment seemed to be disappearing. Perhaps it was being out in the countryside, away from the pollution and stress of the city.

He could stay as long as he needed to, the Hunts insisted, and a job was found for him, preparing for the imminent harvest of wheat at summer's end.

Yet the simple village life was disrupted by events in the capital. The villagers were surprised and angered when Quinneas Raeil mandated the closure of temples across the country and prohibited the possession of religious icons.

Even for Samuel, this was too much. He never contemplated prohibiting people from worshipping, even when he was a young radical. It was much better, he thought, to use the power of reason to convince them of their errors.

What was more, Samuel was almost embarrassed to admit that he had grown to enjoy attending the temple every week and seeing friends from the village. When he heard of the plans for its closure in two days, he was surprised to feel sadness wash over him.

"What if…" Samuel said to the Hunt couple at dinner, "what if we gather the entire village together to protest the closure of the temple?"

"Protest?" said Olive with a puzzled expression. "Whatever do you mean?"

The simple Hunt couple had clearly never contemplated disobedience. It was just the natural order of things that the king or their noble lord – or in this case, Quinneas – commanded, and they obeyed.

"I mean that we gather together to say that we do not accept this decision," Samuel said. "This government has gone against the teachings of Oqci. We shall tell them we shall not stand for it."

"I believe Eston is correct," said Will, suddenly realizing that perhaps the villagers need not do whatever they were told. "But we must do it peacefully, as Oqci would've wanted."

~

THE HEAD PRIEST was informed of the day the temple was to be closed. The date, the letter explained, was strictly confidential. Yet the priest, knowing Samuel's plans, had passed along the information to him and the Hunts.

On the day, Samuel and the other villagers gathered on the main road into the village, just before the temple. Practically the entire village was there, such was the feeling against the government's actions. The hot summer sun beat down upon them as they prepared to make their stand. From his position, Samuel saw several carriages slowly making their way along the country roads. These contained the People's Army members who would strip away all the temple's religious markings and convert it to just another grey building. The villagers were perhaps several hundred strong, and as the carriages drew closer, they made their way into the centre of the road.

"Let us sing a song to raise our spirits," someone in the crowd suggested. "Perhaps 'He Comes Down from the Clouds'?"

A voice began singing the first lines, and soon they all joined in.

The carriages ceased their movement as they came upon the crowd. A small construction team accompanied by three members of the People's Army alighted. The leader of the group walked toward the villagers. They quieted their singing as he approached.

"What are you people doing? Remove yourselves at once!"

They stood strong. Someone in the crowd began singing the song again, and the entire village quickly joined in.

"You will all face arrest if you do not move now!" he shouted over the singing. His two colleagues drew their pistols and approached the crowd.

The sight of the guns caused the singing to die away, and the villagers looked at each other nervously. These were not people accustomed to disobeying orders.

"Please reconsider," Samuel said, stepping forward and looking the soldier directly in the face. He was a young man, probably no more than twenty-five, and his two colleagues looked even younger. "This small temple means so much to our village. It will break our hearts to lose it."

The man looked somewhat moved by Samuel's earnest words. Indeed, even Samuel believed them.

"I am under strict orders to ensure the temple is closed," the man said shakily.

"You don't have to do this. Return to Goldhall, all of you," Samuel said, raising his voice as he motioned to the crew and the other soldiers. "Tell them that you refuse to participate in this cruel and unnecessary destruction."

"I... I can't do that."

"You can!" Samuel said. "All of you can. If everyone refused their orders, these temple closures would cease."

The People's Army soldiers and the crew looked at each other uneasily. "We shall surely be arrested or worse, and others will replace us."

"Whoever tries to arrest you, tell them the same thing I told you. That if they refuse to arrest you, the whole chain is broken."

The man looked back at the others in his group, perhaps wishing someone, anyone, would take his place.

"Have courage," Samuel said. "Have courage to do what is right!"

"I..."

Samuel stepped forward to grab hold of the man's shoulders. "Please," he said, looking him squarely in the eye, "please have faith."

The poor soldier looked behind him again and took a deep breath. He observed the villagers, many holding their hands together, pleading with him. "We shall return to Goldhall," he said dramatically. "And we shall tell the government that we refuse to participate."

The crowd cheered and let out cries of "praise Oqci!"

The men got back into their carriages and turned around, just as they had come.

"Mr. Miller, that was simply wonderful," someone said to Samuel.

"It was surely the voice of Oqci leading you," said another.

A small circle formed around him as people slapped his back. Samuel felt a strange feeling he had not felt in some time, perhaps ever. Was it pride? The satisfaction of doing a good deed for once? Tears formed in his eyes, but he steadied himself before they dripped down his cheeks like a fool.

Samuel knew not whether his words were right. Maybe the men, once they returned to Goldhall, would be promptly arrested – or worse – for having disobeyed orders, and a new party from the capital would return the next day. But, for now, their temple was spared.

YANIS

The People's Army amassed near Winterbridge, where they would cross into Friezzia to make their attack on Fortress Gul. Yanis rode through the lines and examined the soldiers.

He summoned up indignation as he addressed some of the regiments through a speaking trumpet. "The Friezzians have given their message that they intend to keep shielding the princess and the other exiles, that they will continue to support the Soldiers of Oqci. Let us not forget how the Friezzians treated our countrymen and women when they were on our soil. How they attempted to starve us out! How they brutalized us! Shall we not return the favour to them?"

Cheers of "hurrah!" followed. Yanis gave the order for them to press ahead to the Friezzian border defences.

As Yanis marched on, already the sublime walls of Fortress Gul came into view. Surely over two dozen stories high, the walls stretched from the northern coast inland toward the impassable mountains in the south. An imposing skull, itself several stories high, was carved into the wall and looked with its black eyes out toward Estenland's soil.

Fortress Gul was constructed following the Great War to be an impregnable barrier between the two nations. Never again would Estenland be able to cross into Friezzian territory. Or so they thought.

But the sacred creatures supplied the Estenlanders a crucial advantage.

Their forces would attack the fortress from two directions: from the east by land and from the north by sea. As the columns of soldiers approached, Yanis and his officers watched the battle from atop winged horses. He was not able to ride one himself, so he climbed upon the horse ridden by Clem, who had been training over the past weeks.

Clem led the horse into a gallop and they were soon airborne. Up here, Yanis could see the entire terrain of the battlefield and the fortress. The wind rushed all around. He took a short glance at the long drop immediately below, before quickly averting his eyes to look straight ahead.

"Worry not, Dragon Slayer," said Clem, sensing Yanis's nervousness. "It is no different than riding a regular horse."

The Friezzians pursued their usual strategy of an artillery barrage from the safety of the fortress walls. Cannon fire battered the Estenlander forces below, but not for long.

The signal was given and from Yanis's perch among the clouds, he watched his officers on winged horses fly toward the walls, alongside griffins and winged lions.

"This will finish them," Yanis said eagerly to Clem.

The griffins and lions swooped down upon the unsuspecting Friezzian artillery. The helpless Friezzians managed to fire, but before they could reload, it was too late. The sacred creatures were already upon them. Some of their soldiers jumped from the walls to certain death as the griffins approached, their screams reaching all the way up to Yanis and Clem. Other Friezzians who stood to fight were quickly torn apart by the griffins.

Teams of two Estenland soldiers rode atop the winged horses, one to pilot, the other armed. They flew along the battlements and fired on the panicked Friezzians who ran for their lives as griffins and winged lions stalked the walls.

It was all going to plan.

The Friezzian infantry stormed out of the fortress walls, knowing it would be hopeless to wait inside. They quickly assembled into line formation and launched orderly volleys. Exactly as Yanis had hoped.

"Let us go down for a closer look," Yanis said.

"Very well, Dragon Slayer."

Flying closer to ground level, he and Clem watched as their flying horses, lions, and griffins swooped down to attack the vulnerable Friezzian lines. But the Friezzians formed square, their bayonets extended above them and to the side.

The officers, riding the horses and commanding the lions and griffins, descended. One lion crashed into the square, barrelling through the wall of Friezzian soldiers, but doing considerable damage to itself in the process. The soldiers regrouped and surrounded it, stabbing it repeatedly with their bayonets. More griffins and lions were sent down. They too shattered through the Friezzian lines, but to Yanis's surprise the Friezzians regrouped and killed the creatures in their midst.

"It seems as though our Friezzian friends learned something since the last battle," he said.

"They have more pluck than I thought," Clem replied, "but the outcome is assured."

Yanis and Clem descended to the earth. The Friezzians continued to bunch together to withstand the charges of the sacred creatures.

"The war machines," Yanis called out.

The bugler played the signal, and the fleet of war machines lumbered across the open terrain.

Up in the clouds once again, Yanis and Clem watched the Friezzians try desperately to attack the war machines, but their bullets could not pierce their armour. As the Friezzians scrambled to avoid the cannon fire from the approaching war machines and the sacred creatures' attacks, their lines became entirely disjointed.

The Estenlander infantry advanced in unison and began their volley. Clouds of smoke filled the air. Through pockets in the clouds, Yanis glimpsed his own line, standing strong, while the enemy's was scattered. More flying horses, griffins, and lions emerged from the smoke as they descended again to attack the Friezzians.

A bullet whizzed past Yanis, even all the way up there in the sky. His heart pulsed as he gripped Clem tightly. There was no hope of the Friezzians hitting him from so far down below. Their weapons were simply too inaccurate. It would be a million to one chance. And yet...

"Don't they know it is bad manners to fire upon a general?" Clem said, in a bid to calm Yanis.

He let out a nervous chuckle. "Indeed, it is. Very rude."

The enemy's left flank was beginning to collapse. He ordered Clem to fly back down, where Yanis commanded a charge of griffins to completely shatter the flank.

Up again, Yanis watched it all unfold. The charge. The Friezzians scattering in all directions. Unfortunate soldiers who were singled out and torn apart by the griffins. Their infantry forces hitting the centre of the Friezzians from the front and the side.

"It's a rout," Yanis said to Clem. "Victory is ours!"

They watched the war machines trudge straight through the centre of the Friezzian lines, continuing their cannon fire as the Friezzian bullets hopelessly bounced away.

The Friezzians had no answer for Estenland's sacred creatures, nor the war machines, and from high up, Yanis could see the Friezzians retreating on the other side of the great wall.

They had won the battle. But not yet the war.

CHARLOTTE

The metal frame of Charlotte's bed groaned as she sat. She opened the day's *Goldhall Gazette*. Inside was only the worst news. The police continued to search for her. Koralo had been arrested, and in the weeks since Charlotte's disappearance, anyone who had a connection to her had also been detained, including poor Willien. She cursed herself for having dragged them into this mess.

Charlotte had been in this women's boarding house in Iron Town for two weeks. The room was quiet at this time of the afternoon, but it typically housed a dozen other women, each of them sleeping on decrepit, worn mattresses that stank of tobacco and mold. She unthinkingly reached down to scratch at the tiny red bite marks that had made themselves known across her legs. Fleas and bedbugs: their fellow boarders. But at least they provided a temporary diversion from the scurrying of mice in the walls.

She flung herself down upon the bed and gazed at the ceiling. Dear Oqci. What a terrible fate! Yet no one would ever think to look for her here.

Shifting onto her side, she continued reading. The newspaper also gave word about her nation's initial successes in the war against Friezzia. This would give Quinneas an even greater hold on power. The Soldiers of Oqci's random acts of violence against those who sold sacred creatures persisted, as did their attacks against the People's Army. Yet more and more of the terrorists were being apprehended. With Tressa and Aran's support, soon all opposition to Quinneas would disappear.

～

IT WAS at dinner the next evening that Charlotte noticed a curious woman. Even as Charlotte kept to herself, by now she had come to recognize most of the faces of the others. This woman, about Charlotte's age, looked around, watching the others carefully, even as she pretended not to.

It was not at all typical behaviour. Most of the women returned after the day's work, joylessly ate whatever barely edible meal was provided, then retired to bed. There was little time or energy for banter. Yet the strange woman attempted to make conversation, only to be rebuffed.

Charlotte, least of all, was eager to talk to anyone, lest her attempt at a working-class accent be scrutinized too closely. She thus kept her distance. When the meal was finished, however, she lingered on the threshold, out of sight, and watched as the strange woman cornered the last resident to finish her meal.

Charlotte could not decipher everything that was said, given her distance, but she overheard enough. "Listen," the woman said. "Would you like to earn some extra money?" Charlotte's fellow boarder quickly removed herself, perhaps reasoning that the woman had sinister motives.

The women there were as respectable as could be expected. They were employed at nearby factories and shops. This was no brothel. And plainly that was what the other woman was suggesting.

Or was she?

IN THE FOLLOWING DAYS, Charlotte kept a careful watch on the woman. At last, she committed to investigate further during their breakfast of stale bread and hard butter. Charlotte sat beside the strange young woman, smiling as she took her seat.

There was indeed something suspicious about her. Her accent indicated she was of the working classes, but she looked too well-nourished to be a regular resident. Charlotte had developed a theory. And now she would determine if it was correct.

"I fear I might one day break my teeth on this bread," Charlotte said, doing her best to mimic their accent.

The woman laughed and grinned widely, at last having a companion to talk with. "It's more sawdust than grain I reckon," she said.

"Indeed."

They ate the rest of the meal in silence, yet when the others departed, Charlotte waited for the inevitable approach.

"You know," she said, "I learned of somewhere we can earn additional money. I can tell you, if you would like."

"Really? That interests me a great deal."

The woman's expression was one of disappointment – until Charlotte's words registered in her brain. "It does?" she said. Answering her own question, she continued, "Why, yes, of course. Many have been eager to participate." She paused and observed Charlotte closely. "My name is Sky. It is not my real name, but it is better if neither of us knows the other's name."

"It is a sensible precaution," Charlotte said, before quickly wondering whether her vocabulary was too advanced. "We can really earn a lot of money?" she asked quickly.

"Yes," she said. Sky's eyes scanned the room to ensure once more that they were alone. "I have earned hundreds of crowns in only several weeks."

"Hundreds of crowns? But what sort of work shall we be doing?"

"I cannot tell you just yet," she said. "Meet me alone later tonight, and I shall take you to them. I promise the money will be worth it."

Charlotte nodded. "I shall await the visit with excitement."

DELLIREA

"Do not get your hopes up, Delli," said Yunolarol with that stupid grin he wore so often. "It is but one battle."

Yunolarol dealt out the cards as he and Dellirea passed the time in the palace.

She gathered up the five dealt to her to inspect her hand. Four blue unicorns and one yellow sea goat. A strong start.

By now she had heard the news of Friezzia's recent defeat. She was anxious to follow the progress of the war, yet she knew not what to think about it. On the one hand, she welcomed the possibility of liberation from her imprisonment in Freless. On the other, she feared what would happen to her if Estenland were victorious and she were brought back home.

Yunolarol discarded two of his cards, while Dellirea slid only the sea goat back to the pile. A green unicorn. So close!

"The mobs of Estenlander soldiers will have a surprise awaiting them when they reach Freless," continued Yunolarol as he rearranged his cards thoughtfully.

Dellirea did her best to reveal no interest in his words, focusing intently on her own cards, even as she was eager to learn more. She didn't wish him to know there was something she wanted from him.

As Dellirea inspected the cards, she could not help but be amused at her younger self, concerned that even a humble pastime such as cards could be blasphemous simply because they contained pictures of the sacred creatures.

"Your friend Rodnel has been a great help to us," Yunolarol said. Dellirea's eyes darted up from her cards. He smiled. "Aha, I see I have attracted your notice now."

Blast! She had given herself away upon the mention of Rodnel.

"Yes," Yunolarol continued, "under his guidance, we have built a fleet of war machines. In Friezzia, when a king commands the population to do something, they do it. They do not moan. They do not complain. They do not try to revolt. They simply do their duty, and with a smile on their faces, knowing they are serving their country. As it should be."

"Is Rodnel well?" Dellirea asked, breaking her silence and ignoring his slights toward her countrymen.

A second round of discards. This time she drew a fifth blue unicorn.

"Of course he is," said Yunolarol. "My grandfather promised his good health for cooperation. And he has cooperated."

She was relieved for Rodnel's sake, even if it meant he was collaborating with the enemy.

Yunolarol stared at the ceiling. "My grandfather has not long to live." He shuffled the cards in his hand uneasily. "Then my father will reign. And then one day it will be my turn. With you by my side, Delli, we shall rule this continent."

Dellirea examined the cards in her hand, daring not to look up and meet his eyes.

"When I am king, the world will bow at my feet." He laid down his hand: three blue griffins and two unicorns of different colours.

"Is that so?" Dellirea laid down her hand, revealing her five matching cards. Yuno chuckled when he realized, on this occasion, that he was not invincible.

Yet the frivolities of cards could obscure only momentarily the great stakes Dellirea faced. And she knew not what was worse: to be brought back to Estenland to be executed or to live forever in Friezzia as the bride – or prisoner – of Yunolarol.

SAMUEL

Samuel was feted as a hero following the stand outside the temple. The agents of the government returned to Goldhall to tell their superiors that they refused to carry out the destruction. Samuel hoped this might cause a ripple effect that would bring down the entire government in time.

But tonight was for celebration. Everyone gathered at the estate of a former village noble, which provided considerable space. Of course, Samuel's supporters were all strict followers of Oqci and abstained from alcohol, which meant the party lacked what he would usually consider an essential ingredient, but they had good food and good company, so he could hardly complain.

"Thanks be to Oqci," said Will Hunt, "for bringing Eston Miller to our village!"

"Hear, hear," responded the crowd.

Samuel and Will talked alone as the merriment continued.

"Have you ever been married, Eston?" he asked.

"Why, no," Samuel said. "Though there was someone I once dreamed of marrying…"

"You are a good and decent man," he said. "You possess a kind heart and steadfast courage. You would make a fine husband. My friend, we shall find a wife for you. There are many eligible ladies here who would suit you."

Samuel smiled at the thought. For so long, he had only ever imagined himself with Greta. But now he could at last begin to think of loving someone else. Of making a life with someone else.

"Yes, I would like that."

"I shall keep my eyes and ears open," said Will with a smile.

As the singing of the party began to quiet and the revellers departed for home, Olive pulled Samuel aside. "Eston," she said, "I believe we have witnessed a miracle today. Not only the saving of our temple, but your conversion. You wished to become a true follower of Oqci, and you have!"

It was strange to admit, but Samuel supposed they were right. He was even beginning to forget that his new identity was supposed to be just a ruse.

~

THE NEXT DAY, HOWEVER, THE VILLAGERS' naïve optimism was revealed to be just that. More People's Army soldiers came without warning. Some of the villagers frantically called out when they saw them. Samuel, the Hunt couple, and several dozen others hastily assembled on the path just as before. Again, Samuel thrust himself forward to speak.

As he began his speech, the leader of the group, an older man than the one from yesterday, stopped him. "Those soldiers who refused the government's orders yesterday are now imprisoned on suspicion of treason. We have come to carry out the job that they failed to do. Please stand aside."

The soldiers raised their guns and Samuel knew that this was not a group who could be swayed. Resistance would mean suicide.

Samuel and the others stood back from the road, all holding hands, as the soldiers entered the temple and began tearing apart its interior with hammers and crowbars, removing anything that showed it was a place of worship.

With each crack and crash, Samuel winced. He recalled the fond memories he had of the place even in the short time he had been there. A stone statue of Oqci was lugged out by four grunting men. The villagers consoled one another. They had grown up with the temple, been married there, attended funerals of family and friends. For their whole lives, the temple had been the centre of their village. Even though Samuel didn't believe in Oqci, he knew how much it meant to them... and to him.

Samuel put his hands on the shoulders of his two hosts who had been so kind to take in a wretch such as himself. The final ornaments were stripped from the temple and carried to a large wagon, where they would be taken to Goldhall to be destroyed or melted down.

"Let us be strong," Samuel said to the Hunt couple, who wiped away tears.

But he felt so weak.

YANIS

Yanis bit off a chunk of chicken drumstick while butter and juices trickled down his chin. Devon and Clem and some of his other officers sat in the commander's room of Fortress Gul, enjoying a well-deserved meal, cooked with food ransacked from the fortress's supplies. Yanis gave the rest of his soldiers free rein to take what they could from the fortress. Let them eat and drink well tonight, Yanis thought; soon they would march to Freless where the real battle would take place.

An aide entered to report on the scouting of the Friezzian defences. "High Commander, our scouts have spotted the Friezzians preparing sacred creatures for use in the coming fight."

"Hmmm," Yanis said. "It would appear they are learning from our success." Devon and Clem chuckled at this. Yanis set down the chicken and took a sip from his glass of beer, leaning back in his chair. Not as good as an Estenlander brew, but it would suffice. "It is no matter about the creatures. We have far more than them." He took another sip.

"High Commander, there is one more thing. Our scouts also report formations of war machines in the Friezzian lines."

Yanis nearly choked on his mouthful of beer. How did they…? "It was Rodnel!" he huffed, making the realization. "He must have been the one who designed them. Turning on his own people. Shameful!"

"What else can be expected from a noble?" said Devon as the aide looked on.

"Thank you for your report," Yanis said, dismissing the aide, "but worry not. They have fewer creatures and fewer war machines than we do."

The aide exited and Yanis continued dining, not letting on

that he was slightly shaken by the news. The Friezzians had the advantage of the defensive terrain. And they already had experience defending against the sacred creatures, which his side did not. This would be a much more difficult battle than the one at Fortress Gul.

~

THE PEOPLE'S ARMY marched in columns as before, passing villages just outside the limits of the capital. There was the slightest chill in the air as they marched, signalling the arrival of fall. Already they could see the factory smoke rising above nearby Freless. The respite at the fortress days ago had recharged Yanis's force for another battle.

The war machines traversed the dirt roads of the countryside well. The Estenlander scouts informed Yanis that the Friezzian army awaited, camped out on the high ground outside one of the villages. This would be their last stand.

Yanis tried to assume an air of confidence as he rode behind their line, even if private doubts crept into his mind. This battle would be crucial. If they managed victory, the Friezzians would be forced to relinquish the princess and Yanis would return to Estenland a hero. And if they lost... well, it was best not to think of it. His mind turned back to the consequences of victory. It would mean he could at last resign his position as head of the People's Army. The military life was no longer for him. And he yearned to see Nadeni again. How much time they had spent apart! But it was better than her being here, Yanis knew.

Soon Yanis caught sight of the Friezzian blue soldiers, still far outside of firing range, awaiting them in the fallow fields.

Before they could move into formation, dozens of Friezzian winged horses and winged lions flew toward the Estenlanders from above.

"Form square!" Yanis called out.

The lions swooped in to attack. Yanis's soldiers scrambled to take their positions. But too late. The lions crashed into the lines, dealing great damage, clawing at his soldiers before flying off again.

The Friezzian horses hovered in the air with their officers commanding the lions. They used two-man teams on the horses, just as the Estenlanders had.

Damn Friezzians! Could they not have an original idea?

They should have seen the charge coming. Yanis should have seen it coming. And now the lines were in chaos. They needed to counterattack.

Yanis quickly flew high above with Clem.

"Let us take the fight to the Friezzians," he called out as he drew his pistol.

"You sure that is smart?" Clem said to him. "It might be better to remain behind the lines."

"Am I not the Dragon Slayer?"

Clem hesitated. "Very well."

Clem flew them toward the Friezzians and into the fray. Yanis fired in vain as one of the Friezzians' flying horses whizzed past. Yanis and Clem spun around and Clem took out his lance. They flew ever nearer to the other team atop a flying horse. The Friezzian aimed his pistol and fired, missing Yanis widely. As he reloaded, Yanis took a shot. Another miss. He and Clem peeled away.

Turning back around, they flew past again. Nearer. Nearer. A clash of steel as the pilots' lances crossed, but neither gained an advantage. A dozen winged horses, some Estenland's and some Friezzia's, soared in circles in the cloudy grey sky. Yanis could not keep straight which were which. Shots rang out from all sides.

"We need to get back down to the ground," Yanis shouted to Clem. The gunfire from below had already created large clouds of smoke. Yanis's head spun. They had flown around in so many circles and it was ever more difficult to see where his own lines even were.

"Where in Oqci's bloody name are we?" shouted Clem.

They hovered in the air, trying to determine their location.

Out of the corner of Yanis's eye appeared a Friezzian team on horseback flying toward them.

"There! There!" Yanis shouted to Clem, who had not seen them. Clem frantically tried to fly away. A pistol fired. A direct hit into Clem's head. Blood and brains splashed upon Yanis as Clem slumped forward on the horse.

"Clem!"

Yanis fired a shot to ward off another pass from the Friezzian duo.

A bloody indent in the back of Clem's head dripped down upon the horse, which now flew aimlessly. Yanis needed to take command of it, as best he could.

There was no choice. "Goodbye, loyal friend," Yanis said as he pushed Clem's limp body from the horse. Yanis cursed how his stupid decisions cost Clem his life. He only hoped Clem's body crash-landed upon a Friezzian far down below. It was what he would have wanted.

Yanis made his way to the front of the horse. He was completely untrained in flying horses. But he grasped the reins, hopeful he could manage it.

The horse flew wildly in all directions. The world spun. Smoke was everywhere and Yanis could barely tell which way was up. He yanked the reins, yet they continued flying erratically. He could not get the hang of it.

More and more Friezzian soldiers circled in the air.

He was going to be killed up here, he realized. By the Friezzians. Or by his own incompetence. He just needed to find a way down. Somehow!

Yanis pointed his pistol toward any enemies who approached. "Get back, you cursed Friezzians!" he shouted into the emptiness of the sky.

Glancing down below, Yanis saw the long parallel lines of his battalions clashing with theirs. The Friezzian side had managed to withstand a charge of their sacred creatures. The Friezzians already had experience dealing with the attacks. The Estenlanders had none. And their own lines had been rattled by the Friezzian charges.

After much experimenting, Yanis slowly grasped the way to make the horse move how he wished. He needed to get back to ground level to command the battle. At last, he approached the earth and his horse gracefully trotted to a smooth landing, behind their lines.

Yanis dismounted and tried to take a step. He immediately collapsed to the ground. The entire battlefield was rotating. Even as he sat still, the earth moved below him. Yanis braced himself with his forearms upon the ground and put his feet underneath him, but he instantly toppled over again. On the ground, Yanis vomited, from the dizziness and from the smell of blood and guts and excrement and gunpowder that filled the air. He heaved again as he tried once more to climb to his feet.

"Have some water, Dragon Slayer," said Devon, rushing toward him and handing him a flask. Yanis gulped it down. Eventually, the world stopped moving and he took Devon's hand to get back to his feet. Yanis ordered immediate reinforcements to the left flank, where his lines were becoming disjointed. A Friezzian griffin attack came before the reinforcements could arrive, cutting the line into further chaos.

"Send our griffins!" Yanis shouted to anyone who would listen. A unit of griffins was sent. The two sides of griffins charged at each other and paired off in battle as bullets rained down from the Friezzians riding flying creatures above. More and more soldiers, and more and more dead sacred creatures, dropped from the air and onto the battlefield. Yanis wondered what Oqci would think of such horrors, if he were indeed real.

Yanis's side was struggling. The Friezzian griffins had gotten the edge. Thoughts of retreat crossed his mind. The Friezzians' war machines made their way onto the battlefield, slowly but surely. Dear Oqci. This could be the end of them.

"The war machines! Bring out our war machines!" Yanis shouted. Devon dutifully signalled for them. This would be their only hope of avoiding a rout.

The Estenland war machines lumbered across the muddy fields and launched preliminary fire. Yanis's soldiers let off volleys at the Friezzian war machines. The bullets ricocheted off their steel shells.

"Devon," Yanis said, over the cacophony of the battle, "I fear we might need to retreat if this attack does not succeed."

The trudging of the Friezzian war machines filled Yanis with dread. One of them came into range to fire. The outside cannon was aimed toward him.

But then…

An explosion inside crumpled its exterior walls and sent smoke pouring out from every hole. The war machine was now a piece of flaming wreckage in the middle of the battlefield.

More of the Friezzian war machines approached, but when one tried to fire a shot, it too destroyed itself. Helpless soldiers struggled to make their way out before they were consumed in the blaze.

What was happening?

The battlefield was strewn with dozens of ruined Friezzian war machines. But Estenland's still functioned.

"Press ahead!" Yanis urged.

The Friezzian troops looked all around them, their discipline shattered as they struggled to understand why their vaunted war machines had failed so spectacularly. As they did, Yanis's infantry and sacred creatures were given new life. They pressed the advantage. The Friezzians, dispirited, threw themselves on the ground in surrender or fled in panic.

Devon stared at Yanis, unblinking, his mouth gaping open. Other soldiers nearby looked at Yanis as if he had conjured the destruction of the enemy war machines through magic.

The battle had been won… although Yanis knew not how.

CHARLOTTE

Charlotte met the strange woman called Sky later that night as planned. She led Charlotte through a maze of city streets in Iron Town, splashing along in the small puddles of rain – or at least Charlotte hoped it was just rain. The streetlights from the main roads did not penetrate much into these alleyways, leaving them in near darkness. As they rounded corner after corner, Charlotte was becoming disoriented.

Did she truly think this plan through? What if it was not at all what she imagined?

"Are… are we safe, Sky?"

"Of course," she said, turning back. "Trust me. It's not much further now."

A rat scurried across their path as they continued, until they finally came to an inconspicuous door off a narrow alley.

Charlotte's heart raced. Terrible thoughts about what could be behind the door flooded into her mind. She hoped she was right.

"This is the place?" Charlotte asked.

"Yes." Sky reached into a bag and pulled out two black masks lined with gold. She handed Charlotte one of them. "Put it on." Sky pulled the other mask over her face.

Charlotte's worries washed away once she had donned her mask.

Her suspicions were right! How foolish she was to doubt her instincts.

The door creaked open, and Charlotte and Sky descended rickety stairs into a dark and grimy basement. Before them were twenty other mask-wearing individuals, seated on wooden chairs: the Soldiers of Oqci, in the flesh. Through the interrogations of the captured members, Charlotte knew that they were mostly composed of former nobles, but evidently they didn't mind paying those at the margins to be their pawns.

"You have brought before us someone who wishes to join?" said the central masked figure, a woman.

"Yes, Sun," said Sky, tilting her head before her. "This is Silver. She is a humble woman, yet I have spoken with her and have found her surprisingly intelligent. She desires to join us."

Surprisingly intelligent? That was a nice compliment, Charlotte supposed. Poor Sky didn't have the faintest idea who she really was!

The one they called Sun turned in Charlotte's direction. "We shall ensure all your needs are met should you wish to join us. No more will you be forced to live in poverty and hardship! But you must do what we ask of you. You must not waver. You must not bend. Sky has been a faithful servant to us. She has always carried out her duties faithfully. And she has been greatly compensated."

Charlotte looked to Sky, who nodded.

"I am willing to do whatever you ask," Charlotte said.

"It is a wise choice, Silver," said Sun. "We should be glad to have you as a fellow Soldier, but you must first earn our trust."

"Of course."

"There are now vendors who sell sacred creatures," continued Sun, "as if they were some kind of common trinket. No different than a cheap widget that is hawked on Market Street! These vendors make a mockery of our faith. What we require of you, Silver, is to kill one of these vendors, to prove your loyalty to our cause."

Ice ran through Charlotte. The thought of killing someone… she couldn't! Behind their masks, Charlotte felt the eyes of the Soldiers of Oqci bearing down upon her.

"It is not so bad," Sky whispered to her. "Just think of the money. That's what I did."

But Charlotte cared not for money. "Is… is there another way to win your trust?"

Sun shook her head and sighed. "Sky, why have you brought

me this woman? She is plainly not serious. She is plainly not willing to do what is necessary."

Sky struggled for words. "I… I have disappointed you…"

"Maybe there is another way," Charlotte said, reaching her hands up to remove her mask.

"Keep your mask on!" Sky said, as she tried to grab Charlotte's hands. But Charlotte evaded her.

"Yes, maybe I could earn your trust another way," she continued as she pulled off the mask. The stares of the masked crowd felt heavy upon her. "I am not some poor woman… but rather, I am Charlotte of Evesbury."

Gasps filled the room.

"You could benefit from having someone like me supporting your movement," she said firmly. "Could you not?"

Sun walked toward Charlotte and brought her face inches away. "It is you," she said. "It is you. I did not recognize you for a moment."

"I believe we have a common enemy, have we not? Quinneas Raeil."

DELLIREA

Yunolarol moved his food about his plate. He had barely eaten any of his oats and onions. A part of Dellirea enjoyed seeing him squirm like this.

"Estenland's forces will be here soon," he said tersely, perhaps sensing her thoughts. Maybe she had not sufficiently concealed her smile. "It's only a matter of time before we surrender. You should be worried too. Do you think they are going to welcome their former princess with open arms?" He snorted. "Think again. They will take you prisoner and do the same to you as they did to your parents."

"That may be so," Dellirea said. "Though at least I shall be in my homeland."

The warfare had been terrible. She thought of the two sides slaughtering one another on the battlefield. And now both sides using the sacred creatures! Did they not share the same faith? Were the doctrines of Oqci not supposed to teach them peace? She thought about the lessons their faith supposedly taught, and yet... it seemed that people twisted Oqci's words for whatever reasons they wished. And sometimes they even used them to justify sinister practices.

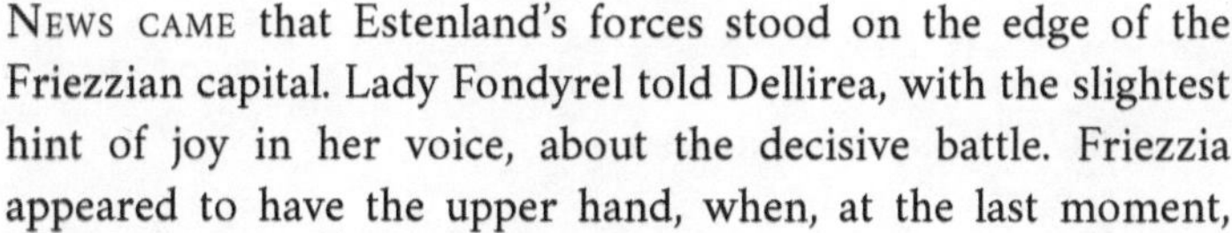

NEWS CAME that Estenland's forces stood on the edge of the Friezzian capital. Lady Fondyrel told Dellirea, with the slightest hint of joy in her voice, about the decisive battle. Friezzia appeared to have the upper hand, when, at the last moment, Friezzia's war machines inexplicably failed.

"How could that be?" Dellirea said. "Rodnel is a genius crafts-man. He could not have designed defective machinery."

"I know not," said Lady Fondyrel, "but Rodnel entrusted me with a letter to give to you once the war concluded."

"A letter?"

She handed Dellirea an envelope. Dellirea quickly tore open the seal and read the contents.

Dear Lady Zendar,

This letter bears sad news, I fear. By the time you read this, I may no longer be on this earth. If the stories of Oqci are true, I hope I am with him in the Cloud Kingdom.

I designed and built the war machines for the Friezzians, just as I had done for your father. Yet I added one surprise. The cannons were engineered to cause an explosion within the war machines as soon as they were fired. If things unfolded as I imagined they would, this would cause a disaster within the Friezzian lines at the pivotal moment, ensuring victory for our nation.

Again, if things unfolded as I imagined they would, the generals would have quickly realized who was responsible for the malfunction and would have had me executed. But it would be a small price to pay, as Estenland would already have been victorious.

I write you this letter to say goodbye to you, Lady Zendar, but also for you to show those back in Estenland, so that the people might know the sacrifice I have made for our country, and for you. I did it so that you might return to your homeland. I plead for mercy for you and beg the rulers of Estenland to honour my sacrifice by refusing to enact any cruelties upon you.

Lady Zendar, you are a good and kind person, with a noble spirit. I pray my sacrifice was not made in vain.

Your friend,

Rodnel, Count of Summerstone

Tears dripped onto the paper as Dellirea read. Oh Rodnel! What a brave soul. She clutched the letter to her chest and hoped its plea would be heard.

"What news does it bring?" asked Lady Fondyrel.

"Sad news."

Lady Fondyrel hugged Dellirea. She understood.

THE IMMINENT CAPTURE of the capital led King Hyazaral to offer peace. He relented to Estenland's demands to relinquish Dellirea, along with the other exiled nobles that Friezzia had been harbouring. He would also pay a massive indemnity to cover the damages caused by the Friezzian army during last year's siege. It was that or be conquered completely. It was only a matter of time before Estenland accepted the deal.

At last, she would be going home.

Yunolarol rapped upon her door. His eyes were red. Had… had he been crying? He lurched stiffly at the threshold to Dellirea's room, gripping the doorframe, unsure whether to enter.

"It seems we shall not be marrying after all," he said. He stared off down the hallway. "I… I am disappointed. I hope that you are not too disappointed by this news."

Disappointed? He couldn't be serious, could he? Yet there was no hint of irony in his voice.

"I think I shall survive it," Dellirea said. She paused for a second. "Besides, I prefer ladies."

There was that same dumb face of his, his mouth hanging open, unable to process what she had just said.

"Goodbye, Yuno," she said. "I wish you well."

She meant it. Maybe one day he would find happiness, though she was glad it was not to be at her expense.

Lady Fondyrel interrupted her parting with Yunolarol and informed her that she was to gather her things at once and prepare for the trip home. As Dellirea did so, Lady Fondyrel watched her. "Princess," she said, "be strong as you return."

"Thank you, Lady Fondyrel," Dellirea said. "I hope you get justice for what happened to you and your husband. Somehow."

"I have given up all hope for justice in this life," she said. "If there is an afterlife, and if Oqci sees me fit, then perhaps I shall find justice there."

Dellirea embraced her. Dellirea had been frightened of her when she first arrived, but now Dellirea realized how fond she had become of her. Perhaps Lady Fondyrel was correct about the afterlife. For her sake, Dellirea hoped she was.

At the designated time, King Hyazaral arrived at her room. His presence caused Lady Fondyrel to meekly lower her head, even as he said nothing. Hyazaral led Dellirea through the hall-ways to the outside of the palace. All along the route were members of the royal family and the court nobles, who stood silently as they walked past.

At last, as they approached the gates of the palace, Dellirea saw the carriage that would take her away. She was to go with the one who was known as the Dragon Slayer, Yanis Haller.

Hyazaral looked at Dellirea before she left. "I know not what they have planned for you back in Estenland," he said coldly, "but I hope for your sake it is not the same fate suffered by your parents or your friend Rodnel."

Dellirea knew to what he referred. But she refused to betray any emotion. "Thank you for your hospitality during my stay," she said. "I learned much here."

"Hmm," he grunted. "It will be the last time I trust an Estenlander."

And that was all. Dellirea turned to walk out the palace gates.

There she saw Yanis, dressed in a smart green, white, and yellow uniform, with two officers on either side of him. She found herself impressed. Hearing of a "people's army" filled her with thoughts of wild, undisciplined soldiers butchering all who were in their path. Yet Yanis and his colleagues were as well-dressed and well-groomed as any noble officers.

"Greetings, Ms. Zendar," he said. "I shall be escorting you back to Estenland."

"Thank you," she said, unsure of how to act in the presence of someone who was once her inferior, but who was now, she understood, her equal.

Dellirea stepped into the carriage and took one final look at the imposing palace that had been her home for several months. She had meant what she said to Hyazaral. She *had* learned a lot there. She had learned something about the cruelty of kings, and she had learned something about herself.

Their carriage, surrounded by horses and sacred creatures and soldiers, set off through the deserted streets of Freless. It would be a day's journey to the border, and from there a railcar would transport them the rest of the way to Goldhall.

Yanis sat quietly in the carriage, simply looking out the window as they passed down a thoroughfare that might in other times be lined with vendors and shoppers. Now, however, not a soul was outside, save those in the convoy.

"What will happen to me once we return to the capital?"

"That will be for Quinneas Raeil to decide," he said, "not me."

"But if you did have the chance to decide," Dellirea said, "what then?"

He looked at her with kind, weary eyes. "You were always caring toward the people," he said. "You have a good heart, Ms. Zendar. If it were up to me, no harm would come to you."

This did little to brighten her spirits. She bit her lip in thought. From his words, it sounded very much like harm would come to her once they returned.

YANIS

For long stretches of their carriage ride back to Estenland, Yanis and Dellirea said nothing. But Yanis watched her closely the whole time, observing her expressions and movements. She cared more for the people than all the other members of the royal family put together, he knew. Even if she held some of the same backward views as other members of her class, she was essentially good.

She looked out the window with sad eyes. Yanis had never seen her up close before, but she looked much different than the innocent girl he had imagined. She was hardened, made more mature, by everything that had happened.

"Mr. Haller," she said, breaking their long silence, "can I trust you?"

"You can."

"I wish to show you something."

From a handbag, she pulled out a letter and gave it to Yanis. He read it carefully. It explained the mystery of why the war machines had malfunctioned in the battle. Rodnel was not the traitor Yanis thought him to be.

Once he finished reading, Dellirea asked whether he thought the letter would make a difference.

"I shall show it to Quinneas Raeil and plead for him to take its contents into account. I can promise no more than that."

"Thank you."

But Yanis feared his promise would not be enough. Would Quinneas show her mercy? When had he ever shown mercy?

Yanis could only do what he could. He must return her without incident, and thereby accomplish his mission. It would be the last mission he would undertake. Clem's death weighed heavily on him. He no longer had it in him to continue leading the People's Army or to participate in this revolution. He would live out his days happily with Nadeni and put everything else behind him.

~

QUINNEAS, along with Aran and Tressa, was there to meet them at the palace following their long journey. Yanis helped Dellirea step down from the carriage as throngs of people watched outside the gates.

Dellirea had a steely look in her eyes as she marched toward Quinneas. Quinneas nodded to Yanis and then said to Dellirea, "Greetings, Ms. Zendar."

Her face remained impassive as she said simply, "Greetings."

"You will be held in the palace to await trial for treason," Quinneas said, before commanding some of the People's Army soldiers to show her to her room in the palace.

"You have done well, Dragon Slayer," Quinneas said to Yanis as Dellirea was led away.

"Thank you," Yanis said, leaning closer so that neither Aran nor Tressa could hear, "but I have important news I wish to tell you regarding Dellirea. It concerns her trial."

"Go on."

"Dellirea showed me a letter in which Rodnel, the former Count of Summerstone, explained that it was him who sabotaged the Friezzian war machines, ensuring our victory in battle. He sacrificed himself for Dellirea in hopes that you would show her mercy."

Quinneas frowned at this revelation. "It was an honourable thing for Rodnel to do, but it says nothing with regard to Dellirea's treasonous activities. I would appreciate it if you kept the contents of the letter to yourself. We shall talk more after my speech tonight."

Yanis's fears were confirmed. The letter would do nothing to sway Quinneas. He had already made up his mind about the princess's fate. There was to be no stopping him now. How foolish Yanis was to betray Charlotte those weeks ago!

"Yanis," continued Quinneas, "I wish you to remain at the

palace, to ensure Dellirea is kept under careful watch. And I wish for you to attend my speech this evening. It is an important speech, announcing Dellirea's capture and how she will soon face justice."

"I must see Nadeni," Yanis said. "We have been apart for too long. I must return home, and I shall then join you this evening."

"It is not possible, I'm afraid," said Quinneas. He patted Yanis on the shoulder gently, as if he were but a friend. "Your presence is needed here too urgently. Once the speech is concluded, you will see Nadeni."

"Will she not be attending the speech tonight?" Yanis asked.

"I have asked her to watch from the crowd," said Quinneas. "The Soldiers of Oqci will wish nothing more than to disrupt this important speech. And your attention must be focused squarely on preventing them from doing so."

Yanis understood. It would only be a matter of time before he and Nadeni were reunited, he told himself. They had been apart for weeks. What was a few more hours? Yanis reluctantly agreed to remain at the palace until after Quinneas's speech. But how he longed to see her again.

THAT EVENING, Yanis stood upon the stage next to the three Emergency Committee members. He could only count the seconds until he saw Nadeni.

"Fellow citizens," Quinneas began, "our revolution is nearly complete! We have the last remaining traitors in our midst. The most important, Dellirea Zendar, is now being held inside the palace. Like her parents, she betrayed the revolution. She betrayed the revolution and supported heinous terrorist activities. And she must be punished!"

The crowd cheered at this. Aran and Tressa, standing on either side of Quinneas, looked out adoringly at the crowd, smiling in a way that repulsed Yanis.

"Bringing her to justice is a critical step in consolidating our revolution! But," he continued, growing quieter now, "fellow citizens, bringing Ms. Zendar to justice is not the end of the revolution."

What did he mean? The crowd grew silent in anticipation, as did Yanis.

"To fully entrench the revolution, to fulfill our nation's destiny, to prove that Estenland is a grown-up nation… we must return to the Dragon Isles! We shall prove that a democratic nation can accomplish something a brutal monarchy never could. Working together, arm-in-arm, we shall gain control of the dragons!"

Wild cheers filled the square. All around, tricolour flags waved fervently.

Yanis could hardly believe what he was hearing. Return to the Dragon Isles? Had Quinneas gone mad?

"I wish you to lead the force," Quinneas explained after the speech as he and Yanis met alone in the king's former council chamber. "Discovering this new sacred creature and bringing it under the nation's control… It will be the culmination of everything we have fought for."

"Quinneas, if I may," Yanis said, "this attempt to conquer the Dragon Isles… It is the very thing that caused the revolution in the first place. It violates all of our principles."

"No, Yanis. You must understand. It is different this time. The previous mission was imposed from the top, from the king onto the people. This time, the collective will of the people *demands* that we conquer those islands."

"Collective will?" Yanis said. "I am sorry to be bold, but are you not just substituting your own will for that of the people?"

Quinneas recoiled in surprise. "Our program, with myself as the chief representative, was endorsed by the people in the most recent election. Did you not hear the fervent cheers during the speech? I am the embodiment of the collective will."

Yanis shook his head. Quinneas had become delusional with his power.

"As the leader of the Emergency Committee," Quinneas continued, "you are under my command. And so I order you to begin preparations for taking the islands. With your experience there, and with the sacred creatures and the war machines at your disposal, I know you will be successful."

Quinneas intimidated him, yet Yanis knew he could not carry out the mission.

"I… I shall not do it," Yanis said, trying to summon confidence. "I cannot accept your authority. I intend to resign my command of the People's Army. I shall speak out against your leadership."

Quinneas sat back in his chair, contemplating Yanis's words. "Yanis, I feared that you would lose your nerve." He shook his head and sighed. "You have always possessed a timidity that I hoped you would have outgrown when given the leadership of the People's Army. I feared that when you learned of what I asked, you would be too cowardly to do what needed to be done. So before you returned from Friezzia, I took the precautionary measure of detaining Nadeni, in the event of such disobedience."

"You did what?" Yanis said. "Is she safe?"

"She is quite safe. But if the mission should fail, or if you should refuse it, I'm afraid harm will come to her…"

"You monster."

"… and your unborn child."

This shocked Yanis into silence.

"Oh, you didn't know?" said Quinneas. "Congratulations, Yanis. You are going to be a father. Assuming you do what I ask."

Yanis never realized his evil could have run so deep. He stood and took a step toward him. "I should kill you right here."

"You are too cowardly to do it, Yanis," Quinneas replied calmly, remaining seated. "Besides, harm will come to Nadeni and your baby if anything should happen to me. So it would be wise for you to obey my orders."

Yanis realized Quinneas was right. How foolish he had been to leave Nadeni behind! Assuming that she would be safer in Estenland than with him!

"But," Quinneas continued, "when you successfully carry out

the mission, a reward awaits. I already promised to begin the transition to independence for New Selver – or Umiri as they call it. But if you are successful in your mission, you and Nadeni will be appointed as the leaders of New Selver. You two can live happily there – with Estenland's support, with my support – ruling as you like."

Quinneas was right that Yanis had no option but to undertake the mission in order to save Nadeni and his child. Try to rally the support of the People's Army against Quinneas? Would they even support Yanis?

It was too dangerous. Quinneas would kill Nadeni before Yanis even got the chance.

Yanis regretted everything he had done. He had emboldened Quinneas and all this time had acted as his personal police force by leading the People's Army. Worst of all, he had turned in Charlotte, the only reasonable hope of stopping him.

Where was Charlotte? As far as anyone knew, she was on the run. But where?

Yanis knew that he needed to find a way, somehow, to communicate with her, wherever she was, to apologize. And to plead with her to save Nadeni and to stop Dellirea's execution.

DELLIREA

When Dellirea arrived back in Goldhall, tears filled her eyes. Tears because there were many times in Friezzia when she believed she would never return home again. But they were also tears for the inevitability of her fate. The palace, where she grew up, was now a monument to the cruelties of the revolution. She thought of her mother and father and brother, and how she would soon join them in the Cloud Kingdom, if the stories of Oqci were true, and if she were worthy despite her transgressions.

At the palace, she was imprisoned in one of the former noble apartments. It was hardly different from her time in Friezzia, she thought, even though she was on her native soil. Her requests for information from the guards were met with protests that they were under strict orders not to speak with her.

After several days of waiting, Quinneas at last came to her room. "Ms. Zendar," he said, "I shall not speak to you long. I only come to inform you of your upcoming trial for treason. You conspired to escape to Friezzia to help the government there and you conspired to help support terrorists who fought against our government."

"I did no such thing," she said. It was true she had left Estenland, but she knew not what he meant about helping terrorists. She certainly had never helped the Soldiers of Oqci, if that is what he meant.

"That will all be decided during the trial," Quinneas said. He paced around her room, towering above her. "The trial will take place in two weeks' time. You will be appointed a lawyer to represent you. Your guilt will be determined by myself and the two other members of the Emergency Committee. Rest assured that we shall examine the evidence impartially before rendering our judgment."

"Please don't fault me for finding that difficult to believe."

"Whether you believe it is irrelevant," he said. "I am animated by nothing but the desire for justice. I don't expect a child like yourself, born into untold privilege, to understand that feeling."

As he exited her room, she called out, "I understand justice much better than you do."

THE ONLY OTHER visitor to Dellirea's room was a young, bespectacled, nervous-looking man who introduced himself as Penn Harper, her lawyer. "My job will be to ensure the law is followed in your upcoming trial," he said as he laid out a stack of papers on the desk in her room.

Penn was not a man who inspired confidence, but she felt reassured at least to have someone representing her interests. He explained how Quinneas would lead the prosecution, and then he and the two other members of the Emergency Committee would determine her guilt at the trial's end.

"Why, that is an affront to all principles of justice," Dellirea protested. "How could I possibly receive a fair trial under such conditions?"

"They will be completely impartial," he insisted. "Mr. Raeil and the others will follow the law precisely. I shall ensure it."

She realized now that her lawyer was no more than a lackey of Quinneas.

"Now," he said, "please tell me the extent of your correspondence with the Soldiers of Oqci so I can begin to prepare your defence."

"The extent was zero," she said. "I never corresponded with them."

"Ms. Zendar, as your lawyer, it is essential that you tell me the truth so I can best represent you. You may be given a reduced sentence if you are honest with the Committee."

She sighed. This was clearly hopeless. "I am telling the truth."

After she and Penn debated back and forth, he eventually relented. He merely said he would be there on the day of the trial to ensure her interests were represented. But she had already resigned herself to her fate.

CHARLOTTE

"Has Oqci forsaken us?" asked Sun.

None of the other members were willing to answer. Charlotte and the others gathered around a large room of what was once a noble family's residence, now abandoned.

Charlotte lived there temporarily with some of the other members, including Sun. But they had to always keep moving, before the People's Army could discover their location.

"It is true that times are difficult for us," Charlotte said finally, when no one else would speak, "but we shall find a way."

This only produced scattered grumbles from the others, all except Charlotte wearing a mask.

The growing arrests of their members had greatly weakened them. However much they wished to overthrow Quinneas's government, they simply had not the weapons nor the people.

The members grew silent again. No one had responded following Charlotte's comments. After having revealed her identity to them, the Soldiers of Oqci accepted that she could be a valuable ally, even if they didn't entirely trust her. They agreed to lodge Charlotte in exchange for her help, whatever that might be.

But in truth she had no solutions to their current impasse.

"Charlotte," said Sun finally, "you have contributed little in the weeks since we have been sheltering you. What exactly *is* your value to us?"

The masked eyes all turned to her.

"I shall discover a solution," she said. "I promise. I know Quinneas Raeil better than anyone. I understand how he thinks and what he will do."

She struggled to believe her own words. She needed to gain

time, but soon the other members would realize how hollow her promises were.

"Very well," said Sun. "But the matter is urgent. Let us trust in Oqci to guide us. Fellow Soldiers, just think what will happen once we kill Quinneas! We shall place Dellirea back on the throne and undo all of the horrible changes brought by the revolutionaries. Those responsible for the revolution will face justice. The natural order will be restored."

Charlotte swallowed hard at this. What would happen to her then? Her only choice was to help them for now. And once Quinneas was dead and Dellirea rescued, what then? That would be for later. For now, the situation was growing desperate. Koralo and Willien languished in prison and Charlotte feared their deaths were not far off.

CHARLOTTE CONTINUED to think of a solution as she learned of the imminent departure of the People's Army to the Dragon Isles. They were led by Yanis Haller, the so-called Dragon Slayer. Part of her wished he had been killed in the war against Friezzia, but another part of her – a naïve, childish part – wished to believe there was still some good left in him.

If Yanis had any remaining sense, any remaining decency, surely Quinneas's plan to send them to the Dragon Isles would have convinced him of the evils of this government.

He might be their last hope.

If he did have regrets, there would be one way for him to notify Charlotte: the place by the stream. The place Yanis had proposed to Nadeni. The place Charlotte and Yanis discussed when she first suggested the plan to stop Quinneas. It was unlikely, but if ever Yanis was going to make contact, it would be there.

Charlotte rushed to speak with Sun privately. She found Sun in her study. Even there, she insisted on wearing a mask. It was too dangerous otherwise, she always said. If any of the members were captured, they might be tortured and reveal the identity of the leaders. Even Sky, Charlotte's companion from the boarding house, claimed she knew not Sun's identity, although Charlotte had her suspicions of who Sun really was.

"I might have an idea," Charlotte told Sun. "It involves communicating with Yanis Haller. But you need to trust me. I need to go into the city, alone, to do it."

"Haller? That foul man?" Sun spit.

"If my intuition is correct, then I know a way that Yanis might try to contact me. What other options have we?"

"If you believe that vile man can help us achieve our goals," she continued, "very well. But remember, Charlotte, if you betray us, we shall hunt you down."

Sun's unblinking black eyes from under her mask made Charlotte shiver.

"I shall not betray you," she said. "I promise."

CHARLOTTE DEPARTED to Iron Town and followed Yanis's directions to Hope Stream. Yanis and the army were leaving tomorrow. Perhaps it was foolish to believe in him, but he was Charlotte's only hope.

No one would recognize her, yet she still felt vulnerable leaving the estate. A carriage brought her to Iron Town. She alighted and traversed the city streets, careful to avoid eye contact with the passers-by.

Yanis had told her exactly where to look those months ago. She followed the stony trail along the water, just as he said. The birds fluttering back and forth across the trees and the gentle hum of the stream almost made it a peaceful scene. But inside Charlotte was only chaos and nervousness.

She moved aside a low-lying branch as she continued along the path. Another branch stuck out and caught itself on her dress. She fumbled with it as she untangled herself.

How silly all this was!

She continued on the path, feeling more and more hopeless.

But there! The point that jutted into the stream. It was

exactly as Yanis described. And there was the tree in question, just before the point.

Charlotte practically shook as she approached it. Preparing herself for disappointment, she reached down into the hollow of the tree. A folded letter!

Thanks be to Oqci, Charlotte thought. Thanks be to the Dragon Slayer!

The seal came apart easily to reveal a note written in his hand.

Charlotte,

I must be brief. All I can say is that I am sorry for my actions. I was a fool to betray you to Quinneas.

I know not where you are or if you will receive this message. But if you do, there is an unguarded cache of weapons belonging to the People's Army at the coordinates on the opposite side of this letter. I have enclosed a key necessary to enter. I hope this is of use to you.

A personal note: Quinneas has imprisoned Nadeni. Please help her if you can.

Yanis

Charlotte flipped over the letter to reveal the numbered coordinates.

She was stunned reading it. Surely this was a trap. Yanis had betrayed her already. Why not once more? But if he was sincere, the weapons could be essential in stopping Quinneas.

101

DELLIREA

Dellirea awakened from a restless night's sleep. Sun streamed through the curtains.

Today was the day of her trial.

Penn Harper, her hapless lawyer, came to her room to accompany her. She hardly needed his help to know the way to her father's old council room, where the trial was to be held. As she entered, she was struck by the absence of his portrait that once hung in the centre of the room. Now there was only the tricoloured flag of the revolutionaries.

Waves of memories flooded into her mind of the many council meetings she had attended there, not least the fateful one in which her father had decided on the expedition to the Dragon Isles. How different things would have been…

At one side of the table were Quinneas and the two other members of the so-called Emergency Committee, introduced to Dellirea as Tressa Smith and Aran Potter. On the other side were her and her lawyer.

Quinneas read the charges of treason against her. "How do you plead?"

Before Dellirea's lawyer could say anything, she said, "Not guilty."

With that, Quinneas began the questioning. "What was the purpose of your family's travel to Friezzia?"

Was it best to be honest? Or try to evade the charges? She knew she was doomed regardless, so she decided to be honest. "We were escaping the revolution. I had no part in the plans, but the goal was for the Friezzian government to help my father regain the throne in exchange for making Estenland subservient."

"Very good," said Quinneas. "See, there is no reason why this should be difficult. Now, why did you send support to the Soldiers of Oqci when you were in Friezzia?"

"I never supported that group. I was disgusted to learn of their actions, and I would never support them, ever."

Quinneas folded his arms. "You were doing so well just a moment ago by telling the truth about your escape to Friezzia." He pulled a handful of papers out of a folder on the table. "We have direct communication, in your hand, pledging support."

Quinneas passed her a letter to examine.

It was indeed a letter that was signed with Dellirea's name, but it was not in her handwriting. "It is a crude forgery."

"Our experts have determined its authenticity," said Quinneas.

Penn turned toward Dellirea and whispered, "Are you sure you didn't write it?"

Some representation!

"Yes, I am sure I would remember such a thing," she said loudly, so everyone could hear. "This entire trial is a farce."

"The legitimacy of the trial is not for you to determine," said Quinneas.

Over two hours, Quinneas, and occasionally Tressa and Aran, peppered Dellirea with questions. Had she ever sent funds to factions resisting the government? Was she angry about her parents' executions? Did she resent the revolutionary government? Did she believe it was legitimate?

She gave her most honest answers, knowing it mattered not. At least Oqci might remember her honesty when he decided if she should enter the Cloud Kingdom.

It came time for Penn to make a closing statement on her behalf. "Today, we have heard from Ms. Zendar that she did not willingly participate in the treason against our government during her escape to Friezzia."

What was this?

"She had no part in making the plans and could have had no reasonable way to stop them. Furthermore, the evidence presented of her communication with the Soldiers of Oqci is of questionable veracity. I therefore urge the members to vote 'not guilty.'"

Dellirea could hardly believe it. Penn at last showed some kind of competence. If she had won him over, then perhaps she had also won over Tressa and Aran. From Quinneas's face, she could see he was not swayed, nor was he pleased with Penn's performance. But the other two were harder to judge. A small part of Dellirea held out hope.

"It is now time for us to vote on the charges of treason against Ms. Zendar," said Quinneas. "I vote 'guilty.'"

That was unsurprising.

"Mr. Potter, how do you vote?"

He hesitated. He and Dellirea made eye contact. She pleaded with her eyes that she was innocent of the concocted charges.

"Guilty."

"Ms. Smith?"

She did not hesitate. "Guilty."

Penn looked at Dellirea with sympathy. She had let herself hope for just several seconds, and now the crushing reality once more set in.

"It is a unanimous verdict of guilty," said Quinneas. "With these votes, we move to the question of Ms. Zendar's punishment. Ms. Zendar, would you or your counsel like to make a final statement before our vote?"

"Yes, I would," she said. "I see no point in begging for mercy. But just know that justice will come to you all, one way or another. And when it does, in your last moments, I hope you will think about me and remember these words."

"Is that all?" asked Quinneas impatiently.

"Yes."

"Very well. Then we shall vote. I vote for the death penalty by hanging. Mr. Potter?"

"I, too, vote for the death penalty by hanging."

Penn placed his hand on Dellirea's, but she quickly pulled away before anyone could notice. For a moment, she could only think of his safety even as her death sentence was being read.

Quinneas must already be displeased with him, but to show open sympathy with Dellirea could lead to a similar fate as hers.

"Ms. Smith?"

"Death penalty by hanging."

"It is passed unanimously," said Quinneas, with a satisfied tone. "The jury has determined that Ms. Zendar will be executed as a result of her crimes against our nation."

Penn looked at Dellirea with a brief look of sympathy, but no more. He realized what she had already realized: that he could do no more for her and he should only preserve himself now.

With Dellirea's death assured, her short life flashed before her eyes. There was so much she wished to do, so much she wished to experience, but would never now get a chance. At least she would soon be reunited with her family in the Cloud Kingdom.

Yet in the back of her mind, she could not suppress the feeling that these were only pleasant stories told to children.

102

SAMUEL

When Samuel received word that the princess was to suffer the same fate as her parents, he thought about the conversation he'd had with her almost a year ago. Samuel, a miserable wretch, had insulted her when she was only trying to help those rendered homeless during the siege. She was so sweet and kind, yet he had truly been a bastard toward her. She was condescending, it was true, but she meant well.

"What shall we do?" said Olive as they sat around the kitchen table discussing the news.

"We have a happy life here," Will said with a resigned expression. "We should simply make the best of our life while we can. Whatever is happening in the capital cannot be stopped."

Samuel thought of those supposed noble friends of his, pelted with rotting fruit and vegetables before being hanged in front of the bloodthirsty mob. He couldn't bear to imagine the same thing happening to poor Dellirea.

"No," Samuel said suddenly. "No."

The other two turned to him with wide eyes.

"We must go to Goldhall – all of us, all of our village – to protest the action. We reached those young men several days ago, did we not? It was true that others replaced them, but what if we went directly to the capital and made our case. We could reach the executioner and anyone else and plead with them to stop!"

The Hunt couple looked hesitant.

"Perhaps," Samuel said, unsure if he completely believed what he was going to say next, "perhaps it was Oqci who brought me here for this very reason. Perhaps it was him who put me through all of these trials, all of this suffering, in order to lead me to this point."

"Yes," Will said, looking deeply at Samuel. "Yes, this could be Oqci's plan for you, for all of us!"

Could it be true? Could it be his destiny?

SAMUEL and the Hunts gathered with the entire village in the former noble's house to plan, just as they had those weeks ago. There he described his idea for the protest. They would all travel to the capital to arrive the day of the execution. Once there, they would march toward the gallows and tell the executioner to cease his actions at once. A chain of resistance would foil the plan to execute Dellirea and, with luck, end Quinneas's reign.

One skeptic in the village asked whether the plan would work. Was this not just more naiveté?

"It might be," Samuel said. "It might be. But we must trust in Oqci."

Olive and Will expressed their strong agreement and soon the whole village settled on the plan.

Samuel knew not how much he believed what he had said, or if he really even believed in Oqci. But he believed in belief, that much he knew.

103

CHARLOTTE

"It is surely a trap," said Sun, when Charlotte told her about Yanis's letter. "I cannot bear to put my faith in a degenerate such as him!"

"I too have my suspicions," Charlotte said. "Yet I believe he is telling the truth. It is a chance we must take. It may be our only hope to stop Quinneas."

"Hmm," Sun grunted.

Just then, one of their comrades burst into the room. "We have just learned that Dellirea has been found guilty and is to be executed!"

Charlotte and Sun both sat in silence, absorbing the news. They had known that such an outcome was probable, yet now their mission became much more urgent.

Sun turned to Charlotte. "We have no choice, it seems, but to trust the Dragon Slayer."

THAT EVENING, under the cover of darkness, a group of four – three other Soldiers of Oqci and Charlotte – set off to find the weapons. In this case, the three were permitted to remove their masks, since otherwise they would be too conspicuous in public. Charlotte was surprised to learn one was a minor noble whom she knew indirectly; the other two she knew not.

They followed Yanis's directions to the east of the city. Their carriage, led by four horses, pulled behind it a large cart which, if the information was correct, would soon be filled with weapons.

They travelled slowly through the quiet country roads, ensuring there was no trap. They came at last to the abandoned farmhouse. Charlotte's heart pounded as they circled the building from a distance. If it were a trap, Yanis would have Charlotte sent to Quinneas, or even worse, Sun would think she had betrayed the group. Either way would not end well for her.

"There seems to be nothing amiss," Charlotte said. "There is no one around."

"Very well," said the nobleman known to her. "Let us two proceed while the others wait here."

With that, the two crept toward the farmhouse, each carrying a lantern and their heads darting in every direction for signs of danger. But none were forthcoming.

Charlotte's companion held the lantern to the door. She fumbled with the key, but to her surprise, it worked. She pushed open the door and held up her lantern to reveal dozens of crates. Charlotte lifted the lid of one. Stacks of rifles filled the crate. Bullets and gunpowder were to be found in another.

"There is grey powder here," said the nobleman from across the room.

"What is that?" Charlotte said, knowing little about weapons.

"It's an explosive," he said. "It contains a charge dozens of times stronger than that of gunpowder."

"Dear Oqci."

"Yes," said her companion. He stepped out of the farmhouse and waved over their carriage.

They began loading as many crates as their cart could hold.

104

YANIS

Devon Black leaned against the railing of the ship as he and Yanis stood upon the deck, breathing in the salty air. "It is our destiny. *Your* destiny," he said. "To show the world what a democratic nation can do. Capturing a dragon! Who better than the Dragon Slayer to lead us?"

Yanis wondered whether he should confess the reality to Devon. That he was leading the mission only because Quinneas was holding Nadeni hostage.

"Is something the matter?" asked Devon when Yanis failed to return his cheer.

"It is just that I feel decidedly ambivalent about returning," Yanis said. "Much personal tragedy has taken place on this island."

"I understand," Devon said, his cheerful mood dented by Yanis's sombreness. "But," he said, "the men feel a sense of confidence. With you as our leader, we shall not fail. Think of what it will mean once we have succeeded. For our nation. For our revolution. For you!"

Yanis did think of it. But he cared not at all for glory, nor for Quinneas's promise to place himself and Nadeni upon the throne of New Selver. He only wished Nadeni and the baby to be safe. If he returned to Estenland, he would ensure their safety and then lead a force to overthrow Quinneas.

But that was for the future.

"I shall not attempt to dissuade the soldiers if my presence makes them feel confident," Yanis said. "But Devon, between you and I, my heroism is all a fraud."

Devon shook his head. "Your modesty is just further evidence of your greatness, Dragon Slayer."

Dear Oqci. Yanis realized that Devon was deluded with these fantasies about him, about the revolution. Devon's eyes were trained upon the islands, which were beginning to peek above the horizon.

$$\sim$$

As they approached, Yanis recalled how he and Calina had joked as they walked through the forest, how she had picked up those mysterious blocks that revealed an ancient civilization, how he had felt hope and excitement for the future. It seemed an eternity ago.

Their transport ships – hauling the war machines, herds of sacred creatures, small cannons, and soldiers – departed from the warships and groaned as they washed ashore. It was all so familiar to Yanis as they stepped onto dry land, but everyone else looked around with wide eyes, pointing this way and that, chattering incredulously.

"Let us press forward," Yanis said, motioning the group ahead. The pathways they had cleared, the fires that had once burned, were all distant memories as the forest had regenerated itself. But there was no time for reminiscing. Yanis was anxious to see how the war machines would handle the island terrain.

They rolled down the ramps onto the beach and struggled across the sand. Once they got further inland and onto solid ground, however, they moved more easily. A party of soldiers went ahead, cutting a path through the forest for the war machines to enter, just as Yanis had done when he landed a year and a half ago.

The familiar buzz of insects filled his ears as they progressed deeper into the island, but they quieted following a distant roar. The booming startled some of the creatures, as well as many of the soldiers, who darted their eyes around and gripped their weapons tightly. The keepers of the creatures calmed their flying horses and griffins. They had been training with them for months and they shared a bond. Yanis counted on that bond. The creatures, and the soldiers, needed to maintain their discipline, even as they faced the greatest risk.

They readied for the dragons. The war machines aimed their

cannons toward the sky. The flying creatures took their marks. As at the Battle of Freless, Yanis commanded atop a flying horse, this time ridden by Devon, while drummers and buglers imparted Yanis's commands from below.

The first of the dragons appeared above them. An adult, and a massive one at that. The key was to distract it until one of the juvenile dragons appeared. A group of the griffins and horses flew into the air to harass it. They could do little more than that. Even the griffins appeared like annoying fleas next to the dragon.

As the dragon flailed around trying to extricate itself from these irritations, the war machines and artillery below readied in case of attack. The dragon roared with anger at the creatures, which brought other dragons to its aid. Noticing the intruders on land, one of them breathed fire upon a war machine.

"Dear Oqci," said Devon as the war machine was blackened from the fire. It was his first view of the dragons' power.

Yet the war machine slowly began to move again, damaged, but not gravely so.

More dragons appeared, including some of the smaller, younger dragons. About a dozen dragons circled overhead, battling the sacred creatures in the air, while soldiers fired from below if they flew too close to ground level. Griffins and horses dropped from the sky, killed in the fighting, but the strategy was working thus far.

"Look!" shouted Devon. The juvenile became separated from its companions.

"Now is the time!" Yanis responded. He gripped Devon tightly with anticipation as they watched.

Two riders on two flying horses each carried one side of a reinforced net. They flew apart and spread the net wide. Closer and closer they flew toward the dragon, perhaps no bigger than a large griffin.

"Get it," Yanis said, clapping his hand on Devon's shoulder. "Get it!"

The juvenile attempted to flee, but it was no use. The two riders converged, wrapping the dragon in the net. Yanis's heart filled with anticipation. They had almost done it! But he cringed at seeing the helpless dragon, contorting itself and writhing around in the net in a desperate attempt to free itself.

But it was no matter. It needed to be done. The dragon cried out in pain as the riders dragged it toward the ground.

"We've almost done it!" said Devon.

Yanis said a silent prayer of thanks in his head to anyone who would listen. They would soon be returning to Estenland with the dragon. And Nadeni would at last be safe.

Just then, a larger dragon, attracted by the anguished cries from the juvenile, flew toward it. The adult roared. The two riders relinquished the net and flew as fast as they could to safety. But it was too late. Fire swept across the sky, incinerating both riders and their horses and sending their charred remains floating to the earth.

"Fuck!" Yanis shouted.

Devon manoeuvred away before the dragon could turn its sights on him and Yanis. Instead, the dragon flew near the ground and hung in the air, breathing a sustained breath of fire upon a war machine. The soldiers below fired upon the dragon, but it would not relent even as its body was showered with bullets. The war machine maintained its structure but ceased its movement. The men had surely been roasted inside from the heat. After the fire stopped and the dragon flew away, one of the soldiers, his face a bright red, limply exited the war machine and collapsed after two steps. None of his other colleagues managed to escape.

"What shall we do, Dragon Slayer?" said Devon.

Thoughts of retreat crossed Yanis's mind. This was a hopeless endeavour. But what about Nadeni? If he returned having failed...

But was it worth sacrificing all of his soldiers' lives for this fruitless quest?

CHARLOTTE

Sun cast her gaze around the crowd of Soldiers, all masked aside from Charlotte. "Soldiers," she said, "tomorrow will be a day of reckoning. Tomorrow, those bloodthirsty revolutionaries will gather to watch Dellirea's execution. But they will be in for a surprise when they find that it will be *they* who die that day!" Sun threw her head back with laughter. Some of the other Soldiers laughed, but more reservedly.

They had gathered in the basement of the Luvir Galleries. It was from there that they would carry out their plan. It was only two blocks from Karazin Square: the perfect location. And not a soul visited the galleries now, ever since the Baron of Luvir closed them out of spite after demands during the revolution to open the galleries to all citizens.

The plan was to haul the grey powder in a wagon into the middle of Karazin Square and detonate it from a distance, killing all of those who gathered. In the chaos, a small team would storm the podium to kill Quinneas and rescue Dellirea. Charlotte had volunteered to be part of that group. She hoped that it would be her who drove a dagger into Quinneas's heart. It would be a more merciful death than he gave her brother and was probably more than he deserved.

But the plan would surely kill hundreds of people. Sun's indifference to the slaughter of innocent people disgusted Charlotte... yet what was the alternative?

~

On the morning of the execution, Charlotte exited the Luvir Galleries, wearing her aletolium necklace under her shirt for luck. She walked through the square one final time and contemplated what was to come. The square was beginning to fill with spectators for the imminent execution. A few clouds dotted the sky; the autumn air was a little cool. A throng of the green-uniformed People's Army soldiers paced around the edge of the stage and the gallows, where Quinneas would soon stand triumphant as Dellirea was hanged.

But there was no jubilant singing and dancing among the crowd. In fact, the mood of the crowd was sombre. In small circles, the people held hands and said quiet prayers to Oqci to save the princess. Sun, and the rest of them, had gravely misjudged the crowd, Charlotte realized.

Returning to the galleries, Charlotte hurried down the wide, eerily empty hallways, past paintings and sculptures from the great masters, past the native artwork from Ozenzal, past the giant wooden heads from western Otela, and down into the basement of the galleries where the grey powder crates were stored. Dozens of Soldiers stalked the basement corridors, carrying weapons and talking about what was to come.

Charlotte found Sun and pulled her aside into a vacant room. Artifacts not displayed in the collections, draped in white cloths, stood all around them like ghosts.

"We must reconsider the plan," Charlotte said. "The crowd is not at all like we thought. They are peaceful. They disagree with the execution as much as we do. Hundreds of innocent people will be killed if we go through with our plan!"

"We must move forward regardless," Sun said flatly. "If the people are faithful followers of Oqci like you say, they will be martyrs and live with Oqci in the clouds. Their deaths will be for a worthy cause: the restoration of the monarchy and the restoration of balance in our society. It is the only way."

"This is wrong," Charlotte said. "You must reconsider."

"If you knew what was done to me and to my family," she said, her voice rising, "you would understand why I can show no mercy, why Quinneas and the rest must be defeated."

Her words were Charlotte's final clue. She was the wife of Richard, Duke of Saundley!

"You're Solorina, aren't you?" she said. "This isn't about

'restoring balance' to society or the other slogans you spew. It's about revenge, isn't it?"

"My daughter… my husband… brutally murdered!" she said, removing her mask. "All caused by these radicals. With their poisonous ideas. Look what they have done!"

"I, too, have seen a family member killed before my eyes. And no one wants to see Quinneas face justice more than me. But please, we must harm no more innocent people."

She shook her head. "There is no choice. Things are set in motion now that cannot be undone."

"I cannot allow you!"

Charlotte spun to leave, to warn the crowd, but Solorina grabbed her right arm before she could. She pulled out a pistol and pointed it at Charlotte, shaking her head. "I knew you were not to be trusted. I knew you would betray the noble class, just like you did time and again throughout your sorry life."

But her grip on Charlotte's arm was tenuous. In one motion Charlotte pulled away her right arm and with her left hand knocked the pistol from Solorina and onto the floor. Solorina reflexively turned to grab it, but Charlotte burst out the door and into the hallway.

"Stop her," Solorina shouted.

"Help!" Charlotte screamed, as the footsteps of her pursuers echoed down the hallway.

106

SAMUEL

"Let us say a prayer to Oqci to give us strength," Samuel said as they bowed their heads. The group of villagers knelt in Karazin Square and prayed, having made the trek from Farnestead that morning. They would need the strength to make their stand once the proceedings began.

Keeping his eyes open during the prayer, he spotted a woman who seemed familiar. Was that not Charlotte of Evesbury? She had shorter hair than before and was not at all dressed like a noblewoman. She wore a shirt and trousers rather than a dress. But the face was unmistakeable. Memories flooded into his mind of her flailing her fists at him after he had shot Quinneas. What was she doing there? She was reputed to have been on the run, but would she be so bold, like him, to appear here?

He told the Hunts and the rest of the group that he was going to step away from their prayer circle for a moment. Samuel followed the woman. She walked with purpose for several blocks before inconspicuously slipping into a side door of the Luvir Galleries.

Had not that place been empty for months? Samuel lingered outside the building to see if she would return, but after several minutes, he decided she would not.

But his curiosity was piqued. Samuel looked around to see if anyone was watching. No one paid him any mind. They were instead fixated on what was soon to happen in Karazin Square. With no one watching, Samuel slipped through the same door Charlotte had entered and found himself at the end of a cavernous hallway.

Just then, a woman's screams came from the floor below. Samuel raced down the stairs to the dim basement of the galleries. Two masked figures hurried down the corridor in front of him, completely overlooking him. The Soldiers of Oqci!

He crept slowly down the hall and peeked in the direction the figures were running.

Another shrieking cry of "help!"

A single pair of footsteps echoed in the hallway behind him, coming in his direction. Samuel slipped into a recess in the wall, out of view. Just as the figure passed, Samuel sprang out, tackling the Soldier. A pistol flew out as they both crashed to the ground. Samuel scrambled on his elbows to reach where it had fallen as the Soldier gripped his legs. Samuel ran his fingers around the dark floor. At last, he grabbed the weapon and spun onto his back just as the Soldier stood. Samuel fired. The figure dropped to the ground. Samuel climbed to his feet and ran in the direction of the screams.

107

DELLIREA

Dellirea imagined how her mother and father must have felt as they were marched before the crowd in the moments before their deaths. She had heard the reports about the vile behaviour of the people. She had prepared herself for the worst. For being taunted and humiliated by the bloodthirsty masses, in the same way her parents had been. She asked Oqci, if he were there, for strength.

"You will soon meet your beloved Oqci," someone called, to laughter, as she was walked across the stage by two guards. She wore the same simple white garb as her parents had on the day of their execution. The white, it was said, represented justice. "Get ready to have your neck snapped, princess!" More laughter. These people had villainous grins with crazed looks in their eyes.

Dellirea closed her eyes and tried to block out their cruel words. But then there were cries of "we love you, princess" and "be strong, princess." She opened her eyes. Most of the crowd clasped their hands together in prayer. Those who shouted vile comments were far outnumbered by well-wishers.

Quinneas, standing next to the podium, traded glances with her and the crowd, alongside his two toadies, Aran and Tressa. An expression of distress appeared on his face. The crowd's reaction was evidently not what he had hoped.

As Dellirea assumed her place on the gallows, Quinneas stepped to the podium to make a speech to the gathered crowd. "Fellow citizens, today we gather to once again defend our revolution from its enemies. Today, Dellirea Zendar, daughter of Aramal, will be put to death for her treasonous activities."

There were some scattered cheers but many in the crowd shouted, "Shame! Shame!" The guards who surrounded the edge of the stage clutched their weapons uneasily.

"Our revolution requires sacrifices," he went on. "Dealing with traitors is never pleasant, but bloodshed nourishes the soil from which our revolutionary society grows."

While she awaited the end of Quinneas's speech, Dellirea thought over her short life. Wasn't it true that she had been naïve? That she passed through the world without a deeper understanding of what it was like for ordinary people? That she deluded herself with the magical stories of Oqci? Perhaps the truth was more complex, as Kephalos believed.

At once, screams of panic came from the far edge of Karazin Square. Figures in dark costumes and masks ran through the crowd as the people scattered. The Soldiers of Oqci? Dellirea stood on her tiptoes to watch. Some of the guards rushed down from the platform and out into the crowd. What was happening?

YANIS

Nadeni's face flashed in Yanis's mind. And the image of their unborn child. But to continue was futile. Quinneas would blame him for the failure to complete the mission, but he had no choice but to call for a retreat as the forests around them burned. He would face Quinneas and take the consequences, but he could not in good conscience continue to sacrifice his soldiers.

"The situation is too grave," Yanis said to Devon. "Let us return to ground level." As they descended, he gave the signal to the buglers who played out the call for the retreat.

"It is the right decision," said Devon. "Quinneas will understand that we gave our all."

Oh Devon! He had no idea what Quinneas had done. What he might yet do.

The war machines began to move steadily back to the beach and the sacred creatures returned to the ground. They began their procession to the ships as the dragons continued circling overhead.

A long line of machines, creatures, and men snaked toward the beach as scattered fire covered their retreat. Yanis stood at the back of the line, praying for it to hurry.

A dragon flew toward the end of the line, landing dozens of paces away without unleashing fire upon on them. Yanis raised his pistol and the others on the line raised their muskets.

But... there was someone sitting atop the dragon. A rider? Were his eyes deceiving him? The figure jumped down while the dragon remained still, its eyes fixed on Yanis.

"Hold your fire," the woman's voice shouted as she walked toward them with arms outstretched.

"Calina?" Yanis said in disbelief.

It was her, although she looked very different.

CHARLOTTE

Two of the Soldiers backed Charlotte into a corner of the dusty corridor. "Help!" she shouted again.

A gun shot down the hall drew the Soldiers' attention. The figures looked uneasily behind them and back to her.

"I shall take a look," said the one to the other.

Before he could take two steps, there was a loud bang. The figure fell to the ground. When the other turned his head, another bang. He collapsed as well. The two figures lay flailing on the ground as blood poured from their chests.

Charlotte's gaze turned to the man holding the pistol. She could not forget the face, even with a beard and in the dim light.

"Samuel Nox?" she said. Surely she was dreaming.

"You have a good memory, Lady Evesbury," he said. "As do I." He reached down to grab the fallen men's pistols, taking one for himself and handing the other to Charlotte. It was covered in blood. "Let us hurry!"

They raced through the hallways and leaped over the bodies of other dead Soldiers. More, however, ran toward them.

"We need to rescue Dellirea. We need to warn the people," Charlotte shouted as they ran. "The Soldiers have stored crates of grey powder down here in the basement and are planning to detonate them in the square."

Soldiers ran toward them from down the corridor.

"You get back to the square," said Nox. "I shall cover you."

She nodded to him and bounded toward the exit.

SAMUEL

Samuel fired down the hallway at the charging Soldiers. One of the shots hit. He dove behind the corner and ran further down the hall.

But he needed to stop them from bringing out the grey powder.

He dashed through the basement, knowing not where he was going. As he lingered, he saw one of the figures rushing through the hall. He peered from behind the corner to see him enter a room and return carrying one of the crates. Samuel leaped out and fired, above the crate and into the figure's head. The Soldier collapsed and the crate clattered to the ground.

The sound alerted more Soldiers who raced down the hall toward him. Samuel ducked inside a room where two dozen of the crates sat, piled high against the wall. Several Soldiers entered with pistols raised. Samuel backed against the crates, extending his gun to hold them off.

He was cornered.

A group of five masked figures surrounded him. A woman, unmasked, stood in the middle of the group. "Don't shoot him," she urged.

Samuel recognized her. It was Solorina. And it was the same voice he had heard the day the auctioneer was killed at the market.

She glared at him. "If you leave now, we shall let you live."

Samuel looked behind him at the pile of crates, filled with grey powder. "Get back," he shouted. He waved his pistol back and forth across the crowd of Soldiers. "Get back!"

"Leave now," she said as she stepped forward. "We don't wish to hurt you."

The figures beside her continued to wait, with their pistols raised, but Samuel could not hold them off forever. They would soon rush toward him. And he could not let them carry out their plans.

An itch began to make itself known upon his back. He felt the urge to scratch. But then he stopped and smiled to himself. He knew now that there would never be a need to scratch again.

He had done all he could. Charlotte would have made it to safety. He prayed she would be able to save Dellirea. The future of the nation would be safe in their hands.

If Oqci were real, Samuel asked his forgiveness for his past wrongdoings and to take mercy upon him. If he were not, Samuel could only hope that those he left behind would remember him as having, at least this time, done something of value.

Samuel turned his pistol away from the crowd of Soldiers and toward the crates.

"Stop!" Solorina shouted as she lunged toward him.

Samuel fired. A blaze of red shot out, engulfing them all.

111

CHARLOTTE

The sun made Charlotte squint as she rushed through the exit. The sound of gunfire from inside the Luvir Galleries caused members of the crowd to stream in all directions in panic.

Charlotte ran toward Karazin Square, ignoring the chaotic screams all around her.

Two Soldiers of Oqci chased after her outside the galleries. She blocked out the fear as her feet pounded on the stones. There were grunts followed by a crashing sound behind her. She turned back. Some members of the crowd had tackled the Soldiers.

But there was no time to thank them. She could hear Quinneas's voice in the distance giving his speech.

Closer and closer she ran toward the square. The sight of the black-clad Soldiers caused people to scream in terror. Realization of what was happening spread throughout the crowd. Quinneas stood on the stage, darting his head in every direction at the chaos at ground level. His great day was ruined.

Two People's Army guards stood high atop the stage, keeping watch over the princess, as the rest of the guards fought back the crowd from storming the stage. Some rode winged horses, others led griffins.

Charlotte needed to reach the stage, but how? Hundreds of people battling with guards and their sacred creatures stood in the way.

Just then came a massive boom. Charlotte felt it more than she heard it. The entire earth shook. A rush of wind knocked her to the ground.

Ringing filled her ears as she climbed uneasily to her feet. Turning back, she saw a giant cloud of smoke pouring from where the Luvir Galleries used to stand. It was two stories of rubble now. The explosives! Was this Nox's work?

All around her, people lay on the ground, still in shock from the blast. Others clutched their hands over their ears from the pain. The sun was quickly blotted out from the white smoke, and a cloud of ash fell like snow.

People hurried past, their clothes and faces entirely caked in ash. Charlotte ran her hand through her hair, which too was coated in ash.

As the crowd ran this way and that, she spotted a winged horse trotting around wildly. It must have dislodged its rider in fright from the blast. Memories of Silver Justice, the horse she rode when she was younger, rushed into her mind. She jogged toward the horse and looked into its gentle eyes. It ceased its frantic movements and returned her gaze, becoming perfectly still. It understood her desire.

She climbed atop its back and petted its mane. It trotted, then galloped, and then lifted off into the air. The smoke was so thick she could barely make out the flaming rubble of the galleries below. Nox and the Soldiers of Oqci inside were surely all dead.

Charlotte coughed as she flew ever deeper into the smoke. She could barely see several metres in front of her. She counted on her knowledge of the square, of the palace. How many times had she walked it? How many times had she ascended that stage outside the palace gates?

Anguished cries and scattered gunshots sounded from below. At last, a spire from the palace peeked through the smoke. She was getting closer. She guided her horse around and they began their descent. She pulled on the reins to steady it just as they exited the smoke, the rear of the stage now in view.

Two guards, still shaken from the blast, did not see them approach.

Gaining speed as they descended, the horse landed with full force upon them, disabling them. Quinneas appeared as a ghost. His green overcoat and piercing black hair were covered in ash.

He stumbled toward Charlotte with a look of shock etched onto his face.

"Help!" he cried out, though there was no one to hear his call. The stage was engulfed in the cloud of ash.

When he realized who sat atop the horse, his eyes widened. He turned to run. Charlotte's horse charged, gaining momentum in the short distance. Quinneas's long strides were no match for them. Her horse rose up on its hind legs and brought its front legs with full force upon Quinneas, trampling him.

Charlotte slowed the horse down and turned back. She dismounted. Quinneas was on all fours, his face bloodied. He tried to crawl across the stage, away from her. No guards could rush to his aid. Charlotte took out the pistol that Nox had given her.

"Charlotte?" he said, rolling onto his back to face her, his eyes full of fear. "Please! Have mercy upon me!"

"I'm going to give you a quicker death than you gave to Brondin."

"Please, Charlotte. Please, don't do this!" he pleaded as he crawled backward with his elbows.

His words momentarily caused a pang of sympathy within her. The snowy ash fell upon them as Charlotte looked down at Quinneas and thought of the man she once loved. The man she stood beside as they – together – led their country through the revolution.

But there was no time for reminiscing. She knelt down. "I'm sorry, Quinneas," she said, forcing back tears. "It is time for you to face justice."

His expression was resigned. He was too weak to escape. Charlotte pointed the pistol at his heart and pulled the trigger.

112

YANIS

"Yanis?" said Calina as she walked toward him. The other soldiers stood stupefied as the dragon eyed them with suspicion. Calina was dressed in animal pelts and what seemed to be turquoise metal on her arms, legs, torso, and face.

"I... I thought you were dead," Yanis said.

"I thought you were dead too."

They looked at each other. As she came closer, Yanis saw that the metal was not just adorning her skin but somehow attached to it.

There was so much to say, but neither of them could figure out how they could possibly begin. They both just stared at each other in shock.

"You are in charge here?" she said at last. She looked at the long convoy of war machines and creatures that twisted through the flaming jungle.

"I am," Yanis said, ashamed that he was the one responsible for this carnage.

"Tell your forces to leave this place. I know not what your purpose is here, but you will all be killed if you persist."

Yanis motioned to Devon to continue the retreat. The war machines and sacred creatures resumed their slow march back to shore, leaving Yanis and Calina alone.

"How?" he said simply. "How?"

"That day, I was sure I was dead," she explained. "I woke to find myself buried beneath the stone blocks. An intense, throbbing pain pierced my whole body. I remember once, when I was little, I touched my fingers for just a moment on a hot stove, before recoiling from the pain. I never forgot that sensation. The feeling was like that, but over my entire body, without any hope for relief. The pain and I became one. The aletolium from the stones had somehow fused into me from the heat of the dragon fire."

She extended her arms for Yanis to see. Long sheets of the turquoise metal coated her arms. Half of her face, too, was covered in the aletolium.

"I managed to clear away the rubble, stone by stone, freeing myself," she continued. "I explored the island. Dead bodies lay scattered and small fires continued to burn in the forest. I searched for you, or any other survivors. Yet I could find no one else alive. And I worried the dragons would soon find me."

Yanis stared at her face as she told this story and all the terrible memories of that day returned, although he now saw them in a new light.

"I walked around the island, starving. I ate some fruit to nourish me. At last, one of the dragons returned to find me. I was sure it was the end for me. It flew toward me, but with a wave of my hand, it stopped. I motioned for it to land. It obeyed me. Other dragons came near. I could control them too. It was, I realized, the aletolium inside me. They understood whatever I commanded."

The pieces began fitting together in Yanis's mind. The priests and nobles used the metal in their jewelry and it was said that they had a deeper relationship with the sacred creatures, although no one had ever made the true connection. But Calina – she had such a concentration of the metal in her body that she could even control dragons with a wave of her hand.

"The second time Estenland's forces attacked, I was still learning to control the dragons. One of the dragons was killed in the fighting, but the Estenlanders eventually retreated."

"I know," Yanis said regretfully. "I was there."

Calina stared at him for a second, seemingly still trying to believe that he was alive.

"Why did you not return to Estenland?" Yanis asked.

"What was there to come back to?" she said, looking him in the eyes. "The person I loved was surely dead. And I feared what might happen if I returned. How a desire to control the dragons would overtake the population and produce great strife."

Yanis thought back to everything that had happened as a result of the discovery of the dragons. All the upheaval. He conceded that she was right to be fearful.

"And you," she said, "what are you doing here? How did you come to lead this force?"

Yanis shook his head at the magnitude of everything there was to tell. "There was a revolution," he said. "The king was overthrown and killed. And I played a major part in it. I command this army now."

She looked beyond him at the war machines trudging slowly to shore and the brushfires burning around them. "Some revolution."

"It started with glorious ambitions," he said, "but it all fell apart. A madman took control. I should have seen it. I should have stopped it. But I shall return to Estenland and right the situation."

Calina looked at him with that expression that he had once loved, that slight smile on her lips. "Will you come back here once you've done that?"

Yanis knew not what to say. Thoughts of Nadeni, and their child, flashed through his mind. "I'm sure that we shall see each other again someday," he said as tears filled his eyes. "I promise."

They embraced for some time, neither of them wanting to let go. But Yanis knew that they must.

113

DELLIREA

Dellirea wondered if it was not Oqci himself descending on a winged horse through the clouds of smoke to free her from her captors.

But when she saw the rider, it was perhaps even more spectacular than if it had been Oqci.

Was she dreaming? Was this not Charlotte coming to rescue her? No, this must be a dream!

The cries of agony from the two guards, their limbs bent in unusual ways as they writhed on the ground, returned her to reality. The screams of Quinneas and the crack of a gunshot even more so.

Charlotte, her hands and shirt bloodied, rushed to Dellirea, leading her winged horse. "Hurry, princess," she said, as she stepped onto the horse and extended her arm to Dellirea. "Get on."

Dellirea said nothing as she climbed onto the horse. She could only stare at Charlotte in awe.

The winged horse dashed forward and lifted off into the air. The remaining guards were overpowered by the crowd before they could stop them.

Dellirea gripped Charlotte's waist and pulled herself close, feeling the heat of her body and the pounding of her heart.

Karazin Square, which moments before had been packed with people gathered to witness Dellirea's death, was now a scene of chaos. Beyond the square, fires raged all around where the Luvir Galleries once stood. For just a moment, Dellirea thought of all the priceless art that must have been destroyed in the blaze. But then her mind turned to all the people who must also have been killed.

The wind rushed around them, blowing Dellirea's hair

wildly. They drifted up through clouds of smoke, but Dellirea knew not where they were going.

"Charlotte, thank you for saving me."

"You're welcome, princess."

She laid her head gently on Charlotte's back and clutched her even more tightly. "Please, call me Delli."

∾

THEY FLEW for some time over the city before landing in the leafy rear gardens of an estate.

"Where are we?"

"This is my old home," said Charlotte, climbing off her horse. "No one lives here anymore. We shall be safe for now."

Charlotte tied up her horse in one of the empty stables that must have once held their sacred creatures. But then she stopped and just stared out into the gardens, now becoming overgrown with weeds. Charlotte ambled slowly down one of the footpaths, as if in a trance, putting her hand out to let it gently pass through the leaves.

"We cannot stay here forever," Dellirea said, as she walked after her. "Quinneas is dead, but his supporters will persist in searching for us. What shall we do?"

Charlotte turned back quickly, awakened from her daze. "I know not," she said curtly. "I need to think. Let us go inside." Charlotte walked briskly past her and into the manor as Dellirea struggled to keep up. Charlotte climbed the stairs and turned into a bedroom before stopping at the doorway, again, just staring, leaning on the doorframe.

"Are you all right?"

Charlotte said nothing as she walked to the bed and collapsed, face down. She put her face on the pillow for several seconds. Dellirea knew not what to do. Charlotte then turned to Dellirea, her face wet from tears. "I only wish this revolution to cease."

Charlotte looked almost like a child then. Dellirea sat on the bed beside her and placed her hand on her back. "All will be well," Dellirea said softly. "I had an idea. Let us travel to Selver. It is my family's ancestral home and I believe we shall be safe there."

Charlotte sat up. "We shall name you queen," she said, wiping away the last of her tears, "if you will accept it. And if you pledge to rule with the support of the Great Chamber."

"I shall."

"In this way," Charlotte said, "we can at last bring the revolution to a close."

~

CHARLOTTE APPEARED in a better mood after having rested for several hours. In the early evening, they climbed onto Charlotte's horse and galloped into the air once more. The trip to Selver, Dellirea hoped, would not take long. Selver was not far from Charlotte's estate, probably only three hours north by a carriage ride.

Dellirea suggested going to her family's palace in Selver, yet Charlotte told her that the revolutionaries had desecrated it. No one lived there now. But Dellirea was sure they would still find supporters in the town.

As they flew, memories flooded into Dellirea's mind of her fateful voyage to Friezzia. She thought of Rodnel, and how he had given his life for her. She hoped, for his sake, that the Cloud Kingdom was real.

"Charlotte," she said as they flew, the cool night air whipping past, "do you believe in the stories of Oqci?"

She thought for some time. "I'm afraid I don't, Delli. I can only believe in humanity, although even that is difficult sometimes. Do you?"

"I don't think I do either. Not anymore."

It was the first time she had admitted to anyone, even herself, that she didn't believe. But it was freeing to finally say it aloud.

Dellirea had visited Selver only a few times, always for a funeral, when someone would be buried in the family plots. When she was only a baby, when her grandfather, Andamar the

Great, died. When she was five, when her brother died, and several other times since then, for the funerals of distant cousins whom she had never met.

Charlotte had never been to Selver, so Dellirea guided her in the moonlight. After an hour in flight, the distinctive pointed roofs and brightly coloured houses of the town appeared. The city sat upon a rolling slope on the north coast of Estenland. She directed Charlotte toward the town square, which overlooked the Sea of Dreams. At one end of the square was the temple, once one of the most beautiful in all Estenland, now denuded of its statues and its stained-glass windows. Dellirea shuddered to think of how their palace would have been debased in the revolution.

There were few people in the square at that hour, just the last of the vendors who were packing their wares for the day and others out for an evening stroll. For them, the arrival of a winged horse excited considerable notice. Shouts of "it's the princess!" brought a small but enthusiastic crowd all around them as they landed.

Dellirea stepped off the horse. "Greetings, friends," she said to the group of about two dozen who had circled around.

"We knew you would return, princess!" people called out. "We always had faith!"

"Thank you for your support," Dellirea said, with Charlotte standing beside her. "I would wish to speak with you all, but we need to act quickly."

She explained that they needed to speak with any remaining family members of hers and any of the town leaders. They must issue a proclamation: that the constitution previously agreed before her parents' execution was still in effect – and that she was now the legitimate queen of Estenland.

114

YANIS

As they landed in New Selver following the retreat, Yanis was rushed to the outpost's command room. It was urgent, the People's Army aide explained as they walked.

In the command room, Yanis was informed of telegraph messages that reported that Quinneas was dead, that the princess had been rescued moments before her execution, and that a huge explosion had killed most of the Soldiers of Oqci. What did it all mean? Yanis stood around a conference table alongside Devon and some of his other closest officers as they heard the news.

"Dear Oqci," said Devon. He held his head in his hands. "Quinneas! What a terrible loss for our nation!" He turned to Yanis. "We must return to Estenland at once. The revolution is in grave danger. With Quinneas gone, the People's Army is needed more than ever."

Yanis nodded but said nothing. He did not wish to let on his joy at the news of Quinneas's death. And he needed time to think. What now?

Devon's words took a moment to register in Yanis's mind. But then he began to understand the possibilities in what he said. The People's Army could take charge. Yanis could take charge.

More and more telegrams arrived. One brought news that it had been Charlotte who killed Quinneas and rescued Dellirea. Another, from Tressa and Aran, the only remaining members of the Emergency Committee, demanded Yanis's return to help capture them.

All the chaotic news seemed to overshadow what many had just seen: that Calina was alive and able to control the dragons.

"How shall I respond to the Emergency Committee, Dragon Slayer?" asked Devon. "Shall I tell them they have our support?"

Tressa and Aran were no rulers, Yanis knew. They were as bad as Quinneas, if not worse. He needed to think.

"I…" Yanis began, but he knew not how to continue.

"It should be you to lead," said Devon. "It should be you as our king."

Yanis concealed his smile. Perhaps this was what his life was building toward. With the People's Army at his back, there would be nothing stopping him.

Just then another aide rushed in. "High Commander Haller, there is an urgent telegram, for your eyes alone."

"From whom?" Yanis said.

"From Charlotte of Evesbury."

Others in the room gasped. Yanis hurried to read it.

Yanis,

I hope this message finds you soon. Thanks to your help, I have killed Quinneas and rescued Princess Dellirea. I am now in the town of Selver with the princess. We have issued a proclamation that Dellirea is the legitimate ruler as constitutional monarch. I believe that is the only hope for a return to stability.

We have received word that Nadeni is still being held. We shall help her upon our return to Goldhall.

Yet Tressa and Aran still rule and our safety is not assured. I ask you to send a message to the People's Army that you support Dellirea's claim to the throne and that you call on all of your soldiers to do so as well.

Please hurry back.

Yours,
   Charlotte

Yanis was at once heartened, stunned, and disappointed by this news. Nadeni was alive! And his directions to the weapons cache must have helped Charlotte. But it appeared Charlotte and Dellirea already had plans to take power.

As Yanis folded the message, he wondered if it were already too late for him.

"What did it say?" asked Devon. "What did that traitor to our revolution want?"

Yanis sat down in his chair in thought. The eyes of Devon and five other officers were hot upon him.

What to do? Support Tressa and Aran? Support Dellirea and Charlotte? Try to claim power for himself? Thoughts of Nadeni, of Jackson, of Calina, circled through his mind. Yet he was all alone, without their guidance. What to do?

Yanis rose to address his officers, knowing in the back of his mind that they could mutiny against him right then and there, if they found his words unsatisfactory.

"Charlotte confirmed what we already knew: that she killed Quinneas," Yanis said slowly. "What is more, she rescued Dellirea, and Dellirea has proclaimed herself queen."

Devon shook his head. His face grew furious. "How dare she? Proclaim herself queen? She has no right! We must return immediately. We must bring Charlotte and Dellirea to justice. Tressa and Aran have shown themselves unable to preserve our revolution. Dragon Slayer, will *you* lead us? Will *you* proclaim yourself king?"

Yanis thought back to yesterday on the island. In some ways, it was where everything began. In others, it was where everything ended.

But seeing Calina alive again reminded him of who he once was. What he believed. And what he must do.

"I shall not," Yanis said. "I shall not name myself king."

"But… but we must punish those traitors," said Devon.

"Devon, if Charlotte is a traitor, then I am a traitor, too."

A shocked expression came across Devon's face. "No. Do not say such a thing, Dragon Slayer!"

The other officers looked at each other. Some withdrew their pistols from their holsters, unsure if they would need to use them. Devon, for now, did not grab hold of his gun.

"I ask for your trust, all of you," Yanis said.

The others appeared confused. They looked to Devon for guidance. He narrowed his eyes and gripped the pistol in his holster. "What do you mean you are a traitor, too?"

Yanis took a deep breath, knowing it could be one of his last. "Please, before you act, you must listen to me. Quinneas kidnapped Nadeni. He threatened her life if I did not complete this mission. He threatened her life, and the life of our unborn child. He was a monster! He needed to be stopped. Charlotte is no traitor!"

The officers muttered words of disbelief to each other. Devon was frozen in shock.

"I was the one who supplied Charlotte the weapons to stop Quinneas," Yanis said. "Devon, when I had you move that supply of arms to a farmhouse outside the city for safekeeping, I did so for Charlotte to find, with the hopes that she could somehow use it to stop Quinneas."

Some of the other officers gasped at this. Devon could only stare at Yanis. He looked to be on the verge of tears. Everything Devon had believed, everything he had worked toward, was falling down all around him.

"Look at what horrors the revolution has brought us," Yanis continued. "We risked our lives and lost many of our fellow countrymen on Quinneas's futile mission to the Dragon Isles! Was he not just like the king? Was it not right to overthrow him?"

The officers looked back and forth at one another, continuing to grip their guns with hesitation.

"I am no great leader," Yanis continued. "But have we not been through enough? We must end this madness now. With Dellirea as queen, I believe our country can return to stability. Dellirea has my support. And I plead for all of you to support her as well."

The others were silent for several moments. Finally, Devon stepped forward to speak, his eyes still watery. He placed his hand upon his heart. "If you support her, then I shall support her as well."

One by one, the others returned their guns to their holsters and pledged their allegiance.

"Let us prepare our return to Estenland," Yanis said. "Send a message in reply that Charlotte has our support. Issue a directive to the People's Army that their loyalty is to Dellirea, not to the Emergency Committee."

"We shall see that it is done, Dragon Slayer," Devon said.

ANTICIPATION AND NERVOUSNESS swirled inside Yanis as he made the familiar trip by rail to the south of Otela. He looked at his timepiece. Could this cursed train not move faster?

Back in Estenland, with the People's Army behind him, together they would help Dellirea stabilize the country after the bitterness of the revolution.

And what of Nadeni? Yanis prayed she would be safe for several days more. He longed to see her again. And soon to see their child.

Yanis closed his eyes as the train chugged along. There was nothing to do but wait.

His thoughts circled back to Calina. It was painful to say goodbye so soon after meeting again. After each of them had only just learned the other was alive! He knew that he would see her again someday... although he knew not when. Mismatched thoughts of her, Nadeni, and the dragons danced through his mind as he drifted to sleep.

115

CHARLOTTE

"Hurrah!" Charlotte shouted, upon reading the telegram.

"What is it?" asked Dellirea.

They sat alone in an office in the town hall, which had acted as their temporary headquarters since their arrival in Selver.

"The Dragon Slayer has agreed to support us," she said.

The response over the previous days to their proclamation had been promising. Safe in Dellirea's family's ancestral city, they could build a base of support from which to govern. With Yanis's declaration that the People's Army would support Dellirea, and already a faction in the Great Chamber saying they recognized her leadership as queen of the constitutional monarchy, an end was in sight.

Yet Tressa and Aran continued to find supporters. They still ruled through the Emergency Committee and claimed to be the legitimate government. But their reign would come to an end once Yanis returned to Goldhall. Charlotte and Dellirea learned he was unsuccessful in his mission to capture a dragon, but they knew no more than that. Now it was time to focus on the task before them.

"Delli," Charlotte said, "we must begin to make our return to Goldhall. Yanis will soon arrive, and we must be there when he does."

"Might we stay here one or two days longer?" said Dellirea. "We have only just arrived in Selver."

The answer vexed Charlotte. She worried Dellirea was growing too content staying there amongst her supporters. A distant cousin of hers had been housing them, but they could not remain there forever.

"There is no time to wait, Dellirea," Charlotte said. "The situation demands strong leadership."

Dellirea had a hurt expression on her face and lowered her head. Charlotte regretted her tone. It had been too strong, as if she had been talking to a child.

After some time, Dellirea said, not gazing up from the floor, "I love you, Charlotte."

"You love me?" Charlotte said, stunned. "What do you mean you love me?"

"Ever since I first saw you, I knew that I loved you."

"I know not what to say, Delli. I… you are only a teenager! And… in any case I prefer men."

"I know," she said, almost whispering, still focused on the floor. "I know. It is impossible. Yet still I wished to tell you."

Charlotte had always taken Dellirea to be a strict follower of Oqci. And Oqci's teachings never talked of anything but relationships between men and women. Yet already Charlotte had learned of Dellirea's disbelief in Oqci. And now this revelation. Charlotte looked at her there, sitting glumly, and she saw her in a new light.

Charlotte walked close to her and put her hand on her forearm. Dellirea looked up at her. "You will find someone better than me, Delli. Believe me."

Dellirea smiled wearily before saying, in a serious tone, "Let us prepare our return to Goldhall."

Dellirea insisted that before they went, they visit her family's ancestral palace. The townspeople had said that the revolutionaries had ruined much of it, but Dellirea wished to see for herself.

The stories were true. Debris and shattered glass lay upon the grounds outside the palace. Trees were toppled over and the gardens overgrown. Some parts of the palace were blackened from fire while all the doors had been kicked down.

Some brave townspeople, Charlotte and Dellirea were told,

had done their best to defend it, yet it was futile. Walking inside, everything of value had been stripped away. Dirt and dust and rubble covered the floors such that one struggled to walk. Dellirea said nothing and betrayed no emotion as she toured the hallways.

They went outside to the family cemetery. Centuries of the Zendar ancestors were buried there, even the terrible King Sera. Charlotte walked several paces behind Dellirea as she looked at each of the names and ran her fingers over the gravestones, many of which were smashed or cracked. Dellirea stopped longest at her brother's grave. Her mother and father were not buried there, as she knew, but in an unmarked grave in the woods outside Goldhall.

The downfall of the monarchy had at last come to Estenland, as Charlotte had long hoped. And this was the wreckage it had produced. She still hoped for a time when they would no longer need a monarch, so she saw no conflict in supporting Dellirea's claim to the throne for now. Dellirea would soon be queen, Charlotte believed, yet nothing could ever be the same as it once was.

116

YANIS

At last, the ferry reached the port of Goldhall. From the deck, Yanis could see a procession of the People's Army there to greet him, as were Charlotte and Dellirea. And Nadeni.

She was safe. Praise Oqci, she was safe!

Yet horrible ideas flashed through Yanis's mind. Would she be upset with him for leaving her behind? Would she blame him?

Yanis leaned against the railing nervously. He could not make out her expression from there. He waved to her, tentatively, as he waited for the ferry to dock. He felt a sense of relief as she waved back.

Yanis raced off the ship and through the crowd toward her. When he reached her, he threw his arms around her for some time, neither of them saying anything. As they broke away, Yanis looked down and smiled at her belly.

"I'm so sorry, Nadeni," he said. "I should have listened to you. I shouldn't have left you behind."

"Not to worry," she said as she hugged him again. She pulled away to look him in the eyes and smiled. "All is forgiven, Dragon Slayer."

"I was unsure I would ever see you again," he said. "Not for the first time."

"We must not make this a habit," she said, "although it seems it has become one."

"Yes, but we are together now, and I promise we shall not separate again."

Yanis greeted the others who awaited his arrival. Charlotte told him that when she and Dellirea had arrived back in Goldhall, they had freed the prisoners, including Nadeni, Charlotte's previous husband, Willien, and Koralo. But not, Yanis learned,

Dellirea's aunt and uncle, who remained imprisoned after the betrayal of her parents.

With the People's Army's support, the followers of Tressa and Aran were growing fewer each day. Yanis's return would mark the end of their reign, he knew.

"Charlotte," he said, "I can never truly redeem myself for betraying you. I shall forever regret it." He turned to Dellirea, "And to you, Your Majesty, I too have wronged you, by handing you to Quinneas to face certain death. To both of you, I pledge to use what influence I have to support the new government."

Charlotte spoke first. "It is true that I shall find it difficult to ever forgive you, Yanis. But we must put the past behind us as we work together to build a more just society. We can yet fulfill the highest ideals of the revolution."

Yanis nodded and shook her hand. It was the best outcome he could have hoped for.

"Mr. Haller, I knew you had no choice in the matter," added Dellirea. "As Lady Evesbury said, together we can build something new. As queen, I shall not repeat the mistakes of my predecessors."

Yanis climbed atop a small pile of crates to address the People's Army soldiers, with Devon at his side. "Let us march toward the palace!"

He stepped down and told Devon to arrange for a carriage to take Nadeni.

Nadeni waved him away. "It is unnecessary. I am far from helpless. I shall walk with you."

Yanis began to interject that the walk would be too strenuous, but he stopped himself. He smiled and nodded at Nadeni, always a fighter, ever since he met her.

They encountered no resistance on their march and entered the palace unopposed. Any supporters of Tressa and Aran must have fled. Charlotte called for the Great Chamber – previously rendered irrelevant by the Emergency Committee – to re-form. They would then discuss the future of the government.

～

IN THE EARLY EVENING, after ensuring the safety of Charlotte and Dellirea, Yanis and Nadeni walked alone along Hope Stream, where they had become engaged. They had barely had time to speak when he first arrived and there was so much to say.

Nadeni told him of her time in the prison. How Quinneas locked her away in a small, dim cell. How she began to lose hope.

"The People's Army soldiers treated me poorly," she explained. "Quinneas must have told them I was sending confidential information about the People's Army to the Soldiers of Oqci."

"I'm sorry you had to endure that," Yanis said. "All because of my foolishness."

"But there was one soldier who treated me kindly," she continued. "He ensured that I always received enough food and that my health was looked after. He told me that he could not believe I would do that which Quinneas had accused me of. I must have recruited him to join the People's Army, although I did not remember him." She paused. "Which was surprising since he was a curious man. He wore metal braces upon his legs and walked with great difficulty."

Metal braces on his legs? Could it be?

"Do you remember the man's name?" Yanis asked.

"His first name was Ronar I believe."

Yanis chuckled.

"You know him?"

"I do."

Old Ronar! With the People's Army growing to such a size, Yanis had no idea he had even joined. Yet he would see to it that Ronar was rewarded for helping Nadeni.

As they continued walking, he had much to tell Nadeni of his own adventures. He told her of the travel to the island. And the fight with the dragons. He paused when he came to telling her of Calina. He knew not exactly what to say.

"There have already been rumours of someone who survived the first expedition," Yanis said. "Someone who lived on the island and controlled the dragons."

"Yes," she said, "I have heard. Did you know that woman?"

Yanis nodded. "She was a scientist on the first mission." He stopped and looked down at the stream. "I knew her. Yes, I knew her."

Nadeni placed her hand upon his shoulder. She understood without him having to say more. She understood that Calina was the one whom he thought he had lost. The one who had made him so protective of Nadeni. Too protective.

One day he would tell her the whole story. But not now.

As they resumed their walk, Yanis gazed at the gently flowing water. One of the good things the revolutionary government did was to prevent the factories from discarding their waste in the stream. It was beginning to return to the cleaner state that Yanis remembered from his youth.

Suddenly, the head of a sea goat rose up. Then another. And another. The thoughtful stares of the mysterious sea goats fixed on them. What did it mean? Were these the same sea goats from the prison moat, recalling the time they helped him save Nadeni?

"It's a sign!" said Nadeni playfully. But a sign of what? Yanis wasn't sure.

The sea goats dipped their heads back into the water, and they continued their walk.

"Yanis," Nadeni said seriously, "I fear that we have been responsible for perpetrating, directly and indirectly, some great injustices."

Yanis stopped and looked deeply into her eyes. There was to be no consoling her, or himself, for she spoke the truth. He simply caressed her arm.

"And yet," she continued, "I hope that we also managed to do some good. And we might yet do more. I hope that our child will understand all that when they are older. I hope they will be proud of who we are, and what we have done, despite our flaws."

"They will be."

∾

As Yanis lay in bed that night, his thoughts turned to the sea goats. Then to Calina. How the aletolium had become one with her body, allowing her to control the dragons. On the second expedition, when the dragons attacked them, debris from the ruins shot everywhere from the dragons' fire, and Yanis was bloodied from its spray.

Could it be that some portion of the shards of aletolium entered his body too? Even though it was only a small amount, it would explain why the sea goats helped him that day at the prison, and why some of the sacred creatures seemed to listen to his commands.

As the theory ran through his head, it seemed satisfying. He was not divinely blessed after all, but – not for the first time – the simple recipient of good fortune.

DELLIREA

With Yanis, the famous Dragon Slayer, returned and the People's Army supporting Dellirea, the opposition withered away. Tressa Smith and Aran Potter fled the capital, but they would soon be brought to justice.

A majority in the Great Chamber voted to end the powers of the Emergency Committee and passed a measure to hold a referendum on the future of the country. The choices were to have Dellirea leading the country as queen with the support of the democratically elected Great Chamber, or to have no monarch at all.

Charlotte told her that she thought the people would support the first option. Dellirea hoped she was right. She was ready for the great responsibility. The entirety of her short life prepared her for it.

Oh Charlotte! Dellirea did not regret telling Charlotte that she loved her. Perhaps Charlotte thought she was silly for saying it, but it felt good to tell her. Maybe she was right that Dellirea would find someone else better than her. But, for now, she could not imagine the possibility.

A PUBLIC RALLY in support of Dellirea's side in the referendum took place in Karazin Square. Yanis and Charlotte both joined her on the stage. Dellirea contemplated how many memories, mostly bad, had been formed in that square.

"Fellow citizens," Charlotte said to the people, "there can be no going back to our old system of government. Cruel, abusive monarchs can no longer be allowed to rule. But we must also protect ourselves against those cynical politicians who would play upon our worst instincts to gain power for themselves."

The crowd, made up of rich and poor, cheered her words.

"As you know," Charlotte continued. "I have long opposed monarchy, but I believe we need someone who represents the best of us to act as the symbol of our nation. This person will inspire our elected leaders as they guide the nation. This is why I ask for your support today to place Dellirea Zendar upon the throne as queen, to govern with the support of the Great Chamber."

Following the applause from the crowd, Dellirea stepped to the podium and brought the speaking trumpet to her mouth. A flutter of nervousness passed through her as she looked at the hundreds of people gathered, awaiting her words. It was the first time she had addressed such a crowd. Yet this was a speech she was born to give.

"Fellow citizens," she began, "my grandfather was known as Andamar the Great. He performed many deeds that we still celebrate. But, myself, I know too well the dangers of aspiring to greatness. Haven't we all seen the dangers of where it can lead? How it can seduce us? How it can allow us to overlook the suffering of others if it serves our goals? How it can make us do things that we knew were wrong even as we told ourselves they were right? No, friends, greatness is not something to which I aspire. But goodness is. If you will have me as queen, goodness is all I shall aspire to. And I shall consider myself to have been a success if one day I shall be known simply as Dellirea the Good."

YANIS

It was a pleasure for Yanis to cast his ballot in the referendum for Dellirea. He smiled at the thought of his younger self, who would surely be outraged at him, voting *for* the monarchy. It was an imperfect compromise. In time, perhaps they might reach a point where they would no longer need a king or queen. But the events of the past months proved that they were not yet at that point.

The referendum was won by Dellirea. In a convincing victory, seventy-nine percent of the population voted to support her. At last, their revolution had reached its end.

At the swearing-in ceremony, Yanis stood next to Nadeni, both of them in their People's Army uniforms. She held their son, who was now two and a half months old. They named him Maandi, after her father.

The air was crisp, but the sun shining down upon them took away some of the chills. A large crowd, bundled in coats and hats, gathered in front of the palace to watch.

Although Charlotte had told Yanis privately of Dellirea's doubts about the religion of Oqci, nonetheless Dellirea wished to be sworn in with the Book of Oqci. It was good to preserve the traditions, she said. Even if the stories were not literally true, they still had their value.

Dellirea placed her hand confidently on the book and spoke aloud her oath. She pledged to faithfully rule the nation as queen and respect the constitution and the Great Chamber. A stable peace was before them, after months and months of strife.

The ceremony was almost at its end, when, at once, they were all covered in shadow.

Instinctively, Yanis clutched Nadeni close to him as they both gazed upward.

But it was no more than a passing grey cloud.

For the briefest of moments, however, his eyes deceived him. Instead, he imagined it must have been a dragon overhead, with Calina watching down upon them. What she might have thought of them then... Yanis knew not.

EPILOGUE

GRETA

Greta handed the director a large stack of papers.

"*On the Origin of the Sacred Creatures?*" he said, examining the cover page.

"That's right."

He stroked his beard and flipped the pages.

The decision had already been made by the editor to publish the book. But the director of the publishing company wished to meet Greta first. It was an unusual step, but it was an unusual book. It was still controversial, even in the time since the revolution, to say that the sacred creatures were natural, not divine.

"Dedicated to the infamous Samuel Nox?" the director said, looking at the dedication page.

"My former mentor," she explained. His expression betrayed that he was hesitant. "Yes, he *was* a deeply flawed man. But he was ruined by something for which he could not be completely faulted. Who among us would not have done the same in his position? And was he not also capable of heroism? Charlotte of Evesbury claimed that he sacrificed himself saving her from the Soldiers of Oqci."

"Very well," said the director.

Greta's book took inspiration from Nox's findings from his early dissections of the murdered creatures. His careful drawings showed unique markings in the creatures' cells, not present in other animals. After the law was changed to allow the examination of creatures who had died natural deaths, Greta had studied the creatures further and confirmed his initial findings. The cells of the creatures had somehow been altered.

The book also drew upon the firsthand accounts by soldiers on the most recent mission to the Dragon Isles. One such, authored anonymously, was called *The True Story of the Dragon Woman* and described Calina Gray, the scientist who survived on the island for a year and a half, unknown to the rest of the world. Her flesh had become one with the aletolium, which allowed her to control the dragons.

The director continued to scan his eyes over the manuscript, nodding as he went.

Some ancient, advanced civilization must have lived on that chain of islands, Greta said in the book. This civilization, she surmised, had engineered the creatures by technology far in advance of Estenland's own, making use of the aletolium, and then, for a reason yet unknown, the civilization collapsed. Perhaps Oqci, if such a figure existed at all, transported the creatures from the island. But he was not divine. This was only a myth that had developed later, over many hundreds of years.

The director at last came to the end of the work and smiled as he read aloud the final words: "In the end, the creatures were created by humans, by the inhabitants of that ancient civilization. But, with technology that advanced, would it truly be wrong to call them gods?"

ABOUT THE AUTHOR

Nathan G. Alexander is a writer and historian based in Ottawa, Canada. He teaches history at the University of Ottawa and holds a PhD in modern history from the University of St Andrews in Scotland. He is originally from Fort Erie, Ontario, Canada.

instagram.com/nathgalexander_writes